The Doves of Ohanavank

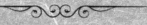

Vahan Zanoyan

Copyright © 2014 Vahan Zanoyan
All rights reserved.

ISBN: 1499582749
ISBN 13: 9781499582741

Library of Congress Control Number: 2014909772
CreateSpace Independent Publishing Platform
North Charleston, South Carolina

Chapter One

Our house in Saralandj has two rooms. Before our parents died and Martha got married, one served as bedroom to the eight children. The other had our parents' bed in one corner, and otherwise it was the kitchen, dining room and bath for all of us. We have no indoor plumbing. Our kitchen and bath have only one appliance, the manure-burning stove in the middle of the kitchen section of the second room. Almost every task is done by hand.

Now that there are fewer of us, my siblings have offered me my parents' bedroom, they say because I slept there with my mother the night before Ayvazian's men took me away. The remaining six now share our old bedroom.

My name is Lara Galian. Today I turn eighteen. I'm not big on birthdays, but my family wanted to do something special for me. My four older sisters and three younger brothers still live in this impoverished village. Saralandj used to be my home too, until everything changed and I moved to the city after being freed. My oldest sister, Martha, is married and has a three-month-old baby girl, Ani. The second oldest, Sona, got engaged a month ago. My oldest brother, Avo, is fourteen months younger than me, but, as the oldest son, he is now the head of the Galian household.

Six months ago I was a prostitute in Dubai. When they took me there I was sixteen. People would stare at me. My manager would say it was because of my age and good looks, but I never understood what that meant. My father and mother used to talk about the legendary beauty that I had inherited from my great aunt, Araxi. That didn't mean much to me either, because I never met Araxi Dadik.

In Dubai, I received around twenty clients a day, mostly foreign workers from Asia and other parts of the Middle East. Then my captor negotiated a contract with Ahmed Al Barmaka, a very rich and influential man, and I became exclusively his and lived in his estate. It was a relief not to have many clients every day, and although Ahmed treated me well, I guess with affection and maybe even respect (in that profession, one can never be sure of respect), the fact remained that I was his property, whom he had bought and paid for.

I betrayed his trust and ran away. I betrayed others too, including some who had been kind to me, to get away from that life and return home.

But home is not what it used to be. My mother died while I was away. I knew she was ill and it was one of my worst fears that I'd never see her again. The fear came true. Avo, who is the closest a human being has ever been to me (possibly next to my father), is different. Before Sergei Ayvazian killed my father and took me away, I had never seen Avo angry. Now he is angry all the time. He drinks, sometimes too much, he smokes, and he has participated in the killing of six people before turning seventeen. He killed these people because of me, two of them in my presence and one with my participation; he did it in order to protect our family and avenge my father's death.

Avo has changed physically too; he has grown, his skin looks darker and more weathered, his face has hardened, is bonier and more angular. He is handsome and looks a lot more like my father now than he did two years ago. Like my father, his beauty does not seem to belong to the present; with his wild curly hair, large black eyes and eagle nose, he looks like some mythical character from ancient Armenia.

It is March, and it is still winter in Saralandj. There is a small hill of snow at the side of our house, where my brothers have gathered the snow shoveled from around the house; it reaches half way up the kitchen window. The snow starts to melt during sunny days, but then everything freezes at night, and once in a while it still snows. Spring does not arrive here until well into April, and in some years even into May. Nevertheless, the villagers are restless after four months of winter inactivity, and have started venturing out, getting ready for spring. Gardens are being raked and, by the more impatient, even tilled for late April planting, stables are being cleaned, and the remaining bales of grass and hay, gathered in late summer and early fall to feed the animals in the winter, rearranged, aired and re-stacked.

All my sisters and brothers work in the garden and the stables. Avo does most of the heavy outside work. Aram is the youngest and is the only one who still goes to school, but he is not exempt from doing his share. My sisters are also busy indoors, getting the house ready for spring; not much gets washed around here during the winter months, because it is very cold and heating large quantities of water on the small manure-burning stove is cumbersome. It is old and rusty, and its stovepipe, which passes through the first bedroom as its only source of heat, has many tears and holes, which Avo keeps repairing. Besides, they have to make sure that the stock of dried manure will be enough for heating the house all winter, and they don't want to take chances until winter approaches its end, when they can be sure that they will not run out.

I miss the smell of this house. It is a combination of dried manure mixed with hay—our main fuel—smoke, sweat and the lingering aromas of cooking and spices. As much as anything, it is this smell that signifies home for me. I missed this smell when I was overseas, first in Moscow and then Dubai, and nearly as much as my family, it was this smell that I yearned to return to.

It reminds me especially of my father, who, even though dead, was the most important influence in my life during my eighteen months in forced prostitution. I recalled the countless tales that he used to tell, and the stories that he used to read to us during holidays. My father always had something to say about any situation; he spoke casually, without showing any presumed import in his message, and I later came to understand that it was that style that allowed every word to sink in, without questioning or resistance from any of us. He simply talked and we simply listened. I probably wouldn't have made it back home had it not been for my father's words and the strength that they gave me.

Almost nothing has changed in this house physically since I left for the first time two years ago. Our old bedroom has the same five beds, made a long time ago by my grandfather, from wood and plywood. The only difference is that now only six of my siblings sleep there, so only my two youngest brothers have to share a bed. Other than that, every detail is the same as when I left.

The other room has not changed either, except that next to the picture of my father on the wall over the bed, now also hangs the picture of my mother. After her death, Avo chose an old photograph of her, enlarged it, made a frame from the pruned branches of our apricot tree, and hung it. That is all. Other than that, everything—the stove, the bed, the low dining table with the low stools around it, the pots and pans stacked together in one corner, the shelves holding the jars and sacks containing food preserved for the winter, the dishes and tea cups lined up along a single wooden shelf, the large pot where we heat water for baths and where we do laundry—all are exactly where they have always been. This became my bedroom after I returned home from Dubai, and it is mine every time I visit from Yerevan. No one else sleeps here. They just use the room to cook, eat, bathe, and do laundry.

No one in this house, let alone in this village, knows or could possibly understand what I've been through. Most women in this village will know only one man in their lifetime, with the exception of the rare widow who remarries. I have been with more men than the entire female population of this village combined, probably a hundred times over. I used to keep track of the number in my little spiral-bound green notebook, but I stopped when I reached the first several hundred men, within a few months of my abduction. I tore those pages from the notebook. There did not seem to be any point in keeping track, and besides, it was depressing me.

Although no one here knows exactly where I've been and what I've done, everyone who knows my family has lurid opinions, and some are not far from the truth. Fortunately, I do not have to admit to anything; I treat the rumors for what they are, no matter how close to the truth they may be. My sisters do not ask any direct questions of me, and they try their best to ignore the rumors. In my presence, they act as if nothing has changed, which is not difficult for them, because in fact very little changed in their lives when I was gone, except for the fact that I used to send a lot of money home, which helped them get back on their feet financially after my father's sudden death.

But dealing with Avo is different. He has killed for me. He and I pushed Sergei Ayvazian down a five hundred meter cliff, from the same spot where my father was pushed after he refused to let them take me away and manage my career as a 'model.' That was in Sevajayr, a village far from here, in Vayots Dzor, a different region of Armenia than Aragadzotn, where Saralandj is. Avo also killed Ayvazian's nephew, Viktor, and four of their bodyguards. He could never have pulled that off had it not been for two people—a crusty revolutionary called Gagik Grigorian, who was a friend of Papa's, and a Swiss-Armenian investigative reporter called Edward Laurian, who somehow got tangled up in our family saga. We call him Edik.

Avo knows more than anyone else, and suspects a lot more. Six months ago, when he first brought me home, he waited for a couple of days for me to recover, and then he asked, point blank, if I had been raped and whether I actually had been a model in Greece, as Ayvazian had promised, or whether the more sinister rumors of prostitution were true. My only request was for him not to ask where I had been and what I had done. I told him that in time I may be ready to tell him certain details, but I asked that he let that be in my own time. I could tell from his face that the simple fact that I did not deny anything confirmed his worst suspicions. He stared at me for a minute, then turned his back and left without saying another word.

I know I owe Avo more. Sometimes I think that telling him either an outright lie or the full truth would have been kinder than leaving things hanging like that. He is deeply involved in my story, and now has his own difficult story. His life and his future have changed irreversibly because of me, and not for the better. But I could not bring myself to outright lie to him, nor could I tell him the truth. I'm not even sure I can repeat the truth to myself. How could I look Avo in the eye and tell him that Sergei Ayvazian brutally raped me the first night that they took me, that his nephew Viktor and his bodyguards subjected me to all kinds of indignities in Moscow in the following few days, that a Ukrainian prostitute called Anastasia taught me the basic skills of the trade, and I started working as a prostitute only a few days after leaving home? Then in Dubai I was a prostitute, and later became a local dignitary's concubine?

How could I look Avo in the eye and tell him that all the money that I sent home, that helped the family recover from its debts, came from my captivity and degradation?

My return home last fall was not uneventful—actually, Edik might say that is the understatement of the year. I had to convince the manager of Ahmed's concubines, Ms. Sumaya, to let me secretly go home for a few days while Ahmed was away on business in Beijing. I later found out that she and two of the other concubines in the estate, Natalia and Farah, wanted me gone anyway, because they felt threatened by Ahmed's deepening interest in me. It turned out that they were plotting to have me 'disappear.' So instead of a ticket directly from Dubai to Yerevan, Sumaya routed my flight through Istanbul, where an Armenian trafficker called Abo was to meet me. As I understood the plan, Abo would then put me on a flight to Tbilisi, where I would catch the train to Yerevan.

Of course I never intended to go back to Dubai once I got home; that was my part in the web of deceit. Sumaya, in turn, had planned for Abo to put me on a flight to Moscow, accompanied by one of his soldiers, where I would be met by Natalia's uncle, who, in turn, would take me to Krasnodar and make me 'disappear.' Apparently they paid Abo a lot of money to execute that part of their scheme. But Abo had ideas of his own. He wanted to make a deal. He'd return me to Ayvazian, in exchange for access to the lucrative sex trade in Dubai, from which he had been blocked for years. So I did not head home as I had thought, nor to Moscow as Sumaya had thought, but back into Ayvazian's hands. Abo had assumed that Ayvazian would then return me to Ahmed Al Barmaka and save face in Dubai. Instead, they brought me back to Armenia, and took me straight to the remote village of Sevajayr, drugged and bound.

That is where Ayvazian and his men were once again taken by surprise. Just when they felt that they had finally regained control over the situation, Avo shows up with Gagik, in the middle of a deserted village road on the way to Sevajayr, where no outsider ever appears; he causes Viktor Ayvazian's car to roll off into a ravine, killing him and his driver on the spot, and then brings Sergei Ayvazian and his bodyguard tied and gagged to the safe house where they were holding me and another woman. How on earth did Avo, a sixteen-year-old kid from Saraladj, almost four hours away from Sevajayr, happen to be on the same deserted road as the Ayvazians at the same time on that fateful afternoon? No one could even begin to understand the truth, unless they understood Edik Laurian's and Gagik's involvement. And that has not happened.

But my country is a small place. And even though a dozen or so corrupt and greedy oligarchs control its economy and trade today, it is home to one of the oldest civilizations on earth, with a culture and history that goes back several thousand years. I myself would not know this had my father not read to us for hours on every holiday. But all that did not matter when Ayvazian, one of the most ruthless and venal of these oligarchs, wanted to recruit me into his network of prostitutes. Apparently he thought a sixteen year old with my apparent allure would be a great asset in his business.

Ayvazian had no friends. Many feared and hated him, and no one liked him. That made it easier for the investigators to close the case of his death as an unresolved murder, as I found out later.

But the rest of the oligarchy could not be as complacent about these deaths as the law was. The six deaths in Sevajayr on that fall afternoon were so shocking, so unprecedented, and so inexplicable, that every other oligarch in the country was immediately on full alert. Their first concern was to make sure that this was not some kind of vigilante strike against oligarchs in general; but soon they started to focus on the potential spoils. They had only an inkling of the type of business that Ayvazian was into. He had managed to keep his operations secret and the competition out. Thus began the race for who among them would fill the void left by his death. With Viktor, his nephew and top lieutenant, gone also, there was no heir apparent in Ayvazian's family that could take over the businesses he had left behind.

Avo is not the only person with whom I have not come clean. I have not yet begun to honestly face my own emotions. While away, I had only one obsession: to get back home. There never was the slightest doubt in my mind that this is what I should, and would, do. Even during the most comfortable period of my exile, when I lived in my own villa on Al Barmaka's estate and accepted the flattering expressions of his devotion, I had only one thought: to get home. Home was what I knew. My life in the village with my family defined me. At heart, I was afraid that if I did not return soon, there would be no going back; I would be too changed.

Once the intoxicating effect of the extraordinary events in Sevajayr faded, after that magical night that we spent in Edik's house in Vardahovit, which was the first night of freedom that I had since my abduction, and after we returned to Saralandj, I tried desperately to force myself to truly return: return and belong, return and embrace, return and become part of this village, this family and this reality again—and I failed.

I failed, not because anything has physically changed here, even though Mama has passed away. I failed because I am different. And although I reject the thought, I know deep inside that I wonder if I did the right thing by returning. Of course if I had stayed a common prostitute prowling the nightspots of Dubai under the management of our pimp, Madame Ano, and under the supervision of Viktor Ayvazian, I would never have these doubts. But the experience of Al Barmaka's estate was life-changing. I realized its significance then, but that did not change my resolve to return home. Quite the contrary, I saw my vastly improved situation as an opportunity to escape. The doubts about where I really belonged began to haunt me only after my return.

Edik Laurian and Gagik Grigorian have somehow become an integral part of our lives. That is another novelty; before I left home, we had never had such people involved in our lives. Everyone we knew was from the village or a close relative. Gagik lives in Ashtarak. He has lived here all his life, and was close to my father. He is wild and crazy, with an intensity about him that I have not seen in any other man. They say he was a revolutionary who fought in the Karabagh war. His nickname is *Khev Gago*—Crazy Gago. He strikes me more as a crazy philosopher than a crazy revolutionary, but Edik says that's because he has mellowed with age. Ashtarak is only around thirty minutes from Saraladj, so he visits often.

Edik is different. Although he is not from here, he is more interested in what happens here than anyone I know. He is interested in our family, in me personally, in Avo, in the country and he is obsessed with what Ayvazian did to me. Unlike *Crazy Gago*, Edik likes to talk to me. He is a journalist, has been all around the world, a poet, a hunter, and perhaps a bit of a revolutionary himself. I wouldn't be surprised if he turns out to be a little *Khev* too, just like Gago.

Chapter Two

I t took His Excellency Ahmed bin Abdullah bin Saif Al Barmaka several months to figure out what had happened. He finally put enough pieces of the puzzle together to form an idea, even if he had to assume certain details. The maze of schemes and counter schemes, every single one of which had blown up in the schemers' faces, was so intricate and interwoven, that, without the full cooperation and confessions of the schemers, there was no way to discover every detail.

What matters to him most is that Lara had in fact campaigned hard to go home. The fact that Sumaya had plotted with two of his other concubines to get rid of Lara surprised him, but was less significant.

Sumaya, Natalia and Farah are dismissed and gone. He has brought a Chinese woman, whom he was bedding when Sumaya called to inform him that Lara had escaped, with him from Beijing. She now occupies Natalia's villa.

That was a little over six months ago. The news hurt him deeply then, and the pain has not eased with time, as he had hoped. He never understood *why* Lara had wanted to escape. Keeping concubines was a way of life for him. None had ever wanted to escape before. On the contrary, they competed for his affection and aspired to have their contracts renewed. Most became emotional and cried when their term ended. So it had never occurred to Al Barmaka that any of his women could be unhappy being with him. Why then would Lara, to whom he was getting attached and whom he treated better than he had ever treated a concubine, want to escape?

She was hauntingly beautiful, very young and, although she was a prostitute, there was an innocence about her that disarmed Al Barmaka. She simply did not fit the mold of the sex worker. It was not just her youthful face and truly magical eyes—large, charcoal-black, with a depth that pulled Al Barmaka in and held him long after he had stopped looking into them. It was her mannerisms, her way of moving, so desirable, so seductive and yet so simple and innocent, or perhaps so seductive *because* it was so innocent. It was later, much later, that Al Barmaka would discover that it had been that same captivating beauty that had made Ayvazian notice Lara in the first place, resorting even to murdering her father in order to achieve his objective of recruiting her.

Lara had been the only one among his concubines whom he allowed to call him by his first name. He had arranged for her to take Arabic lessons, and even though he had not thought about any specific plans, he certainly had intended to keep her much longer than the one-year term he had approved. "What is amazing about this girl," he had confided to one of his cousins, "is that she stays with you long after you leave; her *feel* stays with you."

Al Barmaka does not know what exactly he will do next regarding Lara; all he wants to do now is find out as much as he can about her and why she left. He also knows that the Chinese girl is not a replacement for Lara. The hard truth is that no one could replace Lara.

Replacing Sumaya is proving to be difficult as well. She had been with him for more than eighteen years. First as his lover, later as the manager of his concubines. She ran the ladies' quarters with superior skill and effectiveness, and was devoted to his needs. It took a lot to convince Al Barmaka that Sumaya had been involved in the plot to get rid of Lara. The manager of his private office, an Indian man in his mid-forties called Manoj, had suggested the possibility of her involvement early on, but he had dismissed it as vicious intra-staff rivalry. But as more details of the episode had come to light, it had became clearer to him that it would have been next to impossible for Lara to leave the compound without Sumaya's assistance. Al Barmaka feels the void left by Sumaya every day. He plans to replace her with an experienced manager from China, but the process is proving to be more time consuming than he had imagined.

His only source of information about Lara in Dubai is Ano, the middle-aged woman who manages all of Viktor Ayvazian's prostitutes. She is zaftig, with a disproportionately large behind, making the tight pants that she wears less than flattering. She dyes her short, curly hair dirty blond, and has turned bright red nail polish into one of her distinguishing features.

The death of the Ayvazians has wreaked havoc in Ano's life. After over a decade of working for them, she suddenly is alone, which presents an enormous opportunity for her to 'inherit' the Ayvazian empire in Dubai, but at the same time poses risks that until that day she had not had to worry about. Local protection, for one, had been Viktor's responsibility. And although in her everyday dealings the buck stopped with Viktor, she knew that there is more to the Ayvazian empire than Viktor. Someone could show up anytime and hold her accountable.

Ano is trying to sort all this out when she is summoned to visit Al Barmaka's office. The time and date are precise. She knows enough about Dubai and Al Barmaka's influence to know not to argue. The summons reaches her around noon, for a two o'clock meeting on the same day. She knows that Viktor met with Manoj and Sumaya after Lara disappeared, before Al Barmaka returned from China. And she knows that he had to concede to everything they demanded. If Viktor had to give in, who is she to resist? She makes up her mind to go with the intention of answering their questions as truthfully as she can. She has nothing to hide, either about Lara's disappearance or about the Ayvazians' death. Her activities in Dubai are well known to the authorities, and she knows some key people, as she has been involved in freeing the girls from jail on occasion, as well as in helping close the deal with Al Barmaka on Lara's contract. She also has heard that Sumaya was fired for her involvement in Lara's escape, so this clearly was an inside job, and she would not be under suspicion. Her only concern then is to make sure that she continues to operate in Dubai with the twenty-plus girls now working for her.

Manoj arranges to meet her at the entrance of the Al Barmaka compound. The office is deliberately built right outside the main gate, to receive visitors without having to invite them inside, thus avoiding the tedious formalities of registering guests. It is roomy but simple; the large window-mounted air-conditioning unit blasts away, and the solemn faces of the rulers of the confederation keep watch from photographs on the wall across from the couch.

Ano is invited to sit on that couch, offered tea or coffee, which she declines, and then is left alone. The reception room has not received much attention over the years. She notices scratches on the elaborate wooden coffee table, wear and tear on the carpet, and several stains on the couch. It is clear that Al Barmaka himself would not receive visitors here, and even Manoj would not hold his more important business meetings in this room.

Manoj arrives fifteen minutes late, looking rushed and frazzled, his dark skin glistening with perspiration. He greets Ano hurriedly, does not apologize for being late, and sits on a chair next to the couch. His trademark show of manners and flowery compliments, which used to annoy Sumaya to no end, are gone. Men like Manoj do not hide their distaste for meeting women like her. They consider it unbecoming of their social status and demeaning, even though it is Manoj who handled the finances of Al Barmaka's concubines. The hypocrisy revolts Ano, but this is not the time and place to reciprocate his attitude.

"His Excellency wants to find out more about the background and whereabouts of Ms. Leila," says Manoj. "I expect that you'll tell us all that you know." Leila is the Arabic name that Al Barmaka had given Lara.

Ano has come prepared to face questions about Lara's escape, possibly additional queries about the connection in Istanbul who handed her over to Ayvazian, or perhaps questions about who in Dubai could have in any way been involved in her escape. These have been the main themes of questioning in the past, which led everyone to believe that he was intent on solving the mystery of the security breach in his compound. But it now looks like that is no longer His Excellency's main interest. Her whereabouts? Does this mean that he is now trying to get in touch with her, after turning down their offer to return her to him, saying his home was not a prison?

Ano's antennas are up. This could be worth a lot of money. Had Al Barmaka accepted Lara back when they offered to return her, they would not have had to refund $75,000, three quarters of the price he had paid for her exclusive contract for one year. But he demanded a refund and Viktor transferred the money right away. So now he wants her back? Does he expect to just get her back for free? The answers to Manoj's questions are quite simple. And although Ano had decided to play it straight, the nature of the inquiry has already changed things.

"Her background and whereabouts," she repeats deliberately. "Well, her background is in the file that was submitted to you when you signed her contract. I am not sure what more we have. As for her whereabouts, now that Mr. Ayvazian and his nephew are both dead, that will be difficult to ascertain."

"Her so-called file," snaps Manoj, "has nothing in it and you know it. One paragraph, giving her age, the name of her manager in Dubai and her country of origin. The rest of the twenty pages contain only photographs. Surely as her manager you have a lot more information on her background. Let me repeat. I expect you to fully cooperate with us on this matter."

"What exactly do you want me to do?" asks Ano to give herself time to think about how to raise the issue of payment for her help.

Manoj checks his watch and shows his impatience. "Let us start with what should have been in her file, but was not: where in Armenia is she from?"

"All I know is that she is from a poor village." Ano has assumed a minimalist manner of responding, as if in a deposition by a hostile lawyer.

"Which village? Surely you know the name of the village!"

"Actually, I don't. I could try to find out, but without Viktor it will not be easy. It will take time, and... resources." Given Manoj's impatience, she wants to start negotiating before the opportunity is lost.

But Manoj is in no mood to play along.

"Look," he snaps again, this time more forcefully. "I really don't have time for this. So this is what we're going to do: I will give you twenty-four hours to answer the following specific questions. If you fail, your operation in Dubai will end and you personally may come under investigation for illegal activities. I hope it is clear to you that in the meantime you cannot leave the country. If you try, you will be arrested on the spot." Manoj stops for a few seconds to let that sink in, then continues. "My questions are: first, where is Ms. Leila from, the precise name and location of her village; second, what are her family circumstances, in other words, status of her parents, how many siblings does she have and their ages, and their economic circumstances; third, the full name and contact details of this so-called Mr. Abo, who handed Ms. Leila to Ayvazian in Istanbul. You have until—he checks his watch again—precisely two-thirty in the afternoon tomorrow.

Call my secretary at this number with the answers." Then he hands her his secretary's card and, without another word, leaves the room.

Ano sits there for a minute, stunned, before one of the aides comes in and, with a smirk that Ano knows is meant to mock her, escorts her out.

Chapter Three

There is an old proverb that goes something like this: "Everyone has three ears: one on the right side of their head, one on the left, and the third in their heart." I remember my father telling us this. "Few have developed the habit of listening through that third ear," he said. "But it is often more important than the other two put together."

Based on my experience, it is women, more than men, who listen with the heart. That is not always an advantage. Those who use only the ears on their head can be better off. The third ear often exposes unhelpful truths and, even worse, falsehoods. There are those who swear by it. But I am not sure it is as reliable as it is made out to be. It is possible to mishear with the heart, sometimes with devastating consequences. Unlike the two ears on the head, the third ear is subjective; it serves different functions for a woman in distress, a woman in love, a criminal, a mafia boss, a shrewd politician… It does not always serve its master well, unless the master is focused and selfish, and even then, it can still mislead.

My father had an evolved third-ear. "The third ear keeps doors open," he used to say. "What you hear with your head is what people say, which may or may not be the truth. You hear this or that, who did what; you hear possible or impossible; you hear what happened. But the truth is never that simple, and it is what you hear with your third ear that gives you the depth, that turns the 'no' into a 'yes', the impossible into possible..." We were kids then, and had no clue as to what he was talking about.

Now I understand the wisdom behind those words. And I believe that it was his ear of the heart that got him killed. Without that ability, he probably would not have been so suspicious and would have let Ayvazian take me the first time he asked. But even after refusing to give me up, without his third ear, he probably would not have accepted Ayvazian's invitation to visit him for a day in Martashen, which gave Ayvazian the opportunity to take him to Sevajayr and kill him. He saw the danger in going, but he saw a bigger danger to all of us in refusing Ayvazian twice in the same week. Of course no direct threat was made; he heard it with his third ear.

The only other man I know who can use his third ear is Edik Laurian. Al Barmaka may have the gift, and he did tell me something similar once, but I was not really paying attention at the time. As I think back about specific moments with him, I have to admit that the man demonstrated a rare ability to listen, even to unspoken words. But there were also moments when he was just like any of my other clients—totally third-ear-deaf.

Edik is different. It seems that he is always listening with all three ears. *Always*. That must be an incredibly exhausting way to live. I am not sure I could handle that, twenty-four hours a day.

Avo has invited *Khev Gago* and Edik Laurian to my birthday party. This is not a party like the ones they have in the city, but rather a family gathering with friends coming to eat and drink. The only difference from any other day is that there will be more people at the table and better food. There will be nothing to mark it as a birthday, other than possibly a toast or two. The fancy parties with decorations and presents in colorful wrapping paper with bows and ribbons, which have reached certain well-to-do homes in Yerevan, have not reached Saralandj yet, and I am thankful for that.

It is ten a.m. and I am still in my nightgown, lying on my parents' bed. The others have been up for hours, but have not come into the room in order not to disturb me, forgoing their morning coffee and breakfast. I have grown to cherish my morning hours alone. I did not know what solitude was when I was taken from home at sixteen. Not only did eight of us share a cramped bedroom, but we could at anytime barge into our parents' room for any reason. The concept of privacy simply did not exist, so we never sought it and wouldn't know how to miss it. But during the months that I spent in my own villa in Al Barmaka's estate I developed not only a keen sense of privacy, but also an appreciation of solitude. Solitude does to the soul what sleep does to the body—it restores it, mends the wear and tear, pacifies the inner storms, creates a space that is yours.

This is all the time alone I'm going to get today, until late at night when everyone leaves and I go to bed. My sisters, and maybe even Avo, would want to bathe before the guests arrive, and then they have to start preparing the feast. This room will go through various transformations, as it is set up for its various functions one after the other. At the end, it will look its best as the dining room, cleaned, tidied, and made to accommodate around a dozen people in the space and at a table that can reasonably accommodate no more than four or five diners with any measure of comfort. That will not affect anyone's joyful mood; here, the more crowded a room at times like this, the more festive the atmosphere. Space is irrelevant. It is all about sharing joy, not space.

I decide to get out of bed. Although the fire in the stove has been out for a few hours, the lingering embers have kept it and the pot of water over it warm. My rings are on the table, and I debate whether I should wear them both. One is the simple thin band that belonged to Araxi Dadik, my great aunt whose fabled beauty I am supposed to have inherited. She died in Siberia way before I was born. My mother gave me the ring the day I left home. She said my father had wanted me to have it; she said he loved me very much, and with me he felt a special tie to his past. Throughout my time away from home, the ring, in turn, gave me a link to my past. I always had it with me, either in my pocket or in my purse at first, and then I started wearing it permanently.

The second ring is much fancier. It is thicker and has a large emerald. Ahmed gave it to me in Dubai. "I hope you'll always wear it," he said. It is beautiful, but entirely out of place in Saralandj. In Dubai, I needed Araxi Dadik's ring as a link to home; but here, do I need Ahmed's ring? Do I really need any link to Dubai?

I re-start the fire and wash up hurriedly, using all the warm water in the pot, which I refill from the bucket in the corner. I change, put Araxi

Dadik's ring on my middle finger, place Ahmed's in my purse and walk out.

The girls rush in first, to start tea and coffee, and I feel a pang of guilt for holding them up for so long. Martha arrives to help with the preparations, having left three-month-old Ani in the doting care of her mother-in-law. She is still the oldest sibling and, although married, when present is the boss in the kitchen. At the same time, preparations start for heating water for baths. It is amazing how that empty, quiet room is transformed in a matter minutes into a beehive of activity. If there was any doubt in my mind that I did the right thing by moving out, it is now gone, even though this was not the consideration behind that decision. My decision to move to the city and live alone is more complicated, and to this day I do not dare articulate the reasons out loud, even to myself.

There will be *khorovadz*, the traditional Armenian mixed grill of pork, eggplants, green peppers and tomatoes. During March, none of these vegetables are in season, but Avo is determined to make the full spread, so he has secured everything from the greenhouse in Ashtarak, the largest city in the region. There will also be grilled potatoes and onions, and all types of appetizers of dried meats and cheeses. There will be trout, Armenian *Ishkhan,* boiled with special spices, and several types of salads—chicken salad with sour cream, potato salad with olive oil and lemon, beet salad with sour cream and onions, cabbage salad, and grated carrot salad with raisins and walnuts. Making the salads is time-consuming, so fortunately for the girls, the grilling is done outdoors, and it is the men who assume responsibility for it. They gather by the fire with a bottle of vodka, tasting the smaller pieces that cook faster directly from the fire with a piece of lavash, and drinking. The first bottle of vodka will be consumed before they even sit at the table. That is the more pleasant part of the feast for the men.

By two o'clock the family is gathered. Martha's husband, Ruben, arrives with a large tray of dried fruits and nuts, compliments of the in-laws. Sona's fiancé, Simon, arrives with two bottles of vodka. Avo has already started the fire at the stone grill in front of the house, and is chain-smoking. Martha has brought a dozen additional skewers, as the ten at our house won't suffice and reusing the skewers runs the risk of letting the first batch get cold.

By the time *Khev Gago* and Edik arrive, the fire is ready, and Avo has placed the potatoes and onions on the grill; he has also had his first shot of vodka. I watch them embrace from the window. My youngest brothers are gathering more wood for the fire, and my brothers-in-law are helping Avo, which basically means hanging around, poking the fire unnecessarily every now and then, and giving unsolicited and unnecessary advice.

All that will stop now because *Khev Gago* immediately takes over the grilling.

"Where is the rest?" he asks, inquiring about the meat and the vegetables. Then he looks up toward the house, notices me standing at the window watching them, and waves. *Khev Gago* has small, intense, fiery eyes. Edik told me once that he was far more skinny and crazy when they first met back in the late eighties. He was an idealist and did not understand the meaning of compromise. He has mellowed a lot since those days, says Edik, but the old flame is still in there somewhere, and one never knows when it will erupt.

"And where are the women?" asks Edik laughing, "I did not drive all the way from Vardahovit just to see you guys!"

I cannot help smiling when I hear him. So typical of Edik to ignore the norms and protocols of this conservative culture, and not only get away with it, but do so with the affection of everyone present. Avo, Ruben and Simon smile too, and ignore him. Edik turns toward the house and waves to me.

"I'm sure there are enough women in that kitchen," he yells, "come down." Edik is taller than *Khev Gago* and a bit heavier. "It's all the wine I drink," he said once in way of explanation of his widening waist. His hair is graying around the temples, and his large, dark-brown eyes always seem to have bags under them. I told him once that the village women believe that the bags could indicate some problem with his liver and he should have it checked. "Those have nothing to do with liver problems; they are a sign of age and wisdom. It will be a long time before you get bags like that," he said, winking at me.

Avo walks up the stairs to the house to get shot glasses. He throws his cigarette away before entering the house. I have asked him not to smoke inside while I'm visiting and he accommodates me. The smell of cigarettes reminds me of the first night when Ayvazian raped me, and I find the memory of clients with heavy cigarette breath intolerable.

"You go back out and tend the fire," I tell Avo, taking the glasses from him. "I'll bring these down, with something for you men to eat." Avo smiles and lights a cigarette the second he crosses the threshold.

I fill a tray with sliced sausages, cheese and pickled cucumbers and cabbage, which is a favored accompaniment to vodka for seasoned drinkers. I add the shot glasses and some bread, and walk down to greet the men. Edik moves forward to take the tray from me, which is another breach of custom that everyone ignores, and then gives me a hug and kiss on both cheeks, yet another breach which, in different circumstance, could easily have led to a quarrel.

"I have a present for you," he says, smiling from ear to ear. "I hope you like it." And he takes a small volume from his coat pocket and hands it to me. It is a copy of Daniel Varujan's *Pagan Songs*. Varujan is one of the most prominent Western Armenian poets, and was killed during the 1915 genocide. Turkish soldiers arrested him along with several other writers, took them to a secluded wood, stripped them, tied them to the trees and proceeded to cut them slowly with knives. Their screams could be heard from a distance for hours, according to some witnesses. His *Pagan Songs* is a celebration of love, power, lust, sex, courage and life. It celebrates the pagan traditions of Armenia, which he presents as the antithesis of the Christian defeatist, turn-the-other-cheek, live-life-in-fear mentality. Edik says even though religion has lost its omnipresence in Armenian life today, that mentality dominated Armenian culture for several centuries, weakening it politically and militarily. He considers Varujan not only one of the greatest poets, but also one of the important influences on his own writing.

I notice that he gets distracted for a minute. Sometimes I catch Edik staring at me so intensely that I wonder what he is thinking. Right now, my smile touched him, I know it, and I wonder if I should have been more reserved. I take the book, look at the cover, and hold it to my chest.

"*Shnorhakal em*, Edik jan." I am thankful. Then I go to greet *Khev Gago* and my brothers-in-law.

Chapter Four

"How much do we tell him about Yuri, and when?" asks Laurian pulling Gagik aside.

"We better do it now. He'll be too drunk after dinner," says Gagik. Then, looking over his shoulder at the group around the fire, he adds, "I don't know…maybe this is not the right time and place."

"He needs to be warned," says Laurian. "Maybe we can give him a heads up now, without destroying his mood on Lara's birthday. Let's leave the long discussion for later."

"I'll go get him," says Gagik. Laurian walks around the corner of the heap of snow and waits.

"You remember Hamo?" starts Laurian after they arrive. "Ayvazian's bodyguard that you pushed down the cliff in Sevajayr?"

"Yeah, what about him?" The first hints of slurring are already apparent.

"Well, he has this brother, Yuri, who has returned from Moscow recently. He worked for Ayvazian too, but was based in Moscow. He doesn't know about what happened here, and nothing about you and Lara, yet. But he is asking questions. The reports of his brother and Ayvazian falling off the cliff at the same time have intrigued him."

"Is he asking about Lara?" says Avo. That is what matters most to him.

"Not yet. But we think he knows about your family. What exactly, we don't know," says Gagik.

"If he's not asking about Lara, let him ask all he wants," says Avo. "It doesn't matter now, does it?"

"Probably not. But we thought we'd let you know, in case he gets close, that's all. What you need to remember is to keep calm. Do not show any emotion to these people. If anyone shows up asking if you know about the Ayvazians, just look them in eye and say no. If you act angry or uneasy they'll know you're hiding something. We can talk about this more later; let's not take away from the festivities today."

With that, Laurian puts his arm around Avo's shoulders and they walk back to the fire. Lara, who has gone inside at this point, notices the three of them come around the corner, and leaves the kitchen to join them. She wants to find out what was that all about, and her best chance is Laurian; neither Avo nor Gagik is likely to tell her much.

♌ ♌ ♌

Carla Ayvazian is in her father's study in Yerevan, the same room where they brought Lara two years ago. The study is part of a one-bedroom suite attached to Ayvazian's main residence, with a separate entrance.

This is where sixteen-year-old Lara was overwhelmed and intimidated because everything was so opulent, and because she had arrived there straight from their house in Saralandj. Not much has changed in the room in the past two years. The maroon velvet sofa is still there, so are the overstuffed chairs, the cupboard of heavy crystal and the thick drapes at the windows. The only addition is a wooden desk, placed in front of the windows, behind which Carla sits, with her feet resting on top of the desk. Sergei Ayvazian had no use for a desk, but for Carla it is critical; without it, the room feels bare to her, no matter how heavy all the other furniture is. As importantly, if she is to succeed in taking over the family business, she needs an imposing position from which to greet visitors.

On the wall opposite the desk, in Carla's direct view, is a large framed photograph of their home in Martashen, the largest village in Vayots Dzor and Ayvazian's hometown. He loved the place, and spent as much time there as his work allowed. He loved that photograph too, which shows the acres of fields and mountains around their mansion. Carla never understood her father's infatuation with the countryside. She's been to Martashen only once since her father's death, to attend his funeral. She is a city girl. She has thought of getting rid of the photograph several times and replacing it with a painting or a photograph of her father, but something has stopped her each time.

Carla is thirty years old, somewhat heavyset, with a slightly asymmetrical hourglass figure, where the bottom half is a bit larger than the top. She is not pretty, but attractive in a crude, sensual way. Her short dark hair and minimal make-up accentuate her masculine features, and the serious, almost stern, expression on her face suggests she's not to be taken lightly. She is Ayvazian's only child and, while no one either in her family or among her father's business associates has given her a second thought as a potential player, she is determined to take over the reins and rebuild the business.

But first Carla has to find out who killed him and where the pieces of his business are hidden. Her mother, a lonely and apathetic fifty-four year old woman, who long stopped caring what her husband did, can be of no help, as her father told her next to nothing about the business he ran, and she was not interested in finding out. They had barely spoken in the past several years. She lived in her own world, socializing only with a few of her female friends and a distant cousin, and even that infrequently. Carla does not remember her parents ever doing much together. In the early years, when she was still a teenager, they used to go to visit relatives or attend weddings together. But in the last ten years or so, even those events were rare and far apart. What had survived as a family activity was the New Year's Eve celebration, which, at their home, involved close to one hundred people, and did not allow much direct interaction between her parents. Her father would be busy entertaining the guests he had invited, and her mother would be busy with the relatives and making sure that the table was properly tended by the staff. For as long as Carla can remember, her mother was bored and indifferent.

There is, however, one distinct memory imprinted in Carla's mind. It is a comment that her father once made to her mother. She was barely seventeen, her parents' bedroom door was open, and she heard her father say: "You don't know how I wish Carla was a boy." She waited for a minute outside the door to hear her mother's response, but there was only a barely audible mumble that she could not understand. "Oh, why am I wasting my breath on you," came back her father's voice. "What would you know about any of this anyway!" Carla then heard footsteps and was about to move away from the door, when she heard her mother's voice. "Don't you ever let her know that's how you feel," she said; her voice was still low, but much clearer this time. "Let it stay with all the things that you keep to yourself. Don't you understand that she needs a father more than you need a son?"

Carla turned away and hurried to her room. That was the most she had ever heard her mother tell her father, and the fact that she showed concern for her feelings was a revelation to her. She had rarely done anything that showed concern for Carla's wellbeing, other than the minimal and expected motherly duties, which were often performed as much to impress others as for Carla.

To her surprise, she was not upset or emotionally distraught by her parents' exchange. Back in her room, she processed the information calmly and objectively, which made her feel so empowered that the entire experience became another revelation. She had discovered something important about herself. This was no longer about what her father or mother said; this was about her identity, her independence, her choices, her life. She decided, then and there, that she would be the one who controls men, and not the other way round. *Don't you understand that she needs a father more than you need a son?* Her mother's words replayed in her head and sounded like a dare. Her father needed a son; there was no doubt about that, because he said so. But her mother's assertion that she needed a father was so clichéd that she understood, for the first time, that she in fact did not. "You're wrong, dear mother," she thought in defiance. "He does need a son much more than I need a father."

That night Carla lost her virginity. She telephoned a twenty-year old acquaintance, the son of one of Ayvazian's associates, and asked him to come over. Ayvazian was out, and her mother was in her room. She could hear the sound of the TV from behind the closed door. She took the young man by the hand and led him to her bedroom, shut the door, and told him to undress. When he hesitated, she adopted her stern look and said, "Now!" The young man was afraid—afraid of what her father would do if he found out, but equally afraid of her. Then he saw her undressing, and began to focus.

"Now listen carefully," she said, as a superior talking to an underling. "This is my first time, so make sure I enjoy it. I want to enjoy sex for a long time, so I can't have a bad first experience. They say the first experience sets the tone." She watched him for a second, looking him over from head to toe. He had taken off his shirt and trousers, and was standing in front of her in his underpants. He was well built, muscular, and moderately handsome. His chest was bare, but his legs and thighs were covered with thick, curly black hair.

"How much experience do you have?" she asked.

At this point he was so intimidated that he did not know how to answer.

"Look," she said impatiently, removing the last of her clothes and standing in front of him. "I know nothing about sex first hand. Now show me what you have." And she pointed at his crotch.

Eventually, the young man gathered enough courage and confidence to do what he was told. He had been with a couple of middle-aged prostitutes, but he had not been confronted in this manner by any woman, let alone by a seventeen-year-old virgin whose father was a feared oligarch. After getting over the initial shock, he found Carla's confidence and bossiness arousing. He was not an experienced lover, but knew more than Carla.

Carla's curiosity was not easy to satisfy. She wanted to learn everything about the sensual pleasures. She pushed him hard with her questions, some of which embarrassed the young man and went beyond his own knowledge. Finally, tired more than satisfied, she helped him sneak out.

At the time, that was her only way to take control of her life. Changing anything else would have been costly, with no advantage. She liked the house where she lived, enjoyed the financial privileges of being the only child of a wealthy man, liked the school that she attended, and loved the fact that her parents were too absorbed in their own worlds to pay much attention to her, or even to each other. She was happy that they did not have time for each other, because that minimized the possibility of another discussion about her. This was the ideal environment for her to build a life for herself, secure and protected by the family, but without the interference that she knew other kids her age were subjected to.

If there was one additional thing that Carla wanted, it was to know more and to become involved in her father's business. She believed that she could be as good, if not better, than her cousin Viktor. She did not think Viktor was particularly smart—"He lacks intuition," she once told her mother.

But Carla was not allowed into Ayvazian's world. How could the largest and most secretive human trafficker in the country allow his teenage daughter into his business, when he was abducting, raping and selling young girls her age around the world? So he dismissed her gently when she approached him the first time, soon after overhearing his comment about needing a son. She asked him again on her twentieth birthday, and this time he was not as gentle. But the message was the same: "Get out and stay out. Go to college, get married, open a shop and sell cosmetics to girls your age if you want, and I'll fund it for you, but stay out of my own work."

A lot has changed in her life since her teenage years. She has graduated from college, which she attended mostly for the social interaction; she has had many more lovers, both men and women, all picked by her on her own terms, and has grown addicted to sex. She has also started three different businesses with her father's capital, just for fun, all of them stores selling women's apparel, and all three profitable. But she's too bored with the lack of challenge to visit the stores regularly, and has handed them over to managers who give her monthly financial reports. Once in a while, she likes to spring a surprise visit on her managers.

Now she sits in the very room that only six months ago she was not allowed to enter, and ponders the possibilities of taking over the operation. The biggest challenge for her is figuring out where all the pieces are hidden—what exactly belonged to her father, where are the various sources of income which now someone, somewhere, is enjoying but which belong to her, who were her father's debtors and how much did they owe him? People like Ayvazian don't just get killed; so the last thing he would have worried about is keeping a record or a will.

Yuri knocks and enters. He sees her at the desk, her feet up, the hem of her purple dress fallen to mid thigh, sheer stockings glistening in the late afternoon light, and smiles as warmly as he thinks is appropriate without reducing his stature as a tough guy. He is in his early forties but looks younger; he is trim, muscular and, unlike most of Ayvazian's other henchmen, does not shave his head. His thick, pitch-black, heavily gelled hair is combed straight back, highlighting his wide forehead. His face is not handsome, with small eyes that look ever so slightly crossed, especially when he concentrates on something, and a chin that looks a bit too long for his face, but it is also a face that is hard to forget. Yuri has a presence, and, had he been a bit less muscular, he would look as much like a men's fashion model as a muscle man.

"You're late," says Carla.

Yuri walks over to her, lifts her chin with his forefinger and kisses her on the mouth.

They have figured each other out pretty well in the past few months, both as lovers and as collaborators. Carla decided early on to start her investigation with her father's employees. She slept with most of the younger ones, and gathered as much information as she could from them. They did not know about each other, even though they all worked for Ayvazian, which shed some light on Ayvazian's style of management. No one knew everything, not even Viktor. Carla decided to keep it that way, and rarely disclosed what she found out from one source to another, even when such disclosure would have helped the second source in his work. Little by little, clue by clue, she started getting a picture of the breadth and depth of her father's operations, and the soldiers who made it all possible.

Yuri had arrived from Moscow soon after his brother's shattered body was collected from the boulders at the foot of the cliff in Sevajayr. He had been one of Ayvazian's main men in Moscow for years, but he had not met Lara during the several months that they kept her in Moscow. Lara was not only a special case because of her youth and stunning beauty, but also a very difficult case. She had been raped and thrown into the market in Moscow straight from Saralandj. She had gone through the motions, but had not accepted her new reality as a prostitute. She had not understood the role, let alone shown any ability or willingness to play the courtesan. But her youth and beauty made her by far the largest potential earner for Ayvazian, and Viktor had wanted to handle her himself, relying on a Ukrainian prostitute called Anastasia to break her in.

So when Yuri arrived in Yerevan, he did not know about Lara or the Galians. He came to find out what had happened to his brother Hamo, and to try and exact some type of compensation from the Ayvazians. Hamo was killed on active duty, after all. When he first appeared at the Ayvazian's door, he did not know what to expect. He knew that the only family that

Ayvazian had was his wife and daughter, and assumed he'd deal with the wife. But Ayvazian's wife refused to see him; she told the maid to take him to Carla.

"I have some news," says Yuri, leaning against the desk, facing her and putting his hand on her knee. That is all the explanation that he's prepared to give for being late. Carla likes that side of Yuri. She has intimidated most of her father's other underlings, and has stopped seeing them because of it. The ideal balance, it seems to her, is to be strict enough to make a man realize she's boss, but leave him enough confidence and sense of control to allow him to perform, both on the street and in the bedroom.

"Well?" she says, "now you want to take your time telling me?"

"Have you heard of someone called Samvel Galian?"

"No. What about him?"

He leans closer to her, allowing his hand to slide a few inches up her thigh.

"He visited your father in Martashen around two years ago. Then they went to Sevajayr together with Hamo. There was an accident, and the man fell off the cliff, exactly the same location where Hamo and your father fell."

Carla shifts in her chair, uncrossing then re-crossing her feet; her movement causes her skirt to slide a bit further up her thighs. She looks at him for a few seconds with no expression on her face. Yuri knows she's processing the information, but Carla never asks the obvious questions directly. In that, she is different from her father, who loved to bombard people with questions, often allowing them no time to answer.

"What else do you have?" she asks.

"Galian is from a village near Aparan, called Saralandj. Haven't been there myself, but they say it is poor and backward. He has a large family— eight children. The wife's dead too."

"I guess you'll have to get your shoes muddy," says Carla. "It's worth checking."

"There's more," says Yuri. "I cannot be a hundred percent sure of this yet, but some of the people on your father's payroll in Aparan think that Viktor and his bodyguards visited the Galians on more than one occasion."

"You think that's related to the sex trade or some other business?"

"Could very well be the sex trade, even though I know we used to avoid cases like this, where the girl lives at home with her parents. But I just found out that Viktor used to wire money to the mother from Moscow. What else could that be for?"

"You tell me, Yuri, what else could that be for?"

"Well, in theory, it could be many other things, but I doubt your Papa was in business with this Galian guy, because he was too poor. Besides, he died in Sevajayr."

"How much money was Viktor wiring them?"

"I am still checking the details."

"What's taking so long to check, Yuri?" Carla says a bit too calmly. "Didn't you run everything in Moscow?"

"Carla, no one ran 'everything' anywhere under your father. He had a lot of people working for him, each knows very little, and is not willing to talk. Why should they tell me anything?"

"Why should they tell you anything? How about because you know how to ask?"

"They're scared. The only two bosses they ever knew are both dead. They don't know me. To them, probably even talking to me is risky."

"Now, now Yuri," she says softening her tone and putting her hand on his to stop it from sliding further up her thigh. "You can be more persuasive than that."

She then takes her feet off the desk and stands up, leading him by the hand to the maroon velvet sofa. "A lot more persuasive," she says, "both with them and with me..."

Chapter Five

"May you be naked, as a poet's soul!
And beneath that pagan nudity of yours
May man suffer yearning,
                    unable to touch you..."

That is a verse from Daniel Varujan's opening poem in his *Pagan Songs*, entitled *"To the Statue of Beauty."* I've been reading the collection of poems every day since Edik gave it to me. *Naked as a poet's soul...* spoken to the statue of beauty. Every time I read something like this, I wonder what it would be like to have an hour with the author. Just one hour, over a cup of coffee, to get a glimpse of *his* naked soul...

I know Edik would have a lot to say about that. But we have not had the chance to talk privately for a while, at least not about poetry. Gagik and Edik seem to be worried about Yuri. Edik thinks that sooner or later they'll figure things out, and wonder how I managed to return home after just eighteen months. No girl working for Ayvazian has ever done something like that.

And then there's this other oligarch, Manvel Aleksyan, whom everyone refers to by his nickname, LeFreak. No one knows how the nickname came about, but it stuck. Edik thinks it was a French journalist who coined it. At any rate, LeFreak was one of the Ayvazian's competitors. According to Gagik he is trying to find out how to get his hands on the business Ayvazian used to control. The problem is that as he digs deeper into Ayvazian's business, he may stumble upon my story. So the whole notion that once we got rid of the Ayvazian menace we could live in peace, a notion that Avo had believed and worked for, has now come into question.

Fortunately, Avo is too busy with the countless tasks of spring to give a lot of thought to Yuri and LeFreak. Aside from his normal duties, he also has to deal with his pig farm. That was Gagik's idea. Pork prices have risen; the government has started a program to import a good quality special feed mix from Holland, they say with no hormones or chemicals, which, when mixed with local chaff, makes an excellent feed which many small farmers in the region are now using. Avo is excited about the pig farm. So much so that he agreed to borrow money from Edik to start it. With Gagik's help, he bought twenty pregnant pigs last fall, expected to deliver in a few weeks. That will keep him busy all spring and summer, and hopefully out of trouble, even though in our family, trouble has always found its way to us.

As for myself, I will be happy to spend the warmer months far from Avo's pigs, in my rented room in an apartment in the outskirts of Yerevan, with an old lady who lives alone. It is a two-bedroom apartment on the eleventh floor of an old Soviet-style building. The elevator goes up to the tenth floor, and we have to go up the last flight of stairs on foot. This can be difficult for my landlady, *Diqin* (Mrs.) Alice, who is in her late seventies, so she does not leave the apartment often. Her husband has passed away, and her two sons live and work in Russia. They send her money every month, but she says they are waiting for her to die so they can sell the apartment. They have no desire to return to Armenia, she says. I sense the bitterness in her voice, but I can't tell whether it is directed at her sons or at the country. Too many people leave these days out of desperation.

Bitter or not, Diqin Alice is among the few fortunate ones. Many old ladies her age have become homeless, abandoned by family members who do not have the means to care for them. Edik says that these old women would have been better off under the Soviet system; in spite of all its faults, he says, the Soviet system provided basic economic security to the elderly. I wouldn't know much about that. I was born after that system collapsed, but my father did not have anything positive to say about the Soviet days. Our family paid dearly during those years, he used to say, especially during the reign of Joseph Stalin. But I guess none of that matters much to anyone in Armenia today, unless you are talking to someone like Edik, for whom everything seems to have some relevance, no matter how old or distant.

My room is small but comfortable. I have a narrow wardrobe and a single bed, a window that overlooks a small park and, unlike Diqin Alice's room where the walls are lined with countless family photographs and small hand-woven carpets, the walls in my room are bare. I share the kitchen and bathroom with her, and help her with household chores. The rent is low, around twenty dollars a month, and she asks me to use it to buy her groceries. I do, and I give her the receipt, because she is always surprised how little it buys. She remembers the food prices of a different era. With the amount of money that I sent home before escaping, and with what I brought with me, I can afford to keep a place like this in Yerevan for a very long time.

But why am I here and not at our home in Saralandj? It is, after all, not really the pigs. After struggling for eighteen long and excruciating months with one aching obsession, namely to return home, why am I not at home? Why was it so easy for Edik to convince me to sign up for two courses at the history department of Yerevan State University, and for one English language course? I later heard that the professors were bribed to let me audit the courses, but I did not want to ask Edik about it. I'm sure he was the one who had done the bribing, even though he argues against bribery and corruption with a passion. Why was I so eager to have an excuse to move to Yerevan?

Sumaya told me once that she had long stopped wanting to go home, and that my desire to return reminded her of when she still missed home. "I now miss the days when I used to miss home," she said. "There's something sweet about missing home. It gives one hope, and I've lost that now." That touched me deeply then and I felt close to her for opening up to me like that. But I also swore then that I'd never get to that point, I'd never stop missing home.

But missing home is one thing and being able to return an entirely different thing. Sumaya was right. It is easy and sweet to miss home when you're away. And it gives you hope, because you constantly count on the nostalgia, no matter how painful, to drive you to freedom. Without the nostalgia, hope is lost because you no longer have something to look forward to. But all the missing, the pining, the obsession, and the life sustaining hope is lost the minute you return. It's done. You're back, against all odds, having conquered incredible obstacles, having beaten people a thousand times more powerful than you...and then you ask, now what?

It is difficult in Saralandj. My family never confronts me directly, but there are the silent stares and unspoken questions on my sisters' and brothers' faces. Village gossip can be ruthless. And although the gossip is about me, the malicious tales deliberately reach my brothers and sisters, hurting them, as much if not more, than me.

There is a difference between the solitude that I enjoy and the loneliness from which I suffer. The loneliness is anchored in hiding the truth, in the fear of being rejected, in the inability to share my story with a single soul who can relate to it. I have known girls who could not handle that kind of loneliness. It pushed them into such severe depression that they were unable to have any social interaction. In the most severe cases they became suicidal.

ℒ ℒ ℒ

Soon after I found this place, I met a girl on the bus coming home one night. She is my age, and lives in one of the buildings around here. We take the same bus from center city Yerevan, to the same bus stop. After seeing each other a few times on the bus, we started talking. We were both careful and reserved at first, starting with a simple nod the second time we saw each other, then a smile and a hello, and then taking a seat next to each other and striking up a conversation.

Her name is Anna, and she is from a village in the Lori region in the North. A year ago, when she was seventeen, her parents agreed to marry her off to a man in his thirties from a nearby town. She says she was horrified, because she did not like his demeanor, but had no say in the matter. Soon after they were married, her husband, who used to work in a butcher shop, lost his job. He tried to earn money by buying foodstuffs from nearby villages and selling to shops in the town, but could not make enough. He started drinking heavily, and asked her to get money from her parents. She went home once for help, but her father refused to give her money. Her mother didn't have any money herself. Her husband started beating her and telling her how useless she was.

One day, he came home drunk and asked her to come with him. "I'll take you to see someone," he said. "Just do whatever he tells you." He dropped her in front of a house in the outskirts of town, where a man was waiting for her. They went in the house, and it turned out that the man expected to have sex with her, because he had already paid her husband for it. Anna was horrified and tried to run away, but the man grabbed her and raped her. "I paid your pimp a lot of money for you," he kept yelling.

Her husband was waiting for her when she came out. She refused to get back in the car with him. She was shaking with shame and anger, but he was acting as if nothing unusual happened. "Since you cannot earn money any other way, this is what you'll do from now on," he told her. "Get in the car right now!" Anna refused, and started screaming, threatening to tell the police what had just happened. She screamed so loud that her husband, wanting to avoid attention, drove away. "Fine, walk home!" He yelled as he left her.

Anna did not walk home. She walked to the bus stop and caught the last bus to her village. She went home, but her father refused to accept her. "Go back to your husband," he said. "Married girls don't run away from home like mad dogs."

I cannot imagine how any father can treat his daughter in that manner. Anna spent that night with her aunt. The next morning she borrowed some money from her and took the bus to Yerevan. Her aunt arranged for her to get in touch with her sister-in-law, and she found a job as a sales girl in a women's clothing store. Her husband found out that she was in Yerevan, but could not find her. He visited the aunt's sister-in-law, who denied having seen her. A month later Anna moved to a room like mine, a few buildings down the road from me.

Now Anna lives in constant fear. Her husband can show up anytime and force her to return. No one can stop him from abusing her if he finds her—neither her family nor the police. She believes the only reason he has not found her yet is his fear that she'll tell the police the story of how he sold her for sex. She uses a different last name to rent her place and at work.

Anna's story has made me realize how lucky I am and how great my own family really is. My father would never have treated any of his daughters like hers treated her. My sisters and brothers have accepted me in spite of the stigma I carry. I have heard stories of angry brothers who slit their sister's throat when they found out that she had worked as a prostitute; that is a matter of family honor in some of our villages. I have not faced any of these threats. I have been welcomed.

And yet I cannot accept their kindness. I often find it crueler than outright rejection. It gives me no room for retaliation, for escape. It gives no justification for my being in Yerevan, rather than at home. No one asked me to leave; they all asked me to stay.

It has always been easier for me to deal with those who have wronged me than with those who have been kind. It is not easy to reject kindness.

My father used to say that there is a pathway between hearts. "Wisdom is taught by love," he'd say, "that's why it cannot be taught in schools. Wisdom gets transferred through that pathway." I was young then, maybe twelve or thirteen, and he would look at my baffled face, kiss my forehead, and add: "Lara, the pathway between hearts is real; it can be very busy with traffic. One day you'll understand. When you do, do not turn a deaf ear to it. Right now, don't you feel a pathway from my heart to yours?" I would throw my arms around his neck and hold on to him. He was so real, so solid, and so eternal…my father would never have told me to go back to an abusive husband.

I worry about Avo the most. I know he is struggling with the 'family honor' thing, even though he won't say a word about it to me. Deep inside he knows where I've been and what I've done; of course, not any of the details—that would certainly drive him off the edge. But he knows the basics. He knows, and yet he still calls me "*Kurig*," sister. He hugs me and acts in deference whenever I'm around; and all that anger in him, which sometimes explodes and is enough to blow up our entire village, is never directed at me, even though I know it is about me, it is *because* of me.

I used to see Avo in my dreams when I was in Dubai. He would appear angry and old, and he would always seem rushed and distracted. We would be somewhere in the fields of Saralandj. He would come and say, "*Kurig jan*, Mama is very ill," and then he would disappear. These were scary dreams; I would wake up in a cold sweat, trembling. What is amazing to me is that now, in real life, he looks like he did in my dreams. This is even scarier than the dreams.

I look at my older sister Martha and see how happy she is. She still has the old happiness that I had before my abduction. Her husband Ruben is kind and decent. Their baby daughter is a delight. They live a hard and difficult life, in primitive conditions. The work that Martha does in a day is more than women in much of the world do in a week. But she is happy. She loves life, and that love radiates from her face, through her smile, even from her tired eyes at the end of a long day. My other sisters have the same joy of life, in spite of their miserable living conditions. Only Arpi remains withdrawn and quiet, burying herself every night in books that she brings home from the Aparan Public Library. But melancholy is her nature; it is not unhappiness.

My sisters' happiness is what I tried to come back to. I remember in Moscow when Anastasia was trying to explain to me that what we did was not so bad, that I could be big in that business, and how jovial and happy she looked all the time. I remember fighting her, resisting even my own inner curiosity to understand her joy, I remember thinking, "I want the happiness I left behind, not yours."

The question that I don't want to face now is whether I *cannot* have that happiness back, or I no longer *want* it back. It is much easier to believe that I cannot have it back; that takes the moral burden away from me and puts it on something else. That would be very convenient, if it were true. But the demon that haunts me every day is this question: What if I no longer want it back? What if I have outgrown all this?

Anna and I have become friends. Some evenings, after she leaves work, we go out and walk for hours in Yerevan, in and around Republic Square, up Abovian Street and Mashtots Street, by the Monument, and once in a while on Northern Avenue, which neither of us likes. It is a short stretch of pedestrian promenade between the Opera and the National Art Gallery, and it is the most artificial and superficial part of Yerevan. It is a new development, boasting the most expensive real estate, and showing off stores of the biggest names in fashion in the world. It is not part of Armenia. But Anna and I walk there sometimes anyway, just to see, to compare, to listen to the street musicians performing, and, once in a while, to indulge and have a cup of coffee in one of the coffee shops for a price that would exceed

Diqin Alice's monthly grocery bill. It does not matter where we go. I like her, even though I have not yet told her my story.

One night I invite her to my room and read her Daniel Varujan's poems. She is amazed at the language, the thought, the strength of emotion. She asks me to read over and over the first verse of the poem, *"To The Dead Gods."*

> *Under a cross glorified by blood,*
> *Whose arms drip sorrow over humanity at large*
> *I, defeated, mourn your death through the bitter heart of my Art,*
> *   Oh Pagan Gods...*
> *Thought is dead, and Nature bleeds*
> *Only boredom survives, ornate with its crown of thorns...*
> *Man has fallen under the giant heel*
> *   Of a Hebrew God, deaf and still...*

I am surprised that Anna is so taken by that verse. Christianity is not as big in Armenia today as it was historically. Religion was banned during the Soviet rule. But Armenia was the first country in the world to adopt Christianity as the state religion, back in 301 A.D. Edik says for several centuries Armenians took the Christian teachings literally, especially teachings like turn the other cheek and love your enemy. So they lost everything to invading armies. He says that is the context in which Varujan's *Pagan Songs* should be understood.

Anna knows nothing about all that, and yet she memorized that verse. Varujan is intense. I guess it is that intensity that is so appealing to Anna. I make a note to introduce her to *Khev Gago* one day. He is intensity personified, even though often detached. His intensity is his own, unto his own. Edik, on the other hand, is intensity personified and *connected*. His intensity is for all. I'll introduce her to both, because I've made up my mind to befriend Anna fully. I probably can help her; I have a feeling that one day she will need my help. And I think it is possible to build a pathway from my heart to hers.

Chapter Six

Yuri is frustrated as he drives back to Yerevan. He has spent the entire day in unproductive meetings with a couple of Ayvazian's henchmen in Aparan, who he suspects are now on the payroll of another oligarch and feel no need to cooperate with him. He gets the feeling that they are taking the time to talk to him in order to record his questions, and that those questions will one day come back to haunt him. Ayvazian's influence in this region is lost, and it is not clear to whom.

He passes through Ashtarak, the capital of the region and *Khev Gago's* hometown, wondering whether he should stop for a bite. It has been over eight hours since he's eaten, even though he's had countless cups of coffee. Aside from the two former employees of Ayvazian, he's gone to see the head of the Aparan post office, an elderly, soft-spoken and docile man named Artiom, who, around two years ago was Samvel Galian's boss, when Galian worked at the post office for $25 per month. The postman had no light to shed on either the Galians or on Ayvazian; he sounded as though he descended to Aparan from outer space yesterday. Of course Yuri knows better, because the money transfers to the

Galians were made through the post office, but he keeps his mouth shut. In this deadly game, it is as important to understand the lies and the liars as the truth, because the lies, if one understands them, can often reveal more than the truth.

He decides to stop at the restaurant of a hotel in Ashtarak. It is mid-afternoon, the slow period between lunch and dinner, and the place is quiet. There are two men at one of the tables at the front of the restaurant, one in military fatigues facing the door, the other in jeans and a brown jacket sitting opposite him. Yuri immediately senses from their body language and the slight pause in their conversation that his entrance may have meant something to them, and he is pretty sure that the reaction is not because of his unusual looks. He gets the uncomfortable sense that the men recognized him. He's been asking enough questions around Aparan and Ashtarak to attract attention.

It would be too awkward to leave. He passes them and sits at a table further inside, facing the door, so that now he can see the face of the man sitting across from the one in fatigues. Their eyes meet for a second. The waitress approaches him with a menu.

"Not everything on the menu is available," she says. "Would you like to eat or just have something to drink?"

Normally Yuri does not waste time being nice to waitresses, but today he smiles politely.

"I'm starving," he says. "What do you recommend?"

"The *sbas* is good," she smiles back, referring to the traditional yoghurt soup with wheat and mint.

"That will do fine," Yuri smiles again. "A bowl of *sbas*, some bread and some sausages if you have them."

"Very well. And to drink?"

"Just water for now."

When she returns with a basket of bread and utensils, Yuri slips a thousand dram bill for her on the table. "That's for the good recommendation," he says.

"Thanks," she says with a warm smile, "but don't you want to taste the soup first to be sure?"

"No need. I trust you already."

This is an unusual exchange, and the waitress is intrigued and cautious at the same time.

When she brings the soup, he asks her to wait a minute while he tastes it. He takes a spoon, and looks up to her.

"This is excellent indeed," he says, "I knew I could trust you."

"I'm glad you like it." She starts to leave, but he stops her again.

"I have a small question," he says, lowering his voice. "I hope you don't mind. Are those two gentlemen over there from around here?"

The waitress looks toward the table for a second. "Can't say for sure," she says. "This place is on a busy road as you know, and we get a lot of people passing through. Do you want me to ask them?"

"Oh no, no need. I was just curious. So they are not regulars here, right? Otherwise you probably would have recognized them."

"The fact is, I myself am not a regular here. I work only three days a week. So it is possible that I've missed them even if they have been here."

Yuri eats quickly, visits the restroom and leaves, dropping another thousand-dram tip on the table, and hoping that that will create enough good will for her not to mention his queries to the two men.

The waitress watches as Yuri's car pulls out of the driveway, then walks over and puts her hand on *Khev Gago's* shoulder. "What was that all about?"

"You tell me, Houri jan," says Gagik. "Edik was watching him and he says he was quite generous with you."

"That he was," laughs Houri, who is one of Gagik's cousins. "He wanted to know whether you two fine gentlemen are from these parts. That seemed to matter to him."

"Be careful with him," says Gagik. "He's been in Aparan a few times, but not here until now. Let me know if he shows up again."

"Will do. Can I get you two anything else?"

"Thanks," says Laurian standing up. "I need to get going. See you two soon."

ᘓ ᘓ ᘓ

Yuri has confirmed Viktor's visit to the Galians and heard the conflicting and garbled rumors about the Galians' daughter, ranging from the 'successful model in Greece' version to 'prostitute' and many variants in between. There is no doubt in Yuri's mind that the Ayvazians recruited a Galian into prostitution. Although nothing specific in the rumors ties her story to Ayvazian, the pattern fits perfectly, even if not a single detail in the rumors is true. People would be afraid to include Ayvazian in rumors anyway, even after his death, and it is not the details that matter, but the very nature of the stories, involving modeling and prostitution. That, and the confusion surrounding it, is trademark Ayvazian.

But in spite of the overwhelming evidence of a link, the thought that the Galians may have been in any way involved in the Ayvazians' and Hamo's killings does not even cross Yuri's mind. Peasants, and vulnerable ones at that, simply do not go around killing powerful people. The most likely explanation remains that the killings were planned and executed by another oligarch. So Yuri does not think a visit to the Galians would add much to what he has already learned.

He decides the time has come to go back to Moscow for a few days. Not only are his inquiries in Armenia raising more questions than they are answering, but also some of the leads point to Moscow.

"I'll go see how persuasive I can be in Moscow," he tells Carla that night, accepting her challenge. Carla smiles like a schoolteacher sending her star student on an important mission, even though Yuri is ten years her senior. She has started paying Yuri a salary. He no longer receives anything in Moscow; his paymaster there was Viktor, and he did not hang around Moscow long enough to find out what is left of Ayvazian's operation.

Moscow indeed proves to be easier to crack. Yuri goes to the apartment that Ayvazian kept in a relatively poor section of town, and finds that the housekeeper, a middle aged woman called Nono, whom he's known for years, is still there. It is the same apartment where they kept Lara before taking her to Dubai. Yuri has initiated many recruits in that apartment over the years, and knows that Nono is more than a housekeeper. She's also drill sergeant, disciplinarian and mother hen, as the circumstances require. The new recruits sometimes need to be convinced to accept prostitution as their new way of life. So they are raped and beaten, until they see that there is no way out, and succumb to the new reality. Once the rapes and the beatings are done and the men leave, it is Nono who takes over, cleans up the mess and makes sure that the girls do not do anything desperate, such as try to escape or even worse, make clumsy suicide attempts. She talks to them, alternating between the dangers and futility of fighting their new fate, and the bright future ahead if they simply fall in line.

Nono confirms that Lara was there and that she was eventually handed over to Anastasia. Yuri knows Anastasia too; he has collected from her for Viktor in the past, before Viktor started giving her more leeway and freedom.

But confirming that Lara Galian was there is only a peripheral curiosity for Yuri. He notices that Nono does not seem to be affected by the Ayvazian killings. Everything seems normal in the apartment and in Nono's demeanor. She does not look stressed, nor is she acting as if anything is amiss. She is talking to Yuri as the landlady entertaining a visitor, confident and in control.

He then asks the question that has been haunting him.

"Nono," he says looking her straight in the eye, "who is paying your salary now?"

Yuri feels that technically, with both Viktor and Sergei Ayvazian gone, he should be in charge of the operations in Moscow, even though that was never made clear to anyone by Ayvazian and could easily be challenged. Had Nono not known Yuri, and seen him in action with Viktor in the past, she would have no reason to answer his question. Even knowing his past, she is under no obligation to answer.

"One of Viktor's men," says Nono finally, and Yuri is glad to see that she manages to overcome her initial hesitation.

"Anyone I know?"

"He is Russian," says Nono, somehow resolving in her mind that there can be no harm in telling Yuri the truth. "His name is Nicolai. I have seen him with Viktor here many times. Once he, Viktor and Sergei had a long meeting in this apartment. I remember because Viktor asked me to leave for a few hours. Do you know Nicolai?"

Nono's words hit Yuri hard. His mind soars with the imponderable possibilities. He should have wondered about this situation much earlier. He now realizes that by rushing to Armenia to seek compensation for Hamo's death, he may have passed up a much larger prize. Once again, he is amazed at how little he knows about his former boss's operations. He did not know about Nicolai's existence. He always thought that the key people in the business were all Armenian.

Then it occurs to him that now Carla is playing by the same rules. The flow of information is one-way. Until now, he had assumed that she does not know anything more than what he tells her. He realizes in a cold sweat that he has no idea who else Carla has engaged as informers, and, why not, lovers?

Nono is staring at him. Does he look like he's just seen a ghost? He gathers himself quickly and returns to the moment.

"Is Nicolai also paying the rent here?" he asks, ignoring both Nono's question and surprised expression.

"As far as I know, yes. One of his assistants was here and he also took care of all the utility bills. Now everything goes to them."

"Has there been a lot of activity?" Seeing that Nono does not understand the question, he adds, "Have they brought girls here in the past few months?"

"Oh, yes. More than ten girls, almost all Ukrainian and Russian. Only one Armenian girl since the Ayvazians died."

"And everything is handled by Nicolai? Is there anyone else running things?"

"Well, there are others that come here, but I think they are Nicolai's assistants. I cannot always be sure who is who. Every time someone comes who has the key and knows my name, I assume that Nicolai has sent him, just like the understanding was with Viktor."

Yuri decides that he can go no further with his investigation without getting to the source of the money; he has to figure out who is collecting it and where it is going. He chides himself again for not having done that as soon as the Ayvazians were killed. How many girls are left working for the Ayvazians, who runs them, who collects? How could this Russian he has never heard of take over Ayvazian's operation in Moscow? If he has not, whom does he work for? The end of the string making up this tangle is the money, as usual. And the prostitutes are the source of the money. Time now to pay Anastasia a visit.

Chapter Seven

Edik has written two poems about secrets. They contradict each other, professing quite different philosophies of life. In the first, he talks about how secrets imprison people, how man remains captive to his own secrets as long as he needs to keep and protect them. Your secrets encircle and restrain you, he says, they dominate you, until you no longer have memories, only secrets, and in order to keep them, you create new lies and new secrets, until you *become* your secrets. The implication is that freedom only comes from screaming secrets from the rooftops, until there is no longer anything to hide, even though the poem doesn't say that in so many words.

In the second poem, he talks about how secrets liberate you, how they are all that you have, the only things that you do not share, do not bequeath, do not give away, and the only things that will in the end go with you to your grave.

He read both to me, and then asked which of the two I preferred. He was in an unusual mood that afternoon. We met on campus. As we sat on a bench, he took two folded sheets of paper from his coat pocket and started reading. He was more serious than usual, appearing almost in a dark mood, and it seemed he had come specifically to read the poems to me.

The second poem reached deep into my heart. "It is your secrets that liberate you," was the recurring line. He read it with such force, such conviction, or maybe it sounded like that to me because that is exactly what I wanted to hear.

> *It is your secrets*
> 　　　　*that liberate you*
> *do not confess!*
> *do not expose!*
> *. . .*
> *confession is for the weak!*
> *for those who do not have the will*
> 　　　　*to endure*
>
> *. . .*
> *I want you to live*
> 　　　　*with your secrets*
> 　　　　*within your secrets*
> 　　　　*by your secrets*
> *I want them to be*
> 　　　　*your sanctuary*
> *I want them to be*
> 　　　　*your only refuge...*

I did not answer his question then. I thanked him and promised to read them again. I was taken as much by the topic of the poems as by the forcefulness of the two opposing views.

"Why did you write about secrets?" To me, that was a more interesting question than which poem he or I preferred.

"We all have secrets," he said. "*All* of us," he stressed, looking me in the eye. "The difference between people is how they handle their secrets."

I read and think about them often. *I want them to be your sanctuary*...or are they my prison, Paron Edik? You have no idea how many secrets I have, how I protect them, how they've taken over my life, how I live in the dark prison that they have woven around me, through layers and layers of barbed wire surrounding my soul, my life. Do my secrets liberate me? Maybe yours do, but mine do not. It is your first poem on secrets that I should relate to and memorize. But why do I remember the second? Why do I repeat the verses of the second every night, and choose to forget the first?

The time for a final reckoning with all my secrets will come, and that is a scary thought. I am not talking about reckoning as in confession or facing death. I do not feel I have to explain anything to anyone, except to myself, and, someday, to Avo. By far the most difficult demon I have to face is myself. Why do I want to feel liberated by secrets, why do I want to start loving my secrets so much? I no longer want to feel like I'm imprisoned by them. I want to feel at home with them. That desire is difficult to understand.

Yes, the most difficult demon I have to face is Lara Galian. And maybe Avo. I'm responsible for his rage. He's fighting the Lara Galian demon too, in his own way, which may be a much more difficult fight than mine. At the end of the day I can look into the mirror and face myself; whom does he face?

I'm so glad Edik came up with the idea of taking courses at the University. I would have had no other legitimate excuse to move to the city. Besides, it had been my father's wish to see his children graduate from college, so I had an added justification.

But I do not need to pretend and turn this into yet another secret. The history courses I am following are boring, but I am enjoying the English language class. Edik says understanding our own history is the most important thing we can do. Frankly, I don't see the point; I mean, I don't see the point from an everyday practical point of view, even though if I begin to think beyond the everyday like he does, maybe there is a point to understanding it all.

Do your secrets imprison you, or do they set you free? Today, as I struggle with several situations at the same time, that, and only that, is the question. And you'd be mistaken if you think that the question is academic and irrelevant. If I cannot feel at home with my secrets, then I cannot feel at home anywhere. Even my most important memories, which are the voice and stories of my father, now appear to me in the framework of my secrets. They acquire meaning only through my secrets; I understand them only in the context of my secrets. What did they mean before I had so many secrets? What did they mean to him? What do they mean to my brothers and sisters? I find it impossible to even imagine. If even his sayings and stories are now woven into my secrets, then nothing is left from the old Lara Galian. Nothing.

It is your secrets that isolate you
whatever you feel
wherever you are
with those who love you
or with whom you love
you remain alone …

Leave it to Edik to sum it up in a few verses. What exactly did he ask me to choose? Did he want me choose between his poems, or between two Laras, between two lives?

I thought a few times about reading the poems to Avo, but then gave up the idea. Avo is not the poetic type.

ଅ ଅ ଅ

Anna asks me more about Saralandj and about my family. I repeat the names of my sisters and brothers, starting with the oldest, giving brief explanations; "Martha (married, one daughter), Sona (engaged), Arpi (quiet and reserved), Alisia (a delight, I used to share a bed with her when we were young), Lara (me, I smile), Avo (the man of house, I smile again. He is tall and handsome, I add, too bad he's younger than you—now Anna smiles), Sago (quiet and reserved), Aram (the smartest Galian kid, he probably can teach more to his schoolteachers than they can teach him)."

"And your brothers-in-law?" she asks.

"Ruben, Martha's husband, who is wonderful; Simon, Sona's fiancé. I don't know him well yet, but he seems very nice."

"Wow!" Anna exhales. She is an only child. Her father has treated her as if she was an enemy, and her mother has been powerless to help her.

We are having a light supper at a coffee shop near the Opera.

"Have you heard from your aunt's sister in-law?" I sense that Anna is depressed thinking about her father and husband, and I want to remind her of the one person who has helped her.

"We talk once a week. The important thing is that my husband has not tried to contact her again. I'll be so happy if he's given up on me, but I think that's wishful thinking on my part."

"You never know," I say hopefully. "We're both still young, you know. We can do a lot with our lives. You've had a very bad experience, of course. But that's all it is, one really bad experience."

"Which is not over yet..." Anna lowers her voice.

Is living in fear like living with secrets? Anna is no less a prisoner of her constant fear of being found and reclaimed by her husband, than I am a prisoner of my secrets. But, according to Edik, secrets can also set you free; not so with fear. Even Edik could not write a poem showing how fear can be liberating. Overcoming fear may liberate, but not fear itself.

"There is only one way to be rid of your fear of this man," I tell her, also lowering my voice. "You have rights, you know. You can divorce him, and he cannot touch you after that."

"Divorce him?"

"Sure. Divorce him, and you'll divorce your fear of him." I know that probably it is not that simple, but I know that technically I am right.

Can one divorce one's secrets too? I guess so, by just disclosing them. The problem is that exposing secrets doesn't really get rid of them. Everything is still there; it's just not a secret anymore. Divorcing a secret doesn't kill it, it multiplies it, it increases it by as many times as the number of people you tell it to, and then even more as they start telling it to others. Before you know it, the secret you try to kill by sharing it multiplies like a virus.

"I had not thought about that," says Anna, looking at me as if I just opened her eyes. "How do I go about doing that?"

"I have no idea," I say. "I haven't even been married yet! But I have some incredible friends, Anna. You'll meet them one day. They'll help us figure this out." *I haven't even been married yet*, my dear Anna, but I've been forced to have sex with well over a *thousand* men, and that is something that you'll never understand, and I can never tell you. There is no 'divorcing' that particular fact.

Anna looks like a huge weight has been lifted from her shoulders. She looks a lot prettier when her face is not distorted by stress. She has cut her hair very short since moving to the city, which makes her eyes look larger and more expressive, and when her face relaxes, they dance in an amazing transformation.

Anna has seen a way out, a ridiculously simple and obvious way out. I can tell, from the 'I just saw the light' look in her eyes. Then she throws her arms around me and kisses my cheeks. She is so emotional that some people in the coffee shop notice and turn around to look at us.

"You're the sister I never had," she says, no longer whispering.

I feel I now have a confirmed friend, one whom I may be able help. Anna, with her reaction, has taught me the joy of helping someone whose plight I understand, and I have not even done anything yet. I've just given her an idea, about which I myself know little.

As I think about my discovery, I realize that it is so simple, as simple as the advice I gave Anna, and yet it had not occurred to me before. Then I see something else: Could it be that this what Edik feels? Everyone I know who knows Edik has, at one time or another, raised the question—Why does he care? Why is he so engaged, so connected to everything? There is absolutely nothing in it for him personally, and yet nothing seems unimportant to him. Why *does* he care?

I think I just stumbled onto one possible answer. *The joy of helping someone whose plight I understand.* But does Edik understand my plight? Why would he give me those two poems otherwise? Who is Edik anyway? We know very little about him. He does not have to be here. Why does this man bother with me? With us? He has helped Avo, Avo has spent several days in his dacha as his guest, we all spent that magical night in his dacha after we killed Viktor and Sergei Ayvazian and their four bodyguards, he drives four hours each way from Vardahovit to visit us in Saralandj, he lent the money that Avo needed to start his pig farm, and the resounding question remains: *Why?*

Is it really because it feels good to help someone whose plight you understand? But how on earth did he even begin to understand our plight, especially mine, even before he met me? Gago says he is the way he is because he is *connected.* But I do not believe that's all there is to it. Perhaps this has to do with that third ear, the ear of his heart.

Chapter Eight

Manoj Gupta has run many odd errands for his boss over the ten years that he has been in Al Barmaka's employ, most of them in familiar territory, covering the Middle East, Asia and, once in a while, Europe. But he now has the uneasy feeling of entering entirely unfamiliar ground, even before leaving Dubai, as he boards the Armavia flight to Yerevan. It is presently the only airline that has a direct flight, and he opts for the unknown airline against the more complicated routes via Europe on airlines that he knows.

He is the only one in First Class, which has two rows of four seats each. The aircraft is old and run down, the chairs squeak and shift on the floor bolts, there is rust on the armrests and tears in the dirty carpet. Although the First Class cabin is empty, economy class is full, and he guesses that the airline is doing well on this route, and so does not understand this degree of neglect. The flight attendants look bored and unmotivated. What Manoj does not know is that Armavia is controlled by yet another state-supported oligarch, who is running the company into the ground. This syndrome, which baffles outsiders when they encounter it, and disgusts locals, who leave the country in droves, somehow survives.

It is a short flight, and Manoj keeps himself busy by reading about the country he is visiting and going over a stack of business documents. Before he knows it, they land. Being the first to disembark, he gets into an empty passport control line and, having no checked bags, is in the car sent by the hotel within minutes of touchdown.

Manoj finds himself not just transported to a different country, but to a different world. From a hot and humid desert, he has landed in a cold, mountainous country, where the lowest point is six hundred meters above sea level, and well into spring there are still patches of snow at the side of the streets. While Dubai burns in forty degree Celsius heat only three hours away, he had watched with fascination from the window of the descending plane an almost magical winter landscape. He starts wondering if Al Barmaka did in fact have a business strategy in mind, for the first time giving him the benefit of the doubt that the alleged business motive for the trip may not have been just a cover to send him here to find Leila. He is in fact scheduled to see several businessmen to discuss trade and tourism, in addition to a planned trip to a village called Saralandj. His attempts to find a street address for the Galians' home have been futile. "There are no street maps for small villages in Armenia," the Armenian Embassy clerk in Abu Dhabi tells him. He does not want to disclose his interest specifically in Saralandj and the Galians to the Embassy yet, so he cannot inquire further. All they tell him is that, "Small villages don't have street names. A family name is enough to locate any house in any village. If you have both the first name and family name, even better."

He checks into the Marriott hotel at two-thirty in the afternoon. The food on the plane was inedible. He decides to stay in the hotel for his first meal in the country, and goes to a restaurant in the lobby. The menu has some familiar items, while others sound too exotic for him. He goes for what he knows: a cheeseburger with fries. He's been told to avoid raw vegetables and tap water. But Manoj is from India, even though he has lived in the Middle East for most of his life. Until several years ago, while his parents were still alive, he used to visit family in India. He can handle foods that will make most foreigners sick for weeks. So he is not too concerned about water and raw vegetables, but he orders a Coke anyway.

He's had a few fries and a bite of his cheeseburger when a man in his early thirties approaches his table.

"Welcome to Armenia, Mr. Manoj," he says enthusiastically in a heavy accent, smiling broadly, and not bothering to introduce himself.

Manoj is taken by surprise. The young man adds, "My name is Armen. I am your driver, and I'm at your service. Again, welcome." The explanation answers a question for Manoj, but does nothing to reduce his surprise. He had called the driver earlier to say that he has arrived and that he'll call back with the schedule. The idea that a driver he's never met before can identify him so easily, and just barge in, is unheard of in Dubai. Drivers usually do not even come in; they wait outside until the boss is ready for them.

But Manoj takes a liking to Armen almost immediately. Maybe it is the relief of having someone who works for him in this foreign environment, or maybe it is Armen's relaxed, simple demeanor, which somehow transcends all class barriers. He has not seen such behavior anywhere else: not in India, where the class consciousness is far too strong to permit this type of casual interaction, not in the Middle East, where the local VIP versus expatriate hired labor distinction is even a thicker wall, and not in Europe, where the old, stuffy aristocratic class structure, reincarnated as service sector protocol, dominates. He stops wondering how the driver found him, recognized him, and what gave him the nerve to walk in and greet him as if he was an old childhood friend. He takes one more look at Armen's beaming, ready-to-serve smile, and smiles in return.

"Thank you," he says. "Good to meet you. You'll be with me for the next three days, right?"

"Twenty four hours a day!" responds Armen with another huge smile. "What's the program?"

What's the program? No hired help has ever talked to Manoj like this. Spoken as if he's excited about an outing with an old friend. After a decade of service to Al Barmaka, he has never dared to address him in such an informal manner.

As his nervous tension melts away, Manoj starts to laugh. He chuckles, first in short bursts, and then more fully. Armen starts to laugh with him, which reinforces Manoj's good mood. What the hell, he might as well befriend this driver for a few days. That may serve him much better than a more formal relationship.

"The program," he says, still chuckling, "is…wait, what was your name again?"

"Armen"

"Armen. Okay. The program, Armen, is that we start with a lunch other than a cheeseburger and fries. Where can we get a good lunch that will not kill me by this evening?"

"A local lunch!" says Armen laughing. "Come, we go to the Dzor."

"We go where?" Manoj is still laughing.

"To the Dzor," repeats Armen. Then he realizes that he might be expected to explain further and adds, "Mr. Manoj, there are only four places one can be in Armenia. *Dzor*, which means valley. *Sar*, which means mountain. *Kaghak,* which means the city, meaning Yerevan; and *khaghakits durs*, which means outside the city. That is all. You cannot be anywhere other these four places in Armenia!" Armen looks like he has just solved the mysteries of the Universe. "So," he adds, "the closest local restaurants are in the Dzor. Fifteen minutes from here. I know a good one by the bank of the river. You'll love the food and I guarantee that it will not kill you."

"Let's go!"

Armen reminds him of the smart, enterprising but underprivileged youngsters in Mumbai, whose only asset is their wit, and who manage to scrounge a living in the streets, appearing always happy and full of energy, but in reality they live much darker lives when they end their public day and return to the privacy of their living quarters, which, for the lucky ones could be a room in a deserted building, and for most others a street corner partially protected from the elements.

ꝗ ꝗ ꝗ

Lara Galian freezes at the top of the stairs as she leaves the University building, no longer aware of the fresh breeze after the stuffy lecture hall. She stares down at the woman waving to her. This is the last place on earth she would have expected to see Anastasia, her coach when she was first thrown into prostitution in Moscow. Anastasia is more conservatively dressed than she used to be in the hotel bars in Moscow, but still stands out. Her posture and overall attitude are not those of a student.

Lara continues down the steps and walks up to her. Anastasia smiles enthusiastically. She looks genuinely happy to see Lara.

"Lara, *aziz jan, vonts es?*" That's exactly how she used to talk to her two years ago. Lara, dear, how are you?

Lara does not want to be rude, so she returns the smile, but she does not want to engage Anastasia as if everything is the same.

"How did you find me?" she asks, guiding her out of the University grounds and starting down the street.

"I'm good, am I not?" grins Anastasia. But Lara senses that she is nervous, and is trying hard not to show it. She does not respond, waiting for an answer to her original question. Anastasia remains silent, but picks up the pace a bit.

"How?" repeats Lara, looking at her as they walk.

"I'll explain everything," says Anastasia with another wide smile, and this time there is no doubt in Lara's mind that the smile is fake. Anastasia isn't just nervous; she is afraid. "Right now, act like you're happy to see me."

Lara had almost forgotten the feeling—the feeling of being constantly watched, followed, the sense of permanent fear of more beatings and rapes. She feels her head spin and a cold sweat dampen the hair on the back of her neck. She does not want this. She will not have this again, no matter what. A wave of blinding anger begins to well in her chest.

"Happy to see you?" she says with such sarcasm that Anastasia looks away. "What are you doing here? I do not want to be dragged into any of it again. What do you want?"

"Let's get in a taxi," says Anastasia nervously. "We're being watched. I'll explain everything when it is safe."

Before Lara can say anything, Anastasia stops a taxi and opens the door. Her hands are shaking and her eyes are pleading with Lara to get in. "Please, *aziz* jan," she repeats. "I'll explain everything."

Lara gets in and scoots over; Anastasia follows. "Just drive," she tells the driver. "Towards the Monument." The 'Monument' in popular parlance refers to the statue of 'Mother Armenia,' on a hill overlooking Yerevan, which, in 1962, replaced a statue of Joseph Stalin, built as a memorial of victory in World War II. Anastasia takes her cell phone from her pocket, turns it off and sits on it. Then she leans close to Lara and whispers.

"I'm sorry you're upset, but at least hear me out. Someone I used to know a long time ago in Moscow, who worked for the Ayvazians, says the Ayvazian family is back in full control. He says all old debts have to be paid."

"What does that have to do with me? I have no debts to anyone."

"Don't be so naïve, Lara, please. This guy, his name is Yuri, beat me, threatened me, and forced me to fly to Yerevan with him."

"I thought both Viktor and that animal Sergei were dead," says Lara, trying to give herself time to think.

"They are. I thought it had ended with them too. For many months I was keeping all the money, imagine that! Then this guy Nicolai shows up and forces me to pay him. He says he's the new boss. Then Yuri shows up and says the family knows who killed Sergei and Viktor and wants everything back."

The blood drains from Lara's face. They know who killed Ayvazian? That is impossible. They would have been all over Saralandj if they really had known anything. She does her best to recover before Anastasia notices her panic.

"Why did they bring you to Yerevan?" Lara asks calmly.

"To talk to you. To see how much you know."

"How much I know about what?"

"About the killings, and about who brought you back home and how."

"Why should I know anything about the killings?"

"Because they say you returned about the same time as the killings happened."

"So? How could I know anything?"

"They're just checking, that's all. I am not supposed to tell you any of this. I am supposed to befriend you again. Try to make you talk. I am taking a huge risk by telling you the truth. Remember Lara, I was a good friend to you in Moscow; the fact that you hated being there does not change that."

That part is true. Lara remembers the day when Viktor, after being told by Dr. Melikov that she was pregnant, ordered him to perform an abortion. She did not even know that she was pregnant. It was Anastasia who was there when they released her from the hospital. She took her to her apartment and tended to her for the next three days. She fed her, washed her, and talked to her constantly. She tried to put things in perspective for her.

"So what am I supposed to do now?" she asks.

"Let's pretend that we're friends, talking about old times. Just for a few days. Then I tell them whatever you want me to tell them, things you confess to me in confidence and in friendship. That's the only way they think they'll get the truth from you. That's the only reason why they have not come after you directly yet."

"Yet?"

"Lara, anything is possible. A lot depends on what I tell them. So let's think about this carefully."

"What's it with your phone?" asks Lara, changing the subject.

"My phone?"

"You're sitting on it."

"Oh, sorry." Anastasia leans even closer to Lara and whispers in her ear. "I've heard that they can listen in on my conversations through the phone. That's why I turned it off, but sometimes apparently even then they can listen. So I sat on it. That's why I have the window open. The noise from the street should drown our whispers."

"Okay," whispers Lara, "we'll play this game. As long as you understand that I have no intention of going back to that life. I think I'll be happy if I do not see another man for the rest of my life."

"Lara, *aziz* jan, of course. I'm very happy for you, please understand that. I used to tell you that you'd be better off accepting it because you really had no other choice back then. But now it seems that you do. I'm glad, really. But this is all I know. I just want to go back to my clients in Moscow."

"Did they say they want me to work for them again?"

"Where to, lady?" asks the driver. They have passed the Monument and are driving up the road toward the suburbs.

"Go a few more blocks then turn back," says Anastasia. "Can you then wait for us at the Monument for a little?"

The driver grunts his consent and keeps driving.

"They did not say that to me," responds Anastasia. "Honestly. My mission is to find out what you know about the Ayvazian killings and how you managed to leave Dubai and return home. That's all. I'm not here to talk you into being a good hooker, like in the old days..." And Anastasia can barely hold back a chuckle. "You have to admit, we had some good times back then."

"You were having a good time back then, not me," says Lara a bit too curtly, and regrets it. She does not want to judge her; all she wants is to be left alone.

"*De lav*, Lara jan." Oh enough of that, Lara. "Don't you remember the American at the Sheraton? He wanted you for the whole night? He paid a fortune! How bad was that?"

It always amused Lara to hear Anastasia, who is Ukrainian, use colloquial Armenian phrases. Their conversations have always alternated between Lara's broken Russian and Anastasia's broken Armenian.

"Look, I will not lecture you about this, because you will not understand," says Lara, sounding determined and exasperated at the same time. "I have no problem with you doing what you do. I'm happy for you too, as long as you're doing what you want to do. And yes, that night with the American was not so bad, but *only* if you accept that you are a prostitute in the first place. If you don't, that night was as bad as any other."

The driver pulls into the courtyard of the Monument and stops.

"Give us a few minutes," says Anastasia. Then turns to Lara. "Let's walk a little."

They stand at the edge of the courtyard. It is already late afternoon, and it is getting dark. They watch as the city lights turn on in Yerevan below.

"It is amazing how things can look so beautiful from afar," says Lara, staring at the city. "And yet, there is nothing beautiful out there, once you get closer."

"You're as philosophical as ever," says Anastasia seriously. "I remember how I could never make you take anything lightly. I personally don't think anything good ever comes from overthinking. It is the same city, from up here or from down there. It is neither beautiful nor ugly. It is what it is."

Lara looks at Anastasia for a few minutes. 'It is what it is' she repeats silently. How true. Anastasia is okay. She too is what she is. The fight I need to fight is not with her, not even with what she does for a living. The only fight that I really have to fight is with myself.

Lara pulls Anastasia toward her and gives her a big, long hug. "We don't need to pretend," she says, "we *are* old friends. We'll talk about old times all we want. And everyone else can go to hell."

𝒳 𝒳 𝒳

In a black Mercedes SUV with darkened windows, no more than fifteen meters from them, Yuri and Carla are watching the drama.

"You should have bugged her, as I told you," she says.

The girls get back in the taxi and head down the hill to Yerevan. Yuri waits for a few minutes and follows them from a safe distance.

Chapter Nine

Although I believe Edik's offer to Avo and me to call at anytime, with any issue, is genuine, so far I have not asked him for help. Avo has, when he needed the money to start the pig farm, and we both noticed how pleased Edik was to be called upon.

I know the time has come to call him regarding both Anna and Anastasia, but I've been putting it off. I find it difficult to ask for help, even for someone else, even though I know Edik would be absolutely delighted. It is as if once you ask and he comes through, you have in a way confirmed a relationship, which, for some reason, scares me. After what Edik, *Khev Gago*, Avo and I went through only six months ago in Sevajayr, you'd think I'd be over that fear, at least with them, but I am not. The fact is, I did not ask for that day; they just appeared and saved my life, at the cost of having blood on their hands. But I did *not* ask. Maybe that's why, dramatic as that day was, it still does not count as a favor.

Avo helps me end my hesitation. He calls on a Thursday afternoon, all excited, and insists that I come to Saralandj the first chance I get.

"*Kurig jan*," he says—how I love to hear those words from him. *Dear little sister*, words that take me back to the pre-secrets Lara—"We had one delivery already! Eight little piglets, you have to see them. Eight, imagine! They look like little pink rats, attached to their mother, eyes shut, suckling for dear life. It is amazing." He is almost out of breath. I have not seen Avo this animated, except when he is angry, for a long time. This too is a voice from the pre-secrets days. He sees the farm as a venture that is one hundred percent his own, his contribution to our family, not something left over from Papa or our grandfather. Everything else in Saralandj, from the fruit trees to the sheep, even to the household furniture, is from the past.

"Avo, that is great," I say, even though I have no particular interest in seeing the little piglets. "I have class tomorrow, but will try to get there on Saturday. Is that okay?"

"Sure. Just come. This will be great. If all goes well with the other nineteen about to give birth, I probably will be able to return Edik's money in full this fall."

That's something even I can get excited about. Knowing Edik, he probably wrote off the loan in his mind the minute he made it. But paying him back is a huge obligation for us.

"Edik would be interested to hear the news too, you should give him a call," I say, thinking this would be the perfect opportunity for me to talk to Edik.

"Bring him with you," he says with excitement. "Maybe he can drive and pick you up."

I'm glad my going to Saralandj with Edik is now Avo's idea.

ℒ ℒ ℒ

I catch Edik at a bad time when I call. He sounds rushed and distracted.

"Lara jan, so good to hear from you. Can you hold for just a minute?"

"Sure, but if this is not a good time, I can call later."

"No, no, it is fine. One minute." I hear the slightly muffled noise of his hand covering the phone; his voice is still vaguely audible, and it sounds like he's giving instructions to someone.

"Sorry about that," he says, his voice calmer. "Sometimes I have to explain things over and over to Agassi. I'll have to leave Armenia for a few weeks, and there's too much that needs to be done here. Anyway, how are you?"

"I'm fine," I say, beginning to wonder if I should forget the whole thing; he sounds like he has enough on his hands. "If I had known you are so swamped, I wouldn't have called."

"Absolutely no problem. I don't leave till the end of next week. There's plenty of time to plan everything. What's new with you? How can I help?" He sounds so eager and so genuine, that I decide to stick with the plan.

"Edik jan," I say, hesitation still lingering in my voice, "I'm calling to see if I can see you on Saturday, and if we can drive to Saralandj together. But as I said, if you're too busy, it is not important."

"Lara," he says with a chuckle, "I've been waiting six months for this call! Of course I'm not too busy. I can be in Yerevan before noon on Saturday. We can have a quick lunch, and then drive to Saralandj. Would that work?"

"That would be perfect, thank you so much."

"But tell me, what's the occasion?" Of course I knew that he wouldn't be able to wait to find out what's behind my request.

"Avo wants us there," I say, happy to have the pretext. "One of the mama pigs delivered, and I have not heard him so excited for a long time. And there are a couple of other things I'd like to talk to you about. So I thought the drive up there will give us a chance to talk."

"In that case I have a better plan," he says, and I can feel the impatience in his voice. "I will come down to Yerevan tomorrow night. Let's have dinner together—much better for a good chat than a rushed lunch and a drive. That way, we can leave earlier Saturday morning and have more time in Saralandj too."

"Edik, are you sure?"

"Absolutely. I'll call you when I reach my hotel. Most probably I'll pick you up around eight."

"That's fine, Edik. And once again, thank you."

I've had a lot of time to think about how I'll approach Edik, what I'll say about Anna, Anastasia, about Avo, and even about the nature of secrets, and in what order. I have it all clear in my mind, from the first hello to the last good night, and for once I feel like I can finally turn a corner by taking Edik into my confidence, but at my own pace and in my own way.

I dress conservatively. A pair of navy blue pants, beige turtleneck sweater and my light coat. I wear no makeup at all, and tie my hair up in a ponytail. After being ordered for eighteen months to be seductive at all times, I've developed a distaste for any attempt to appear attractive.

He picks me up a little before eight, and drives to one of his favorite restaurants on Toumanian Street. Until we get to the restaurant and are seated, all he talks about is what he is up to in Vardahovit—the new trees that will be planted in a few weeks: poplars, fruit trees, weeping willows and weeping birch, which he has recently discovered and fallen in love with. "There are forests of it in Russia," he says. "They are even more grace-ful than weeping willows." Then he shifts to the irrigation system he is working on, both for the village and for his estate. I find it fascinating to hear Edik talk like a farmer, as if at that moment he neither knows nor cares about anything else.

I should have known that it is impossible to stick to a script when talk-ing to Edik. When it comes to conversations, he can be a force of nature, connecting dots at lightening speed and charting new courses for every train of thought, until the original script disintegrates and even I forget what my plan was.

When we sit down and we order, he shocks me with his opening line.

"There is an American writer," he says, leaning over the table and look-ing very serious. "He wrote a book, *You Can't Go Home Again*. Have you heard about it?"

"No." I say, but the title hits home. Is this about me also, like the poems?

"I don't know if it ever was translated into Armenian, but it's worth checking," he says casually. "I think you'll find it interesting."

"What's it about?" I ask, wondering what happened to my script and how I can get the conversation back on track, but at the same time I'm intrigued by the title of the book.

"The specific story may not interest you. It is about a writer who leaves his hometown and writes a book about it, and makes everyone in the town angry at him, so much so that he cannot go back. But the real message is that no one can go back to his childhood, to his former way of life, even to his family, once he leaves and sees the world."

"And you think I should read the book because that is what I am struggling with?" I sound a little curter than I mean to be. I was prepared to bare a little of my soul to Edik tonight, but not like this, not with the coming home issues, which cannot be discussed without getting into the secrets.

"Well, of course you are," he says so casually that I relax a little. "Aren't you?" He is talking as if we're discussing the weather. Could it be that I am making much more of this than it is?

"Look," he says when I do not answer. "It is the most natural thing in the world. I've felt it more than once, because I've had more than one home that I could never go back to. Everyone feels it when they move from a small place to a larger place."

"There's a lot more to it than that." He sees my annoyance.

"Are you upset that I brought that up?" He sounds surprised.

"Your American writer could never understand my issues," I say seriously, meaning every word. "It is not just a matter of going back to a small place or a former lifestyle. It is also about where you've been, and what you've done. This writer character of yours, did he leave his town voluntarily?"

"Yes." Now Edik is totally focused on me.

"And he did what he wanted to do after he left, right? He decided to write a book, that was his choice, right?"

"Right."

"So how on earth is this similar?"

"It is not those details that are similar, just the impossibility of going back."

"No," I say, realizing that I have taken control of the conversation, even though none of this was in my original script. "That is not similar either, not at all. As I said, there's a lot more to it than that."

"Tell me." And he waits, staring at me, still, focused.

"It *does* matter whether one leaves home voluntarily or not. It matters even more whether one does what one chooses to do while away. And it does matter that one is free to decide when to attempt a return. Either way, it may still be impossible to come back, but the process and the pain are entirely different."

"Tell me," he says, still focused.

"If I had been free to decide when to return, I would have been home the same night I left. The *same* night. I could easily have 'gone home again' if I had had that choice."

He is still silent, intently watching me. This is the most that I have ever told him. I feel that he is keeping still so as not to frighten me, like a birdwatcher careful not to scare away the bird he's watching. He has broken loose a wave of emotions, he knows it, and so do I. Deep inside, I do want to talk to him; it feels good to tell someone all this. It feels good to have someone hear and understand you, someone so intent on listening to your words that he does not move, he just waits.

The waitress brings the wine and opens the bottle. While he tastes, a waiter brings the salad and the Italian cold-cut appetizers. She pours the wine. He lifts his glass.

"This is good, I think you'll like it." We touch glasses and take a sip. The wine is good; it is a dark red Italian wine.

"Tell me more," he says.

"Edik jan," I say after a while, my voice calmer. "I called you with the intention of talking about a few things. You have been a very good friend, and I appreciate everything that you've done for my family and me. But this is not how I wanted to start the conversation. You took me by surprise with your story about the American writer."

"I'm sorry, Lara. But I'm glad that we've finally started talking. Aren't you?"

"I am." He's right. It is a relief. His expression is warm, gentle and attentive, as if he's trying to listen to me even when I say nothing. The notorious third ear is on full alert. I realize that I'm annoyed not because we're talking, but because the conversation did not go as I had planned it. I know how childish that is.

"If this is not how you wanted to have the conversation, then tell me how." He passes me the appetizer plate. "So far, you've known me as a talker," he smiles, "but I can also be a great listener."

I don't recognize the meats on the platter. One cut looks like *yershig*, our sausage; I take a piece on my plate and leave it there. Then I take another sip of wine.

"I wanted to start with the story of my friend Anna." Then I tell Anna's story as he serves more meats and salad on my plate. I tell him everything, at least everything that I consider important. I see a dark cloud gather in his eyes as I tell about her husband selling her and her father's response. But he does not interrupt. The cloud thickens when I describe her constant fear. I tell him about our conversation in the café, about how I thought of him when I helped Anna think of a way out. And then I tell him I want to ask for his help in getting Anna a divorce.

Edik listens patiently throughout. He does not eat, just drinks wine and refills his glass. They've brought the main course, and we have barely touched the salad and appetizers. We're supposed to share the main courses also, one pasta dish and one chef's special sea bass baked with herbs and spices.

"Let's eat," he says, beginning to rearrange the dishes. Then he lifts his glass, toasts me.

"Eat. I process this type of information differently than most people. I don't like to react as the story unfolds. Let it settle in my mind first."

We eat in silence, probably looking like a couple that has just had a fight. Once in a while he looks at me, as if to re-hear parts of the story from my face, and fills our glasses again.

"There is one risk," he says finally. "I think it is well worth taking, but it is a risk your friend Anna should know about before we start divorce proceedings." That is the first thing he says about Anna's story. Knowing Edik, I was expecting a torrent of questions first.

"Tell me," I say, imitating his style. I may even have smiled, because he does not hide his amusement.

"Once she starts the divorce, she'll have to disclose her story to a judge, which means she cannot hide the story any longer, and it will be more difficult to hide from her husband as well."

"Is that one risk or two risks?"

"Actually two, but they are related. If it's only the danger of her exposing him that is keeping him away now, once the story comes out, he won't be deterred any longer."

"But you still think it is worth taking the risk."

"Absolutely. Once the divorce is final, she'll have legal recourse against him. Now she's his wife and he has rights too."

"I agree," I say. "One's secrets may, once in a while, set one free, but fear never can. She has to get rid of her fear of him."

Edik smiles, and tries to lighten the mood by resuming dinner. It is actually very good, and we are both famished. But I can tell that he's still thinking about Anna.

"You've been reading," he says with approval.

"Yes, but I'm surprised you did not have any questions."

"About Anna's story?" I nod. "Sure I do. Many. But not now. I will have to meet her, don't you think? I'll ask my questions then. Then I'll call an attorney friend in Yerevan on her behalf, and we'll take it from there. What I'd like right now is for you to continue."

"Continue?"

"You said you wanted to start with Anna. So we started with Anna. Now continue."

Telling him about the episode with Anastasia is much more difficult, because it is not entirely about someone else. I have to explain who Anastasia is, which means I have to explain what I was doing in Moscow. Maybe they all suspect or even know that already, but I have never had to talk about it to anyone back home.

But I owe it to Edik, Gago and Avo. They were all part of the killings. They need to know, and they need to agree on what story I feed Anastasia to take back to Yuri.

"How much do you know about Ayvazian?" That seems like a good place to start.

"That depends on what you mean by 'know.' Remember, I'm a journalist. Knowledge has many gradations to us, depending on how much solid verification we have for what we know."

"Edik, please. This is important for me, don't get technical. Do you know what he did or not?"

"Okay," he says leaning closer again and looking me straight in the eye. "Would it help if I tell you first what I already know and what I suspect, so you won't have to open the subject?" Only Edik could give me an answer like that, piercing through a hundred layers of fog straight to the precise point.

"Yes," I whisper, impressed and anxious at the same time.

"Then get ready, because I will not beat around the bush, okay?"

"Okay."

"Ayvazian was the largest sex trafficker in Armenia. He specialized in young girls like you. He either fooled them with false promises, like he did in your case, or he outright kidnapped them, and forced them to work as prostitutes. He also trafficked young boys, both for sex and for labor. He had operations in Moscow, Turkey, Dubai and Ukraine, as far as I know, and possibly more. Lara, I know what happened to you. I don't know the details, obviously, but I know he forced you into prostitution. That deserted house we rescued you from in Sevajayr had other captive occupants before you, all young girls, all looking drugged and beaten. So we know. Gago knows too, and Avo. Stop hiding behind your secrets, at least when you're with us. No one is judging you for what you've been forced to do. No one. We are angry and hurt, for you. Do you understand?"

I cannot control my tears. Does he sound like Avo or like my father? The unconditional acceptance is too much to bear. For the first time that evening, he takes my hand.

"Lara jan, it is okay." There is pain in his voice, sympathy in his eyes.

Fortunately, I have to wipe my tears, and it does not look like I pulled my hand away from his for no reason. I look at him for a long moment. I want to say "there's more to it than that" again, but I remain quiet. There *is* more to it than that, but this is not the time. It is past ten-thirty, and I have to get to Anastasia.

They come to clear the table. He orders another bottle of wine. Edik loves wine, and it does not seem to affect him. I've had two glasses of the first bottle, and I already feel the effect. Without asking me, he also orders two desserts for us to share—tiramisu and dark chocolate cake.

We sit in silence for a while. I need to gather my thoughts, and he lets the time pass. They bring the desserts right away. For some reason, the wine takes a bit longer. We wait in silence as the waitress pours it into fresh glasses, and puts two forks by the side of each dessert.

I look at her closely for the first time. She looks like she is in her early twenties. I wonder what her story is. No one would guess Anna's story by just looking at her, so one never really knows. I see the young men and women on campus, and it is difficult not to wonder—what's their story?

Without giving Edik any feedback on his statement on Ayvazian, I delve straight into Anastasia. How we met in Moscow, what she did for me then, how she appeared on campus a few days ago, and the message regarding Yuri and the Ayvazian family. He listens intently.

"She told you Yuri said that the family knows who killed Sergei and Viktor?"

"Yes, but I don't believe that's true. They would have acted differently if they knew. Anastasia thinks they're just checking around."

"Who is 'the family' now?" That's a question I should have asked Anastasia, but didn't. Maybe I was too nervous, or maybe that's just the difference between Edik and me.

"Sorry, I don't know. And I didn't ask. We always assumed that with Sergei and Viktor gone, no one of any importance is left."

It is late, and we're the only ones left in the restaurant. The staff is lined up at a distance watching, waiting to close. Edik pays the bill, helps me with my coat, and we leave. He drives around for a while, in silence. Then he drops me at my building.

"Lara, don't worry. It is good that this is coming up now. Otherwise, we'd always wonder what happened to the rest of the Ayvazians. I'll pick you up around ten, okay?"

"Okay, time to go and congratulate mama pig for eight newborn piglets. Good night, Edik jan."

"Good night, Lara," he says laughing. "Think only of the piglets tonight; don't let Ayvazian disturb your sleep from his well-deserved grave."

Chapter Ten

Laurian picks Lara up the next morning and they head off. She is in her "Saralandj clothes." A pair of old, worn-out khaki pants and a long black sweater that reaches mid-thigh. Her face is again bare of any makeup, and her hair is tied up in a ponytail. She looks rested and refreshed, and she radiates youthful charm in spite of her attempt to appear shy and reserved. "She'll never be able to hide how beautiful she is," thinks Laurian. "One cannot camouflage one's genes, in either direction."

Laurian has a love-hate relationship with driving anywhere in Armenia, and the road to Ashtarak is no exception. The contrast between the natural beauty of the countryside and the horrific conditions of the infrastructure haphazardly imposed upon it shocks him to distraction. This particular stretch is not only beautiful, but it is the stage where some his favorite stories from childhood played out, such as *Arayi Ler* (Ara's Mountain) and Mount Aragats. When he was a kid growing up in Switzerland, he could only picture these places in his imagination. Being here, let alone driving on these roads in his own car, was one of the many impossibilities during

Soviet times. It is the stories that tie him to the place. He feels he owns the stories, so he also owns the places where they happened.

"Look how much damage man can do," he tells Lara, pointing to the potholes in the road and the unfinished buildings—abandoned concoctions of stone and mortar, spread beyond the road like zombies from a horror movie—the old, rusty pipes piled up on the side of the road, and the plastic bottles and bags scattered all over the fields along the roadside.

"And now look at *that*," he adds, pointing to the majestic quadruple peak of Mount Aragats. "We should be ashamed to even face that mountain. We have no right to turn its dominion into such a miserable dump!"

As much as Lara is baffled by his reaction, he is amazed by the indifference of the locals to all this. How is it possible to gain an independent country after seventy years of Soviet rule, and then neglect it to this extent? But Laurian has come to realize that coveting an independent country was a Diaspora obsession. In the Diaspora, he, like millions of his compatriots, lived with the dream of being model citizens of an independent Armenia, instead of working as hard as they did to fit in and become model citizens of whatever country fate had made them adopt. The locals rarely felt this nostalgia.

"Edik jan," says Lara genuinely concerned, "what's the matter? What is bothering you?"

Laurian looks at her for a long moment, but remains silent. She really doesn't get it. She doesn't see that Laurian means what he says; this is not venting spurred on by some deeper problem, which he presumes she believes it to be.

"*Vochinch*," he says. It's nothing. Then he changes the subject. "Have you thought more about what we should give Anastasia to pass on to Yuri?" Lara is still thinking about his outburst and cannot focus on Anastasia. *What was that all about? Look at this, then look at that, and we should be ashamed to face Aragats?* Even as she looks at all the disrepair along the roadside, Lara cannot really understand him. What does he want to do? Clean the whole mess up? Is he mad? Maybe we should call him *Khev Edik*; he sometimes deserves the title more than Gago.

"Not really," she says, returning to his question. "You told me to think of the piglets. So, that's what I thought about."

Laurian bursts out laughing, dragging Lara with him. It is clear that they both needed to lighten up. This contagious laugh is actually a *Khev*

Gago trademark, passed on to Laurian over the years. "You thought about the piglets all night, eh?" he mumbles between bursts of laughter. "Just as I told you to, eh?" And Lara laughs too, happy to have changed the mood, but still harboring an uneasy feeling that something she does not understand is bothering Laurian.

They approach Ashtarak. Late March dominates nature. The trees in the orchards are still bare, with buds aching to burst out, and the snow is slowly melting by the roadside. The birds, mostly black-billed magpies and crows, unsure if spring has yet arrived, act confused, roosting on the bare branches and diving aimlessly into the wet soil, hoping instinctively to find something. Laurian has to make an effort to take his mind off the imposing presence of nature, which Lara barely notices.

"Seriously," says Laurian, "have you thought about what to feed Anastasia?"

"Seriously, no. That is something we all have to plan together."

"Hopefully we can get to it today. After you've had a chance to cuddle with the little piglets…"

Lara hits him on the shoulder. "And after we let you cuddle with the mama," she says laughing.

"Gago will get there an hour after us. That will be enough time for all the piggy cuddling we need. Then maybe we can chat, before Avo gets to the vodka bottle." That is Laurian's first direct comment about Avo's drinking, but it does not surprise Lara. Avo *does* have a drinking problem, and after the candor of their talk the night before, the comment sounds casual and matter-of-fact.

"At any rate," she says, "I agree with what you said last night. This is a good opportunity for us. Imagine being able to stack the deck of cards in a high-stakes game."

"Where did you learn to talk like that?"

"What, you think you're the only educated person I've dealt with in my life?" She smiles, but her mind goes to Al Barmaka, to some of their rare times when he talked about his business. The talks were more monologues than conversations, and she felt that Al Barmaka was thinking aloud rather than talking to her, but some ideas stuck in her mind regardless. 'Stacking the deck' was one of them.

"*De lav*, Lara jan," says Laurian, using the catchall local phrase meaning, depending on context, 'okay, fine' or 'fine, that's enough' or 'okay, I get it' or any number of similar expressions. "So you're wise and experienced beyond your years, I admit. And I agree that this is a chance to 'stack the cards' in our favor. We still need to find the best way to use the opportunity. We will not get it twice."

"Let's start with this question," says Lara, sounding like Laurian in his lecturing mode. "What do you think they are really after?"

"According to what you've told me, they want to know who killed Viktor and Sergei and how they can get their hands on the businesses they left behind, right?"

"Yes, but the key is really the money, not who killed them. I think they want to find out who the killers were because they think it will lead them to the money. Isn't that wonderful? Do you see how off track they already are?"

"What makes you so sure finding the killers is not an aim in itself?" Laurian sounds intrigued.

"Too bad you never got to know my Papa. He was a wise man. He told me once 'you trap birds with seeds, people with money.' It is an old Armenian saying. He believed that money is the ultimate weakness of people. And the paradox is, he used to say, that the richer the man, the bigger his weakness. Ayvazian's family is accustomed to living in a certain way, with many comforts. I'd bet anything that's what they miss. Not their father or nephew."

"Lara, that is brilliant. Do you know what you just did? You analyzed the subject objectively. You did not personalize. I am supposed to be trained to do that, and yet I failed. I assumed that they would be after revenge, just because I would have been if I were in their place. Brilliant!"

"Well, I hope I'm right," says Lara, trying to hide how pleased she is. "If I am, nothing will point to us as the killers, because obviously we don't have that kind of money. That's why I'm not worried too much about the 'who killed them' part. But even the search for the money can haunt us. They may come after me again, simply for money."

"I like your theory, but in this case I think both are factors. In the world of these people, unsolved murders create a credibility problem, which can be a liability. They need to find the killer and take revenge, not necessarily because they miss the deceased, but to reestablish control of the business, and to make sure that would-be competitors understand that they've regained control."

Lara thinks about what Laurian is saying and another thought flashes through her mind.

"In order to regain credibility, they have to *appear* to have found the real killer and avenged their boss, right?" she says, with a slow careful enunciation indicating that she may be onto something new.

"That's right."

"And what matters is to reestablish credibility in the eyes of the other oligarchs, not in the eyes of a bunch of miserable peasants in Saralandj."

"Right again," says Laurian, curious where Lara is going with this reasoning.

"Maybe we can feed them what they need. A really believable story… Something big… something that will keep them busy and engaged…"

Laurian is quiet. They have passed Ashtarak and are headed toward Aparan when he suddenly exits onto a narrower road.

"Have you ever been to Ohanavank?"

"No," says Lara, "But you want to go there now?"

"It's right on the way. Have you heard the story?"

"No." Lara is disappointed that they're making a detour to see an old monastery, when she is anxious to get to Saralandj.

"You'll love the story, I promise. Something you said reminded me of it. We can learn from it. Bear with me."

They reach the medieval monastery in several minutes. It is an imposing structure right at the edge of the gorge carved by the Kasagh River, and the walls are tiled with red and black tuff stone.

"It took centuries to build this." Laurian is excited like a schoolboy.

As they approach the main gate of the church, around a dozen doves take flight from the bell tower to the right.

Laurian grabs Lara's arm and points to the doves. "Remember that," he says. "They're part of the story."

Inside, Laurian slows down for a minute and lets the peace and quiet of the church envelop him. Lara is affected too, looking at the imposing columns at each side of the altar, the walls lined with some of the most intricate *Khachkar*s she has ever seen—literally, stone-crosses, referring to the large slabs of stone with intricate carvings of crosses, which are prevalent all over Armenia—and the sunlight entering from the windows around the dome, creating a mysterious atmosphere that refuses to allow indifference.

"When Genghis Khan marches here in the thirteenth century," starts Laurian, "he is determined to slaughter every man, woman and child in sight. The village priest pleads with him to allow the people to go into the church to pray for the last time. The Khan agrees. The priest hurriedly gathers every soul in the village and rushes them into the church. He then enters himself, turns around, bows deeply to the invader and shuts the door." Laurian walks over and shuts the doors of the church. "Now, can you imagine several hundred village folk gathered here, with the knowledge that they are praying for the last time before being slaughtered? Imagine that for a minute, Lara; imagine yourself being here back then, among those people."

Laurian takes a few steps toward the altar. "Here!" he says, approaching a small wooden door to the right of the altar. "While Genghis Khan thought the people were praying inside, they were actually escaping from here!" And he swings the door open to reveal a small room, with another, smaller wooden door in the back. "That leads to a vast cave below the church," he says smiling from ear to ear. "Believe it or not, this church is built over a cave. And from the cave, it is possible to walk to the other side of the gorge." He opens the inner door and peers down the dark steps, gesturing Lara to do the same.

"After a while, Genghis Khan opens the church doors, and a large flock of doves flies out, over a hundred birds, startling even the great warrior. The priest kept the doves in the church. When Genghis Khan finds the church empty, he thinks the doves are the souls of the villagers, rising to heaven. He departs Ohanavank in considerable haste."

They stand at the top of the hidden staircase, looking down the steps leading to the cave. "They had to use their heads and resort to deceit to save their lives," whispers Laurian. "I think that was what you were thinking earlier in the car, when you were talking about coming up with a believable story to feed Yuri. That's what reminded me of Ohanavank."

She looks at him, wondering how on earth he could find the connection between the medieval tale and their current predicament. But the image of doves and the escaping villagers stays with her.

"Come," says Laurian, "we can see the opening where the cave leads into the gorge from the side of the church. But first, check these two Khachkars. They are believed to be carved by Momik in the fourteenth century. Most of his work is in Noravank in Vayots Dzor, but these two masterpieces have ended up here. One day I'll find the time to study how."

They remain quiet for a long time while driving on the road to Saralandj. They see the scatter of stone homes in the distance, which swallow the road in their clutter and bring it to its end. Beyond the village, old pine and spruce forests spread up the mountainside.

The forests have special meaning for Lara. That is where she ventured when she was a kid, just to find out what was there. Her sisters weren't curious, and her brothers were too afraid to go, even Avo. For them, the world ended with the back garden. To venture beyond, to cross the vast wild fields full of tall grass and thorns, which their father said harbored poisonous snakes, and to reach and actually enter the dark forest, was for them like venturing into another realm. She went alone. That is when she met the trees, really met them and felt their presence. And that is where she discovered, through the incredible fusion of fear and excitement pounding in her chest, a part of herself. The forest, and her father's soothing voice when she finally found her way back home that evening, saying "What did you discover in the forest, Lara?" remained with her throughout her eighteen-month captivity, giving her the inner strength she needed to overcome the odds and escape.

They pass the sign by the side of the road announcing the village name in English and Armenian letters. The English is a post-Soviet addition. The letter "j" in the English version is faded and virtually erased, and the sign reads "Saraland."

"One day, I'll bring along a magic marker and I'll write in the 'j' myself."

Lara simply smiles. This is Edik, restless and eager to fix things. She realizes that last night and today in the car were the only times that Laurian talked to her as an equal, not as a little girl who needed to be protected, instructed and even pampered.

"You know what?" he says out of the blue, "We should ask Sona if she'd like to have her wedding at Ohanavank."

"That's a great idea," she smiles, "I'll convince her."

They enter the narrow single street of the village, the 'torn apart obstacle course', as Laurian calls it, and as they emerge from the cluster of houses, a lone building appears some twenty meters away. That is the Galian house.

"It looks like they have just filled this ditch," says Laurian, referring to the huge pothole usually full of muddy water, that forces cars to stop and the passengers to walk the rest of the way to the Galians. "I'm going to drive over it this time."

𝒮 𝒮 𝒮

Avo has swept the floors and cleaned the pens with water, and then thrown fresh hay everywhere, but the stench is overwhelming nonetheless. There are over fifty pens, separated by metal bar-fences, twenty of which are occupied by expectant mothers. They walk to the one that has already delivered. She is lying on her side, and, just as Avo said, eight tiny pink bundles have attached themselves to her tits, eyes shut, shivering. If one could ignore the overpowering smell, it would in fact be an inspiring sight.

"They should all deliver in a few weeks," Avo repeats. "Then, when the time comes to wean them, we'll distribute them to the other pens. The male piglets will be castrated when they are three to four weeks old, to make the meat milder. Next year, when we get another litter, these will be older and we'll need to build some new pens to accommodate all of them. Of course by then we'll sell more than half." He is so excited that he is oblivious to the smell. He talks of future expansion plans and big possibilities, which include exports, even diversifying into the necessary agricultural sectors whereby one day he will produce the feed he needs. He talks about signing contracts with restaurants and hotels to supply their pork, and even opening a small *Tonratun*, grill-house, in Saralandj and serving fresh clean khorovadz from his own farm.

His excitement is not the biggest surprise; the real novelty here is his forward planning, thinking of the future. People live for the day around here. The future is far too uncertain. Very rarely would the average villager, and most of the city folks too, have the time or inclination to plan anything past today or tomorrow, which consumes all their energies and resources. In order to start thinking ahead, one has to have hope, faith in the days to come. How Avo got that is a mystery to everyone.

"Avo," says Laurian, sensing Lara's unease with staying longer in the stable. "Why don't we go to the house and continue. I love the planning part. Let's sit somewhere with paper and pencil and do some calculations."

"But Gago isn't here yet," protests Avo. He is reluctant to leave the pigs.

"He can visit the stables when he arrives," says Lara. "Let's wait for him at the house."

Back at the house, they bring a bucket of water and a bar of soap and Laurian washes outside. Alisia offers him a towel. As he dries his hands and face, he can still smell the odor of the pigs on him. Lara washes up inside, but has the same problem with the lingering odor, which seems to be absorbed in their clothes.

They sit at the low table in the larger room, and Avo gets a sheet of paper and an old pencil, which looks like it has been sharpened with a pocketknife.

"Feed has been affordable," he starts. "That's why many small farmers are paying a lot of money for a weaned piglet. I have buyers now who'd pay up to 35,000 dram for a healthy piglet! Can you imagine? That's almost 90 dollars!"

"What do they do with them?" asks Laurian, partly to show interest.

"They fatten them up and then sell them for a profit in a few months. A kilo of pork is now 3,200 dram. So by increasing their weight by fifteen kilos, they can double their money!"

"But you can do the same, right? Why sell and give them those profits?" Laurian is beginning to actually focus on the business model.

"One can keep at the most two piglets with household refuse," says Avo. "If you have more, you have to buy feed. It will still be profitable, but not as much. We can do a little of each. Sell some to get cash in, keep and raise others to sell when they weigh more. And we may keep a few as future mothers. The vet will help us choose."

"That's a great strategy," says Laurian.

"What's great is this," says Avo all excited, "if the others deliver a litter of eight, and assuming all survive, the value of this year's brood alone will be almost equal to what I've borrowed from you. Can you imagine? In less than a year, this investment has repaid its debt."

"First, don't even think of repaying anything yet," says Laurian firmly. "It is too early. You have to expand, remember? Besides, all the piglets may not survive, so do not count them before they're even born!"

"I know, I know, but the vet says in the second year, these mothers deliver fourteen to fifteen piglets, and they will be even healthier the second time around. So an average of eight may not be a bad estimate."

It's close to noon, and a phone call from Gagik to Laurian interrupts the meeting.

"I'm on my way," he says, "and I have some visitors following me. I ran into them in Aparan. They were asking for the way to Saralandj, the Galian's house. The driver is Armenian. The passenger is an Indian guy. He says he's from the Middle East, but would not say what business he has with the Galians."

"You've passed Aparan already?" Laurian tries to gauge how much time they have before Gagik and the foreign visitor arrive.

"Just left town. We'll be there in ten minutes, fifteen if I drive slow."

"Drive even slower," says Laurian and hangs up.

This can't be good news, thinks Laurian. Someone from the Middle East visiting the Galians can mean only one thing: A connection from Dubai coming after Lara. He does not know anything about Lara's experience in Dubai, so has no basis to even guess who the visitor could be.

"Avo, please forgive me for a minute," he says, "I know we're not done yet, but we have to stop for now. I need to ask Lara a question."

Laurian would have preferred to talk to Lara in private, but he could not possibly ask Avo to excuse them.

"Edik, what is it?" asks Lara nervously.

"Some guy who says he is from the Middle East is headed this way. He has an Armenian driver. They were asking for directions to the Galians, Gago ran into them, and they should arrive in fifteen minutes or so. Do you know anyone who would come all that way looking for the Galian house?"

For the second time in a week, Lara goes through the same shock as when she first saw Anastasia at the foot of the stairs at the University. Her past indeed seems to be coming back to haunt her.

"Where in the Middle East?" she asks, aware that it is a stupid question, but she needs time to think. If she had been alone with Laurian, she probably would have immediately given him her best guess of who the visitor was. But she does not know how to break any of it to Avo.

"I have no idea," says Laurian. "But if I had to guess, it would be Dubai. And it has to be about you. Sorry, Lara, we don't have much time, what is your best guess here?

"The driver is Armenian, but the guy asking the questions is not?"

"That's right. Gago said the guy looks Indian."

"Indian? He cannot be from Ayvazian's organization."

"Then what?"

"Let me talk to this man first. Then I'll tell you what I know."

"Kurig," says Avo who has been quiet so far, "how did these people reach Saralandj? Who are they? Why are they after you?"

"Avo, *kyanks*, let me talk to him first. I have no idea till I talk to him."

"They have come to Saralandj!" exclaims Avo, and looks like he immediately regrets his outburst. The pain on Lara's face is clear as day. Laurian notices it and intervenes.

"Avo, let her talk to him. There is no harm in that. And then we'll figure out what to do. There is other news that we need to talk to you about, and we never got the chance. We'll have a busy day."

Manoj has seen poor villages in India, but is still shocked as they enter Saralandj. The streets are so narrow that the car barely avoids rubbing against a fence or a wall; the village homes must have been built when the mode of transportation was the donkey, he thinks. The muddy potholes, the chickens running around, children staring from windows, all add to the eerie feeling he has. How can beautiful Leila come from a place like this? What would Al Barmaka think if he saw this?

Manoj snaps photographs of the road from the car without lowering the window, since he is not sure how the villagers might react if they saw him taking pictures. Still, he needs Al Barmaka to get a visual impression of this place. A woman is sweeping the mud away from her door front into the street. A few villagers are squatting under a walnut tree, smoking. A three-year-old boy is chasing a cat down the road and into an alley.

A couple of dogs bark at the car and run toward it, then, having done their duty, drift away, looking bored. The road presents a challenge, but Armen does not seem fazed by any of it.

"I bet you don't see places like this in Dubai," he says, laughing.

"No, not in Dubai, but I've seen similar places in India." He does not want to make any negative comments.

"Aside from the introduction of electricity, which was a big Soviet program, this place has not changed in six-hundred years!" says Armen.

"What do people do here? I mean, what's the source of their livelihood?" He knows Al Barmaka will ask him the same question.

"Agriculture. They keep animals—sheep and cows, largely—the fruits and vegetables that they grow are for their own consumption, I think their only cash crop is wheat, but I'm not sure."

Gagik drives slower than usual. He is not sure how the driver following him will manage the road. As he leaves the village, he is happy to find the big ditch filled. It would be even more awkward to have the visitors walk the last twenty meters.

Lara, Avo and Laurian are waiting outside when they arrive. Gago waits for Manoj to get out, and they walk together toward the house. Lara has not met Manoj, but Manoj has seen her pictures. He politely nods at the two men, and addresses Lara.

"A very good afternoon to you, Ms. Leila," he says, exercising his famous charm. "I trust I find you in good form and in good spirits. My name is Manoj Gupta. I work for His Excellency Ahmed Al Barmaka."

Manoj is speaking English. Lara has learned enough in the past two years to be able to communicate. That was the language they used in Dubai, and her classes in the past few months have helped polish her English more. Avo does not understand a word, Gagik a few words, and only Laurian is fluent, and amazed at the flowery greeting.

By now the driver, Armen, who was checking under the hood of the car, has joined them, and briefly greets everyone. It is an awkward moment, with five men and Lara standing on the wet ground in front of the melting pile of snow, all, except Manoj, with serious and uncomprehending expressions, and Manoj doing his best to keep the kind smile on his face and make it look natural. Some of Lara's siblings are watching with interest from the kitchen window.

"Hello," says Lara at last. "What can I do for you?"

"Uh…is there a place where we can talk? I promise I won't keep you long. I just need to pass on a message from His Excellency."

Lara remembers how she was expected to call him 'Your Excellency' until he asked her to call him by his first name, and how amused he was as she struggled with the Arabic heavy 'H' in Ahmed.

Her first instinct is to say "we can talk here," but she realizes immediately how rude and inhospitable that would be. After all, the man has somehow managed to arrive here all the way from Dubai, and is doing his absolute best to be courteous.

"Just a minute," she says to Manoj in English, and then shifts to Armenian and turns to Avo. "We need to invite him inside for a coffee," she says. "He says he has a message for me. Edik is the only one who will understand what is being said, so there's no point in everybody coming in. Is it okay if only he joins me while I talk to this man?"

Avo is uncomfortable, but realizes that what Lara is suggesting makes sense. He nods. Lara gestures for Manoj and Laurian to follow her, and walks up the several steps to the house. She asks Arpi and Alisia, who rush away from the window and pretend to be busy with kitchen chores, to leave. They scurry out, blushing heavily.

"Can I offer you a cup of coffee?" she asks, once Manoj and Laurian take seats on the stools by the low dining table.

"Many thanks, Ms. Leila, that is very kind of you indeed," beams Manoj, "but absolutely no need to go through the trouble. I will not be long. I need to get back to Yerevan soon."

Lara joins them at the table.

"This is a close family friend," she says pointing at Laurian.

"Edward Laurian," says Laurian, extending his hand. "Good to meet you."

"Good to meet you, Mr. Laurian." Manoj uses every diplomatic bone in his body to hide his discomfort with the whole situation—the room, the smell, the presence of Laurian, the other men waiting downstairs. It is time to deliver his message and leave.

"His Excellency is very concerned about you, Ms. Leila," starts Manoj.

"Mr. Manoj, my name is Lara," she interrupts.

"I'm very sorry, of course, I meant no offense, it's just that that's how His Excellency always refers to you. Once again, my apologies."

"That's fine, Mr. Manoj." She has already regretted bringing up the issue of the name.

"Thank you, Ms. Lara. His Excellency sent a message to say that he cares about you deeply. And… he'd like to see you again."

Lara is terrified when her heart suddenly starts to pound. She did not expect, nor want, to react like this. She worries that Manoj and Laurian will notice that her hands are trembling, raising her nervousness by a few notches. *It's just the guilt*, she keeps telling herself. *I betrayed the trust of a man who treated me kindly. That's all this is…*

"Mr. Manoj," she says, keeping her hands firmly clasped together in her lap, and staring at the table. "My going back to Dubai is out of the question. I am now enrolled at the University and cannot leave Armenia."

"Your going to Dubai is not necessary, Ms. Lara," says Manoj, very much aware of the change in her. "His Excellency will be delighted to hear that you are now enrolled at the University. I am sure he will be amenable to visit you in Yerevan."

Laurian's curiosity is now piqued as to who His Excellency is. But his role at this meeting is simply that of an observer, as it would have been unthinkable to leave Lara alone in what is partly a bedroom with the stranger. Meanwhile, Lara is at a loss as to how to answer. It is Manoj who breaks the silence again.

"Perhaps it would be best if he could call you first, Ms. Lara," he says with the gentlest smile. "He asks your permission to call you, and, if you agree, for your telephone number."

Lara looks at Laurian for the first time since they've come to the room. He nods—the slightest tilting of the head, his approval being communicated more through the expression in his eyes than through his nod.

"I have no objection if he wants to call," says Lara finally. "You may have my mobile number. It is best to call during the week, when I am in Yerevan. Please give my regards to His Excellency." Manoj enters her number into his cell phone, and carefully repeats it. Getting that number makes him feel like he has found a hidden treasure. Then he stands up.

"Ms. Lara," he says extending his hand, "please accept my deepest gratitude for your affirmative response. His Excellency will be very happy when he hears from me. With your permission, I must now leave."

Lara and Laurian stand up and walk him out and down the stairs. Avo, Gagik and Armen watch them. Laurian joins them and stands next to Avo, giving him a reassuring nod, indicating that the meeting went well and there is nothing to worry about, while Lara walks Manoj to his car. Armen opens the door for him and he gets in.

"Excuse me, Mr. Manoj," says Lara approaching the car before Armen gets a chance to close the door. "May I ask you a question?"

"But of course, Ms. Lara, anything."

"I was just curious, how is Ms. Sumaya?"

"Ms. Sumaya, along with the other…uh…ladies, has been dismissed," says Manoj casually. "His Excellency no longer requires their services."

"Thank you. I wish you a safe journey." And she walks back to join the men waiting by the pile of snow.

Chapter Eleven

Edik looks amused. He barely manages to restrain the smile that's struggling to burst across his face, but his eyes give him away.

"No woman," he says with exaggerated theatrics, raising his right hand as if he is giving a sermon, "*No* woman, in the *entire* Republic, has *ever* been addressed with as much reverence, as much courtesy, as much respect as this stranger addressed Lara today." The smile breaks free.

I feel my face grow hot, and wonder if I'm blushing. Thankfully, I am in the process of making coffee, so I can keep my back to them most of the time.

"*De lav*, Edik jan," I say putting the pot of water on the stove and turning away again to fetch the cups and saucers. "Don't exaggerate."

Avo and Gago still have no idea what has gone on and maintain their serious and impatient expressions. Glancing at them briefly, I set the cups on the table and turn my back again, thankful that Edik is acting the way he is. That will go a long way to lighten the mood.

"I said no woman in the entire Republic," says Edik laughing, ignoring me, "but now imagine a young lady, who smells like she has been rolling in the stable with the piglets and their mama, being addressed like she is the queen or some princess or the first lady…"

I instinctively bring my right arm to my nose. The sleeve of my sweater is saturated with the pigs' odor.

"That is right, Ms. Lara," he says, then, shifting to English, he adds "and please accept my deepest gratitude for your affirmative response." His imitation of Manoj is so good that I start laughing too.

Funny as this is, it is uncharacteristic of Edik, and even Gagik, who knows him the best, is somewhat surprised. Usually Edik is the sober one, taking seriously details that the others dismiss or laugh about, analyzing all the implications and consequences until everyone starts to roll their eyes. And here he is amused, acting like a clown, and not a bad one at that.

"So when are you two going to tell us what the story is?" asks Avo. He is still impatient, but the extreme gravity seems to have lifted from his face.

"Lara jan, it's really your story," says Edik. "I myself am dying to know. Who is His Excellency?" He is not joking around anymore. My mind registers two new observations about Edik: he has read Avo well, and he is a good manipulator. I'm glad he's on my side.

"His name is Ahmed Al Barmaka," I start, trying to sound as casual as I can. "He is a very wealthy and influential man, and has many important government positions in Dubai. That's why they refer to him like that."

"What does he have to do with you?" asks Avo.

I hear the water boiling and get up again to add coffee and watch the pot. It's good to have something to do while I tell the story.

"I was with him during the last three months before I came home. It is from his palace that I escaped." I know I need to choose my words carefully, but there is no roundabout way of telling the basic facts. Avo looks confused.

"You escaped from his palace?" he says, scratching his head. "Why? Was he beating you? But wait, why were you in his palace in the first place?" How much of this do I need to spell out? *Common, Avo*, I plead in my mind, *figure out the rest yourself!* Then I decide to take the plunge. I take the coffee pot off the stove; I won't be able to watch it and focus on what I need to tell Avo at the same time. Then I sit opposite Avo.

"Avo jan, listen," I say looking at him, as if the others are not in the room. "Ayvazian sold me to him. I was his. He never beat me, or mistreated me in any way. He is the only person in those horrible eighteen months that treated me with dignity and affection. That is the truth. So why did I escape? Because I wanted to come home, Avo. I wanted to see Mama before she died, remember? I missed you and our sisters and brothers. Because I did not like being sold. Do you understand?"

There is total silence in the room. Edik stares at me, then looks at Avo. Gagik has his head in his hands and is looking down at the floor. I expect a burst of anger from Avo. But his eyes are surprisingly soft. I feel affection and love in the way he looks at me, not anger. My short-fused kid brother, whose rage I feared even before returning home, is now looking at me with affection. I was so convinced that he'd be unable to accept where I've been and what I've done, so sure that he wouldn't be able to stand being in the same room with me, to look at me, if he knew the truth. I was wrong.

This is going to be a day of many surprises and many revelations. It will also be the day when the healing starts. If Avo can still look at me with love and acceptance, maybe I no longer have reason to fear my demons so much. I do my best to control the tears that are welling up in my eyes, but fail. His eyes are wet too.

"That is the truth, Avo jan. Do you understand?" I repeat.

"I understand, *kurig*." I burst into sobs at the sound of that word.

Edik gives me a few minutes to gather myself, and then jumps in.

"That explains the way Manoj was talking to you," he says. "The courtesy that he extended to you is actually coming from his boss." I know what he is trying to do. He wants to reinforce, for everyone's benefit, that I was treated well and with dignity. Avo needs to focus on that aspect now, before his mind starts wandering into darker scenarios.

"Now we all know he was polite," says Gagik finally breaking his silence. "But did he want anything?"

"Al Barmaka wants to talk to me," I say, skipping the 'wants to see me' part. "He asked if I would give him my permission to call me, and for my number. I said yes, he can call me, and gave him my number. If he wants to call, let him call."

"He requested your permission to call him," repeats Gagik looking impressed. "His Excellency requested your permission…"

"That is exactly what he requested," says Edik, "But there is a lot more on the agenda today." He checks his watch. "It is almost two p.m. We need to go somewhere and talk, so the rest can use this room. Let's go to Ashtarak and have lunch there. My treat."

I know Avo is dying to learn more about Al Barmaka, and, probably much more important for him, how I intend to handle his continuing interest in me. I know this from the way he is looking at me, I hear him with that third ear. I cannot let him wonder like that. I have released a few secrets, and I like the feeling. I find clarity liberating.

As I am thinking about the effects of freeing secrets, I remember another conversation with Al Barmaka. He used to tell me that in the Middle Eastern culture, it is ambiguity that provides safety. No one should be made to be very clear and final about anything, he would say. It is the same in Asia, he'd say. "The Chinese and Japanese don't like the 'yes' and 'no' words. Clarity is too deterministic, and so, once spoken, those words immediately restrict one's options. Only ambiguity offers options," he would say. "But it takes great skill and sophistication to manage ambiguity, my lovely Leila… Simple people cannot handle it. Simple people need a yes or no answer."

None of that made any sense to me then, because I could not relate to what he was talking about.

But in the last two days, I have discovered the liberating properties of clarity. In my case, ambiguity did not provide safety. It provided constant uncertainty and unnecessary fear. Maybe I am not sophisticated enough. Ambiguity may hold options, but it also houses the loose ends, which are not always liberating. It is clarity that Avo needs right now.

"Avo, I know this man's visit has troubled you," I say, intending to clarify as much as I can without creating new anxieties. "I am as confused by it as you are, but I will tell you the truth, as I know it. I suspected that Ahmed was falling in love with me in Dubai, but I never thought that he'd track me all the way to Saralandj. I'll be honest with you about something else, Avo jan. I feel bad for betraying his trust when I ran away. He was in China. He did not deserve to be treated like that. I should have at least explained to him that I wanted to go back home. He would have understood. But at the time I was afraid that he'd hand me back over to Ayvazian. So I betrayed him. Now I don't think that he would have handed me over to Ayvazian, and I don't know what will happen next. If he calls, I'll talk to him, and I'll let you know what he says. Okay, Avo?"

I know I have done the right thing. Avo believes me, I can tell. He looks relieved, and grateful for the explanation. A little clarity has gone a long way. I now believe more strongly that this is the beginning of the healing process.

$$\mathcal{L} \quad \mathcal{L} \quad \mathcal{L}$$

We spend a few hours at the restaurant in Ashtarak, briefing Gagik and Avo about Anastasia's visit and discussing strategies of how to best use the opportunity. Then Gagik and Avo head back to Saralandj, with a promise from Gagik to visit the new family in their pen, and Edik and I leave for Yerevan. We agree to have dinner together that night, and meet with Anna the next day before he returns to Vardahovit.

Chapter Twelve

Carla is in the bedroom of her father's private suite. This is where Sergei Ayvazian raped Lara on the same night that his men took her from Saralandj. This is the room where Anoush, the housekeeper that they kept at the time, and who they've since let go, tried to clean up the mess, making a shell-shocked Lara take a bath and go to bed, telling her that this is how things are, and that they will be this way from now on, that she'd better get used to it. Lara, clutching Araxi Dadik's ring in her hand, shut off the world around her, and, for the first time in her life, experienced the feeling of being alone.

Carla has introduced important changes to the room; she has added a large high definition TV, where she watches her large collection of porno films. More than half of her collection is supplied by Yuri. She has made him make at least one special trip to Moscow just to procure a few bondage films. She avoids using the Internet for fear of being detected. She does not trust the authorities.

Carla's latest obsession is bisexual threesomes, after finding out that having another woman in bed along with Yuri is more satisfying than having Yuri alone. And Yuri does not mind.

But on this chilly afternoon she has only Yuri as company. He has been attentive as usual and succeeded in satisfying her seemingly insatiable desires. They lie in bed, silent for a while. Yuri stirs first, and goes to the bathroom to wash his face. When he returns, she's sitting up in bed, with the sheet pulled up to her shoulders. The expression on her face is pure business, as if the past half-hour did not happen.

"You need to fly to Dubai," she says. "And the sooner the better. There are three direct flights a week. Catch the next one, I think the day after tomorrow."

Yuri hates surprises, especially when they involve last minute, rushed tasks. He looks at her for a minute, his irritation showing, and starts getting dressed.

"It's important," says Carla. "Viktor had made some large investments in Dubai. All his files must be there, probably with Ano, who, by the way, is still running more than twenty girls for us. We have far too much at stake that is still up for grabs."

That gets Yuri's attention.

"He's made investments? Aside from the girls and Ano?"

"I believe so. My mother, who normally knows nothing about the business, remembers my father saying that he bought a large piece of real estate in Dubai. She does not know what. He never said anything more about it to her, other than that Viktor handled everything for him."

"The documents were not in your father's papers?" asks Yuri, wondering how he is going to uncover Viktor's acquisitions without a paper trail.

"Nothing here. Nothing at Viktor's place either," Carla says, then, seeing his inquisitive look, adds, "I had his place searched. Everything is here now. Nothing about any property in Dubai. So I have to assume he kept the paperwork there. It makes sense, he'd need those documents there, not here."

Yuri knows better than to ask whom she hired to do the searching and the confiscation of Viktor's papers. He had asked a similar question once, and Carla had walked out of the room without saying a word, with such a chillingly disapproving look that he learned never to ask again. She has already volunteered a lot by telling him about her search.

The next day Yuri applies for a visa at the travel office suggested by Carla, and gathers as much information as he can about Dubai, including Ano's coordinates and piecemeal records of past income flows, some of which seem inconsistent and in conflict with each other. He also checks Viktor's passport—issued under the false name of Viktor Arakelian, which Viktor needed to get back into Dubai after being deported once—to check for the latest entry and exit stamps into Dubai. Viktor had been in and out of Dubai, and then to Istanbul, only a few days before the accidents in Sevajayr. Yuri finds that interesting. Could part of the mystery surrounding the deaths of Hamo, Viktor and Sergei be concealed in Dubai somewhere?

ৎ ৎ ৎ

Dubai swelters in forty degree Celsius heat. As Yuri leaves the air-conditioned airport, his breath catches. It is not just the heat, but the humidity that he is not used to. In the few minutes that it takes for him to get into a taxi, his clothes feel wet. He checks in to the Emirates Towers, one of the more expensive business hotels on Shaikh Zayed Road. He showers, and calls the laundry service.

Ano is not amused when Yuri calls. She's had major problems with the girls in recent weeks. They have gotten wind that Viktor is no longer there, and started to question Ano's authority. Some have outright defied her and are no longer making payments. Others have added new conditions, including more independence, cell phones that they can use to call overseas, and of course much lower percentage payments from their earnings. She's had to accept most of these demands.

She has called 'Ali the Enforcer' for help, but without success. Ali is the most feared disciplinarian. He serves many pimps, bringing insubordinate prostitutes into line with just a single one-on-one session. The girls are terrified of him. Ali has been cooperative with Ano in the past. It was he who drove Lara to Al Barmaka's house after the deal was sealed. But now he ignores her, often by not returning her calls, and on the rare occasion that he does answer a call, by saying he is far too busy. Ano suspects that some of the girls have gone to work for him, accepting his protection.

When Yuri calls, Ano is aware that the operation is slowly but surely slipping from her grasp. He is rude on the phone, talking as if he owns her and everyone who works for her. He says he represents the Ayvazian family interests and summons her to his hotel for an urgent meeting. Given everything else that is going on, Ano decides to go, as one never knows, this may present a solution to some of her problems, even if it creates new ones in the process.

"How do I know you are who you say you are?" asks Ano once they sit at a remote corner of the hotel lobby.

"Viktor flew to Dubai on September 12 last year, stayed one night, then flew to Istanbul from here. The Moscow office has been wiring money to the family of one of your girls, who, as we understand it, somehow escaped on your watch. Now, how would I know all that if I am not who I say I am?"

"You don't have all your facts straight," says Ano, but realizes that the man does know too much to be a stranger to Ayvazian's business.

"Ano, neither you nor I have a lot of time to waste. So let's do this right," says Yuri, looking dead serious. "Before Viktor was killed, the Ayvazians' income from Dubai, after all expenses and fees, exceeded one hundred thousand dollars per month. Some months, it was much higher, closer to one hundred-and-fifty thousand." Yuri knows that he's taking a chance with these figures, which are based on piecemeal accounts, but even if he is wrong, the orders of magnitude make enough sense to him to be worth the risk, if it means Ano will fall into line faster. "Now, as you know, for six months the Ayvazians have not received a penny. You must be a very rich woman by now, Ano, at someone else's expense."

"First, let me say that you are way out of line, and if you really want to do this right, as you say, you better get back on track real fast, or I will leave right this moment," says Ano, looking equally serious, and waiting for Yuri to respond.

"Go on," says Yuri. "I get the point."

"Good. Now listen carefully," continues Ano with renewed confidence, "because I do not feel under any obligation to explain this to you even once, let alone repeat it for you later. I have not seen Viktor for over six months. I have not heard from anyone claiming to represent the Ayvazians until you show up. I have not heard about you and have no idea who you are or how you got your hands on the information that you have, which, as I said, has some of the facts wrong. Finally, the business that you are referring to is nowhere as profitable as you suggest. I have lost more than half of our girls in the past few months, and I have lost most of the local influence and protection that we used to have when Viktor was around. I struggle every day to keep the operation going against all odds, all alone, and here you are accusing me of getting rich at someone else's expense. You have some nerve, Mr. Yuri."

Yuri is impressed. Ano must need something, because otherwise she wouldn't have bothered to say as much as she did. She must be giving him the benefit of the doubt that he does work for the Ayvazian family. That is the only authority she would recognize.

"I work directly for Carla, Sergei's daughter, Viktor's cousin." Yuri is hoping that he'll finally be able to discuss business with Ano. "Before that I worked for Sergei and Viktor, and was based in Moscow. Carla is the only one left, and she has already reclaimed almost all of her father's businesses," he lies. "Now her attention has turned to Dubai."

"And how do you intend to reclaim what's here?" Ano makes no attempt to hide her sarcasm. "By just parachuting into Dubai and throwing accusations at me? There is no physical asset here that you can just take and carry back with you, Mr. Yuri. There are women and relationships, and both are dwindling. If Carla wants her father's business here to be what it once was, she better send me someone who understands how to operate in this environment, and do it soon. Someone who can give us the necessary protection. Can you do that? Can you do what Viktor used to do? If so, I'll be happy to turn everything over to you."

"Ano, let's leave the girls and local protection aside for just one minute," says Yuri, realizing that he will soon come to a dead end in the conversation. "Did Viktor keep an office in Dubai?"

"Why would he need an office?"

"Did he keep any documents?"

"He has a safe in my apartment. I don't think there is anything important in it. He has not opened it for years. I don't know the combination. It gathers dust in my closet." Even as she speaks, Ano realizes that perhaps she is too quick to volunteer the information, but it is too late.

"How large is the safe?"

"Not very big." She draws a one cubic foot space in the air with her hands.

"I'd like to see it," says Yuri.

"I cannot let you near it or near anything else of Viktor's until I have proof that you are who you say you are."

Yuri is annoyed and glad at the same time. He's glad Ano is so protective of the details of the business, even if she's doing it to protect her own interests rather than Viktor's. If it's this difficult for him to pull anything from her, it must be the same with anyone else.

"How am I supposed to prove that?" he asks.

"That's your problem, Mr. Yuri. Now if you'll excuse me, I have a business to run." And Ano stands up to take her leave.

"Wait," says Yuri. "Please sit down. If Carla Ayvazian talked to you directly over the phone, and confirmed who I am, would that satisfy you?"

"How can I be sure who I'm talking to over the phone?" asks Ano.

"You must have Sergei's home number somewhere, right?" says Yuri after thinking for a minute.

"I've never called him, but yes, Viktor gave it to me a long time ago, in case of an emergency."

"Do you have it with you by chance? Like in a phone book in your purse, or in your mobile?"

Ano checks her cell phone. There, saved under SA-Big Boss, is a Yerevan city number, with the '10' area code indicating it is a city landline, not a mobile phone. She nods.

"Call the number. Ask for Carla. Then ask her to verify who I am. I will not say a word. Do you agree that there is no way I could set this up to trick you?"

Ano stares at him for a minute, then, without saying a word, dials the number.

"Ms. Carla Ayvazian, if possible."

"Speaking. Who's this?" Carla sounds even ruder than Yuri.

"This is Ano from Dubai. I used to work with Viktor."

"I know who you are. How did you get this number?"

"Viktor gave it to me a long time ago, for emergencies."

"Then this better be an emergency," says Carla curtly.

"There's a man here who says he works for you and wants access to some of Viktor's things. I will not give him anything unless you confirm he is who he says he is." There is defiance in Ano's voice, which she feels is justified. After all, she's doing Carla a favor by being careful.

"Is his name Yuri?" asks Carla.

"Yes."

"I sent him to Dubai, Ano. I'd appreciate it if you cooperate with him." Carla's tone has changed.

"Can you please describe Yuri?" Ano wants to enjoy the feeling of calling the shots for a few moments longer. Carla is impressed. Is this loyalty or self-preservation?

"He has thick black hair slicked back, a long face and is kind of ugly," says Carla, smiling to herself.

"Yes, that's him." Ano smiles too, looking at Yuri for the first time since she placed the call. "How much do you want me to cooperate with him? I mean, he wants to have the safe that Viktor kept in my apartment. Also, the business here is in grave danger. We can lose a lot."

"Cooperate fully, Ano. And I'll make sure that you are rewarded. Explain to Yuri what needs to be done there to get things back in order, and it will be done. I appreciate your holding the fort in this difficult period."

Spoken like the real owner. Ano thinks she'll probably lose everything in Dubai in a month or two anyway, so there is no harm in playing the role of loyal retainer. She has made close to half a million dollars in the last six months, in addition to her normal fees. It would have taken her over five years to amass that kind of money. There can be no accounting for all that; if they want her cooperation now, they'll have to forget about the past.

Yuri spends the next few days learning about the setup in Dubai. He is alarmed at how much the business has suffered. He finds the challenge of rebuilding control in an environment that is totally unfamiliar to him daunting. Ano is helpful to some extent, but the more she explains, the harder the task appears to him. Dubai is a complicated place. There are no clear rules, and among the many ambiguous rules the strongest are the unwritten ones. Yuri is used to more structure.

Opening the safe is another major challenge. He has managed to bring it to his hotel room, but he cannot crack the combination lock. If he had been in Moscow this would not be a problem. He'd have a locksmith open it for him in an hour.

A substantial bribe to the Lebanese concierge solves his problem. Within a few hours an old Indian man appears at his door. In half an hour he leaves, on the desk a wide open safe.

Yuri sifts through the papers and then stares at a document. It is the sale-purchase agreement of a villa at the famous Palm development. 2.8 million euros paid in cash. The deal was concluded four years ago. It is unclear where the villa stands in terms of completion, but at the time of purchase they were still dredging for land reclamation. There is a deed of trust, as well as a separate representation agreement signed with a certain Mr. Jawad Ghanem, the agent who brokered the deal for Viktor. His office address and telephone numbers are listed on the agreement.

Chapter Thirteen

"Which do you prefer?" I ask, looking Edik in the eye. "Clarity or ambiguity?"

"I'm not sure I understand the question," he replies. "Clarity or ambiguity in what?"

"In everything," I say, doing my best to adopt his style of talking. "For example, do you prefer the words 'yes' and 'no,' or the words 'maybe,' 'it depends,' 'it's unclear'?" I persist.

"It depends," he says with a smart-ass smile.

"Would you please take my question seriously?"

"Lara, I'm an investigative journalist," he says a bit defensively. "What do you think? Of course I prefer clarity in all things."

"I'm not talking about your professional life. Would you also prefer to have clarity in all things in your personal life as well?"

It finally occurs to him that I am not engaging him in light conversation.

"What is this all about?" he asks, giving me that focused look that he gets when he wants to hear more of what I have to say.

"Okay, let me put it this way," I say, ignoring his question. "Does ambiguity give you more options than clarity? What I mean is that once things are clear, or once you accept them to be clearly one way or the other, is there any room for maneuver? On the other hand, if they are ambiguous, you keep your options open, don't you? I mean, you can weigh alternatives, hold out on clarifying until you know better how you want to represent things."

"Ambiguity does not give you options," he says, with finality, like he really knows what he's talking about. "It gives you time to think. And sometimes time to think is more important than options. Depends on what you're facing. But the options themselves... well, they're either there or they're not, ambiguity cannot create them."

"But it gives you time to think," I repeat, sounding like I've seen the light. "Edik jan, that is brilliant!"

He looks confused. What is so brilliant about that, he wants to ask. And that is exactly where his brilliance lies. Oh how I want to say this to Ahmed, who thought ambiguity offered options. It just buys you time, my dear Ahmed. It allows you to put off decisions, which creates the illusion of having options. That is all. It can never create new options.

"Of course," adds Edik casually, as if he has overlooked a simple detail that may or may not be worth bringing up, "if you are not sure which way to go, buying time can be valuable. Don't ever underestimate the importance of time, Lara. After all, that's all we have on this earth."

That's all we have on this earth. Time. I'm no longer hearing Edik, but my father. And every second that passes will never return. We can never live the same second twice. He used to talk like that about time. So much so, that I became obsessed with the passing of time, and started recording things in my spiral notebook, just to keep track.

I come out of my reverie and see him staring at me with such intensity that I shudder.

"Are you sure you're only eighteen?" he asks sardonically.

"Ha, ha, ha Paron hundred-year-old Edik," I chuckle. But I know what he is asking. Am I eighteen?

Again I think, ambiguity buys you time. Not options. You need clarity to see the options, those that are there already, or those you may have a chance to create. Either way, without clarity, you can neither recognize what's there, nor create what's not there. It is clarity that enables options, not ambiguity. Ambiguity buys you time—oh how I love that phrase.

Edik is still staring at me. God knows what my face looks like right now. It is late Saturday night, and we have returned to Yerevan, showered and changed the clothes still reeking of pig, and then met at a jazz club on Isahakian Street to go over the events of the day. The music is loud, especially when the band plays. During the intermissions, when they play recorded music at lower volume, we can hear each other more easily. Overall, in spite of the noise, this is a good place to talk.

I feel I have to give an explanation of what prompted me to ask the questions, which also provides a good opportunity to bring up Ahmed again. I tell Edik a little more about him and what he used to say about ambiguity versus clarity, his view about the whole Eastern culture thing, and how I thought he used ambiguity to his advantage in business negotiations.

"In a complicated negotiation," Edik says, "I can see how keeping things ambiguous can keep options open. There's no advantage in clarifying your position prematurely."

"Anyway," I say in a tone that suggests we can now bring this topic of conversation to a conclusion, "maybe that's what he meant. I've been thinking about it in the past few days. In my case, clarity has been good. I'm glad some things are now out in the open. And thanks for helping move the process forward. I wouldn't have been able to get this far if you had not been such a good listener."

"You're welcome, but not everything is out in the open, right?"

"Of course not," I say as casually as I can. "It is not possible to have everything out."

"You told Avo you feel bad for betraying Ahmed's trust. Is that all that's bothering you?"

I'm glad the lights in the jazz club are dim; otherwise, he'd see me blush. I hate to blush. It's like your own body turns into a snitch and exposes you, in plain view for everyone to see, without warning, and there's nothing you can do to stop it.

"He was kind to me," I say. "He did not deserve to be treated like I treated him. I was obsessed with getting back home. I had a feeling. I had to get home before something happened to Mama." Then I add, "And I could not be sure, or take the risk, that he would allow me to leave if I asked."

"I've been debating whether I should tell you this," he says, "but I think this is as good a time as any to bring something up. It is people like Al Barmaka that grease the wheels of Ayvazian's operation. They create the high-end demand for what Ayvazian sells, and they have the money to spend. I will keep an open mind about him because you do not seem to hold a grudge. But I want you to know that without people like him, the Ayvazians of this world would not find this business so worthwhile. You do see that, don't you?"

His words hit hard. Which Ahmed should I think about? The one I knew personally or the broader role he plays in the sex trade?

"I cannot think of him as the same as Ayvazian," I say, aware that my voice is shaking. "There is no similarity between how those two men have treated me."

Edik does not push the issue, even though I have not responded to his comment. Then I find myself volunteering more about Al Barmaka's estate, my villa, Sumaya, the other girls. I talk about how he used to treat me, I describe both his moments of extreme kindness, and his desert-hardened, dispassionate behavior that sometimes abruptly reminded me where I was and who I was, and who he was. And then, how it would start all over again, how just when I would be very clear as to my role in his house, he'd spring such an incredibly touching surprise, that I'd start wondering again. I tell Edik about the night he brought the CDs of an Armenian singer with the deepest, most velvety voice, who had an Arabic song followed by an Armenian song on the CD, and how moved I was that night, because Mama used to sing that Armenian song. And then, of course, the wake-up call would follow about who he really is and what my role is.

"Sounds like he was hiding behind ambiguity in dealing with you as well," says Edik when I finally stop talking. "He couldn't decide about you, so he wanted all options open, at all times."

I had never thought of that. I always assumed that Ahmed knew exactly who he was and what he wanted, since he owned everything around him, and that the duality in his treatment of me was very much part of him, something that came naturally to him, and to which he did not give a second thought. I was the one suffering from the ambiguity created by it, no one else.

"You think so?" I wonder how much of my soul Edik is actually seeing through this conversation.

"It's the best explanation, given what you told me earlier," he says casually.

"And now?" I ask, hoping that he'd be able to shed some light on the latest events. "Does this mean he's seeking clarity? Is that why he sent Manoj?"

"Hard to tell. You disappeared suddenly. Maybe he wants to know what happened."

"He sends Manoj all the way here because he wants to know what happened?" I sound disappointed.

"Obviously, he cares about you, otherwise he wouldn't bother to find out anything." He has noticed my disappointed look. "But I wouldn't jump to the conclusion that he is ready to make a clear choice. Have you thought about the possibility that maybe he enjoyed the old ambiguity so much that he wants it back?"

"No, I have not thought about that or any other possibility yet."

"You see, assuming that he had no reason to rush into anything, the ambiguity that you describe was perfect for him. He could be as romantic with you as his mood called for, and then he could create the distance, giving himself whatever protection he felt he had to have. He had everything. And then one day, when he's looking the other way,"—and here Edik gives me one his devious smiles—"you run away. So why wouldn't he want all that back, exactly as it was?"

"Because he cannot have it all back," I say. "It can never be the same again; he can never buy me again, can he? So how can it ever all go back to the way it used to be?"

Edik gives me a frustrated look. I *know* that's not what he's talking about. It is not whether it is possible or impossible. It is whether that's what's he's after. I *know*. But I still have to say it out loud, more than once if necessary, as much for my benefit as for anyone else's, that things can never go back to the way they were.

"Just keep an open mind, Lara," he says after a long silence. "Don't rush to second guess his motives, don't overthink it. Let it come to you, at its own pace, and take it as it comes. He'll call you soon enough."

That's good advice, even if it is much easier for him to give than for me to take. It is also a good way to end the conversation about Ahmed. I've spoken about him much more than I intended to anyway. Edik is right; there are too many imponderables in this story to allow meaningful speculation.

It's time to revert to where we had left things in Ashtarak, which is why we have agreed to meet tonight.

"We had a good start in Ashtarak," he says. "It didn't take much to bring Avo and Gagik into the loop."

"We still need to find a plausible story. I cannot tell you how exciting it is to plan this."

"One thing that we don't control in this process is the timing. They cannot keep Anastasia here indefinitely. They're losing money by her not being with her clients in Moscow. They'll increase the pressure on her."

"Oh, she'll probably start working here," I laugh. "I know Anastasia."

"Regardless, we don't have very long."

"We need a good villain. The right villain."

"Then we're in luck," laughs Edik. "No shortage of villains in Armenia these days."

Edik drops me at my apartment. We agree to meet at noon on Republic Square. Anna has managed to get permission to take her lunch break outside the store, and will join us. After that, he has to rush back to Vardahovit. This two-day excursion has been ill-timed for him, considering his forthcoming trip overseas.

Chapter Fourteen

Jawad Ghanem is in his early fifties, heavyset, balding, with bright white hair around his temples, and an equally white pencil-thin mustache, which almost glows over his dark skin. He arrives at the hotel accompanied by a man around twenty years his junior. Yuri watches them as they approach the pre-agreed location in the lobby.

"Mr. Yuri?" says Ghanem extending his hand. "This is my assistant Ramsey. He is fluent in Russian, in case we need a translator."

"Zdravstvuyte Yuriy" says Ramsey. His Russian is formal, with a heavy Arabic accent.

Ghanem's precaution of bringing Ramsey along is not baseless. When Yuri had called, he could barely understand his broken and heavily accented English. But he made out enough of what Yuri was saying to understand that it involved the property of Viktor Ayvazian at The Palm.

Ghanem is aware of the type of business that Viktor was in. Even though it has been four years, he remembers the transaction. Payment in full, all cash. It smelled of money laundering like nothing else. It was rare that someone would pay in full for a real estate project that was still a concept. The investor could only stare at the waters of the Gulf and visualize the development, based on an architect's rendition. This was one of the larger villas. Ghanem remembers Viktor well. He did not negotiate on the price. He was quite eager to conclude the transaction and make payment.

"I represent the Ayvazian family interests," starts Yuri once they are seated and have ordered coffee. He starts in English, but finds the effort too tedious, and asks if he could shift to Russian. Both Ramsey and Ghanem eagerly agree.

"You may, or may not, know that Mr. Viktor Ayvazian was in an unfortunate automobile accident, and passed away around six months ago," continues Yuri in Russian, and waits for Ramsey to translate.

Ghanem looks like he did not know about Viktor's death. He has not seen or heard from the man since the transaction. Investors usually call to ask about progress and to check if everything is still on schedule. Not Viktor.

"I am very sorry to hear that," says Ghanem in Arabic. "May God be merciful toward him." Ramsey translates into Russian.

"Thank you, Mr. Ghanem. As you can imagine, his family would like to have his assets transferred to a family trust." Yuri waits for the translation, and continues. "Viktor was not married, and his parents are also deceased. His only family is that of his uncle, Sergei Ayvazian, who unfortunately died in the same automobile accident, but is survived by his wife and daughter."

There is an important lie in Yuri's account. Viktor was married. He and his wife no longer lived together, as their relationship had gone sour soon after their wedding, and she had returned home to Leningrad in less than a year. But they had not bothered to formally divorce. So, legally, they were still married. This could complicate matters if it ever came out. Yuri is confident that they can produce adequate documentation that would show that Viktor was single when he died.

Ghanem listens, his face showing nothing but the gravity called for by the news of the deaths. But he knows that Yuri is out of his league in Dubai. No one will buy this story. If Viktor is dead, and has no immediate family, then the property could be tied up in courts for a long time.

"There should be no problem," he says, with a very kind and sympathetic smile. "The inheritance rules in Dubai are clear. If there is no legally binding will, then the property goes to the next of kin, in a specific order, and specific shares to wife, children, parents, etc. Since Mr. Ayvazian did not have a wife nor children nor parents, we shall seek legal counsel and determine what needs to be done in this particular case."

The unintended advantage of having a translator in situations like this is that it gives each side time to think. A direct one-to-one dialogue, by its very nature, requires that one is more spontaneous. Both Ghanem and Yuri are grateful for the extra time.

Yuri is flustered by Ghanem's statement, but does his best to show relief instead of anxiety. The process sounds complicated. Without the proper support to grease the wheels of the bureaucracy, this could take years to sort out. He can imagine that a similar situation in Russia would probably take decades.

"Mr. Ghanem, I am relieved that the law is clear and that the rightful heirs will be protected. And I am thankful that we are facing this unfortunate situation in Dubai, rather than in some other country where it would not necessarily be the law that determines the outcome. But how can we expedite the process of settlement? I mean, a widow and an orphaned daughter have no other recourse than to claim their rightful inheritance."

Ghanem is amused. Yuri is out of his league in more ways being a fish out of water in Dubai. He probably believes that he is being sophisticated and diplomatic in his approach, but Ghanem has seen the best of them in action, and is not impressed. The poor widow and orphaned daughter of a pimp and money launderer? He looks at Yuri's hair, greased and combed back, his unusual face, that of a gigolo, and smiles sympathetically again.

"Mr. Yuri," he says, standing up. "I assure you that we'll take the plight of the widow and daughter into consideration. Family matters most. But before we can start anything, the courts in Dubai will need the death certificate of Mr. Viktor Ayvazian, his marital status, proof of the legal identity of the heirs, and formal documentation that you represent them. You understand of course that this is meant to protect the interests of the legal heirs."

Yuri's first attempt to start 'extra-judicial negotiations' has failed. Ghanem is leaving. He stands up also, in an awkward manner, having been taken by surprise by Ghanem's sudden and abrupt way of bringing the meeting to an end.

"Thank you for meeting me here," he says, "but what are the next steps?"

"No problem, Mr. Yuri," says Ghanem. "My office is next door," and he points at the second of the Emirates Towers twin buildings. "As for the next steps, please secure the documents I mentioned. Only then can we talk about concrete actions."

With that, Ghanem walks out, not waiting for Ramsey to finish translating his last sentence.

ℒ ℒ ℒ

Manoj's office is inside the walled compound that houses Al Barmaka's mansion, the villa guesthouses, one of which used to be occupied by Lara, and the staff quarters. It is only a five-minute walk from the mansion, but Manoj drives there. It is already too hot and humid to walk.

Al Barmaka receives him in his private study, off the first floor living room.

"The mission was largely accomplished," starts Manoj. "I saw two of the businessmen, the third had left the country on a last minute trip, and I saw Ms. Leila and her village. Where do you want me to start?"

"Tell me about Leila."

Manoj recounts the story of his visit to Saralandj, describing the roads, the village, the Galian house, and the meeting and conversation with Lara. He hands him her phone number and shows him some of the pictures that he snapped of the village.

"This is where she lives?" asks Al Barmaka in amazement.

"Yes Sir. Well, that's where she's from. She now lives in Yerevan and is enrolled at the University. She was home for the weekend. Unfortunately, I could not take any pictures of their house. It would have been too awkward."

"Did you meet any of her family?"

"A brother, two sisters, and a couple of family friends. One of them joined our conversation. He is not from Armenia, but he speaks Armenian."

"Who is he?" asks Al Barmaka, wondering what someone 'not from Armenia' would be doing in that village.

"I'm not sure, Sir. His name is Edward Laurian. That's all I know. He attended the meeting, but was quiet. I guess they did not want to leave me alone with Ms. Leila."

Al Barmaka stares at the pictures of the village for a long time.

"Why would she leave this place to go there?" he asks, half to himself, half to Manoj. Manoj is not sure whether he should answer.

"Did you get any clues?" asks Al Barmaka after a few minutes.

"No Sir, sorry. Our conversation was short. She said to give her regards to His Excellency, and that she would not mind if you called her. She also asked me to call her by her 'real' name." That briefly gets Al Barmaka's attention, but he does not say anything.

"Anything worthwhile to discuss regarding your other meetings?"

"It's an interesting country. Good development potential. It is around fifty years behind Switzerland in terms of development, but has the same potential. Three hours from Dubai, and you can be on snow covered mountains."

"Any industry worth considering?" Al Barmaka's interest in the conversation has already waned.

"Some mining, but the real potential is in the service sector, possibly tourism. The place is landlocked, with some unfriendly neighbors. Trade is not easy."

"Have some initial due diligence done on the country, political risk, investment potential, etc. We'll revisit later. Anything else worth reporting?"

"Just one more thing, Sir. Ms. Leila asked that you call her during the week, when she is in Yerevan. I'm not sure why she prefers it that way."

"Thank you. Keep a close eye on the people who used to run Lara here. Report to me any new activity, no matter how insignificant."

"Yes Sir," says Manoj. He already has arranged round the clock surveillance of Ano.

༄ ༄ ༄

Back in his office, Jawad Ghanem goes through the dusty files of Viktor Ayvazian. Aside from the cash payment in full, there is nothing unusual surrounding the transaction, and even that is not entirely unheard of in Dubai. Nevertheless, he calls in his legal counsel and asks him to do a quick background check on Ayvazian with the immigration authorities and with the courts handling expatriate affairs.

Within two hours his legal counsel returns with interesting information. It turns out that Viktor Ayvazian was deported from Dubai around two-and-a-half years ago. Aside from a few legal violations, he had offended the system with his loud and careless behavior and had argued with his local protection, and even refused to make payment on time on at least one occasion. But a couple of months later he returns with a new passport, under the new name Viktor Arakelian. The authorities know that Ayvazian and Arakelian are the same person, but they let him get away with it. By then, through Ano, he has already paid off all his debts and reestablished his old protections.

But the legal counsel's attention is quickly drawn to the fact that, a few months after that, Viktor Arakelian enters Dubai again, this time with a wife—a young woman called Lara Galianova, who, according to her Russian passport, is twenty-one years old at the time. After that, Viktor Ayvazian's status is restored, even though he continues to enter Dubai with his fake passport.

Yuri does not know about Lara Galianova, because he was kept out of the loop. When Viktor was getting ready to bring Lara to Dubai, she was only sixteen, and Dubai laws did not allow single women under thirty-one years old to be issued entry visas. Viktor knew that a fake passport showing her to be thirty-one would not be believable. So he had a passport forged that showed her to be twenty-one, and also produced papers showing that Viktor Arakelian was married to Lara Galianova. That is how Lara entered Dubai, accompanied by her legal husband, Viktor Arakelian.

Jawad Ghanem ponders the situation for a long time. The legal owner of the villa in the Palm has been deported once from Dubai, has returned under an assumed name, has a wife under the assumed name, but is supposed to be single under his real name, and now he is deceased and his uncle's family wants the villa.

≈ ≈ ≈

Ano has given Manoj most of the details involving Lara, including both her real and fake names and ages. She has also mentioned that, as a pure formality to secure her entry visa into Dubai, Viktor had forged marriage papers for her.

When Manoj gets his informant's report that Jawad Ghanem was seen meeting a man who had been also seen with Ano earlier, he gives him a call. Al Barmaka's family owns Ghanem's real estate firm, and Manoj handles their accounts, and represents Al Barmaka on the board of the firm.

"I thought I had seen everything in this business," says Ghanem, "but even I have to admit that I've come across a new one—the first in a very, very long time. If this case interests you, you are welcome to the entire file."

Chapter Fifteen

"They say you cannot find a calf under an ox," Edik tells Anna as he takes his leave. I know he likes her. His handshake is long and his voice is warm. "Finding solutions is sometimes easier than we think, if we don't waste time looking in the wrong places."

"Thank you, thank you very much," says Anna. "For everything."

Edik gives me a short kiss on the cheek, winks, and rushes out of the café. He has already paid the bill and tipped the waitress. He has a long drive to get to Vardahovit.

"Lara jan, thank you *soooo* much. He's amazing. Now you have to tell me why he does it."

"What do you mean?" I ask, even though I know what she means.

"Who in this country today will help anyone, especially a total stranger, if he does not expect something back?"

"He expects nothing back," I say with finality.

"Then why?"

I shrug my shoulders and turn my palms up. "It's the way he is, that's all."

Anna's not convinced, but drops the subject. Edik called his lawyer friend, a certain Mr. Thomas Martirosian, while we were at the café, and explained the situation briefly. He then made an appointment for Anna to see him on Wednesday next week, at noon so it coincides with her lunch break. He told Anna not to worry about any fees, because Mr. Martirosian would do this as a favor for him. Anna accepted the explanation, but I know he will end up paying for the legal costs of Anna's divorce.

It is a pleasant Sunday afternoon. The weather seems to have taken a break from its normal late-March madness, the wind has subsided to a light breeze, the skies have cleared after starting the day cloudy and drizzly, and the air smells fresh and full of promise. Unfortunately, Anna has to rush back to work. She'll be late as it is.

I take a long walk, crossing Republic Square and walking up Abovian Street, left on Northern Avenue, past the Opera and then back on Toumanian Street, wandering aimlessly, looking in shop windows and watching people. Random phrases from the various conversations of the past few days ring in my ears, and once in a while a verse from one of Edik's poetry books intervenes in the cascading thoughts. If there is a pattern to this cacophony, it is buried so deep in my subconscious that I'll never be able to find it. And it does not matter anyway.

I arrive home by early evening and help Diqin Alice prepare supper. We eat together, with very little to say, and then I retire to my room. I read for several hours and then fall into the deepest, most restful sleep I've had in over two years. The thoughts, voices and flashbacks must have worn themselves out during my walk.

$$\it{2} \quad \it{2} \quad \it{2}$$

The week is relatively uneventful. I've been expecting Ahmed's call by Thursday, before the weekend begins in Dubai. I know he spends Friday with his extended family of siblings and more than a dozen nieces and nephews. He never visited me on Fridays. Even though he is not religious and has broken many social customs, he likes going to the mosque on Fridays, just to uphold tradition, which he views in an entirely different light than social rules. Tradition, especially aspects of it that are tied to a glorious past, is worth upholding. Ahmed thinks of himself as an Arab nobleman, the heir to a period when Arab culture reached its zenith. He especially loves to imagine himself as a modern day prince descended from eighth-century Andalusia, the height of Arab culture, literature, music and science.

And then the call comes.

I see the '971' country code on my phone, which is the United Arab Emirates. "Hello?" I say, aware that my voice is trembling.

"*Habibty*." My dear love.

"Ahmed, is that you?" What a stupid question to ask. Who else would call me '*habibty*'?

"Leila, how are you?" Then there is a hesitation, followed by another question. "Shall I call you Leila or Lara?"

"Ahmed, I am Lara now." I feel foolish again at the way that sounds. Then I make matters worse by adding, "I remember the days when I was Leila fondly, Ahmed."

I want him to know that I hold no grudge against him, or against the name he gave me, and that the name 'Leila' is not a bad memory. But I still sound stupid.

"*Habibty*," he says, and I believe he uses that word to avoid choosing between Lara and Leila, "there is so much to talk about, but none of it can be said over the phone."

"Ahmed, I am very sorry for the way I left." I begin, and he tries to interrupt me with something like 'none of it matters now,' but I am too nervous to hear exactly what, and I feel the need to finish telling him what I need to tell him, so I talk over him, drowning his words with my voice. "Ahmed, stop! Please listen to me. I was wrong. I mean, I'm sorry for treating you the way I did. I should have told you the truth."

"Are you done?" he asks, and waits. So do I. Am I done? Is that all I want to tell him?

"Well? Are you?"

"I'm sorry," is all I can manage to say.

"Lara," he says, and I know he deliberately uses my real name, "stop feeling sorry for the past. You must have had your reasons. None of this would make any sense otherwise. Let's go forward. Listen carefully, Lara. Forget *everything* about the past. Everything. Do you understand?"

"No, I don't," I whisper into the phone. And I really don't. Forget everything?

"I want to see you again," he says. "Just Ahmed Al Barmaka meeting Lara Galian. No intermediaries, no contracts, no deals. Just a meeting of two people."

Just a meeting of two people? Can he really forget that he bought me from a pimp?

I wish Edik was here to tell me to stop being childish. I want to hear him say that Ahmed is not at fault for the way he met me, that he did not know me before he bought me, that he got to know me afterwards, and he's been trying to live up to what he discovered about me since then. But that is probably even more childish. Nothing changes the fact that he bought women, even if most of them wanted to be bought by someone like him.

"I cannot come to Dubai."

"I know. I'll come to Yerevan. I need some time to arrange schedules, because I want to come for at least a few days."

"Ahmed, it cannot be like it used to be." I'm not sure myself what I mean. Do I mean, 'visiting me in Yerevan cannot be the same as visiting me in his villa in Dubai?' Or do I mean, 'we cannot be lovers like we used to be?' I don't know what I *want* it to mean.

And I finally see what an incredible haven ambiguity really can provide.

"It does not have to be any specific way, Lara. I want to see you. Let's talk face to face. It may take me a few weeks to free up the time. Or I can come for just an afternoon; I can do that earlier, if you prefer that."

"No, Ahmed, please don't do that. Take your time." I create yet another ambiguity—am I saying an afternoon is too short? Take your time and come for a longer visit? Or am I saying take your time to plan, so you don't disrupt your schedule?

"Okay then," he says. "I'll call again soon. And I'll see you soon."

Before I finish saying, "Okay, Ahmed," he hangs up. That's the other side of Ahmed that I remember well. He decides. He acts.

ॐ ॐ ॐ

A popular saying around here is, 'the bear knows seven songs, all seven are about honey.' It applies to Avo these days. All he talks about are the pigs and piglets. Six more have delivered, one a litter of nine, the others some seven, some eight. The rest will deliver by the end of next week, he says. The vet has been there often, and says the newborns are healthy, and will survive, if the new mothers don't crush them during feeding due to their inexperience.

Avo has left the responsibility of planting the garden to my sisters, who also take care of the sheep and the cows. Sago and Aram help, but they're too young for most of the tasks. I feel guilty for not being there to help out, but I cannot see myself making a real contribution. Before I left home over two years ago, both of my parents were alive and I had four older sisters, so I did not have any experience with tending to the animals. And a month after my Papa passed away, I was taken. So it has been my sisters and brothers who have learned to keep the house and animals in Saralandj in the past two years. Every time that I've tried to do something while in the village, my movements have been so awkward, clumsy and slow, that my sisters have laughed and taken over from me.

Meanwhile, Avo has agreed to sell to three different farmers from Aparan a total of fifty piglets, when they each weigh ten kilos. So it will be almost two months before he can deliver any piglets and get paid. But he will get the top price of 35,000 dram per healthy piglet. That is more money than Avo has ever earned. He has already borrowed against that future income to stock up on extra feed, because he expects feed prices to start rising a bit once all the farmers in the region start fattening their animals.

I am happy that Avo has found something positive to spend his energies on. Both Edik and Gagik have expressed concern about Avo's anger and his drinking. I have seen it myself. But both seem to be under control when he is absorbed in his farm.

Alisia is my main source of home news and gossip. She is closest to me in age. We are also just close. She has always been the most jovial and energetic among my sisters. She tells me that Arpi is more and more withdrawn into herself, and that she reads all the time.

"She barely even talks to anyone," she says. "Every minute that she's not working, she's reading. She's finished the entire works of Teryan and Sevak, and now has started reading Raffi. She'll read the whole collection of ten huge volumes!"

She tells me that Avo has not drunk all week, which is a major thing at the house. She also tells me that she thinks he has an eye for Ruben's younger sister, Hermine. Alisia, who turned nineteen a few months ago, giggles like a little girl when she says this. Both Avo and Hermine are too young, but one never knows. In the village, a lot of couples get married before they are eighteen. She also tells me that she does not have any interest in meeting a man anytime soon. First, she says, we'll marry off Sona, then Arpi, assuming she can take her nose out of the books long enough.

"Alis jan," I say trying to laugh like her, "it doesn't work that way. It's not by turn, you know. It happens when it happens."

Chapter Sixteen

The snow has disappeared even from the stubborn corners where the sun doesn't reach. Lara's sisters have been busy. The garden in Saralandj is fully tilled and planted. As usual, tomatoes, cucumbers, cabbage, green peppers, green beans, garlic, onions and potatoes take most of space. What little space is left is portioned off to the main herbs—parsley, mint and basil. In addition, the house is thoroughly cleaned and several large loads of laundry, including all the sheets and pillowcases, are done, ironed and put away.

Avo has been busy too. All the pigs have delivered, and the piglets already have started eating some solid food, even though they are still suckling. It will be another three weeks or so before they are weaned.

Sona and Simon have set the date of their wedding at the end of May. So in about a month she'll leave home. But Simon, like Martha's husband Ruben, is from the village. She won't be going far.

Aram continues to excel at school. Laurian thinks he should be sent to a special school for gifted kids in Yerevan, but Avo is not in agreement.

We need him here, he says. Gagik thinks the real reason is that he does not want to borrow more money right now.

Sago was not good at school and dropped out over a year ago, and he is not particularly interested in any work that is available for him in the village. It saddens Lara to see him like that, scattered, almost depressed, with an indifferent detachment, even on relatively happy occasions. She finds him more worrisome than Arpi. At least Arpi has her books.

Al Barmaka has not made it to Yerevan, but has called several times a week. Lara's initial excitement about hearing from him has waned. If he really wants to see her that much, why the delay? He had said a few weeks, and it has been almost four. Why should it take four weeks to sort out his schedule and free up three or four days?

"I'll have some interesting news for you when I come," he had said during his last phone call. "I'm sorry I've been delayed. This is our busiest time. We're finalizing first quarter accounts, and have a few important audits which require my attention." That is more about his business than Ahmed has ever said to Lara.

"It is okay, Ahmed. Please do not go to any trouble. Take as long as you need."

Edik is about to return from overseas. He has called a few times. He tells Lara that Thomas Martirosian is making progress on Anna's divorce case. There should be a breakthrough in a few weeks.

In the meantime, Anastasia has convinced Yuri to let her go back to Moscow, even though she has not told them much yet. She has convinced him that it will take time for Lara to open up to her, that she's made a lot of progress already, and that if she pushes harder, she may scare her off. She also calls Lara regularly from Moscow.

♃ ♃ ♃

The entire country is getting ready for the May 1 holiday when Avo gets a call from one of the farmers who have agreed to buy his piglets.

"Avo jan," he says, "I'm afraid I have some bad news. I won't be able to buy the twenty piglets as we had agreed."

"What's the matter, Aram *dzadza*, do you need some credit, or to make payment in installments?" Avo likes Aram. He is an old family friend from Aparan, about his father's age, who was close to his parents. That's where the *dzadza* honorific, which is a Russian word meaning 'uncle' that seeped into the Armenian lexicon during the Soviet era, comes from.

"No, it is nothing like that," says Aram. "To tell you the truth, I wish it was. I could have sorted out that type of problem."

"Then what is it?" It is more Aram's depressed tone that has Avo worried than his message.

"Have you checked the price of pork lately?"

"No," says Avo, and realizes that Aram's call is more serious than he had assumed.

"It's down. It was 3,200 dram per kilo, now it's down to 2,500 dram, and many think that it will drop to below 2,000 soon."

"But that could be temporary," says Avo hopefully. "Prices rose during the New Year and Christmas season. Maybe they're now coming down a bit, before we see another rise."

"Avo, we're talking about a forty percent drop in a matter of weeks. No one thinks this is temporary. And it certainly is not small. It changes the entire calculation."

Avo is quiet for a while. He fights the wave of frustration and disappointment that is rising in his chest. He does not want to accept this as a final verdict on his pig farm.

"What is causing the price decline?"

"No one knows for sure," says Aram, "The rumor in the market is that large quantities of live pigs have been imported from somewhere. Some are talking about as much as twenty thousand head."

"Who? How? From where?" Avo is stunned.

"No one knows for sure. But that is not the entire story. You must have noticed what has happened to the price of feed, Avo. You're feeding more pigs than any of us."

"I bought a lot a few weeks ago, thinking that the prices might rise when all the farmers start to buy. So no, I do not know what has happened to the price of feed more recently."

"You were smart to buy early, but I'm afraid that won't help you when you run out. All grades of imported feed have gone up by twenty-five percent. But the worst part is not even that. The price of chaff has gone up from 75 dram per kilo to 150 dram! When feed prices rise like this and pork prices fall by forty percent, how can we still make money at this business?"

Avo's face turns red and his hands start to shake. He recognizes the rage. It is similar to the storm that rose in his chest when he returned home from Vardahovit last fall and found that his mother had just died. It gathered speed and mass in a matter of seconds, first directed at fate, at some invisible force, and then, as it got so strong that he could feel it even in his eyes, Sergei Ayvazian became its target. The frenzy was then transformed into an obsession, which, even after the rage was spent, turned Avo into a cold-blooded killer.

But now Ayvazian is dead, and this time the enemy is truly invisible. Is it fate? Bad luck? The market?

"Avo, are you there?" comes Aram's voice.

"Ha, Aram *dzadza*. I understand. No problem with the piglets, please don't worry."

Just as Avo had managed to control his anger temporarily when his mother died, because he had the burial to attend to and because his family needed him calm and sober, now too he feels he has to save his business first, which means he has to keep a cool head and figure out how to overcome this setback. That is the most immediate task. But not the most important one. By far the most important task for Avo is to identify the enemy. His wrath is aching to burst out.

ℒ ℒ ℒ

Laurian lands in Yerevan in early afternoon. He is anxious to get home to Vardahovit before dark. He thinks about calling Lara and Gagik, but decides against it. He does not want to be given a reason to stay in Yerevan. He gets his car from long-term parking and heads straight out of the city.

No one, not even Laurian himself, has been able to fully understand the Vardahovit phenomenon. It is a tiny village in Vayots Dzor, one of the regions south-east of Yerevan, with around 300 inhabitants, two-and-a-half hours from Yerevan, and thirty-five kilometers from the border with

Kelbajar, a region controlled by Nagorno Karabagh. The roads leading to it are in such disrepair that even the more adventurous travelers tend to avoid the place.

Laurian has bought a mountain plateau of over fifty acres, two-and-a-half kilometers from Vardahovit village. Down in the valleys below, creeks flow south and eventually merge into the Arax River, which marks the border with Iran. It was a major undertaking to build a house on this plain, which stands at two thousand meters above sea level. Moving construction materials, workers and supplies was a nightmare. Laurian had fallen in love with the place. He could have had a mountain house not just anywhere in Armenia, but anywhere in the world, including Switzerland, Spain or Italy, where he had long-standing connections, but he chose this place. "I just feel good here," he says to anyone who asks why.

By three-thirty p.m. he has already reached the roadside restaurant where he likes to stop to break the drive. It is right before the Getap junction, which, for Laurian, signifies the beginning of his 'area,' as he calls this part of Vayots Dzor. Ten kilometers along the road to Getap, and the climb begins through Shatin, Yeghegis, Hermon and finally Vardahovit. That twenty-kilometer stretch is another road with which Laurian has his love-hate relationship. Catastrophic road conditions embedded into a breathtakingly beautiful mountain setting. But for Laurian this stretch has more than natural beauty. It was the crucible for a fascinating part of medieval Armenian history, the relics of which—ruins of fifth-century cities, forts, monasteries, tombs of medieval princes, graveyards of various ethnic groups—continue to keep watch over the peaks, valleys and rivers below, oblivious to the present day neglect around them.

Laurian makes his stop short. A quick coffee, a few words exchanged with Nerses, the owner, and he takes off again. He is anxious to see how many of the spring tasks Agassi, the caretaker who lives in the guardhouse with his wife, Vartiter, has managed to complete.

Late April is magical in the highlands. Every mountainside glows with the bright red and purple of wildflowers, every meadow boasts more shades of green and yellow than any camera or paintbrush could possibly capture, and the overflowing creeks and rivers produce unabashed symphonies proclaiming the exuberance of spring.

Agassi opens the large iron gates and Laurian drives in, waves, and goes straight to the main house, some hundred meters inside the property. He is too impatient to even bring his suitcase in. He quickly changes his shoes and they walk out, inspecting first the newly planted rows of poplars. It is easy to plant poplars. Just push freshly cut branches into the soil, before the buds sprout in the spring. Then it is a matter of watering regularly, and in April and May the rains minimize that task. Agassi has completed the poplar plan—six hundred sticks are lined up in six straight lines in the mud.

In the fruit orchard, the apple and pear trees planted last year have done well, but the cherries and plums have not survived the winter. Agassi was supposed to replace all the dead trees with new saplings. But he has not managed to secure cherry and plum trees from the nursery in Yeghegnadzor, and has replaced everything with walnut trees instead. Laurian is not happy with the choice.

"These are a new sort," says Agassi, defending his decision. "These are the dwarf walnuts. They start giving walnuts in three years. It takes forever for the regular trees to start giving fruit. And these don't grow very tall."

Laurian lets it be, but he still wants his cherry and plum trees.

"Let's drive down to the nursery tomorrow and check what they have," he says. "There is room to add two more rows; we'll do one row of cherries and one of plums."

"*Vonts kuzes*, Edik jan." As you wish. "But we're going to have problems with those again next year. We are too high up for cherries."

"Let's try," says Laurian. "We'll plant a few by the house also, where they'd be more protected."

Then they check the pine trees that were planted last fall, and see that all have survived the winter, with the beginning of fresh new growth already visible. Laurian is happy. He has always wanted more evergreens.

It is already dark when he returns to the house. Vartiter has arrived and is busy in the kitchen.

"How hungry are you?" she asks, and her trademark smile warms Laurian's heart.

"I'm starved, don't go cheap on me tonight. Is Saro in the village?" Saro is the Mayor of Vardahovit, a close friend of Laurian's.

"Should be. You want him to join you?"

"Yes, and why don't you and Agassi join too." Laurian is tired, but not in the mood to eat alone and quietly retire. For him, being back here after a few weeks' absence is exciting and worth celebrating. "Sorry to increase your work at the last minute."

"No problem, Edik jan," laughs Vartiter. She is the most easygoing and contagiously content woman Laurian has ever known.

"Shall I tell Saro an hour?" He likes to chat with the Mayor after each absence, to catch up on anything new in the region.

"An hour is fine. I'll have at least something for you men to start with by then."

"Let's sit in the front." The front terrace is his favorite place, because it has stunning views, including some of the most spectacular sunsets.

He calls Saro, brings his suitcase in, unpacks, sets the laundry aside for Vartiter, and takes a quick shower.

It is close to seven p.m., time to enjoy the magic outside. Vartiter has already set the table, and taken out some of the cold appetizers. Laurian opens a bottle of wine and settles into a chair. Earlier that week he was in Paris. Even though he has traveled all over the world, it still amazes him how quickly one can get transported from a noisy, dirty city, to a place that can inspire awe and boundless peace at the same time.

He takes his first sip of wine and smiles at the vast mountains spread before him, when Gagik calls.

"I'm glad you're back!" he says.

"Just sat down a minute ago," says Laurian. "Landed this afternoon. Drove straight up. How are things?"

"We need to meet," says Gagik, and something in his voice and tone puts Laurian on edge.

"Tell me," he says.

"All hell has broken loose in Saralandj, Avo is up in arms, and I think we may have found the villain we were looking for at our last meeting in Ashtarak."

"Is everything okay with Lara?"

"I've not heard anything, but she needs to meet with us. Maybe we can finalize the message to Anastasia."

"Gagik jan, why don't we all meet here this time," says Laurian. "I just got back, and frankly am not up to driving back down so soon. Even Avo should be able to take one day off. Why don't the three of you come tomorrow and stay the night. We'll cover everything."

"That's fine with me. I'll see if I can round them up."

Chapter Seventeen

have to admit that I am excited about going to Edik's place. Last time I was there, everything was so dramatic that I do not remember much about the place itself. We slept there the first night I regained my freedom, and I was still in a daze the next morning. Edik has invited us back a few times, but everyone has been too busy, or unwilling to go up there during the severe winter months.

Gagik will pick Avo up and head to Yerevan for me. I am expecting them to arrive around nine, so we should be at Edik's place by late morning. We're supposed to return tomorrow evening.

Ahmed calls again yesterday, from Singapore. He says his next meeting is in Manila, and he'll try to fly straight to Yerevan from there.

"I don't think there are any flights from Manila to Yerevan," I say, and immediately realize that I made another stupid comment.

"Sure there are," he says, laughing. "On Air Al Barmaka." He means his private jet. I don't think Ahmed has ever seen the inside of a commercial aircraft.

"Sorry, I forgot about that one," I say, even though he himself has not told me about his airplanes, Sumaya has.

"Well, it was I who told you to forget the past, didn't I?" he chuckles again.

It has now been around seven months since I ran away, and Ahmed still talks as if nothing has changed between us. I don't understand how men can do that. It does not seem to matter to him that I was a captive, that I was not allowed to leave my villa, let alone the compound, without permission and an escort. I was not allowed to use the Internet, or to mail letters, without the sharp scrutiny of Sumaya. It does not seem to matter to him at all that he had bought me, albeit for one year, to be his concubine. How can all that not matter? It is almost all that matters to me.

And I know that if I talk to Edik about him again, he will extract from me the truth, which I have been denying even to myself. That perhaps sometimes I do want to be with Al Barmaka again, without the captivity, without the 'being bought' defining me and our relationship, without the rules and restrictions. Just to be with him. But how can anyone break away from her past to that extent? Simply pretend that the circumstances of our past relationship never existed? How can I move from being his property to his friend, let alone lover, without 'the whore' constantly looking over our shoulders, haunting us?

You can, I tell myself, because it was neither you nor him who made you a prostitute. He never treated you as one, and you never chose to be one. You were forced into this, Lara, and you fought it with everything you had, and you abandoned him and ran away, which is the ultimate proof that you were not the prostitute. So stop telling people you're sorry you ran away. You're *not* sorry you ran away. If you had not run away, Ahmed would have every right to still look at you as his property.

Oh, how I hate these demons! These loud, intrusive, obnoxious lurking demons. They so love to contradict each other, and often they contradict even themselves, just to confuse me. And they succeed.

Avo calls to say they are two minutes away. One flight of stairs by foot, then the elevator, and then into Gagik's car. I have only a small overnight bag. I hop into the back seat, lean over the front to kiss Avo, and tap Gagik's shoulder as a greeting. I feel the excitement of a little girl going on a picnic. Let's go! Let's get out of the city. Let's go to the peaks, to the clean highlands, where there is more dignity than we can find anywhere in in Yerevan. That is what we all need right now. Serenity and peace!

Of course, Avo does not share my enthusiasm. He is somber and serious. He also feels uneasy about leaving Saralandj and his farm. But he need not be. He has given clear instructions to Sago and Aram; surely they can handle the farm for two days.

Gagik drives fast, and we do not stop anywhere on the way. We arrive twenty minutes earlier than we expected. We find Edik walking around in his knee-high rubber boots, his shotgun slung over his shoulder, planning something with Agassi. His face lights up when he sees Gagik's car at the gate. He beats Agassi to it, flings the gate open and gives everyone a bear hug. Then he tells Gagik and Avo to drive to the main house, but holds me back. "You come with me," he says. "I want to show you something."

He has nothing to show me. He just wants me to walk with him to the house.

"What's it with Avo?" he asks.

"He's losing his pig farm. That farm was the best thing that ever happened to him."

"He's losing the farm? How?"

"Gagik will explain everything. It is complicated."

He looks at me for a few minutes.

"I'm so glad you're back here," he says. "It has been too long."

"I know, I don't remember much from the last time."

The walk from the gate to the main house is interesting. He has pine trees planted on either side of the narrow pathway. The apple orchard is on the left, and a small cluster of poplar trees on the right, and before the poplars is Vartiter's flower and vegetable garden, freshly planted in neat rows and columns. It won't be until June that anyone sees what will come to life in that patch.

"Lunch will be served at one," says Edik. "Saro will join us after lunch to say hello. So we have time to talk privately before he gets here. Vartiter has prepared some light snacks to hold you over. But I warn you, if you get full before lunchtime, you'll regret it! You won't want to miss this feast."

We wash up and go to the front terrace. Edik has the large green umbrellas open, as the sun is very strong. We all have coffee and water, and some of Vartiter's sandwiches of cheese, yershig and chicken. Gagik is impatient, and wants to start the discussion.

"I've gathered a lot of new information," he says. "Let me explain the basic facts, before we begin arguing, okay?"

"Okay," says Edik, but he looks confused. He is not aware of the latest development. Avo and I nod.

"This is how he does it," starts Gagik so quickly that it's obvious he's been dying to tell this story for hours. "He has been granted an effective monopoly in certain products for five years. That is his reward for helping out with the last elections." Gagik is animated in a way that I have not seen before. This is not Gagik talking. It is *Khev Gago* talking.

"Gago, stop," interrupts Edik. "Who are you talking about?"

"LeFreak!" screams Gagik, "Who else?"

"Gago, you need to slow down a little," says Edik. "Assume we know nothing and I really don't. So explain from the beginning."

"From the beginning," says Gagik impatiently. "First, I'll explain how he operates in general, and then we'll get to the details of the pork business and Avo's farm. He 'helped' with the last elections. His reward is a five-year monopoly over key agricultural products, including wheat, flour, pork and animal feed. He has his fingers in other products too, but let's focus on these for now."

Gagik stops and looks around, to make sure he has not lost anyone again. His eyes are intense and wild with emotion.

"The customs office has authority to set the reference price for all imports," he continues. "They impose import duties based on the reference price. Now imagine this: Let's say I want to import wheat, and LeFreak wants to monopolize wheat imports. Let's say I have a shipment arriving in a month, and he has a shipment arriving in six weeks. A few days before my shipment arrives, the customs office raises the reference price by fifty percent. I go to clear my shipment from customs, and I am told sorry, the reference price you have there in your documents is no longer valid. Please take all your paper work and go to such and such office."

Gagik stops again, and watches our faces.

"Are you with me so far?"

We all nod.

"Obviously," he continues, "I do not want my shipment of wheat to rot in the storage bins of the customs office, so I go to the office they direct me to. They show me an import duty invoice, which is fifty percent higher than what I had before. Of course, I can contest their claim, because I have documents setting the import fees at much lower levels. But if I do, I am almost guaranteed that my wheat will be eaten by rats before I resolve the issue. So I accept."

The *Khev Gago* gaze pierces us for a second, and when no one utters a word, he continues.

"Two weeks later, LeFreak's shipment is due to arrive. A day before the due date, the custom's office lowers the reference price to a fraction of its original value. LeFreak clears customs by paying a small fraction of the import duties that I paid only two weeks earlier."

Gagik stops for effect. He is not used to talking this long without being interrupted, if by no one else, at least by Edik. But Edik is quiet. Like the rest of us, he sees the scenario clearly.

"So what do you think happens next? LeFreak offers wheat on the market at a huge discount, and he does that at a profit. I cannot compete. If I match his price, I end up selling at a loss. If I don't match it, I cannot sell any of it. So what do I do?" asks Gagik, his small dark eyes flinty. "I'll tell you what most small importers do in this case. They go to *him*. They offer to sell their wheat to him. And oh, he is so gracious, so generous. He agrees to buy everyone's wheat at whatever it cost them, which is substantially more expensive than the price at which he is selling his own wheat. 'So you don't lose money on this shipment,' he says. 'But you have to agree never to import wheat again.' Everyone agrees. Tens of small wheat importers are eliminated from the competition in one afternoon. LeFreak is the king of wheat. In a matter of a few weeks, wheat prices start to rise again. No one understands why. It is the market, they say. Prices fall, then prices rise. Who knows why?"

We all fall silent. Vartiter, noticing Gagik's lively monologue, avoids walking out with the food. I notice her once opening the front door and, hearing Gagik, closing it again quickly. She understands Edik and his rules well.

"He's operated in a similar fashion, with some variations in the details, with flour, animal feed and livestock," continues Gagik. "By the way, he did the same exact thing with cell phones two years ago. That is how he ends up controlling these markets."

"How come this hasn't come out?" asks Edik. "It shouldn't be difficult to expose something like this."

"But it is difficult," snaps Gagik. "First, he personally does not appear in any of it. Everything is done through his people, some of whom are not official employees. Second, the Customs Office is supposed to monitor and adjust the reference price. That is its responsibility. No one pays any attention to the timing of specific adjustments. Third, when he pushes prices of a commodity down, he gets credit for it in the media and even by some government officials. I saw an archived news report from a while back, where some farmers were protesting the sudden drop in the price of flour, and the government official's response was, 'I don't understand what the problem is. We have an open economy. Anyone can compete. That is why our consumers enjoy the lowest possible prices. Would you rather pay more for a kilo of flour? People should be thankful, not upset.' And so our monopolist becomes a hero. And when prices start to rise again, it is blamed on the market forces."

"Gago jan, I have to ask you," says Edik, "how do you know all this?"

"I know a young man at the Customs Office," says Gagik. "He is fed up with what he has seen. Or maybe the senior officials do not pay him a share of the bribes they receive from LeFreak. At any rate, he spilled his guts one night when we were drinking. Then I did some research of my own. The online news services keep the old news broadcasts and talk shows in their archives. It is incredible what you find there. The problem is that no one connects the dots. Each broadcast is viewed and then forgotten. People don't have the habit of questioning. Even when they know what is going on, they just accept it as how things are. You know that better than anyone, Edik jan."

Edik nods slowly. He knows the syndrome well.

Avo and I have been quiet. He's listened without showing much emotion, his face serious, his body and hands still. His only nervous movements have been chain smoking, giving me apologetic looks every time he lights a new cigarette. But we're outdoors, and I don't want to make a big deal of it.

"Now tell me about the prices of pork and pig feed," says Avo.

Vartiter cracks the door open and Edik turns around.

"Ha, Vart is everything ready?" he asks.

"It's ready. Can I bring the food before it gets cold?"

"Yes," says Edik. "Let's take a short break."

I get up to help Vartiter carry the trays out. She has three different stews, rice, roasted chicken, steamed trout, grilled potatoes and onions, and several salads. It is an impressive spread and what makes it more amazing is that she managed all this alone, and timed everything so it is ready in the right sequence.

"Agassi must have been here helping you," I joke.

"That will be the day!" she laughs. "If he had been here, I wouldn't be able to finish anything!" Her laugh flows like one of the clear, bubbling creeks of Vardahovit, and her smile is so warm that I want to give her a hug.

"Here, Lara jan, take this tray with the salads. I'll carry the one with the stews." She doesn't trust me not to spill the stews, and I don't blame her.

The table is set in about ten minutes. Edik, as usual, gets up and helps as we bring the trays from the kitchen. Avo and Gagik don't even notice.

Edik brings two bottles of wine, one red and one white, and a bottle of vodka for Avo and Gagik.

"These are not for now," he says. "We'll have one glass each to start the meal, but drinking won't start till after we're done hearing Gagik."

No one objects. We toast once, and start eating, but Avo is impatient.

"Let's talk while we eat. Gago jan, prices of pork and feed."

"Okay, LeFreak has been planning a total takeover of the pork business for a while. Last winter, his men quietly bought most of the supplies of chaff. His warehouses are full. Today, no matter where you buy your chaff, you are buying it from him. He supplies all the suppliers, and he sets the price."

"But he has doubled the prices and people are talking about more price hikes," says Avo. "At these prices, isn't it cheaper to import, say, from Iran?"

"Sure it is, but if you try, your shipment will be stopped by customs at the border, and, as with wheat, you'll be either asked to pay a fortune in import duties, or you will be faced with such incredible bureaucratic delays that your chaff will be useless by the time you get it out."

Avo lights another cigarette, and is clearly having more trouble controlling his anger.

"Of course he is not interested in wheat chaff. He is doing this to push the pig farmers out of business. By the time chaff is produced again in late fall, he would have already succeeded in his goal. Then he'll be the only buyer of chaff in the market, because he'll be the only one raising pigs.

"Let's move to the collapse in the price of pork. He has imported ten thousand head from Georgia, with another five thousand on its way from the Ukraine. He has paid virtually no import tax. One of my sources says that he may even have used funds from the Ministry of Agriculture that were supposed to provide financial assistance to small farmers. I haven't been able to confirm that yet, but it wouldn't surprise me."

It is already past two-thirty in the afternoon and the sun has moved. Edik gets up and adjusts the umbrellas. We've all had something to eat, but our appetite has not been that great.

"I think we get the picture," says Edik. "But I cannot continue this without another glass of wine and a cigar."

Everyone is ready for another drink. Edik pours the glasses—white wine for him and me, vodka for Avo and Gagik—and raises his glass.

"We have overcome bigger challenges," he says. "Compared with the crimes of Ayvazian, this looks like petty theft to me. We can deal with this guy."

Avo downs his vodka and refills his glass.

"We cannot deal with LeFreak the way we dealt with Ayvazian," he says.

"Of course not," jumps in Gagik, eyes shining. "No two fights can have the same battle plan. We are on new ground here with new players. But there is an important part of the puzzle that involves Lara, and we have not even talked about it yet."

"What does LeFreak have to do with Lara?" says Avo so sternly that I begin to worry. His protective instincts toward me are profound. Nothing is off limits for Avo if my safety is at stake.

"Slow down, Avo jan," says Gagik. "This is important. LeFreak is the most powerful contender for Ayvazian's business. Apparently trading in wheat and pigs is not enough for him; he wants to trade in people now."

I see how Gagik gets Edik's attention with his last assertion. He has cut his cigar and is in the middle of lighting it. He stops, and looks at Gagik with a seriousness that gives me chills. It is amazing how many different personas can exist in one man, and they make their presence known only when something triggers a reaction. The triggers are neither loud nor necessarily obvious. I've seen this is Gagik, who could transform from Gagik to *Khev Gago* in a second, I've seen it in Ahmed, and I've seen it in Edik, which, in some ways is the most shocking, because normally he appears to be the most stable of the bunch. But, at the mention of trading in people, Edik's face turns into that of killer.

"Tell me," he says. That must be a phrase he's picked up on his trip, because I don't remember him using it this frequently before. The cigar is now lit, and a cloud of smoke rises over his forehead like a halo.

"Ayvazian operated through a number of cells. Often these cells did not know about each other. He'd have a few henchmen in each, who kidnapped, beat, raped, drugged, and sold the girls for him. The largest operation was in Yerevan, but he had at least fifteen other cells around the country, in addition to his operations in Moscow, and the main connections in Istanbul, Dubai and the Ukraine. He loved to operate near the orphanages. Only his nephew Viktor knew about every cell, but even he did not know every detail of the operations."

"Gago, where does LeFreak fit into this?" asks Edik.

"I'm getting there, don't rush. These details are important. Most of Ayvazian's men—whether salaried employees or paid on-demand informants—in our region now work for LeFreak. But he has no permanent cell there. As far as I could make out, LeFreak has taken over three different Ayvazian cells and is actually running them himself. Two are in Lori, up north, and one in Kotayk, near Yerevan."

Edik interrupts again, but this time addresses me, not Gagik.

"Isn't Anna from a village in Lori?" he asks.

"Yes," I say, "and her husband too."

"Sorry, Gago, please continue," says Edik.

"Who's Anna?" asks Gagik, distracted.

"Never mind for now, Gago, sorry, please continue. We'll get to Anna before the end of the day."

"As I was saying, these three cells are now operating like before, but working for LeFreak instead of Ayvazian. LeFreak wants eventually to take over everything, even Moscow. The problem is, like Ayvazian's own men, he does not know where everything is."

Gagik has a habit of letting out a long, low-pitched whistle every time he hears something shocking or interesting. Now Edik takes a break from his cigar and does exactly the same. Avo looks both annoyed and confused. He probably does not want the conversation to digress from the pig farm, but at the same time anything involving me is important to him. Besides, he wants to have another drink, but custom requires that we all drink together, after a toast. The sun has moved further west, and the shade of the umbrella slides and the rays fall on my face. I blink and instinctively raise my hand to shield my eyes. Edik gets up and moves both umbrellas, even though the sun is not as hot as it was a couple of hours ago. I cannot help but notice that as soon as the sun hits my face, Edik's eyes light up, and he stares at me. That is another noteworthy moment. His last transformation was from Edik to a killer. But what is this one, which lasted no more than a second? I've seen it before, when I've smiled at him a bit more warmly than usual, or when I've said something profoundly simple and true. I've seen that same look in Ahmed's eyes too, during his more tender and loving moments. And I shudder when I make the association.

"Here is my last little bit of intelligence," says Gagik. "The person running things at the Ayvazian household is his daughter, Carla. She's around thirty, totally ignored by everyone until now, and she is Yuri's boss. She has also recruited almost all of Ayvazian's former henchmen from Vayots Dzor, Ayvazian's home region, and where we have the pleasure of sitting right now." Gagik is animated. "So, we have Carla who has reclaimed everything in Vayots Dzor, and LeFreak who has conquered cells in Lori and Kotayk, and they probably don't even know about each other. Isn't that absolutely fascinating?!"

"It sure is," says Edik puffing on his cigar. "But if they themselves don't know about each other, how come you do? Sorry to ask, but you know I have to."

"I'll get to that in a second," says Gagik. "But first, listen to this." His eyes sparkle more brightly and he can barely sit. "Carla is a nymphomaniac." He stops and looks at me for a second. "Forgive me, Lara jan. I forgot myself for a minute."

"Gago, please go on." I say forcefully. "Either I'm part of this meeting or I'm not. If I am, no need to hold back anything on my account."

"Okay, sorry again," says Gagik sheepishly, but the fire immediately returns to his eyes. "She is addicted to sex. She is sleeping with everyone who worked for her father. My source tells me it is her way of taking revenge on her dad, who kept her away from his business. This is 'showing him,' he says. But I am not sure about that. If that is not her real character, revenge won't just bring it out."

Avo, who as far as I know is still a virgin, is shifting uncomfortably in his chair. His refuge is another cigarette. Edik looks serious, but I know he is suppressing a smile, probably more at Gagik's way of telling the story than at the story itself. And there I am, thinking what it would be like to use men as sex objects, if that is what Carla is into. Why would any woman even bother?

"Now, my dear table-mates," says Gagik, lifting his glass, a moment that Avo has been waiting for, "let me tell you how I know all this. Edik jan, you've been gone for three weeks, right? Give or take a day. What do you think I've been doing in those three weeks? While you were out revisiting your decadent European past, I was here pulling in every favor, contacting every potential source who may owe me something from the old days, spending hours on that computer, trying to connect the dots. I've learned something from you, my friend; all that one needs to do is to bother, to look, to ask. And of course be old enough to have some meaningful connections," and Gago smiles a devious smile. "The rest is easier than anyone may imagine."

Saro walks in, and we all get up to greet him. The embraces are long and warm. He is a friend and a comrade and he knows everything about the events of last fall in Sevajayr.

Chapter Eighteen

"**Y**ou'd be surprised how easy it actually is for a chapter in your life to end, and for a new one to open. The old can die without the earth shaking, and the new can open without even a whimper. Only you can keep the past alive, Lara. Your past does not have a life of its own, so it can continue to haunt you only if you yourself allow it to."

"That's easy for you to say." She stops walking for a minute to admire the view from the eastern edge of the property, the valley below, the steep rise of the mountain on the opposite side and the creek gushing some five hundred meters in the ravine below. "You move from country to country, from assignment to assignment, one thing ends, the other starts. That's how it is for you. But my past can and does stay alive on its own; it follows me, like my shadow."

Laurian stops to face her.

"LeFreak is after Ayvazian's business. So are Yuri and Carla. They really are not after you. I admit, your past happens to have a role—a small one, considering the scale of his operation. But we can handle the LeFreaks and Yuris of this world. You have to handle the past."

"And Ahmed Al Barmaka? If he shows up here wanting to see me, no strings attached, isn't that part of my past that appears without my permission?" She did not intend to sound so angry.

"If you want the *relevance* of your past relationship with Al Barmaka to be over, kill it. Kill it right now, right here," and Laurian waves his arm at the panoramic scenery surrounding them. "The minute you decide the past will no longer affect the present, it won't. Then, if you want to see him again, see him again, but not the way it was before. A new chapter with him can only open if you've already pulled the plug on the old one. But if you haven't, the new chapter will have far too much interference from the old. It will fight you, it will resist, it will make your life a misery."

They walk in silence for a while. Laurian makes a compelling point, but Lara is not at all convinced that what he says is true. Just kill the past in your head, and it dies. That's all? Are there really men with that much inner strength, that much will? Is that even humanly possible? Are we even *supposed* to be able to control our minds and emotions to that extent?

"There is one important point I don't want you to misunderstand," says Laurian. "I am not talking about denial. If you try to deny your past, you're fooling yourself. Besides, a past denied does not die. I am not talking about forgetting it, either. You cannot forget everything. I am talking about looking the past straight in the eye, acknowledging that it happened, confronting it, and then banishing it to a quarantine from which it can no longer have any active role in your life. That's what I mean by 'killing it.' Do you see the difference between that and denial or forgetting?"

Lara nods. That seems even less plausible to her. They pass by the poplar forest and Laurian proudly declares, "Four hundred trees last year, six hundred more this year! A thousand poplar trees fully-grown, twenty-five meters high. Imagine this place then!" Lara is amazed at how quickly the deep thinker of a minute ago is transformed into an overexcited child.

Lara asks, "Aren't they too close together?"

"Not at all," says Laurian. "These trees grow thin and tall. The branches will end up touching each other when they mature, but that is the idea. It will be dark in this little forest in the middle of day!" Lara's mind momentarily goes to the pine and spruce forests of Saralandj.

"I'd like to see it then," she says.

"You will. Let's walk until we reach the end of the plateau. There is a little surprise there for you. On the way back, I'll show you the fruit orchard."

They walk slowly, because the land is rugged, full of rocks, uneven, and covered by thick grass. There are rosehip bushes and wild apple, pear and plum trees everywhere.

"Only the bears enjoy the fruit of these trees," says Laurian. "That's another sight I want you to see. I'll get you back here in the fall when the wild fruits are ripe, and we can keep watch for the bears one night."

"You're kidding, right?"

"Of course not, Lara. I've seen them with my own eyes. We'll choose a night when there is a full moon, so we can really see them. They're magnificent animals."

"It's not dangerous?"

"It can be, if you do something stupid like scaring them or threatening a mother bear's cubs. But if we sit quietly at a good distance and watch, they just ignore us."

They reach the end of the western edge and turn to cross the width of the property. It is narrow here at the tip, and widens gradually toward the house.

"There's your surprise," says Laurian, pointing at a large teak bench right at the edge of the cliff. Lara is surprised.

"You're crazy!" she laughs. "How on earth did you manage to bring that thing all the way here? I could barely walk here!"

"Let's go sit," says Laurian. "This bench has a past that I do not want to erase."

They sit and remain silent for a long time. The view is unbelievable. Rivers, boundless valleys winding through intertwined mountain chains, vast plateaus and meadows and a remote mountain range spread right in front of them, as far as the eye can see, disappearing into a thin mist on the far horizon.

"I call this the 'point of truth and redemption,'" Laurian breaks the silence. "You know what Avo said when I first brought him here?"

"What?" whispers Lara, still awestruck.

"He said your father used to read the Bible to you when you were kids. He said there was a story he remembered where the devil leads Jesus to a mountaintop to tempt him, and offers him dominion over everything that his eyes could see. Avo said that mountaintop must have been a place just like this."

"I can certainly see that." Lara is still whispering, as if in the presence of something that should not be disturbed.

"But that is not the past I referred to," continues Laurian. "We were sitting right here when you made your first phone call to Avo. Remember, when he told you he was in Vayots Dzor, and you were so worried about what he was doing here, and why he wasn't home taking care of your mother?"

"Yes," but Laurian can barely hear her.

"We were sitting right here," he repeats.

Lara's mind flies to Dubai, to Sumaya's villa, where she had used every bit of guile she had to convince Sumaya to allow her to place that phone call. She had not even known that Avo had a cell phone. She had convinced Sumaya to call the post office in Aparan and leave word that she'd call back in an hour to talk to Avo. The post office had sent someone to let the Galians know. And when she had called an hour later, Martha had answered, and given her Avo's phone number. What a saga that was! What heart wrenching moments those were.

And now, she sits where Avo sat during that call, amazed not only at what nature has spread in front of her, but also at the incredible contrast between here and the compound in Dubai. She cannot imagine two more vastly different worlds, both physically and by what they conjure up in her mind.

"My God, Edik jan" she says at last, "what a heavy history to lay on this poor bench."

They sit lost in the seeming infinity spread before them.

"What did you say you called this place?" she asks. "The point of truth and what?"

"And redemption."

"Truth and redemption," repeats Lara. She likes the phrase. "Now Edik, remember you cannot lie to me here. I want you to answer this: have you really been able to confront and quarantine everything in your past as you were telling me to do? Have you really overcome all your nightmares? I *have* to know the truth."

Laurian looks at her for a long moment. There is no way to get around this girl. He is tempted to lie, and even tries to formulate the words in his mind, words that would give Lara a sugarcoated account of how he has managed to do what he has been advocating. But an entirely different word comes out of his mouth.

"No," he says.

"Tell me," she says, dead serious.

"Tell you? Now?"

"Tell me, now."

Laurian hesitates for a minute.

"We were in Spain, on holiday," he starts, speaking more slowly than usual. "With my parents and twin sisters, Arpi and Sirarpi. They were twelve, I was fourteen. We were standing in front of a statue of Don Quixote when we realized that Sirarpi was gone. Just disappeared, in broad daylight. We searched for her for two months. Those two months were the most difficult and trying times for my family. My father stayed in Spain to make sure the police did not stop searching. My mother took Arpi and me back to Switzerland because we were in school, but she would leave us with friends and join him on weekends. The police were not helpful. They said they thought sex traffickers had taken her, and it was rare that they could rescue victims of sex trafficking. Two months after she was taken, they found her in the Casa de Campo Park. There were no fatal wounds on her body. She had died from repeated rapes and beatings…" Laurian stops for a minute to manage the surge of emotion rising in his chest. When he finally catches his breath, he adds: "And malnutrition."

Lara, who until that point had tried to avoid all physical contact with Laurian, throws her arms around his neck, unable to control her tears. Laurian remains still, staring into the vast space ahead.

"That was some thirty years ago," he says at last. "And *that*, my dear Lara, I have not been able to quarantine. I am very sorry. Because I still want *you* to believe that it is possible to put the past firmly behind you, to render it irrelevant to your future."

"Hush," says the eighteen-year-old girl, holding the forty-five year old man more tightly in her arms. "I understand everything. Let it go, Edik jan. Just let it go."

It is almost noon when they get back to the house, having lingered on the bench for a while, then walked back slowly and toured the orchard. Laurian shows her several remnants of Bronze Age walls buried in the thickets. "This place has been inhabited for thousands of years," he says. "I can never stop wondering how they lived here, how they hunted, fought, defended themselves from the elements."

Lara cannot focus on any of that right now. This has been an eventful walk already, with so much to process, from the will to kill the past, to the history-laden bench, to the twelve year old Sirarpi. There is no room for the Bronze Age.

Avo and Gagik are anxious to leave. There is too much to do.

Vartiter has prepared a light lunch, which, after the large breakfast that they've had, does not generate much interest. But Laurian insists that they have something. "You have a long drive," he says. "Eat something light now, and Vartiter will pack something for the road." They know better than to argue with him.

♌ ♌ ♌

Thomas Martirosian, Anna's divorce lawyer, calls Laurian the next day.

"Her husband seems to have some backing," he says. "Are you sure you told me everything?"

"Everything that I knew. I don't even know the bastard's name."

"His name is Hov Samoyan," says the lawyer. "And Hov is not short for Hovannes. Hov, believe it or not, is his full, official first name. His nick name, on the other hand, is Hovo, which is…"

"Thomas, stop," says Laurian, "enough with the name. What makes you think he has backing?"

"The poor soul has been an unemployed hooligan for almost a year. Then he gets hired as a 'bodyguard.' His official title on his papers is 'security officer.' And guess what? He gets a license to carry a firearm. He walks around with a pistol in his belt."

"Who does he work for?" Laurian has an uneasy feeling that he already knows the answer.

"Officially, no one knows. The person who hired him is a nobody, like him. But unofficially, every one says LeFreak is behind the organization that employed him."

"What does his organization do?" asks Laurian, knowing that Thomas will not have a clue.

"Depends on who you ask," comes the answer, instead of the 'beats me' that Laurian was expecting. "Some say LeFreak imports so much from Georgia or through Georgian ports, that he needs a large organization in Lori to help with the logistics of clearing customs and distribution. Others say he is building up muscle because he is planning an expansion. You can believe or disbelieve anything you want. If this guy has the protection of LeFreak, I wouldn't want to rush into divorce proceedings yet. He can badly damage your friend Anna when it all comes out in the open."

"I agree. Put the divorce on hold for now. But I want to find out everything about what our man Hovo is doing. Everything, Thomas, do you understand? Don't worry about the cost, I'll cover it."

"I understand," says Martirosian.

"One more thing," adds Laurian. "Can we put the word out that his wife is trying to formally divorce him, just to see how he will react? His reaction may give us a hint of how to proceed."

"Edik, I have to say that it is dangerous to think about experiments like that in situations like this. But having said that, yes, I can put out the word"

"What are the risks?"

"The risk is that we'll remind him that he has a wife. And now that he thinks he has real muscle behind him, he will get more aggressive in trying to track her down. But the bigger risk is that if LeFreak decides to back him up in the divorce process, we'll have most judges turned against us. He'll bribe them all."

"*De lav*, Thomas," says Laurian. "Why on earth would someone like LeFreak go into that much trouble for a minor underling, a new recruit with no record of any achievement, before you even file for divorce?"

"Just saying," says Martirosian. "You asked about the risks. I had to tell you what the risks are."

"If those are the risks, let's go with it. Put the word out. I am dying to know what he'll do."

Chapter Nineteen

From mid-afternoon until the early hours of the morning Anastasia is usually with clients, and then she sleeps till noon. It is best to catch her soon after she wakes up. I've learned from the days that I used to spend at her apartment in Moscow that that's when she can focus, but she's not yet so awake and full of energy that it becomes difficult to keep her attention on one thing.

She answers after four rings, when I'm about to hang up. Her voice is groggy.

"Anastasia, sorry if I woke you up. Is this a bad time?"

"Oh, hi Lara," she mumbles. I hear shuffling of sheets. "I'm not home yet. Is it urgent?"

"No, sorry, it can wait. When can I call?"

"At least two hours," she says. "If it can wait."

"It can, don't worry. Talk to you soon."

I imagine Anastasia in some hotel room, with a client who was drunk the night before and agreed to pay her an all-night fee. He probably fell asleep after having sex once, and snored all night, keeping

Anastasia awake. But all-night clients do not feel they've had their money's worth if everything ends like that. They have to have sex in the morning, to make the fee worthwhile, even if they are so hung-over that their own body is reluctant. I could never understand that. Anastasia told me once that it is like insisting on finishing last night's dinner the next morning, just because you've already paid for it. I remember feeling so offended by her explanation that I yelled some very angry words at her. But she found the whole thing amusing. She was laughing the whole time, both while telling me her take on the overnighters and when she saw my outrage. I am still amazed at how well Anastasia has adjusted to her world.

I call her back in mid-afternoon.

"Lara, *aziz* jan, sorry I couldn't talk earlier. You won't believe what this guy was like. A small Japanese, maybe fifty, wants me to give him a bath, then a massage, then oral sex, then he wants to fuck. In that order. And then the same sequence in the morning. Everything timed, everything precise, everything…"

"Anastasia, stop," I interrupt. I have waited half an hour too long before calling. She's fully awake, maybe on her third cup of coffee. "Let's skip all that. We need to talk about Yuri. I have some information."

"Oh thank God! Finally! I am suffering in his hands. I never thought I'd be beaten again by these bastards after I managed to calm Viktor down, and here I am back to square one with Yuri. When can we talk? Can you come to Moscow?"

Sometimes it feels like Anastasia still thinks of me as a fellow prostitute. She wouldn't have talked to me about the Japanese client otherwise. Nor would she think that I could just hop over to Moscow. I think perhaps I should test Edik's theory of killing the past on Anastasia first. That would be simpler than trying it on Ahmed. So I bundle up all my past dealings with Anastasia and put them away somewhere in the back of my mind, focusing on where I am now, the past rendered inactive and irrelevant.

"I cannot come to Moscow," I say. "I can talk to you on the phone for some of this, but you may have to come here for the rest."

"Lara, *aziz* jan, if I leave again, Nicolai will kill me; if I don't give something to Yuri soon, Yuri will kill me. Please. How else can we do this?"

"You'll have to have Yuri and Nicolai sort this out. I cannot come to Moscow. Now listen, call Yuri and tell him that there is a very powerful man in Armenia who is after Ayvazian's business. He has already taken over some operations, and a few of Ayvazian's old henchmen now work for him. He will believe this because he knows it is true. This is important, are you listening?" I want to make sure her mind has not drifted somewhere else.

"Yes, I'm listening. That is important."

"Good. Make sure you tell him that Ayvazian's men in Aparan are now working for some other boss. That will give the rest of your story more credibility. Tell him that you asked me to help you find out more about this new boss. Say I promised to help. Then tell me what he says."

"Lara, we cannot even talk this much over the phone. What if they're listening? We have to figure out some other way to send messages."

"Fine, we'll do that. But now tell him that much and let me know what he says."

Half an hour later Anastasia calls.

"He's in Dubai," she says all excited. "So I don't think he was listening to us. He's returning in two days. First to Yerevan, then he'll come to Moscow, he said. So if there is more, you have two days to tell me, *aziz* jan."

Have I managed to really change anything in my relationship with Anastasia by putting the past away? I'm not sure. I would probably have told her the same things, regardless. Maybe the difference is just in my head, and not in her head. But that wouldn't be enough. In order to declare this experiment a success, Anastasia has to stop thinking of me as a prostitute, even as a former prostitute. She should look at me as one of her non-prostitute friends, if she has any, and even if she doesn't have any. Maybe if she stops telling me stories of her clients... I would take that as a step in the right direction.

So, Yuri found his way to Dubai. It was bound to happen, given that he's on a hunt for Ayvazian's assets. I wonder if he'll run into Nicolai there also, or that one is strictly a Moscow takeover artist. Either way, Madame Ano would have had the pleasure of meeting Yuri. I catch myself wondering what has happened to Ano and the other girls, and I get mad at myself. How can I expect others to forget my past, if I still think and wonder about it? I have to stick strictly to my new persona, in order for me to project it, and only it, to the rest of the world. At least I think that's what Edik was trying to tell me in Vardahovit. This is not about denial, he said. Nor about memory. Acknowledge the past, confront the past, kill the past! Then move on, free of the past.

♌ ♌ ♌

Alisia calls when I'm in class. We have agreed that she won't call during class unless it is an emergency. Class ends in fifteen minutes, and my first instinct is to wait. But then I panic. What kind of emergency could they be having in Saralandj?

"Lara, they arrested Avo," she screams. I am right outside the door of the classroom, and I walk fast towards the exit of the building so students in the hallway do not hear my side of the conversation.

"What happened?"

"He slaughtered one of his pigs, filled two large buckets with all the entrails and the blood, drove to LeFreak's house outside Yerevan and splattered it all over the fence and the front gate." She is hysterical. "The security guards almost killed him," she screams between sobs. "They shot at him, to scare him away. Then they beat him up real bad and called the police. He's in jail, Lara! What are we going to do?"

"Alisia, calm down, how did he drive to Yerevan?"

"He borrowed Ruben's truck. He does not even have a driver's license. Just to run a few errands between Saralandj and Aparan, he told Ruben. The police called Ruben about the incident. That's how we know."

"Does Gagik know?" I ask.

"I don't know..." and Alisia starts wailing again. "Lara, they say he was very drunk. He was screaming 'you want to be the king of pigs, Mr. LeFreak? You already are the biggest pig of all! Here! Take this then, the blood of your relatives!' That's what they said he was screaming while pouring the blood on the fence."

"Alisia, there's nothing we can do right now." I desperately want to calm her down. "I'll call Gagik and see what he says. They'll probably keep him a day or two then release him. He hasn't hurt anyone, hasn't committed murder or something serious. So we'll see. I know it's scary, but it's probably less serious than it appears to be."

"Lara, he slaughtered the mother pig in the pen, while the piglets were suckling!" Alisia's wail is deafening. "He dragged the body out, crushing a few of the piglets under her. How can our Avo be so cruel? How can he get *that* angry, *that* drunk?"

Details make you focus better. Alisia's outburst is so powerful that my knees begin to shake and I sit on the steps. She is still ranting, and the phone is pressed to my ear, but my mind is blank. I want to turn off all signals, sounds, visions, and to just dissolve, merge with the earth. Did I make Avo this angry? He learned to kill because of me; did he learn anger because of me too? Does one *learn* how to be angry?

"Lara, are you there? Are you listening?" Alisia seems to be making herself even more hysterical as she tells the story.

"I'm here," I say as calmly as I can. "But I have to go now. I have to see what we can do. I'll call back when I know something. Did they tell Ruben which jail he's in?"

"I don't know, I never asked. I'm so sorry…I know I'm not helping at all. I'm so sorry… I'll pull myself together, I promise."

"Good. That's the best thing you've said so far. None of us can help if we're hysterical. Don't worry, I'll call Ruben myself. You take care of things at home until we sort this out."

Two hours later Gagik and I are at a jail outside Yerevan. It is past visiting hours, and the guard is uncooperative. Gagik tries to reason with him, saying that I am the prisoner's sister, that no one from the family has visited him yet, that at least I should be allowed to talk to him, even for a few minutes. The guard stares at me for a minute, but remains firm. He stands at the gate like a rock, and addresses us so rudely that my blood starts to boil. Could anger be genetic? Then Gagik reaches into his pocket, and approaches him. He slips some banknotes into his hand.

"I'll see what I can do," mumbles the guard. "Maybe five minutes."

Gagik notices my hands shake.

"Don't be afraid," he says, clearly mistaking my anger for fear.

"I'm not afraid," I say. "I want to do to him what Avo did to that poor pig."

Gagik looks at me for a moment, unsure how to react. Then he laughs.

"Anger is a powerful tool," he says. "We used it as ammunition during the war. It is as important as guns and bullets. But, like guns and bullets, one needs to aim it right. The target of your anger should not be this poor guard, Lara. He really does not know any better. Besides, technically, he's right, we're here past visiting hours."

Gagik's words bring me back to earth so fast that I feel momentarily disoriented. And they call this guy 'Crazy?' I'd love to see him when he is really crazy, when he is releasing his anger at a deserving enemy.

The guard returns, a huge, bear-like creature swinging right and left as he walks, huffing as if he's out of breath.

"Come!" he orders. We follow him, and a whiff of his body odor nauseates me. Some of my clients smelled so bad that I had to hold my breath. I literally held my nose while they were having sex with me. This unkempt bear of a man smells like them.

"Wait here!" he says and walks out.

A few minutes later two guards bring Avo in. They release him. He is limping. As I run to him, I see him wavering, and Gagik is quick to join me as we hold him up.

"Did you bring me cigarettes?" he asks. That's when I notice his lips shake like twigs in a storm. Inside his left eye, a pool of blood has filled the space where the white used to be. There is a huge bruise on his right cheek.

I cannot lose Avo like this. This has to end. My problems seem so petty right now. If I'm the one who has been to hell and back, why is it Avo who's in this condition right now? Why is he still in a hell that he cannot escape? I do not need to overanalyze this, but I'm responsible for a large part of it. It does not matter what part and where and how. What happened to me has caused this to happen to Avo. It was the strength of my family that held me together while girls in my situation were becoming unreachable. I shall now try to bring Avo back home, as I came back. Avo has the same fight in him that I had in me. I am now convinced of that. In many ways, he has been forced out of his home, without even leaving Saralandj, as much as I was.

"We have to get him cigarettes," I tell Gagik.

"They'll never let us back in," he says, worried. Then he approaches the two guards waiting by the door.

"*Aper* jan," he says, 'brother', "would you sell me a pack of cigarettes?" He is holding a five thousand dram note, which is probably ten times the price of a pack. The guards look at each other and shrug.

"Sure," says one of them, grabbing the note from Gagik's hand. He hands him a pack of cigarettes from his shirt pocket. Gagik checks it, and

I can tell from his reaction that the pack is not full. He stares at the guard with such intensity that I see the guard take a step back.

"And the lighter," he says, holding his gaze. The guard hands him his disposable *bic* lighter.

"Thank you," says Gagik and walks backwards toward us, still focused on the guard. He puts a cigarette in Avo's mouth and lights it. He then hands him the pack and the lighter. Avo shuts his eyes and takes a long drag. As he puffs out the smoke, he looks at me for the first time.

"I'm sorry, *Kurig* jan," he says. "For everything, and for smoking indoors."

Chapter Twenty

"Did you miss me?" asks Yuri as he enters Carla's study. He looks tired but in a good mood, and he has a large manila envelope in his hand.

"That depends," says Carla, but smiles faintly. She is lying on the maroon velvet sofa reading a magazine. "You sure took your time in Dubai."

"It was worth it." Yuri approaches the sofa.

Carla sits up, and accepts a kiss from him with another faint smile. "Good to have you back," she says, keeping her voice businesslike.

"I have news. Some good, some bad, and some as of yet unclear. Do you want them in any order?"

"Just talk."

Yuri opens the envelope and drops a bunch of papers on the coffee table. The top document is bilingual, with two columns, Arabic on the right and English on the left.

"That's the purchase agreement of a villa in Dubai. Paid in full in cash. 2.8 million euros, four years ago. The deed of trust is in there too. In the name of Viktor Ayvazian. The agent says prices have not risen much in the last four years, but he thinks he can sell it for 3 million euros today."

"So for once my mother knew what she was talking about." Carla eyes the papers. She does not want Yuri to see she's excited about the three million euros.

"The problem is, Dubai has strict inheritance laws. This cannot be yours yet, even if Viktor bought it for your father and with his money."

"Then whose is it?"

"His wife's. Even though Viktor's wife has long returned home, legally they are still married. She gets everything."

Carla slowly moves her eyes from the papers to Yuri, and stares at him for a long moment, waiting for a more hopeful interpretation of these unwelcome facts.

"Of course, no one in Dubai has any knowledge of Viktor's marital status," says Yuri. "I told them he wasn't married. I was told to bring back four documents. First, his death certificate; second, an official paper testifying that he was a bachelor, had no children and was not survived by his parents; third, a paper showing that you, or you and your mother, are the legal heirs; and fourth, a power of attorney from the legal heirs appointing me to handle the inheritance in Dubai on their behalf. The first and last are easy. The second and third are problematic. But if we secure these papers, I can go back tomorrow and transfer everything to your name."

"Who told you to bring these documents?"

"The real estate agent."

"Is he a lawyer?" Carla likes to put Yuri on the spot, to insinuate that he has been less than thorough.

"Uh, I don't know if he's a lawyer." Yuri is annoyed and impatient. "I wasn't about to start talking to lawyers out there. He has handled enough cases like this. I'm sure he knows what he's talking about."

"Where was Viktor married?" asks Carla, ignoring Viktor's last comment.

"Good question," says Yuri, but he still sounds annoyed. "I have no idea. Has anyone met his wife?"

"I haven't. I'll ask my mother. She must have met her. I know she went back to Leningrad. I know nothing else about her. If they were married in Leningrad, it will make matters easier."

"Do you want me to ask around for a good lawyer to prepare the documents?"

"No, leave this with me," says Carla, putting the papers back in the envelope and walking over to her desk. "I want to read these more carefully. Tell me what else you found."

She is wearing a pair of grey pants and a white blouse. Yuri has learned that, generally, her clothes reflect her sexual mood. A skirt is the most suggestive that she's in the mood. A dress is a close second. Pants usually mean that she is not receptive. But these are only general observations he has made, not strict rules. There have been exceptions that have surprised him.

She comes back to the sofa and puts her feet up. Yuri tells her about his meeting with Ano and the state of affairs in Dubai. He also gives an account of the various nightspots that he visited, and his impressions of the market in Dubai, and some comparisons with Moscow. He tells her what he found out about Ali the Enforcer and his new priorities.

Carla interrupts him a few times with specific questions that he cannot answer. "How many girls did we have," she asks, "and how many of those have defected?" Viktor does not know. "Did you find out about the Galian girl? How did she leave Dubai?"

"Yes," says Viktor, happy that he did not miss this one. "She was sold to some local VIP. A lot of money. Ano says one hundred thousand dollars for one year. But when she escaped, Viktor had to refund three quarters of it."

"How did she leave Dubai?" asks Carla again, not impressed with his answer.

"Ano does not know. No one knows."

"I'm sure someone knows," says Carla dryly. "It is you who doesn't know."

But Yuri is tired of talking. He gets up and pours himself a drink from the ornately carved cabinet full of heavy crystal. A generous shot of *Nayiri* twenty-year old cognac in hand, he returns to the sofa, and offers her a sip. When she accepts, Yuri puts his arm around her.

"So now will you tell me how much you missed me?"

"Not today, Yuri. If you had arrived two days ago, I would have given you a different welcome. But not today." The detail in explanation, which is unusual for Carla, is meant to convey to Yuri the message that this is not a convenient time of the month, and that she is not trying to show her disappointment in his results.

ℒ ℒ ℒ

Yuri still looks tired, sleep-deprived and irritable. Anastasia hates that mood in any man, and more so in one who won't think twice about hitting her. He's just arrived at her apartment, again without calling in advance. Clothes are thrown on the chairs and on the floor in the living room, and dirty dishes are piled up in the sink of her small kitchen.

"Call her now," he tells her. She knows he means Lara. She is happy that she has agreed with Lara on a code word to let her know that someone is listening to their conversation.

"Lara, *aziz* jan, it's me, Anastasia," she says, stressing her name. Giving her name is not her normal style of starting a conversation and is the cue to Lara that everything she says is overheard.

"What's the matter?" asks Lara, "You sound like you have a cold. Are you okay?" That is her code phrase to let Anastasia know that she got the message.

"I'm fine now. Was a little under the weather earlier. Have you found out anything new since we last talked?"

"There seems to be total chaos here," says Lara. "Whatever that bastard Ayvazian had in Aparan and Ashtarak is being grabbed by others."

"Any idea by who?"

"No one knows for sure, but most people think it is the animal called LeFreak. People say he has taken over Ayvazian's operations in Lori too. He has been hiring new thugs there. I don't understand why the government protects these criminals."

"Lara, how sure are you LeFreak is behind all this?" Anastasia is repeating Yuri's silent instructions through his lips and hand movements.

"No one can be one hundred percent sure of anything." Lara sounds frustrated. "These people do not appear anywhere under their own name. They have others do their dirty work for them. Ayvazian was the same way. Is there any proof anywhere that he was selling people into slavery? Some say Ayvazian's family is still in control, some say LeFreak is taking over everything, some say that there are other oligarchs pulling the strings from behind the scenes. Who knows? But I wouldn't put it past LeFreak to be behind most of it."

Yuri is now scribbling notes for Anastasia.

"What else do you have on LeFreak?" she asks.

"When I was in Istanbul," says Lara carefully, starting the second part of her prepared message, "I overheard a few things. There is this man there, his name is Abo Arslan. The Ayvazians knew him. They were competitors, and the Ayvazians would not let him into the Dubai market. Abo was talking with LeFreak about starting up in Dubai, and beating Ayvazian at his own game. Abo hated Ayvazian. I mean, Anastasia, *really* hated him. Then I heard him tell his assistant, some Turkish guy, that he'd make a deal with the devil if he had to in order to beat Ayvazian. They were talking Turkish in a corner and I was sitting in a chair at the far end of the room, so they thought I could not hear, and besides, they knew I did not speak Turkish. But Turkish is close to Azeri, and I know a little Azeri, so I heard and understood enough. And then Abo tells his assistant, 'Timur,' he says, 'I think I just found the devil with whom I'll make a deal to kill Ayvazian.' Now, again, I cannot be one-hundred percent sure, but I am almost sure that the devil he was referring to is LeFreak."

"That's incredible," says Anastasia, this time without any prompt from Yuri. "So this goes all the way to Istanbul?"

"Frankly, I did not think much of Abo's comments then, but when I heard LeFreak has taken over Aparan and Lori, it all came back to me. He must have been planning something for a long time. Maybe he was the one behind Viktor's and Sergei's murders. Not that I am shedding any tears for those two bastards, Anastasia. They probably deserved whatever happened to them. But this LeFreak is not any better, that's all."

"Be careful, *aziz* jan. You really don't want to be mixed up with people like that. Stay away, keep your head down."

"All I want to do now is attend classes at the University." They have to have some girl talk, to make the whole conversation more credible. "I am done with that life. If you're happy staying in it, I'm happy for you, my old friend. I will never judge you. But I cannot return to that."

"Good for you, Lara. I knew this was not for you from the beginning. Not everyone can take to this. But I still say you would have been great. You could have built an empire!" laughs Anastasia, recovering her joviality.

"You can keep it, sister," Lara laughs back. "You can keep all of it! There is no power on earth that can force me to go back to that world. Not LeFreak, and not Ayvazian if he were to return from his grave." That too is for Yuri's benefit. Lara wants them to know that she'd be more trouble than it's worth, no matter how lucrative she could have been had she cooperated. "Now I have to go," she says. "We'll talk again soon."

Yuri signals Anastasia to keep the conversation going, but Lara hangs up. Not a big loss; he's heard enough. He'll have a lot to plan with Carla when he returns to Yerevan.

Chapter Twenty-One

Edik often talks about an Irish friend of his who believes that the Irish and the Armenians are similar in many ways—general outlook on life, culture, a sad history captured in sad songs, etc. Edik says his friend is particularly curious about Armenian popular sayings and proverbs, because he claims they could easily have been Irish.

One such proverb is: 'It is better to go into captivity with the whole village than to a wedding alone.' I told Edik that if he asks me about this saying first thing in the morning, I probably would disagree with it. I still love and need my solitude in the mornings, no matter how alien that may be in these parts. But when I look at all that we have to fight against these days, it makes infinite sense.

It is the third day that Avo is in jail. I have visited him every day, taking four packs of cigarettes each time, and have called home regularly to put everyone's mind at ease. His eye and bruises do not look much better, but he seems stronger, a little more steady, and is no longer limping. We've had more time to talk alone in the past three days than in the past seven months. At least that has been one good thing to come from this disaster. I have begun to realize that Avo is deeper and more complex than he appears. For one thing, he takes his role as the 'head of the family' seriously. He sees me as the most exposed member of the family, which explains why a large part of his protective instincts are directed at me. Combine that with the total helplessness that he feels with everything having to do with me, and you get the frustration, which is the cauldron where his anger brews. I've learned that feeling helpless in general—helpless to prevent Papa's murder, Mama's death, my abduction, helpless against LeFreak—is what feeds the rage in Avo. Probably the only time that he felt somewhat in control was in building the pig farm, and that was taken away from him in the end.

I jokingly remind him that I'm older. "Head of the family or not," I say laughing, "you're still a kid. So stop being so serious about everything."

Avo brings up Hermine once or twice during these talks. It is always in the context of talking about Ruben and Martha, but it is obvious that he likes to mention her.

"So how much do you like Hermine?" I ask teasingly, and he blushes. It feels good to make a man blush for a change.

"She's nice," he says and looks away, and I drop the subject.

My main task is to convince Avo to accept LeFreak's condition for dropping the charges: Avo has to paint the entire outer surface of the fence surrounding his house. It is two-hundred-and-twenty meters long, one-and-a-half meters high. Over the wall, there is another meter of cast iron railing, which, fortunately, does not have to be painted. Gagik says that a laborer would charge around five hundred dollars to do the job, so it is not the money that LeFreak is after. "He just wants to humiliate Avo," says Gagik. "To teach him a lesson. Have him think, at least for the three days that it will take Avo to complete the task, that he can't mess with him again."

Had LeFreak been a decent, law-abiding man, says Gagik, he would have approved of his way of handling Avo. Teach the young man a lesson, and set him free, hoping that he gets back on track. Brilliant. Of course had he been that man, Avo would have had no reason to commit the mistake that he made. And this is one of the strengths of these criminal oligarchs.

They know how to make their actions appear fair and compassionate, even as they destroy the livelihood of hundreds of families.

Gagik helps me convince Avo to accept the terms. We secure a provision that Avo can have others helping him, as long as he is there the whole time while the painting is being done. That is important, because what would have taken three days for one man to do, takes just half a day for six men working together. Avo, Gagik, Ruben, Simon, Sago and Aram finish painting the fence in four hours. We all have to fight hard with Edik to keep him out of it. The participation of an expatriate would have raised LeFreak's curiosity, with no added advantage. "What the hell do you know about painting walls anyway?" Gagik told him. "Just leave this one to us."

Edik's Irish friend is right to like our proverb.

Avo is thus a free man after four days in jail, but still he does not have much to come home to.

My life has become busy in the past week. Aside from the incident with Avo, Sona's wedding preparations create new demands on everyone's time, and Anna wants to spend more time with me as her new and only friend. At the same time, we are anxiously awaiting a reaction from Yuri, and I have not even mentioned Ahmed yet, who calls regularly and, when he finally arrives in Yerevan, will create the ultimate distraction for me in the middle of everything else that is going on.

Anna has borrowed Varujan's *Pagan Songs* and reads religiously. But it is not easy to understand Varujan. Not only did he write in Western Armenian, but also his vocabulary is far more advanced and sophisticated than either of us can fathom. So Anna gives me a list of words every few days to look up in the dictionary at the University. I appreciate the opportunity to enrich my own vocabulary in the process, and now that we both understand him better, we realize how boundless his passion is.

Edik calls to ask if we can meet in Yerevan, and wants to have at least one meeting with Anna as well.

"I've been in touch with Martirosian," he says, "but I have not told you two anything because things were still evolving. There are some interesting surprises."

"I'm sure she'd love to see you again. You've made quite an impression on her. She's reading Varujan, the book you gave me for my birthday."

"Good for her," he laughs. "I'll be in Yerevan tomorrow afternoon. Why don't the three of us have dinner this time? You and Anna decide what time and let me know. Do you want to go to the Italian restaurant on Toumanian again, or somewhere else?"

"That doesn't matter to either of us. You decide. I'll call you back with the time."

"Okay, I'll introduce you to a new cuisine," he says. "We'll go to a Lebanese restaurant that just opened on Zakian Street. I hear it's good. Text me the time so I can reserve."

I don't tell him that I was introduced to Lebanese cuisine in Dubai. Some of the most elaborate breakfasts at Sumaya's villa and the most common meals that the staff used to deliver to my villa fresh every day were Lebanese, with occasional Indian dishes thrown in for variety.

The restaurant is small but pleasant. We sit at a quiet corner in the back. Edik asks to meet the owner, a young man called Murad, with a bushy, black mustache and thick-rimmed eyeglasses. They chat for a few minutes. Edik finds out that he comes from a suburb of Beirut called Bourj Hammoud where most residents are Armenian, and that he owned a restaurant there for over twenty-five years.

"Now you will see the ingenuity of the Lebanese cuisine," he says turning back to us. "Here, you can order around twenty dishes by just saying one word: *Mezza*. I used to surprise my Japanese guests in a Lebanese restaurant in Geneva with that. We'd go in, sit down, and I'd tell the waiter 'mezza,' and watch as they start bringing around a dozen cold appetizers, followed by another dozen hot appetizers. 'When did you order all this?' the Japanese would ask, surprised. 'All this' has a name, I'd say. It always broke the ice with new sources that I was trying to tap for information."

"Edik," I say a bit impatiently, "Anna has a surprise for you."

"You do?" he turns to Anna with anticipation. "You'll have my full attention as soon as I order something to drink. Would you ladies have some wine with me, or, since we're here, would you like to try the traditional Lebanese drink? It is called Arak and it is kind of strong, but is excellent with this food."

"You decide, Edik jan."

He calls the owner and makes sure they have authentic Lebanese Arak, and orders half a bottle.

"Now," he says turning back to Anna, "tell me."

Anna starts reciting the first poem of *Pagan Songs*, "To The Statue of Beauty." She recites it by heart, with such skill and perfect enunciation, that even I am surprised. She sounds like a professional actress performing on stage.

Edik keeps staring at her with his mouth open.

"Anna, that was flawless!" he says. "Just flawless. Where did you learn to recite like that? Especially Western Armenian?"

Anna blushes and starts fidgeting with her napkin. "This is the shortest poem in the volume," she says, as if that answers his question.

"And one of the most beautiful! *Apres*! Bravo! Where is that Arak?" He turns toward the service corner, "Now we have something worth celebrating!"

Anna is on cloud nine, and I am pleased that we pulled this off. The Arak comes. Edik mixes in water and the clear liquid turns white. "The Lebanese call this the milk of lions," he laughs. As he pours the Arak for the three of us, they start piling dishes of appetizers on the table.

"Here's to the discovery of a new artistic talent!" he declares. We toast and take a sip. I can see Anna's nose crinkle, but I like the drink. This is one thing that they never served in my villa in Dubai. We could not have any alcohol, even though my mind briefly wanders away to one night when Ahmed showed up with a bottle of champagne.

"I have some interesting news," says Edik, as he explains the dishes and shows us how some of them are to be eaten by hand, or scooped up by a piece of pita bread. "Do you mind if we talk while we eat?"

"Tell us," I say smiling at him. I like him even more than usual tonight, maybe because we succeeded in surprising and impressing him like that. It is easier to like someone when you find that you can please him with a simple, considerate gesture.

"Your husband, Mr. Hov Samoyan, has an interesting new job," starts Edik. "He is a security officer, has a license to carry a firearm, and works for none other than Mr. LeFreak." He turns to me when he brings up that name. Anna is quiet, and has stopped eating.

"Please, don't let any of this kill your appetite. Try this salad," he passes a plate of tabbouleh to Anna. "Now, I have to admit that a couple of weeks ago we did something naughty. I told Martirosian to put the word around that Hov's wife is seeking a divorce and has hired a lawyer to start the paperwork, to see his reaction." Anna's eyes are wide open again, and she has again stopped eating. Edik passes her another plate with a nod, urging her to eat.

"Well, his first reaction was apparently very bad," he continues. "He got angry, and asked some of his new co-workers, all LeFreak's henchmen, to help him find his wife." Seeing Anna's anxiety, he holds up his hand, signaling for her to just hear him out. "The henchmen of course do not take orders from him, nor do they use their muscle without LeFreak's approval. So the word goes back to LeFreak that one of their new recruits has a wife problem, that she has run away to Yerevan and is about to file for divorce, and that he's asked for their help in finding her." Edik empties his glass of Arak, takes a bite of *sujuk*, and starts mixing another glass. He looks at us, staring at him expectantly.

"Well, Mr. LeFreak wants to know the details. Why did she run away, how long ago, etc. The aides advise Hov not to lie. 'He'll eventually find out the truth,' they say, 'and if you have lied, God help you.' So, our Hov actually confesses that he tried to make his lovely young wife work as a prostitute, and that was the main reason why she ran away."

"He confessed?" says Anna, her voice a bit too loud.

"Shhh," says Edik, putting his forefinger to his lips. "Yes indeed, he confessed. But his confession was music to Mr. LeFreak's ears. He asked Hov to come to Yerevan to meet him in person. A great honor, you understand, for the newly hired young thug to meet the boss in person." Edik washes down the sarcasm with another healthy swig of Arak, and takes another bite. He looks at us again, enjoying the suspense he has created.

"In LeFreak's eyes, Hov is up for a promotion. If someone can sell his own wife into prostitution, imagine what he can do with total strangers, helpless girls from orphanages, or anyone vulnerable enough to be either lured or forced into the business. So Hov is viewed as an asset to the future of the organization."

Of course, I understand precisely what Edik is talking about, but Anna does not. "What asset?" she asks. "What organization?"

"Anna, the business that LeFreak is trying to get into is something called sex-trafficking. Have you heard of it? Do you know what it means?"

Anna shakes her head.

"They take young girls and sell them into prostitution. What your husband tried to do to you is actually a huge business, Anna. Hov did not know that when he tried to sell you. But it is a multi-billion dollar business. They fool, steal or convince young girls and take them and sell them. Your husband got a promotion because the boss thought he was a natural."

Edik notices the angst on my face and stops. Why does he have to rub it in like that? The Arak may have a role, and I think Sirarpi has a role too. She is always in the background.

"Sorry," he says, looking at me. "At any rate, LeFreak hears his confession one more time from his own mouth. 'Divorce the bitch,' he says. 'You cannot be tied down with that kind of baggage anyway. Divorce her and move on.'"

Anna's jaw drops at the 'divorce the bitch' bit, but there is also a glimmer of hope in her eyes.

"His boss told him to divorce me?"

"That is exactly what he told him." Edik empties his glass. I have seen Edik drink two bottles of wine without any visible effect. But the few glasses of Arak seem to have made him tipsy already. "So Martirosian is finalizing the papers. He'll have them ready for you to sign in a couple of days. Then he'll send the papers to Hov through his own channels. Once countersigned, you'd be officially divorced from Hov Samoyan. Martirosian says it is a simple case, and you two do not even have to meet, because there are no assets to divide. He is representing in the papers that you have no claims against him, Anna. Are you okay with that?"

"What does that mean?" she asks, and I notice how her voice is shaking.

"It means you have no demands, no compensation requirements, nothing. You get divorced and go your own way. He owes you nothing. Martirosian says that if we want to keep this simple and make sure that you do not have to meet Hov, that is the way to go."

"Of course I want nothing. I just want him not to be my husband anymore... and to leave me alone."

"Anna, I have not met Hov, but people like that are not reliable. I do not want to mislead you with happy scenarios. He may sign the papers and still decide to come after you. Revenge, spite, pride, all factor into it. So we'll take this a step at a time. One positive thing right now is that LeFreak is not using the resources of his organization to locate you, and he has ordered Hov to divorce you. That's good. Let's drink to that!"

And he notices that his glass is empty and starts mixing himself another Arak. Anna and I are still on our first glass. The table is full, just as he said. Little has been eaten so far, and the hot appetizers are cold.

"I'm famished," says Edik. "I have not eaten anything since breakfast, which was at seven this morning." And he digs in with a ravenous appetite, totally concentrated on trying everything on the table. He does not look up and does not say a word, just wolfs down plate after plate. Anna and I watch him, fascinated, wondering how he can focus like that, one hundred percent, first on telling us the news, and then on eating. I also understand why the Arak had such an effect on him, given his empty stomach. Minutes later he looks up, sees us watching him, and starts laughing.

"Sorry, that poem Anna recited spurred my appetite," he says. "I'm done talking, and I'm done eating for now, but I'm not done drinking. So, you ladies tell me what you've been up to."

I look at Anna and smile. "Have you memorized anything else?" I ask, knowing that she knows a few verses from various poems. She hesitates, but then recites the first verse of "To The Dead Gods."

Chapter
Twenty-Two

Yuri feels unsettled by Carla's uncompromising posture. He thinks the priority should be to claim the Dubai villa first, and then focus on LeFreak.

Carla disagrees. "LeFreak comes first," she says. "The villa is not going anywhere." She has assumed responsibility for securing the documents that Yuri would need in Dubai, so he has no control over the process.

"We need the money. You want three million euros to just sit there?"

"Let me handle the money. Has there been any delay in paying your salary?"

Yuri does not say anything, but he is seething. There are moments like this when he resents working for a woman—and not just any woman, but one younger than him, with whom he is having sex. This clearly is not the type of boss that he's used to. He has accepted it, because they have generally agreed on what to do, and it has felt to him more like a partnership than a boss-employee relationship. But Carla does not compromise when there is a difference of opinion. And she can be so curt as to be insulting, as in the way she just mentioned his salary, blowing away the partnership illusion in a second.

Aside from her strong personality, Carla's strength is access to money. She has found in her father's papers the documents of his various bank accounts, including four different accounts in Yerevan and one in Moscow. In addition, Viktor has one account in Yerevan, one in Moscow and one in Dubai. Her mother knows about her father's accounts, but no one knows about Viktor's. Yuri knows nothing about any of these accounts. Carla has signatory authority over her father's accounts, but not over Viktor's. She plans to use the same documents that Yuri needs to transfer the villa to also get access to those bank accounts.

But Carla is convinced that these accounts are only a small part of her father's and Viktor's assets. She expects that there are more real estate investments as well as cash lying around waiting to be discovered. She has already found a large briefcase in the study, which Yuri also knows nothing about. It contained a mixture of US dollars, drams and euros, close to a million dollar's equivalent.

The bank accounts and the cash that she has access to exceed several million dollars, which is enough for Carla at the moment. She retains eight employees on her payroll engaged in the search for her father's assets. She has recovered some sources of income, especially in Ayvazian's operations in Vayots Dzor. For her, chasing the villa in Dubai is far less urgent than removing a major threat right here at home. LeFreak, left unchecked, could destroy everything.

Yuri can think of only one way to gain some control over the situation.

"We need to be better organized to handle LeFreak," he says. "I need a team that I can trust. I need to spend a lot more money than what my salary is costing. I need to bribe, gather information, set up cells."

"Then what are you waiting for?" Carla looks him in the eye. "I approve everything before you take a step. I will give you a couple of men to start with. You can trust them, they work for me," she says, and the tone in her voice makes Yuri cringe. He takes the sarcasm to mean that she has seen through him. "You present me every expense before you incur it, and if I approve, I'll give you what you need. You discuss with me every aspect of the strategy." She waits a minute. "Are we clear on that, Yuri?"

"We're clear." He has to play along while he thinks of ways to sideline her, which he knows will not be easy. Carla knows more than he does, controls the money, and has the personality to run the business. There can be no short cuts to gaining control. But Yuri is determined that eventually he will take over the Ayvazian businesses.

"Good, I'll work on getting the documents we need for Dubai. I've already contacted one of Papa's lawyers. What I want you to do is learn everything about LeFreak. Everything. Start with what that girl is talking about, the operations he is supposed to have taken over in Lori, but don't stop there. Focus on what he's doing in Armenia first, but eventually we have to find out what that Abo character is up to, and what he and LeFreak agreed upon."

"When can I meet the two people you have for me?"

"They'll call you this afternoon."

"We'll need cash to buy information," says Yuri. "We'll have to bribe a lot of people."

Carla stands up and goes to her desk. She unlocks a drawer, shuffles through a few things inside it, and returns with a stack of 20,000-dram bills, around one centimeter thick.

"There's two million dram in there." She tosses the stack on the coffee table. That's around five thousand dollars, and Yuri knows that it won't go very far.

"I can start with that, but you have to understand that we'll be bribing people who are employed and probably paid well, and who know the punishment for betraying the boss. So that won't be enough to buy the information we need."

"There'll be more when you need it," says Carla curtly again. "Just use it wisely. Let me know when you need more. And I want to know details of how much is being spent on which sources."

This has been a tense meeting for Yuri. Usually, after meetings like this, Carla wants sex. But Yuri is cold, and Carla does not seem to be having an easy time shifting moods either. It is not even clear to Yuri that she is trying. He looks at her for a moment, to make sure, and then stands up.

"I better get going then," he says, taking the money from the coffee table. "I'll expect a call from your men this afternoon."

With that, Yuri leaves and shuts the door behind him.

Carla goes back to her desk and sits on her large chair, putting her feet on the desk. The framed photograph of their house in Martashen is still on the wall facing her. She either hasn't gotten around to changing it or perhaps she has chosen not to get around to it. It is the only truly personal thing left from her father. The money and the businesses are not personal. She never thinks of her father when she spends his money. It's all her money now. But the house, which he loved, is his. And Carla, who had no love lost for her father, wants him in this room as she takes over the business. She wants him to see everything that she does in this room. She herself has never thought of it that way, but that is what it is. That is why the only photograph that she has thought of replacing the picture of the house with has been one of her father. But maybe she subconsciously realizes that a photograph of her father would be less 'him' than that of the house; *he* hung this picture here; *he* loved that house.

It is one thing if LeFreak is trying to take over the orphaned Ayvazian businesses, and an entirely different thing if he orphaned those businesses in the first place. If he had been plotting before the killings, as the Galian girl claims, then he could very well be behind the killings. Why would she make any of that up? Why would Anastasia care? How could she possibly make up the conversation that she overheard in Istanbul? Carla knows that she was in fact in Istanbul.

Carla has enough money to buy many of LeFreak's men. She is not so sure about her own men. Can Yuri kill? She needs killers, not just men who beat and rape the girls, to subdue them. A killer is a different animal. A killer kills without anger or emotion; a rapist has both. A killer is not intent on changing his victim's behavior; men who beat and rape the girls are. Surely her father had some killers on his staff. Who are they? Did they die with him last fall? Was Hamo, Yuri's brother, one of them?

Then a thought hits Carla like a lighting bolt. She could kill LeFreak herself. She could stand in front of him and, looking him in the eye, pull the trigger. Bang. Blood, brains on the carpet, and LeFreak is no more. She definitely can kill. No second thoughts, no regrets, no afterthoughts.

And then, as an exercise, she imagines herself shooting Yuri in cold blood. Just to see how it would be. She first imagines him betraying her, to make the scene more realistic—Yuri has changed sides and sold secrets to LeFreak, instead of buying secrets from his men, and he has used her money to build his own team to overthrow her. That scenario has been brewing in her mind for a while anyway, so it is not that difficult to imagine. Yuri deserves to die. Bang. More blood and brains on the carpet; Yuri is no more. This is nothing, she thinks. I can do this.

It occurs to Carla that she has rarely been out of the house. Yuri and the other henchmen that she employs control the streets. All she has is what they report back, which is second hand, filtered information. That is when her first major crisis of confidence hits her. She is not used to this. Doubt is alien to her. She knows infallible, boundless confidence. Doubt, self-doubt, is the ugliest feeling she has ever experienced. It leaves a rotten, bitter taste in her mouth.

That evening Carla calls Yuri and asks him to come over. Yuri arrives half an hour later ready to perform any sexual fantasy that she may have dreamt of. But Carla greets him in a pantsuit.

"Have you ever killed anyone?" she asks.

"What kind of question is that?" he snaps.

"Yuri, it is the question that I'm asking, and I expect an honest answer." Yuri, who has come prepared to satisfy a nymphomaniac, is taken aback by her seriousness.

"I am sorry to disappoint you Carla, but I will not answer your question. And I will go further and tell you that you have no right to ask that question in the first place. Now, if there is nothing more, I have to go. You made me waste valuable time." And Yuri heads for the door. He is still seething from their last meeting. He knows that she needs him, and he is not going to put up with her whims to this extent.

"Stop!" Carla's is so abrupt that Yuri freezes. He turns around and faces her.

"Sit down, please." Her voice is calmer and Yuri marvels at her self-control. He takes a seat on the chair facing the sofa where Carla is sitting, and stares at her with deliberate defiance.

"Now," she says, maintaining the calmer tone, "tell me what's bothering you."

"We need to modify a few things." He runs his fingers through his hair. He has a bright blue silk shirt on with the top three buttons undone, light brown corduroy pants, and a suede jacket. He is wearing cologne. He feels awkward; he is painfully aware that he is not dressed for a business negotiation.

"Go on," she says, in a patronizing tone that adds to his discomfort.

"This is not the relationship that I had with your father. He trusted me more. I had a cut in the revenue that I generated, aside from the fixed salary. I ran things on my own for him, he did not check every detail. If we cannot work like that, then this is not going to work."

"How long did you work for him?" asks Carla.

"Eight years."

"Don't you think that the trust between us will come? I've only known you for a few months."

"Maybe. But we're no longer talking about running routine errands. We're talking about recovering millions and getting rid of the LeFreak threat. You cannot treat me as a salaried employee." Yuri is happy with himself. In spite of his not so businesslike attire, he comes across as serious, balanced and calm. Most of all, he feels he's regaining a measure of control, no matter how Carla chooses to respond.

"What do you want?"

"Ten percent of everything that I generate. A fixed amount of two million drams a month for expenses that I do not have to account for. And I want to hire a few men of my own." Yuri's gaze on Carla is as steady as his voice.

"Whoa! That is quite a list, Yuri. As I said, relationships like that are built over time. I don't mind some modifications, as you put it, but we take it slower than that."

"Depends on what you mean by slower."

"I don't mind paying you ten percent of any *new* business that you generate," says Carla. She has thought about this before calling Yuri over. "Just to be very clear, so there is no misunderstanding later, that has to be both new business and business generated by your own efforts. If I give you leads and use my own sources to help you get the business, you do not get ten percent. If it is not a new source of income, just recovering an old asset that you did not build, you do not get ten percent. Are we clear on that?"

"What do I get in those cases?"

"It depends. It depends on the amount, and the nature of your role. It can range anywhere from two percent, if your role is relatively minor and the amount is large, to a maximum five percent if your role is significant and the amount is smaller. You have to trust me too as we figure this out." Carla waits, eyes fixed on Yuri. After a few second, he nods. Yuri wants to ask what would be his share if he recovered the villa in Dubai, but decides against it. It would be at least two percent, and possibly he can argue for a bit higher, given the significance of his role. Somewhere in the 60,000 to 75,000 euro range. Not bad; he can live with that.

"Let's move to the two million dram in expenses," says Carla. "I concede. I will trust you with that, but I have to see results. If the results are there, I will not question how you're spending the money. If the results are not satisfactory, we revisit this issue, in fact we revisit everything." She waits again. Yuri nods.

"Of course," she adds, "you may consider giving me an accounting once in a while, even though I will not ask for it, as a confidence building measure. I leave that up to you." She waits, looking at him, but he does not react.

"Now, let's come to the most difficult item on your list of demands. You want to hire your own men. That, I am not ready to accept. We either function as one organization, run by me, or not at all. I'm paying for your time, for your expenses, a healthy percentage of the income you bring in, and I am paying the salaries of everyone who works for you. I want to know who they are and I want to approve them before they're hired. You can identify and propose candidates that I do not know, but you have to discuss them with me first and, if I want to meet them, I will meet them first, and then you can hire them only if I give my approval. Depending on the person, I may approve even before meeting them. But that will be my decision. I cannot compromise any more than that on this issue."

Carla knows that Yuri has improved his position considerably through this negotiation, and the last point is not going to be a deal breaker. She herself is happy with the outcome. This will buy Yuri's loyalty for a while, she reckons six months or so, before he gets restless again. And then she'll re-evaluate and decide what to do.

She looks at him quietly for a long moment, but does not wait for a nod. She stands up before he makes any noticeable gesture.

"If we're done here," she says, walking toward the bedroom door, "why don't you pour us a drink and join me inside?"

Chapter Twenty-Three

Edik returns from Saralandj late. He calls to say they now have a concrete plan to liquidate the pig farm, and in a few weeks that chapter in Avo's life will be closed. They will sell everything very cheap, he says. They have already found some farmers who'll buy the mothers as well as the piglets even before they are totally weaned, as long as they look healthy..

"How's Avo taking it?" I ask.

"Not well. He is angry, disappointed, frustrated. The only good news from Avo is that he has reduced his drinking a lot. I'm not sure if he's avoiding getting drunk only in front of us. Ask one of your sisters about that."

"I will, Edik jan, thank you so much for all this," I say, wondering for the hundredth time why, although I now see why what happened to me matters to him. "When will you return to Vardahovit?"

"I'll leave in the morning. No particular time. Do you want to meet for a late breakfast?"

I hesitate for a minute. Breakfast isn't really my thing.

"How late?" I ask.

"Don't worry," he says. "I'm exhausted. I won't be ready to face the day until around eleven. Can you come to my hotel or shall I come pick you up?"

"I'll come," I say. "I'll be there around eleven. You can start without me if you get hungry."

"Okay Lara. *Bari qisher.*" Good night.

The next morning, as I start my routine of making Diqin Alice and me coffee, my phone rings. I answer without checking the number, assuming it is Edik or Alisia.

"*Habibty*," comes Ahmed's voice over the phone. "I didn't wake you, did I?"

"No Ahmed, I've been up. How are you?"

"I am better than I've been for a long time, because I will be with you in two days." He speaks fast, sounds almost rushed. "Day after tomorrow. I'm not sure exactly at what time I can leave Dubai, but it should be sometime in the evening when we land. Next time I call you it will be from Yerevan!"

The small coffee pot where we make Armenian coffee boils over and spills all over the small propane stove. I turn off the burner and put the pot aside. I don't know what to tell him. I don't even know if I should sound happy. I start wiping the stove with a damp towel, which sizzles as it comes in contact with the hot burner. Should I ask him how long he'd be staying, or would that sound too eager?

"Are you there?"

"Yes, Ahmed, sorry, just spilled something in the kitchen," I say. Why do I always end up saying something stupid to him over the phone? But I want him to know that I have been distracted, so he won't misinterpret my lack of reaction to his news.

"Please tell me it was the excitement of me visiting that made you spill it," he laughs. Ahmed has no clue. The things that I agonize over do not even occur to him.

"Give me a minute, I have to put the phone down for just a second." I put the phone down and finish wiping up the mess. Diqin Alice walks in, but I do not want to keep Ahmed waiting.

"Sorry," I say to Diqin Alice. "I'll restart the coffee in a minute. I need to finish this conversation." I leave the kitchen.

"Have you made all your arrangements in Yerevan?" I ask.

"Manoj is coming with me. He's taken care of everything. I'll be there for a few days, I am not sure exactly how many yet. It depends on some of the irons I have in the fire, but at least two. I want to tour some of the country with you. I hope you can make some time for me Lara."

My head is spinning. I think about all the irons that I have in the fire, Anna, Avo, Sona, Anastasia, classes.

"Sure, Ahmed. When you come we can discuss."

"See you soon." And the phone goes dead.

I sit at the edge of my bed for a moment, staring at the phone resting in my open palms in my lap. How am I going to deal with Ahmed here? Where does he want to go on his tour of the country? Manoj must have told him about the conditions in Saralandj. A chill passes down my spine. I sincerely hope he does not have Saralandj in mind. What if he wants to see my place in Yerevan? How can I bring him to this room? What do I do if he tries to get intimate? For three months I slept with him. What do I do now? 'Acknowledge the past, confront the past, kill the past, then go forward free of the past.' Edik's words. They sound good. They have a ring to them that should connote feasibility. After all, if they sound that good, with the rhythm of a military march, then it must be imminently doable. Who am I kidding?

Diqin Alice pokes her head inside my door.

"Amen ban lav a?" Is everything okay?

"Ha, Diqin Alice," I say, jumping to my feet. "I'll start a new pot of coffee. Sorry for the mess." It is good to have a chore to do. I get busy, chatting with her about nothing. We drink the coffee together at the kitchen table. I wash the cups and the pot, and go back to my room to get ready. It is almost eleven. I'll be ten minutes late for Edik.

The breakfast room at his hotel has a big buffet that reminds me of some of the spreads in Dubai, displaying almost everything imaginable on a breakfast menu. I walk in and see him sitting at a table talking on the phone. Several men and a few women turn to watch me as I approach his table. I am so used to this by now that I just ignore it. Edik has a cup of coffee in front of him, but no food. I wave and join him. He signals that he won't be long, and points to the buffet. I'm not comfortable starting without him, but wonder whether he does not want me to hear his conversation. I don't remember ever being like this. Worrying about everything, trying to second-guess what people may want or what they may think. I hate it. When did I start being like this?

I stop worrying about Edik's phone call. I don't want to start breakfast alone. So I stay in my chair and wait for him to finish. There! One less source of unnecessary anguish. The waiter comes carrying a large pot, offering coffee. I accept, and smile amiably at Edik.

"Breakfast is the most important meal of the day," he says, ending the call. He leans over and kisses my cheek. "Are you hungry?"

"Can we sit for a minute? I mean, if you're not rushing."

"Of course. I'm not rushing." He looks me over and takes a sip of his coffee. "I have to cover a story for one of the news agencies." He says. "I may have to go to Georgia for a few days. But that's not until next week. What's new with you?"

"Ahmed will be here day after tomorrow." I take another sip of coffee, put the cup down and then look at him.

"Finally!" He says, with a mixture of excitement and nonchalance that only he can pull off. "I was beginning to give up on him."

"Edik, this is going to be difficult for me." I want him to know, but I am not looking for feedback.

"I know," he says seriously. "But it does not have to be."

"I know the theory: acknowledge, confront and kill the past, then move on."

"Precisely," he says, holding my gaze.

"It's the 'moving on' part that I'm not sure of." I say, even though I am equally scared of all the parts.

"But if you manage the first three, that should be the easiest."

"What if I don't know how I want to move on?"

"Then you take your time deciding, Lara. No one can force you to rush into a decision if you don't want to be rushed."

Buy time, I think. Put off decisions. Not because I want to procrastinate, but because I don't know.

"Will I have time to decide?" I ask more to myself than to Edik.

"Lara, you're overthinking this again. You cannot answer every question in advance. Didn't I tell you once to let it come to you, and then take it as it comes? First see what he wants, when he wants it, and then decide if that is something you also want. Why are you all worked up about it now?"

"It is easier to figure out what you *don't* want than what you do," I say, ignoring his question. In Ahmed's case, that is precisely my problem. I am one hundred percent sure of what I do not want with him. And I am totally in the dark when it comes to what I do want, if anything.

"That is true, but it is also true that the hungry monkey does not dance. Let's get something to eat."

"The hungry monkey does not dance?" I ask laughing.

"That's from my father. Wandering entertainers would pass through his village when he was a kid. They'd play the drums, and they'd have these monkeys that were trained to dance to the drumbeat. And then they would pass a hat to gather money. They'd say the bit about the hungry monkey not dancing while asking for money. It stuck in my dad's head."

We eat in silence for a while.

"Edik jan," I say after he consumes half his plate, "I have an unfair question. But you're the only one I can ask."

"Ask," he says, putting a slice of ham in his mouth. "The reason I love your questions is because they are almost all unfair." He turns to me briefly and winks.

"I will describe to you two opposite sides of Ahmed, and then ask you to give me a single word assessment of him. Just listen first," I say when I see his eyebrow rising. "Side one," I begin. "He bought me as he buys any property. He had a few other concubines in his estate at the time. I was a captive there. I had to adhere to strict rules of behavior." I stop for a second, but he is busy eating. "Side two," I continue, "he treats me better than anyone outside of my family, and of course you, has ever treated me, better than Anna's father ever treated her, better than anyone has ever treated Anastasia. He never makes me feel cheap, never gives me any reason to be offended. He is loving, caring, generous, clean, considerate." I decide to stop there before I start sounding like I'm in love with the guy. Edik's attention is still on his plate. "Now," I ask, putting my hand on his arm, because I want him to look at me at this point. "Is he a good man or a bad man? Just answer with one word. Good or bad?"

Edik takes a sip of coffee.

"Neither." Before I can protest, he adds, "I know you want the good or bad answer, Lara, I know that is the question you're struggling with, but I'm telling you, based on the information you gave me, he is neither good nor bad. I've already told you that it is men like him, men who pay for sex, that sustain Ayvazian's crimes. If I focus only on that aspect, I'd say he's bad. But that's not what you're asking me. He's a man who likes women without complications, it seems to me. He likes sex, and he prefers to buy it. I'm sorry if that makes you uncomfortable. Who else would keep a few concubines? It seems you were more than a concubine, so in your case things were a bit complicated. But 'good' and 'bad' don't enter the picture. He is who he is."

"You're not helping."

"Of course I am. If I had answered you as you wanted me to answer you I would have done you a huge disservice."

"Do you think it was his fault that I met him as a prostitute?" I persist.

"Lara, he is a man who pays for sex; how else could he have met you? I repeat, by paying for sex he becomes an enabler of the crimes that were committed against you. You're looking for excuses to exonerate him from something that even you do not fully understand yet."

"Edik, I need to know how to look at him two days from now. As a captor, or as a..." I want to say lover, but I cannot. I hesitate, and he sees the pain in my eyes. "...gentleman." I say to complete my sentence.

"Do you remember my Irish friend? The one who likes our proverbs?" I nod.

"He told me an Irish saying once, which fully applies here. He said, 'every saint has a past, every sinner has a future.' If saints and sinners cannot be pure good or pure bad, how do you expect your Ahmed to be?"

Edik leaves for his dacha in Vardahovit after breakfast, and I walk up Abovian Street, without even realizing that I am walking to the women's apparel store where Anna works. I have not been in the store before, but I know she works here. I enter and start looking around. Even though the store is quite large, it looks cramped because it has a surprisingly wide selection—from handbags to shoes to clothing of every kind, from sweaters to scarves to dresses to underwear. They even have inexpensive jewelry: glass beaded necklaces, semi-precious stone rings and earrings, and cheap watches. A saleslady approaches me and asks if she can help. I ask if Anna is in. She says she is on her lunch break, and points to the door at the back of the store.

"I can call her for you," she says.

"If it's not too much trouble. I just want to say hello."

She walks into the back room, and comes back out in seconds.

"She'll be right out," she says, and then freezes, looking like she's seen a ghost.

"Madame Carla," she says looking past me at the person who has just entered the store. "What a pleasant surprise!"

"Hello Lucy," says the woman she called Madame Carla, ignoring me. How is business? Maybe we can go inside and talk. Don't you have someone helping you here?"

"I do," says Lucy nervously, "she's on her lunch break inside but she should be coming out any minute."

"Then let's go in."

As they head toward the back door, Anna walks out. Carla passes right by her as she walks in, followed by Lucy. She gives Anna a focused look, her eyes lingering on her face for a minute, and then she looks her over, from head to toe. As Anna walks toward me, Carla stares at her back and, I notice with some bewilderment, at her behind.

Anna does not see any of that. "Lara, hello," she says, giving me a hug.

"I thought I'd come on a surprise inspection, but I see someone beat me to it. Do you know who that woman is?"

"Yeah," says Anna rolling her eyes, "she owns the store. Lucy is scared out of her wits by her. Her name is Carla something."

"Carla Ayvazian," I whisper. "Stay as far away from her as you can, Anna. She's not good news."

"You know our Lord and Master Madame Carla?" she laughs.

"Hush, Anna, lower your voice. I'll tell you about her later, but we should not talk about this here in the store. I'm serious. keep your distance."

"*De lav*, Lara jan, stop being so serious."

I smile. There's no point in making Anna anxious at her workplace.

"I stopped by to say hello," I say. "We should try to get together soon. I may be busy for a few days."

"What's going on with you?"

"It's a long story." I'm anxious to get out of the store before Carla comes back out. I don't think she's seen my face, and I want to keep it that way. "I'll tell you when we get together. Let's have a bite to eat when you get off this evening. My treat, but I cannot afford the type of restaurant that Edik took us the other day."

She hugs me again, and I leave the store before Carla and Lucy emerge from the back room.

I love walking alone in the streets of Yerevan. Solitude in a crowded and noisy street is different from solitude in the quiet of morning. Your aloneness somehow acquires more depth, more consequence when you're in a crowd. Being surrounded by people and tuning them out is in some ways more powerful than not being near anyone. As you switch off what's around you, your mind isolates itself from your own body, concentrates on a problem, and focuses with such sharpness that even your breathing cannot disturb it. But when you're physically alone, you sometimes interrupt your own thoughts; you distract yourself.

I walk down Teryan Street, cross Northern Avenue, make a right on Arami Street and emerge in the beautiful park sandwiched between Koghpatsi Street and Mashtots Avenue. The park is peaceful; the flowerbeds have come to life with the first blooms of spring, and the branches of the weeping willows, with their fresh coat of light-green leaves, swing gracefully in the breeze and impart an added measure of serenity to the park.

I sit on a bench facing the afternoon sun. Someone has scattered bread-crumbs on the lawn and the sparrows are having a feast. Where will Ahmed and I meet? Maybe here, in the park? Will he be considerate enough not to ask me to go to his room? What if he does? Should I wear the ring he gave me? How should I dress when I first see him?

Edik is right, I am overthinking this.

I call him. He has reached the village of Areni, which is famous for its grapes and wine. They've discovered a six thousand year old winery in a cave near there, so folks here have been at this for a while, Edik says laughing.

"I bet you can't guess where Anna works," I say.

"You told me in some store selling women's clothes, right?"

"Kind of, yes, but whose store?"

"Someone I know?"

"Madame Carla, as she is known by the store manager."

"You don't say... How did you find out?"

"She walked in when I was visiting Anna. She did not see me. But she was eying Anna. I think that was the first time she's seen Anna. But she knew the store manager."

"We must be able to use this," says Edik, "but I cannot think now, not in the car. Let's talk later. Have you warned Anna?"

"Yes, and I'm seeing her later this evening. Safe journey, Edik jan."

It takes my mind less than a second to return to Ahmed. This is going to be awkward, no matter how calmly I consider his visit. We were lovers,

I keep telling myself. We had intimate moments. True, I reject the context in which it all happened, but how can I reject everything that happened? I'm like a painter who wants to burn the canvas on which he has painted, but keep the painting itself. And then I realize how off track I am with this line of thinking. I have not painted the painting, I do not understand it, so what part of that painting do I really want to keep?

I remember thinking a lot about 'context' in Dubai. The grounds of Ahmed's compound were so immaculate, the lawns were so perfectly manicured, palm trees and bougainvillea scattered around with such harmony, that the whole place had a sense of fantasy, and if I allowed myself to forget who I was and how I got there, I'd begin to think I was in some fairy tale. That's when I realized that I could not think of what I did out of the context of the place. What I do depends on where I am, I used to tell myself. But does *who* I am depend on where I am also? I used to imagine that the compound was like a chessboard, and I was the queen on that board. What would I be worth *off* the board? So my worth depends on the context too. Off the board, out of the game, the queen is worthless.

If Edik could hear my thoughts right now, he'd ask me again if I'm really only eighteen. But I did not read these thoughts in a book. I did not start to think of these things because some professor gave a lecture about them at the University. These are things I lived through. It has nothing to do with age, Edik jan, nor with what you and others sometimes call maturity. I was entirely immature when I was sixteen—much more than other sixteen year olds in Saralandj or anywhere else. I knew nothing about life. Then Papa died. Then I was abducted and raped and became a prostitute. In a few weeks I had seen more than most women in my village would see in a lifetime. No one is mature or immature by nature. Experience either makes you mature or it doesn't.

Anna's my age, but I can play the role of older sister for her. We go to a café on Toumanian Street. I talk to her about the risks that she faces. I also warn her again about Carla. Then I tell her that someone I knew when I was overseas will be visiting for a few days, and I'll probably be busy with him. Her jaw drops and her eyes open wide with surprise. She did not know that I had lived overseas for a while. She has not met anyone who has *been* overseas.

Chapter Twenty-Four

Hov Samoyan is nervous. He looks at the man facing him and can feel, deep in his bones, that he is way out of his league. The man is much better dressed than he could ever afford, better groomed, with his thick, black hair slicked back and his face clean shaven. He is so relaxed, so at ease with himself, that he exudes a level of confidence and self-control Hov has never known. This man acts like he owns the world, and he probably does.

Yuri has arrived in a black Mercedes SUV with a driver, a muscular man with a clean-shaven head, the typical look of most bodyguards who also serve as drivers for oligarchs. He has waited for the driver to open the back door for him, then stepped out and walked casually to their rendezvous, a small roadside café at the entrance of the city of Stepanavan, with the bodyguard keeping a watchful eye on him and his surroundings.

Hov wonders why they chose to approach him and how they managed to find him. He's not sure if he is being noticed by his superiors, and wonders how he will explain meeting this man. He knows nothing about Yuri, and yet Yuri seems to know a lot about him.

"I think you'll want to see us," the voice on the phone had told him a day earlier. "We already know where you work, where you live, and we know how your wife left you and why."

"What do you want?" is all he could say.

"Let's meet and discuss," said the voice. "You have nothing to lose."

Now Hov looks at Yuri, awestruck, and wonders if he was the one who called to arrange the meeting.

"I'll start with answering some of the questions in your mind," says Yuri. He removes his sunglasses and stares at Hov, who has said nothing yet. They have not even greeted each other, or shaken hands. "It was one of your coworkers who told us about you," continues Yuri. "It did not take much, by the way, just around a hundred dollars, and he told us everything."

Hov wants a cigarette, but does not dare light one, for fear of Yuri noticing his hands shake. He turns toward the bodyguard, who is sitting at the next table, watching them. The bodyguard does not move; he just stares at him.

"I hear you," says Hov, and waits.

"So the first point is that you cannot trust anyone where you currently work. And you cannot even trust what they're saying about you to the big boss."

"I have no problem with the big boss," snaps Hov, and regrets the lapse immediately. Yuri just smiles. He takes a cigarette and offers Hov one, who accepts gladly. Yuri lights them both.

"You have no reason to be nervous," says Yuri, keeping his smile. "They are not watching you here. And we know the boss is impressed by the way you tried to make your wife work for you. By the way, I am too."

Hov takes a deep drag and just stares at Yuri. He will not make reckless comments again.

"At any rate," continues Yuri, "you cannot trust your co-workers. It took us less than an hour to find out everything that we know about you. And the boss may be happy with you now, but that can change fast, depending on how you do and what they tell him about you."

Yuri waits for a minute, to see if there is any reaction. Hov remains silent.

"The second point I want to make is that you can do a lot better than this. Not only are the people you work for untrustworthy, they are also incompetent. The business they are trying to get into is above their heads. Your boss knows how to import wheat and flour and pigs. He knows nothing about the business of people and prostitution. He has no network and no contacts. He is endangering not only himself, but also everyone who works for him, including you."

Hov realizes, for the first time, that he may be at the brink of a new opportunity. Yuri is not here to threaten him, but to offer him something. He lights another cigarette from his own pack, and offers one to Yuri. Yuri declines, but the offer signifies a change in Hov's attitude.

"Before we go any further," says Hov, "maybe you should tell me a little about yourself and what you do."

"We're not there yet," says Yuri curtly. "You'll learn what you need to know when the time comes." Yuri would never admit it, but he has learned a few tactics from Carla. That would have been Carla's retort: never let an underling feel that they can control the agenda. Keep them on their toes and dependent.

Hov shrugs, partly to hide his embarrassment.

"What I want you to do is continue working where you are, but for me. You continue to take your salary from your boss. In addition, I will pay you double what you're making now. So you'll triple your salary as of this afternoon. You report to me every move they make. That is all. Your boss will lose this business soon, and then you'll have a job with us if you don't screw this up. Otherwise, you'll be in the street again, like most of your co-workers." Yuri turns toward the bodyguard, who walks over and gives him an envelope.

"There's 200,000 dram in here." Yuri pushes the envelope toward Hov. "I know you make half that per month."

"How do I know you're not a bigger risk than you say my boss is?" asks Hov, but his eyes linger on the envelope.

"You don't," says Yuri. "Until a few minutes ago you did not know your friends had sold you out. Nor did you know that your boss is venturing into something he knows nothing about. Now you want to know the risk I represent?"

"I want to know that I'm not jumping from the frying pan into the fire," says Hov.

"You're not." Yuri looks and sounds bored. "Your boss has three different operations in Lori. You and your co-workers are supposed to run things here in the Stepanavan area, but so far you have not recruited a single girl, and he is getting impatient. You have a list of six candidates that you are following," says Yuri, staring at his surprised face. Hov nods. "Don't be surprised that I know that. I want you to find out everything about the operation and report to me. Your team will manage to catch some of those girls soon. Some will join easily and start working. Others will have to be persuaded. You will tell me every detail, especially where they get sent, who handles them, who collects and how much. Everything."

Hov takes the envelope and slips it in his inside coat pocket.

"Good," says Yuri. "Aside from the money there is a name and a phone number in the envelope. You call that number and talk only to the person named there. No one else."

Hov nods, and waits.

"He won't last more than a month or two," says Yuri. "Then we hire you directly. Any questions about what you need to do?"

He shakes his head.

"One more thing before I leave. Do you have a picture of your wife?"

Hov looks surprised. That is the last thing he'd expect Yuri to ask.

"Your friends say you're obsessed with her but have not been able to find her. Is that true?"

He nods.

"Do you have a picture?" he asks again.

Hov takes out an old black-and-white photograph from his wallet. It is a crumpled passport-size picture of a girl with long black hair and thick-rimmed eyeglasses. Thick eyebrows are visible from behind the rims.

"How old is this thing?"

"More than two years. Before we got married. She looks different now."

"How different?"

"Her eyebrows are thinner. She changed her glasses too, even though she used the old ones also once in a while."

"That's it?"

"As far as I know."

"What's her full name?"

"Anna Arturi Hakobian."

"I don't promise anything," says Yuri, "but I'll see what I can do to find her for you."

Hov is still surprised by this part of the conversation.

"Why?" he asks.

Yuri shrugs. "Why not?" He stands up. "I'll wait for your calls. Can I take the picture for a while?"

"Keep it," says Hov and stands up as well.

What neither man knows is that Anna looks quite different now. Her hair is cut very short and she does not wear glasses in public. She puts them on only when she has to read or look at something closely. She used a different last name in her job application at the store and with her landlady, neither of whom have bothered to check for an identification card. The store pays her meager salary in cash, and she pays her rent in cash. The only thing that could give her away based on the photograph is her eyes, if one bothers to look closely, past the eyeglasses and the eyebrows.

Yuri is happy with his work of the past week. He has managed to bribe several of LeFreak's men, both in Lori and Ashtarak. He has exposed many of the weaknesses in his human trafficking operations, and has found increasing evidence that LeFreak has been trying to enter into Ayvazian's domain for a long time. He is convinced that there is a general lack of confidence and morale among LeFreak's men, at least among those employed in the trafficking side of the business. Otherwise it would have been a lot more difficult to get information, and it would have cost a lot more. He has used the tactic of gaining personal information on employees from co-workers, and using it to recruit new informers masterfully.

He reports to Carla the success he had with Hov and shows her Anna's photograph. Carla looks at it closely for a minute and hands it back to him.

"I hope she looks better than that now," she says coldly. "Girls her age will end up showing up in one of my stores sooner or later," she adds as an afterthought. "Put a copy of the picture in all my stores. You never know."

The next day Yuri takes a copy of Anna's picture to each of Carla's three stores. "Let me know if she comes here," he tells the managers. "Her full name is written in the back of the photo. If she walks in here, find an excuse to get her address and phone number. Call me immediately."

Lucy, at the store off Abovian, looks at it briefly and puts it on the table in the back room. "Will do," she says.

Chapter Twenty-Five

I walk into the hotel lobby with trepidation. I would have preferred to meet in a café or a park. But at least he did not ask me to meet him in his room. We're meeting in the lobby bar. I am deliberately underdressed. A pair of jeans, one of my favorite turtleneck sweaters and a light grey jacket. I wear flat shoes and minimal makeup. My hair is tied back in a ponytail.

But I am wearing his ring, next to Araxi Dadik's. I probably make a bigger deal of that than he would; he might not even remember that he gave me the ring and asked me to always wear it.

I notice him sitting at a table with Manoj. I have not seen him in western clothes before. He'd always be in his Arabic robes and headdress when he visited me. He looks good. He also has jeans on, a white shirt and black leather jacket. His curly black hair, his high cheekbones, small eyes and goatee are as I remember them. I wonder what Manoj is doing here when I'm supposed to meet with Ahmed, but then I remember Sumaya telling me once that people of Al Barmaka's importance cannot be seen in public alone. It will look like they are idly waiting for someone, which is unbecoming of their stature. They should always either be attended by a subordinate or in a meeting. I watch them for a minute, then take a deep breath and walk toward their table.

Manoj notices me first and jumps to his feet. "Ms. Lara," he says with a wide smile that only he can produce, "what an auspicious day this is that I can see you again, in the presence of His Excellency."

"Hello Lara," says Ahmed and stands up, extending his hand.

"Hello Ahmed." I had debated whether I should call him Your Excellency or Sir, because we are in the presence of others. He had given me permission to call him by his first name, but only when we were alone. But if I am to go forward free of the past, then 'His Excellency' has to die too.

"I do hope that you'll forgive me Ms. Lara," says Manoj, "but I have to attend to a few matters of some urgency. I will take my leave now." With that, he is gone. Ahmed has not moved his eyes from me.

"Hello *habibty*," he says when we sit down.

"How was your flight?" I ask, realizing that I have to get rid of my nervousness.

"It was fine. Thank you. I have waited a long time for this." He looks at me for a minute, and adds, "Seven months and three days, to be precise."

He notices the slight flicker passing over my eyes. I think I control it in just about two seconds, but he notices anyway. He smiles, the slow, knowing smile that gathers like a wave and concentrates in his eyes. Ahmed is not handsome. Even when he smiles, his face is not warm. He has a thin, bony, angular face, a shape that his goatee accentuates. There is a harshness in his looks that used to give me chills. But that's what makes his kind manners, by contrast, even more impressive.

I want to get my practiced words out of the way as soon as possible. "Again, I am sorry for the way I left. I should have talked to you. I had issues to tend to, that's all." There. Done. It is all out. I've said what I came here to say. Perhaps I should just excuse myself and leave.

He waits to make sure I'm done talking. His hands move toward mine and then he withdraws them quickly as he fights an impulse to touch me. In the process he notices the ring, and his smile returns.

"Thank you," he says, looking at the ring, and then returns to where I had left off. "You told me all that already over the phone, remember? If that's all I wanted to hear, why did I come to see you?"

So much for rehearsing my words.

"You tell me. Why did you come to see me?"

"Because I need to understand. What we had should not have just ended. I need to understand why it had to end."

The waiter appears, and Ahmed's smile returns.

"How about a glass of champagne?"

"Okay."

He orders a bottle, probably the most expensive. The waiter speeds away to fill the order.

"You do not understand why it ended," I say looking him straight in the eye, "because you do not know how it started." I know I have his attention. My words come out as a challenge, even though I do not intend them to be.

"I don't know how it started? I think I know how you ended up gracing my life, Lara."

"No, before that. Do you know how I ended up in Dubai in the first place?"

The waiter approaches with the bottle of champagne. He uncorks the wine and pours two glasses, puts the bottle in the cooler, wraps a white linen napkin around its neck and leaves.

Ahmed is too intrigued by my last question to pick up his glass. He keeps staring at me while the two glasses bubble up in front of us.

"How did you end up in Dubai?" he asks.

"Against my will. I was abducted. I was forced to come to Dubai. I did not want anything to do with that life. I spent eighteen months planning an escape." I want to add—*I'm sorry I had to finally succeed after reaching your place*—but I realize how wrong that would sound, and stop myself just in time.

"We have more to talk about than I thought. I did not know that, Lara. And I'm sorry that I never asked. But I always assumed that people were where they wanted to be. That's why, when Ayvazian offered to return you to me, I rejected his offer. My house is not a prison, I said. Whoever does not want to be there, should not be there. And I meant that then, and I mean it now."

"Do you really think that every girl who ends up working in the nightclubs of Dubai is there by her own free will?" I know I am not being fair.

"No, I do not think that. I've heard of some cases. But I myself had never known a case like that."

"At any rate, it is important that you know that I was not in Dubai voluntarily. I was not in that business voluntarily. If you knew the truth, I doubt you could remain indifferent, Ahmed." I'm happy that I got that off of my chest. For me, that is probably the single most important piece of information that he needed to know. And now he does.

"Tell me what happened," he says.

"It's a long story, and I've already told you the bottom line." I want to give him a way out if he is not seriously interested in the story.

"I want to know what happened to you," he says. "But first, let's not let this fine champagne get warm." We lift our glasses and we take a sip.

"Now," he says again, "what happened to you?"

I recount the highlights. My father's death, my mother's agreeing to let them have me, the first night in Ayvazian's house, then Moscow, Dubai and his villa. Snapshots of each phase, as in screenshots from a movie.

He downs his champagne, and reaches for the bottle, but the waiter beats him to it. He refills our glasses and leaves.

"Here's to you Lara." He has a serious and sad expression on his face. "The most beautiful woman I have ever known, both inside and out." He looks so serious that I cannot think of anything to say. We drink. I get the feeling that he's processing what I've told him. He is not ready to react to it yet.

"Now," he says, finishing his glass. "Let's get out of here. Manoj and his Armenian driver will lead the way, and you and I will follow in a separate car. I brought my driver from Dubai, in case we needed to talk privately while traveling around the country. I cannot pronounce the name where we're going. It is supposed to be a ski resort or something. We'll have dinner there."

"Dzaghgadzor?" I say, surprised. It is around forty minutes from the city. The peak of the ski season has ended, but the hotels and restaurants remain open year round.

"Something like that," he laughs. "They're supposed to have excellent traditional dishes."

We walk out of the hotel. Manoj and two men are standing by the entrance. As soon as they see us they scurry toward two cars parked at the front of the hotel, and open the doors. Manoj waits till Ahmed and I get in one of the cars, and then gets in the back seat of the other.

When the cars pull out of the hotel parking lot, he takes my hand, leans over and kisses it, then lets go. The gesture is abrupt, and takes me by surprise. But it does not create any awkwardness; if he had kept my hand in his any longer, it probably would have.

"I have a lot to tell you," he says. "I have news specifically about you. But first, I want to learn a bit more."

"You have news about me?" How can he come from Dubai with news about me? Scenarios involving Yuri and Ano flash in front of my eyes, and then my mind wanders to the way I left and I wonder if there are lingering legal ramifications.

"Don't look so worried," he laughs. "Would I come all the way here to give you bad news? But talk about yourself, your family, your village." He slides back in the seat, puts his head on the backrest, and shuts his eyes. I remember that is how he listened—to music, to me, even to himself. In the villa, as he reclined and shut his eyes, he'd have his hand on my thigh while he listened to music. But his hands are folded on his chest now. "Talk," he says again, "and don't forget that family friend, the one Manoj met in your village."

I imagine Manoj was thorough in his report. I tell Ahmed about Papa, Mama, my brothers and sisters, village life. I talk briefly about Gago and Edik, Edik's dacha in Vardahovit, his bench at the edge of the cliff. I tell him Edik calls it the point of 'truth and redemption.' At that he briefly opens his eyes and turns towards me, then shuts them again. Of course I say nothing about the events of last fall in Sevajayr.

He has not moved again nor opened his eyes. This is good, I think. Nothing we're doing now has anything to do with the past. The past is not here, except for some of his habits, like the way he listens. "Listening is a much more complex human function than most people realize," he had told me once. It was late, he was tired, and he often revealed his personal thoughts when he was tired. "One of my teachers taught me to listen to two separate things: listen to the person talking to you, and listen to what he's saying. If they're not saying the same thing, don't trust either. If they tell you the same thing, trust both." I remembered my father's story of the third ear then and wondered if it meant the same thing. But the thought left me like a flash. I was not supposed to indulge in deep thinking when I was with Ahmed. I was supposed to focus only on his needs.

Here he is now, in Yerevan, listening to me, and at the same time, as a separate process, listening to what I'm saying.

The car stops, and he opens his eyes. I'm done talking anyway. I've told him as much as I can. I've described people and places quickly, in wide brushstrokes, trying to tie them together to give a sense of the community that we have, hoping that I have managed not to bore him. I know he does not want to get involved in his girls' personal lives. Sumaya told me the story of one of his Tunisian concubines, who tried to sweet talk him into helping her father, who was in some kind of trouble back home. He left her villa without a word, and the next morning she was let go.

That same man has now listened to me talk about my family and village life for over half an hour.

The restaurant is a collection of private dining rooms, the size of small one-room cottages, scattered along a slope, with beautifully landscaped pathways between the rooms. The pathways are lined with flowerbeds, and a variety of antique agricultural tools decorate the entrance of each dining room. There are large clay jugs, the type that we still use at home to carry and store drinking water, and there are clay and wooden butter churns, which we also still use to churn butter in Saralandj. I wonder how many other everyday utensils we have which would pass for decorative antiques in this place.

Ahmed and I are led to a cottage. The two drivers and Manoj are in a second cottage nearby. Manoj can express almost any emotion through his smiles, and his smile as he enters the cottage with the drivers shows disappointment, sadness and a touch of embarrassment. I get the feeling that Manoj is not happy about being lumped with the drivers, but he won't insist on taking a dining room all by himself.

"We have a lot to talk about," says Ahmed, checking the inside of the cottage. It is rustic, with crude, solid-wood tables with thick tabletops, and heavy chairs, with small wool carpets serving as cushions. Everything seems to be a novelty to him. "I had come prepared to discuss a few matters with you, not knowing your story. Now that I know some of your story, I can't decide if I should change anything."

It feels strange seeing him here. "I don't know what you're talking about," I say. "But I know it is important that we both understand that my being in Dubai was wrong. You did not know that. You tried to make something happen between us there; at least I felt that you were trying. I appreciated that then, and I appreciate it today. But whatever it was that you were trying to build would have been built on a lie."

"That's not what's worrying me," he says surprised. "Lara, good things come out of disasters all the time. One does not throw away the good just because it was a bad thing that made it happen in the first place! Is that what you want to do?"

His take on this is far too simplistic, but still, I have to admit, I had not thought of it that way before. A crime was committed, it destroyed my life, but something good came out of it. If I accept the good, does that mean I am implicitly accepting the bad from which it came? Interesting take, I think, but way too naïve. Besides, what exactly was the good that came out of the bad? The good according to him? According to me? And I know precisely what the "bad" was in this case, and I reject it. He does not, not entirely. He accepted me knowing that I was a prostitute.

"It is not that simple, and I think you know it," I say, trying not to sound patronizing. "This is not like suffering a setback in one business venture, which inadvertently leads to a better opportunity somewhere else."

Two waiters open the door, each carrying a large tray. There is almost everything except pork. Ahmed, although not a strict Muslim, does not eat pork, partly because Islam prohibits it, but mostly because it is alien to him. He will not be able to taste the famous Armenian pork khorovadz, nor some of the pork sausages.

The two trays are the appetizers. The main courses will come when we ring the bell. The special today is a rabbit stew, says the waiter, in tomato and red wine sauce, cabbage, carrots, potatoes, garlic and a few types of greens. He recommends it strongly. But Manoj has also ordered lamb khorovadz, he says. I translate to Ahmed. Ahmed does not want to be interrupted by ordering food, so he's asked Manoj to arrange a large selection. The waiter asks what we'd like to drink.

"What do they usually drink with this food?" asks Ahmed.

"Cognac, vodka or wine. But I'm not sure you'd like the local wines." I remember one of Edik's comments about local wines.

"Let's try your famous cognac then. I've heard it is good."

Ahmed focuses on the various dishes for a minute, asking me what each one is. I think he's making small talk because he does not want to be interrupted in the middle of something more serious when the waiter returns with the cognac. I feel like lightening the mood too, so, a bit more jovially than I usually talk to him, I describe the various local cheeses, the Armenian *kamadz matsun*, which is similar to the Lebanese *labne* we used to have for breakfast in Dubai, the famous Armenian *basturma*, which he knows about from the Middle East, the traditional large plate of *ganachi*, which includes six or seven fresh green herbs, then I pass to the various salads, and I get more animated as I go, happy to explain to him something from my life…then I notice that he is staring at me, not at the dishes that I'm pointing to.

"Are you listening to what I'm saying or to me?" I ask laughing.

"You remember!" He is moved. He fights another impulse to touch me. "I love listening to you," he says.

I ignore his comment. The waiter returns, serves the cognac and leaves.

"Where were we?" he asks, taking a sip of his cognac. "This is strong. I've had this after dinner, not with dinner. Are you sure they drink this with dinner?"

"I'm sure, but you don't have to. Do you want something else?" and I hold up the little button that summons the waiter.

"No, no, this is fine," he says. "Where were we?"

"We were talking about building something on a crime, and how that was not the same as good coming out of a setback."

"That's what *you* were saying," he says with a devious smile. "But it is okay, let's talk about that. Lara, regardless of how we met, we're not strangers, right? We had something together, and it was not just one night or a day or two, but three months. So, for old times' sake, please just say it, exactly as you feel it."

Is this the moment when I acknowledge and confront the past? I have a direct invitation from the only representative of the past that matters.

"Say it as I feel it," I repeat, having decided to take the plunge. "Here are the facts, Ahmed. You bought me as a prostitute. I was basically your property. Sorry," I say when I notice him cringe, "but that is the truth. Even if I had chosen that… Umm… let's call it a profession, even if I had chosen that life, I was still captive in your beautiful villa. A bird in a golden cage still dreams of the wilderness, we say here. I was such a bird. Now, imagine that I did *not* choose the profession in the first place, and I did *not* want to be bought and sold, and I did *not* want to be anyone's possession. I had to go through those motions, for fear of my life, for the safety of my family and because of the absolute lack of alternatives. Until I escaped. Imagine all *that*, Ahmed, and tell me you don't understand what is bothering me."

I'm not a drinker, and I have never understood when someone says they *need* a drink. Edik says that often, and as much as I respect him, I don't understand why he would need a drink. Avo needs a drink most of the time. But now, for the first time, I feel I need a drink. It's not that I'd like to have one, not that I want one, but I actually need one. I take a large sip of my cognac, and bite into a cucumber. I am so worked up that I don't notice the pained look on Ahmed's face at first. I take another sip, and then look at him, and my heart breaks into pieces.

If one could paint remorse, it would be a painting of his face right now. Deep, pure, true remorse, undiluted, seeking no exoneration, just overflowing from his eyes. The question that I had asked Edik starts to resonate in my ears. Is Ahmed a good man or a bad man? Neither, he said. I wonder if he'd give the same answer if he saw his face right now. I finish my cognac, and feel my head getting lighter. I've learned from Avo and Edik that one needs to eat while drinking. So I start eating to avoid getting drunk. And perhaps to avoid looking at him again. I could not bear to see the pain in his eyes.

He does not say any of the things that I thought he'd say—how he never treated me like a prostitute, how he never thought of me like one, how I gave him so much happiness. Those statements would all be true. But he does not utter them. He is not here to justify anything. He hurts for me, and for himself. That does not change the facts, but it does change my perception of him. Right now, I think he is a good man.

"If I could rewind the clock," he whispers, "I would, and I'd start all over again. Don't ask me how I'd restart, because I don't know. All I know is that I wouldn't want you to suffer like that. You were always different from the rest, Lara. Truly special. That's why I'm here. But I never understood why you were different, until now. This is a revelation for me."

"So here we are," I say with some sympathy, but I know I have not rid myself of the sarcasm, "trying to save a good thing that came out of a bad situation. What is the good in this, Ahmed? What is it that you came here to save? To reclaim?"

"I told you already that I came here to understand why it had to end," he says, and for the first time I sense frustration and even a bit of resentment in his voice. "Who said anything about reclaiming anything?"

"And now you understand?" My voice is gentler.

"I understand why you ran away," he says. The way he ends the sentence implies that he does not understand anything else, including why it all had to end, but he does not say it. Ahmed has probably never been this vulnerable, so he is not familiar with the feeling. He does not know how to cope with it. I even get the impression that he may be regretting making the trip to see me. I don't know what he was expecting to find out, but I know this has caught him by surprise.

"Thank you. Thank you for understanding why I ran away. It has been bothering me that I betrayed your trust."

"Well," he says displaying a characteristic abrupt change in mood, "I still think something good came out of your appalling situation. I met you." He is serious but no longer sad. His expression is no longer remorseful. Then he laughs. "I hope you think meeting me was a good thing also, but I will not ask you that now. Now, I want to focus on getting some sustenance." He refills my glass and we toast. My first impulse is to tell him about the painter's dilemma of wanting to burn the canvas while saving the painting, but I change my mind. It's time to drop the heavy conversation.

We eat and focus on small talk. He tells me about Manoj's research on Armenia, how he was impressed with the development potential, and why he chose this area for us to have dinner. He says Manoj thinks it is worth looking into building a hotel here that caters to tourists from the Middle East. He talks about other business ideas, we ring the bell for the main course and he orders some red wine after all. "The cognac is good," he says, "but we'll have some more after dinner." The only wine they have is the house wine, and it comes in a clay pitcher. Edik wouldn't have liked it, I know, but Ahmed drinks it and says it is good.

Then, totally out of the blue, "So how's your Arabic?" he asks. He had hired one of the most prominent tutors in Dubai to give me private lessons. Sumaya had to be present at every session, because I could not be in the company of another man alone. I was beginning to get good at it. I would surprise and amuse Sumaya with occasional Arabic phrases. She would laugh at my accent, and once in a while correct me.

"*A'atazer, ya* Ahmed," I apologize, "but I haven't kept it up. I have neither the time nor the tutor here." He laughs, happy that at least the apology was spoken in Arabic.

"You said you had news," I say. "You said you had come to discuss a few things, and now didn't know how to proceed."

"Yes, I do have something to talk to you about. But first, tell me how did these people, Ayvazian and his nephew, die?" He asks the question so suddenly that I panic for a minute, and he notices.

"Sorry," I say, recovering my composure, "you took me by surprise. People say there was a clash of some sort between oligarchs. Six people died in one afternoon, far from here, in Ayvazian's region. The nephew and a bodyguard died in a car crash. Two bodyguards shot each other. And Ayvazian and another bodyguard fell off a cliff. I do not know any other details. Why is that important?"

"According to your entry papers in Dubai, you are a married woman. You were married to some Viktor Ara... wait a minute," he says, pulling a piece of paper from his shirt pocket, "here it is, A.ra.kel.ian. I'm not sure if I'm pronouncing that right." I had not given the marriage another thought after Viktor announced it to me in Moscow. "And although you just turned eighteen, your papers in Dubai say you are over twenty-three."

"They manufactured those papers." I stare at him, surprised that he is bringing all that up. "A fake passport and marriage papers. Viktor Arakelian is Viktor Ayvazian. I don't know why he had two passports."

"Because he was deported from Dubai and returned under a different name. We know they are the same person."

"Ahmed, I have to ask again, why is all of this important?" I am wondering if I can get into legal trouble for lying about my age or having a fake passport.

"Because you may be the legal heir of a three million euro villa in Dubai," he says smiling. "You may be a rich woman, and you didn't even know it!" Now he's smiling broadly. "I told you I wouldn't come all the way here to give you bad news, didn't I?"

"I still don't know what you're talking about."

"It is complicated," he says, "but we have ways of un-complicating things in Dubai. Here is the story as I understand it: the real Viktor bought a villa in Dubai more than four years ago and paid cash. Then the fake Viktor married the fake Lara." He sees the confusion on my face and smiles.

"Bear with me," he says, "it gets better. Then Viktor dies. In death, we're all the same, and the fake and real Viktors die together. Apparently, Viktor has no immediate heirs—no wife, no children, no parents. So his uncle's family sends someone claiming the villa for the 'legal' heirs. But they do not know that Viktor was married. By Dubai law, the wife inherits, not the uncle's family. As I said, it is complicated, because we have to transfer the asset from the real Viktor to the fake Viktor by simply showing that they are the same, and then the fake Lara will inherit the villa, and pass it on to the real Lara, because we know they are the same person also. Of course, none of this could be done if the Dubai authorities did not want to uncomplicate things. And I'm telling you that they do want to uncomplicate things."

"I don't want to have anything to do with Viktor's villa." My head is spinning, and not just from the cognac.

"Lara, don't be silly!" He snaps. "You're being childish."

"What am I going to do with a villa in Dubai?" I ask, matching his annoyance.

"I repeat," he says, showing his frustration, "the villa is worth three million euros. I can sell it for you and give you the money. Are you going to ask me now what you're going to do with three million euros?"

I look at him for a long moment. I know he's seeing right through me. The temptation, the struggle. But he does not understand the half of it. Am I supposed to snatch a prized asset right out of Carla's hands? Satisfying as that may be, it would be impossible to keep it a secret.

"Ahmed, you don't know how this country works," I say calmly. "The appearance of three million euros, through this process of uncomplicating the complications, could spell my death warrant and possibly the death warrant of most of my family. What you uncomplicate in Dubai will be re-complicated here."

"There is also a simpler way," he says brushing away my concern. "We have legal justification to confiscate the property on the grounds that it was acquired to launder money. I can still divert the proceeds to you, without raising anyone's suspicions."

"Why?" I ask, looking him in the eye.

"I came here to offer this to you because I thought, as the wife of the deceased, fake or real doesn't matter, you are entitled to have it. Then I heard the truth about your story, and the wife angle lost its luster. But now

I feel even more strongly than before, because this would, in a very small way, compensate for what they have put you through. So you tell me, why not?"

"There are many more answers to the 'why not' question than to the 'why' question. Both practical and ethical, not to mention legal. Let's drop this subject for now, Ahmed, please. It has already given me a huge headache."

"The subject is dropped," he says with a charming smile. "I'm here for at least two more days, possibly longer. Think about it, and we'll talk again."

The only person I know who will understand the predicament presented by this news is Edik. I'll have to talk this over with him.

"There is a lot that I want to see here," he says. "Let's plan the next two days. I understand that there are some rare Arabic manuscripts in your... wait," and he reaches for the piece of paper in his pocket again, "let me see if I can say this, *ma de na ta ran*... did I say it right?"

"Perfect!" I say, clapping happily. "Much better than I pronounce Arabic words!"

"So that's one visit. The Art Gallery is supposed to be good too, that's another visit. Manoj says a visit to the Genocide memorial," he checks his piece of paper again, *"Tzi tzer na ka bert*, whoa! Is a must. So that's another visit. We can do these three tomorrow, then the next day we get out of Yerevan. There is so much to see, you'll have to help me select."

It is late. We decide to leave. Before calling the others, he stands up and takes my hand, pulling me gently to my feet. He holds me for a few minutes, and then lets go. I put my arms lightly around his waist, but I do not give him a real hug.

"Regardless of everything," he says, "I am happy I know you."

I tell Armen, Manoj's driver, my address. They drive and we follow them. When we reach my building, I insist that he not come out of the car.

"Good night, Ahmed," I say. "Thank you for this evening. And by the way, I am happy to know you too."

He leans over and kisses me on the lips. I linger a minute not to give him the impression that I am angry, I smile, then I leave the car.

Chapter Twenty-Six

Laurian is in his beloved poplar forest. He has a bunch of stakes and a heavy hammer to push them into the hard ground. Agassi is helping him stake the crooked saplings, but he shakes his head and rolls his eyes.

"Edik jan," he says, puffing, "have you ever seen a poplar tree that was not straight? You're tiring yourself for nothing. Even the ones that look crooked now will grow straight on their own."

"Sure I have," says Laurian. "Look at this for example," he points to a tree that is almost at a forty-five degree angle from the ground. "How can this poor thing grow straight? Either it won't grow at all, or it will grow crooked. What does it take to push in a stake and tie it?"

"*Vonts kuzes.*" As you want. He knows he won't change Laurian's mind.

A light drizzle, closer to a fine mist than rain, descends upon them without warning. Laurian looks up at the gathering clouds.

"It looks like you won't have to water for a few days," he tells Agassi. "So stop sparing yourself from work and help me finish this row before the rain starts."

"Ha, Edik jan. *Vonts asés.*" As you say.

The drizzle changes to rain, and a burst of thunder erupts with such ferocity that the two men instinctively hold their ears. The downpour follows almost immediately. It is a torrent so strong that there is no point in running for shelter. In a few seconds they are drenched to the bone.

"I told you once that people here get their personality from the weather," yells Agassi over the horrendous noise of the rain. "You won't find a single predictable person in this entire region!" He laughs, amused by the shocked and shivering Laurian.

It is later that afternoon when Laurian finally sees the missed call from Lara. He has walked back to the house, showered, and is sitting at the dining room table with a cup of coffee when he notices it. It came more than two hours ago. He calls back.

"I really need to talk to you, but this is not a good time. When can I call back?"

"Did he arrive?"

"Yes, yesterday evening. We're having lunch now. Can we talk in couple of hours?"

"Of course we can. But is everything okay?"

"Everything is fine. I'll call back."

Although Lara sounds fine, Laurian decides to go to Yerevan. He packs an overnight bag, calls his hotel and takes off fifteen minutes later. He feels he should be in Yerevan while Lara's visitor is in town.

He is about to enter the Yerevan city limits when Lara calls back.

"Can you talk now?"

"Where are you?" asks Laurian.

"He just dropped me at my place. I'm seeing him again in a few hours."

"I'll be at the entrance of your building in twenty minutes. We'll talk face to face."

"Edik jan, you drove down? There was no need." Lara is surprised but also happy. This does call for a face-to-face conversation.

Laurian picks Lara up, drives to a deserted road, and parks the car.

"Tell me," he says.

Lara explains the situation with Viktor's villa and the three million euros. She goes through all the 'complications,' as well as Al Barmaka's 'uncomplicating' scenarios. She explains how Al Barmaka thought she was being silly and childish when she told him she wanted nothing to do with Viktor's money. She explains her fear of retaliation from Carla and her gang, which he well understands. And she touches upon the moral conflict she was having. She even tells him about her fictitious painter and his dilemma.

Laurian listens, interrupting only a few times to clarify the details of the fake and real Viktors and Laras. After around half an hour, Lara ends her story. Laurian waits for a few minutes, thinking.

"Obviously," he says, "you are not sure whether you should accept the money or not. Otherwise, you wouldn't have called me."

Lara is quiet. She just looks at him and waits.

"Let's eliminate two variants of 'not sure.' First, 'not sure' could mean that you want the money, but you need me to tell you it is okay. Is that it?"

Lara shakes her head.

"Second, perhaps you don't want the money, and you want me to convince you that you're not being silly or childish, and making the right decision. Is that it?"

Lara shakes her head again.

"So you really don't know what to do," says Laurian, more to himself than Lara. Lara is still quiet.

"Lara, are you sure you do not want the money? You know how much money that is, right? Can you visualize three million euros? That's almost four-and-a-half million dollars. Do you know how many problems you can solve with that? For you, for Avo, for everyone in your family?"

"I know how many problems I can solve with the money," says Lara, but her expression is stern and uncompromising.

"Okay, I have one more question, and then I'll give you an idea. I want you to explain to me why you don't want the money for yourself."

"*De lav*, Edik. Isn't it obvious?" Lara sounds frustrated.

"Maybe it is, but I want to hear it from you."

"Fine," says Lara curtly. "I'll tell you why, short and to the point. Let's not analyze the obvious to death. First, it is not my money. That 'legal' heir argument is a sham, and we all know it. Even if by some twisted logic it is made legally mine, it is not, and can never be, rightfully mine. Second, I thought the point was to kill the past and move forward. How would I be killing the past if I take that money? Do you want me to finally become the woman that I tried not to be for eighteen months? Third, think of the complications when the Ayvazians find out that their villa is confiscated, and then all of a sudden the Galians are living like kings. Can I take a risk with the life of a single one of my siblings? And believe me, everyone's life would be endangered.

Fourth, Ahmed says it would be a 'small compensation' for the suffering they put me through. In one way, that would be too small compared to what they did to me, but in another way, it is far too much. How many girls like me did they exploit and abuse to amass three million euros, do you think? Why do I deserve that money now, and the others don't?"

Lara has surprised Laurian many times before with her depth and maturity, but she has always looked vulnerable and even weak in his eyes. He's seen her as someone to be protected, coached and advised. He is not prepared for the inner strength and moral fiber that he sees flowing through her words and filling his own soul.

"Any other girl in your position would have taken the money without a second thought."

"Perhaps. I can even give you some examples of girls who would take it in a second—Anastasia for one, Susannah in Dubai, Nadia, Farah, Sumaya, and tens of others that I met in that year-and-a-half. Do you know what they all have in common? They are all real prostitutes. They applied for the job, as some of them told me. Did I? Did I apply for the job, Edik jan? Why would you expect me to react the same way as those who did?"

For the first time, Laurian sees Lara's youth as an asset. *Only an eighteen year old could be this idealistic*, he thinks. A thirty-something would have found it much easier to opt for the money. He leans over toward the passenger seat, grabs Lara and holds her tight. He does not care what it looks like. "I am so proud of you," he finally whispers in her ear, and Lara relaxes, stops resisting his hug, and allows herself to wind down in his arms.

After a few minutes, he lets go.

"Now I know," he says. "Not only do I know where you stand, but I know how you can burn the canvas and save the painting. I really do."

𝔏 𝔏 𝔏

Anna freezes when she sees her photograph on the table in the back room. She instinctively looks around, as if expecting to uncover a bad practical joke. For a split second she imagines Hovo has found her, walked into the store and put the picture there just to terrify her. But no one is there.

She then looks at the picture carefully, at her long hair and thick-rimmed glasses, and wonders if it is possible to tell it is her. Thank God she does not wear glasses any longer.

Lucy walks in and sees her holding the photo to the light.

"Oh yeah," she says casually, "if someone looking like that walks in the store, let me know. Try to get her address and phone number, if I'm not here."

"Who is she?" asks Anna, wondering if her voice is shaking, but relieved that Lucy has seen no resemblance.

"Her name is in the back of the picture."

She flips the photo over so fast that she wonders again if Lucy noticed her nervousness. "Anna Arturi Hakobian," she reads aloud. "But who is she, I mean, what do we want with her?"

"I have no idea. Yuri wants to know. I don't ask Yuri why." She shrugs and walks out of the room.

'Yuri wants to know' means Madame Carla wants to know, thinks Anna, and she's been warned about both. This photo could have come only from Hovo. She has been warned about that risk too. But what good are the warnings? What's she supposed to do now? And didn't Laurian say that Hovo was working for LeFreak? Then how come Yuri is asking about Anna Arturi Hakobian?

Anna is in a cold sweat. She puts the photo back on the table. She goes to the mirror hanging on the back wall, and takes a long look at herself. Very short hair and no eyeglasses are the only changes since that photo was taken. That may be enough to fool Lucy, but not a more observant person. Hovo would certainly recognize her if he saw her in the street. Her parents would recognize her too. The man who raped her could recognize her, even though he was not that interested in studying her face.

She has to call Lara. Overseas visitor or not, this is an emergency.

𝓛 𝓛 𝓛

There is no doubt in Yuri's mind that LeFreak orchestrated the killings in Sevajayr last fall. He could not prove it, but he is convinced. His informants' consistent reports of methodic attempts to take over the Ayvazian operations are a good indication. Hov's reports of the snide remarks of LeFreak's men about Ayvazian, saying what an idiot he must have been to have gotten himself and his men killed, serve as an added indication for Yuri. They sound almost like they're bragging.

Carla listens to Yuri with her feet up on her desk. She's lost some weight in the past few weeks, and takes pride in her new looks. She has stopped wearing stockings since the temperatures have risen in Yerevan in early May. Her skirt slides up her thighs as usual as she shifts her feet from left on right to right on left. Every additional inch of exposed skin adds to her own arousal as much as to Yuri's, but she enjoys building expectation a lot more than he does. Build the pressure and control it at the same time, like pulling an arrow in a bow. Tension like that has its uses.

"We cannot take any chances with this, Yuri," she says, in a tone that would make one think she's in a boardroom in a formal meeting. "LeFreak may be inexperienced when it comes to our business, but he is not a clumsy man. Don't forget that he has built a formidable empire of his own."

"I'm not saying he's clumsy. I'm saying he killed Sergei and Viktor. How is that clumsy? I'm also saying his men are demoralized and frustrated. We have a chance to strike now, and we should take it."

"Yuri, that's why I asked you before if you've ever killed anyone, and you never answered me. You acted like a spoiled child who's denied his candy, if you remember. Why do you think I was asking? Just to be nosey? If you think the time is right to strike, have you also thought of how and when and where?" Carla shifts her legs again, offering a glimpse of her bright red thong in the process. Yuri fights the urge to get out of his chair and have her right there on the desk. But the last thing he needs is another insult delivered in the form of a rejection. He gathers himself and keeps his eyes on hers.

"I have killed before," he says so coldly that Carla takes notice. "And I can kill again, if there is a well thought-out plan that I have faith in, a plan that won't blow up in our faces." Then, keeping his defiant gaze on her, he adds, "Have you?"

Carla ignores the question. He should know better than to challenge her like that, because she has never taken the bait and never will.

"Good," she says, "that will come in handy when we're ready. Leave the planning to me, Yuri. This is not something you can rush. I doubt that his men will suddenly find motivation any time soon. We still don't have enough information about him. His weaknesses and, more importantly, his routine. What does he do on a typical day? Who can take over from him if he dies? What do *they* do on a typical day? I admit that what you've uncovered in the past week has been impressive. But it is not enough to strike. Gather this information and we'll regroup. I have a specific team in mind for this operation."

"Any progress on the documents for Dubai?" asks Yuri.

"Yes," says Carla, but makes sure Yuri sees her displeasure. Only she can change the subject like that, and only she can ask for progress reports. Nevertheless, she explains. "Three documents are ready. He's working on the fourth."

She then takes her feet off the desk and walks toward him.

𝒮 𝒮 𝒮

Alisia confirms Laurian's reports that Avo has moderated his drinking. Actually, moderation is not the right way to describe it, because he avoids alcohol altogether for four or five days in a row, and then drinks a bottle of vodka in a few hours and gets senseless drunk. But at least he does not drink everyday, and he does not get violent when he drinks. He just passes out and sleeps for twelve hours.

Most of the pigs are sold. Only one remains with her litter of piglets. Avo has decided to keep them, using the feed he had purchased before the prices rose, augmented by household refuse, such as potato peels, outer leaves of cabbages, wilted carrots, beets and turnips from their winter storage bin, and as much as he can gather of the same stuff from Martha's house.

The proceeds from the sale of the pigs have generated less than twenty percent of what Avo borrowed from Laurian. But Laurian does not accept any payment.

"Use what you have to cover your other debts," he tells Avo. "The interest will accumulate and it will become a much larger burden on you later. What you and I need to talk about is not the old debt, but a new business plan."

"What's the point?" says Avo. "They'll destroy anything else that we start." He sounds so depressed that Laurian is torn between his feelings of sympathy and anger. Anger not at LeFreak, but at Avo himself, for not showing the will to start oevr, to fight back, for what appears to Laurian as a defeatist, fatalistic resignation and acceptance of conditions as they are. That is the problem with the whole country, he thinks. The LeFreaks and the Ayvazians would not survive for one day if people didn't acquiesce so easily.

Laurian checks his anger by reminding himself that Avo is in fact different from the vast majority of the population. He has shown two major acts of defiance, both violent. One during the killings of last fall, and the second through his attack on LeFreak's fence, an utterly hopeless act driven by nothing other than extreme desperation.

"Of course there is a point," he tells him calmly, "since when do you give up like that? Haven't we overcome much larger problems?"

Chapter Twenty-Seven

Ahmed spends hours at the Madenataran, pouring over not only old Arabic manuscripts, but also ancient Armenian texts written on lambskin, old Bibles with miniature art filling the margins, handwritten and painstakingly copied by one priest over his entire lifetime.

He has done his homework before coming here.

"This is one of the largest repositories of old manuscripts in the world," he tells me, oblivious to the irony of acting as my tour guide in Yerevan. "More than seventeen thousand manuscripts, thirty to forty thousand documents virtually on every subject, and what's most surprising to me, well over two-thousand historical documents in non-Armenian languages, including over a thousand Arabic manuscripts." He catches me watching him and stops.

"Are you listening to what I'm saying?" he asks with a smile.

"I'm listening." I smile back.

I admit to him that this is my first visit to the place as well. He looks at me, surprised at first, then smiles.

"I love it that we can share a first experience," he whispers.

We go to lunch at a French restaurant near the Cascade. He talks non-stop about the Arabic manuscripts, which, he says, include both complete and partial Quranic scripts and life stories of the Prophet Mohammed. "We don't have this many ancient manuscripts in Dubai," he tells me.

After lunch, he drops me back at my place, because I tell him I need a few hours for some personal errands.

"Thanks Ahmed," I say as I leave the car, "I'll meet you in the lobby of your hotel around four. No need to send the car to pick me up." The Mercedes sedan has begun to be noticed in my neighborhood.

♌ ♌ ♌

I don't know why I never thought about the fact that Ahmed and Edik are staying at the same hotel. Edik always stays at the Marriott. That's where Ahmed is. As I walk up the steps to enter the hotel, I wonder what I'd do if they're both there. Do I introduce them? Do I pretend I don't know Edik?

I walk in, and Ahmed is with Manoj as expected, having a coffee. Edik is not around. I wait for them to finish and we walk over to the Art Gallery across the Square. Here too, Ahmed has done his homework.

"There is far too much to see in just a few hours," he says. "Let's focus on the 5th and 4th floors. The 5th floor is the classical Armenian artists and some 19th century art. The 4th is twentieth century Armenian artists." He sees me staring at him again and starts laughing. "All you need, Lara *jan*," he says, stressing the *jan*, "is to think like a tourist. It is all there. But those who live here will never open a tourist flyer!"

"And who taught you to say '*jan*'?" I ask.

"That's how everyone talks around here," he says casually. "That's much easier than *ma.de.na.ta.ran*! Anyway, I think we should start with the 5th floor and walk down. What do you say?"

On the fifth floor, we start from the left wing, which happens to host the Gallery's Aivazovski collection. He is fascinated by the shipwreck scenes. He spends a long time in front of each painting. I hear an occasional 'incredible' or 'genius' coming out of his mouth, but he finds it difficult to let go of one painting and move to the next. He stops the longest in front of a painting of a storm, with a large sailing ship tilted on its side, the mast bare of any sails, waves and mist rising from the ocean, merging with a sky full of thick white clouds, a long log is floating in front of the ship, waves gushing over it—the entire painting is a presentation of concentrated, angry nature and danger. "Look at that," whispers Ahmed, in awe. "Every single point on this canvas is moving. You feel the waves in your bones."

Something else catches his eye. It is a painting of Noah leaving the ark. Noah is in the foreground, in flowing robes, long white hair and beard, accompanied by his sons, and in the background a long caravan of the other family members and all the animals, winding through the wet fields, with Mount Ararat in the background.

He walks closer to the painting. "You can feel the exhilaration, the joy, the victory of having survived the flood, and most of all, you can feel the power of their faith. Wouldn't you love to have this painting in your bedroom, right in front of your bed, so every morning when you open your eyes, you live this same feeling of having survived something huge? Can you imagine that?"

I did not know about Ahmed's infatuation with paintings. During the time that I was with him, he had talked about music, poetry, and sometimes philosophy. He had brought CDs for us to listen together. Towards the end, right before I escaped, he had begun to introduce verses from famous Arab poets, to augment my language lessons. He'd read and translate them to me, then ask me to read them. But his ability to walk straight into a painting and be engulfed by it is news to me.

"On second thought," he says, looking at Noah's painting again, "I could never have this in my home."

"Why?" I ask. "I mean, obviously not this exact one, but a perfect duplicate. The guide below told me you could commission duplicates of the paintings. They will be identical, except for the size, she said. They change the size, otherwise it would be considered a forgery."

"That's not what I mean," he says. "Noah's story is in the Quran also. In Islam, he is considered one of the prophets. God spoke to him. And we cannot have a physical portrayal of any prophet. It goes back to the prohibition of worshipping idols."

A guard walks in to say it is closing time. We have not even finished viewing Aivazovski yet.

We walk out. It is already dark in the Square.

"It is too late to go to the Genocide Memorial," he says. "I will not even try to pronounce the name again. There is too much to see here. I'll have to extend my stay by a day or two." He looks at me, hoping for a happy reaction. I give him a warm smile.

"I think you'll enjoy meeting my friend Edik," I say. "He's like you. Interested in everything."

"I'm not interested in everything, Lara," he says seriously. "Only in the things that are part of you." After a minute, he adds, "Of course, I'd still love to meet your friend."

We walk slowly around the Square and back to the hotel.

"Where shall we have dinner?" he asks.

"You seem to know more about Yerevan than I do," I say, laughing. "You decide."

"Do you feel like anything in particular?"

"No, but I'd prefer somewhere quiet. I have something important to discuss with you."

"Oh? Good news or bad?"

"Would I give you bad news when you've come all the way here to see me?" I ask, paraphrasing him.

He chooses a quiet restaurant on Charents Street. It is around fifteen minutes drive from the hotel. Manoj does not come along. Ahmed's driver will have to figure out where it is from a map, instead of following Armen as usual. He finds the address without any difficulty.

I like the feel of the place. It is an old house turned into a restaurant, with separate dining areas with just a few tables in each. There is also a terrace, where we sit. He orders several dishes for us to share, and looks at the wine list.

"They have some interesting foreign wines here," he says. "What type of wine do you feel like?"

"Ahmed, if you don't mind, I'd rather not drink tonight. I think I still have some of that cognac from last night in my veins."

"That's fine," he says, "I won't drink either."

I don't know why I automatically compare Ahmed and Edik in almost everything. This, for example, would never happen with Edik. For him, wine is more important at dinnertime than the food. He won't go to a restaurant that has a poor wine list, even if the food is excellent. Ahmed does not seem to care one way or another.

We've spent almost the entire day together without talking about us. I think he feels the need for a break from last night's serious conversation as much as I do. His seemingly boundless interest in old and new, and his deep appreciation of the arts remind me of Edik. But the two men could not be more different in every other way. Edik's endless curiosity springs in part from his profession, and in part from his being an expatriate Armenian trying to understand today's Armenia. Ahmed, on the other hand, is first and foremost a businessman. His interest in history and art comes from a nostalgia toward a once glorious history that he fears is lost. He used to talk to me about the Arab renaissance in the first several centuries of Islam with great passion. One way or another, all of his non-business interests can somehow be traced back to that history.

Aivazovski's paintings are still on his mind. His desire to wake up every morning to the same sensation as Noah must have had at the hour when he finally left the ark fascinates me. I wonder what it would be like to have the freedom to think about that kind of possibility. What type of outlook on life should he have for that thought to even occur to him?

Equally surprising is to hear him talk about idolatry. Ahmed is not religious in that way. He does not follow dogma. He has no problem drinking alcohol, even though it is prohibited by Islam. He does not pray five times a day, like he's supposed to. But he won't hang a picture that he admires with his heart and soul in his bedroom. His bedroom, which neither I nor, as far as I know, any of his many other concubines have ever seen, must be the inner sanctum. What is permissible outside the bedroom is not allowed inside. Maybe he does not take a glass of wine to his bedroom either. Or maybe it is something else altogether. I have to stop trying to understand contradictions in a man like Ahmed. He is *made* of contradictions. His being here to see me contradicts his entire way of life.

I remember Sumaya once telling me how everything is attributed to God's will. *Everything*, she would stress. All the beauty, all the ugliness, the fair, the unfair, the good, the bad, everything has one and only one source, which is God. I believed then that she believed that, and that belief helped her cope with every difficulty that she faced. After all, it is God's will. Once you accept that, she'd say, you can answer all the questions that haunt you.

But that did not answer any of my questions. *Did God create Ayvazian too,* I'd ask? *Did He make him do what he did to me? Why?*

Now, sitting here in this quiet restaurant in Yerevan, a place I not only had not been to before, but I did not know existed, a place where I could not afford to buy a meal, while Ahmed probably could buy the entire neighborhood, he looks at me, and I wonder if he's thinking God is the source of this evening, He made us meet, He made me escape, He made Manoj find me, He made him come here to see me.

"You're beautiful when you're deep in thought," he says suddenly. "I did not want to disturb you, but I cannot resist. What's on your mind?"

"Oh, I'm sorry," I say. "I didn't mean to drift. A lot has happened since you arrived that makes me think." He doesn't ask again; he just waits.

"Thank you for your interest," I say. "In the Madenataran, in the Art Gallery, in Tzitzernakabert, in everything."

"And in you," he smiles. "Why don't you want to thank me for my interest in you?" Because I don't understand it, I want to tell him. Because you bought me for sex, and now, is that your interest in me? If it has changed, how has it changed?

"Yes," I say instead, "and for your interest in me." But Ahmed is sharp and shrewd, and he senses that I did not say that with conviction. She did not mean quite the same thing as her words, he's probably thinking. But he lets it be.

They bring several dishes of dolma, cabbage and grape leaf wraps, stuffed eggplants, tomatoes and peppers, yoghurt with mashed garlic, and a couple of salads.

"I was told to order this. It is supposed to be like grandmother makes it." He laughs and serves some onto my plate.

"So how long are you going to keep me in suspense?" he asks after a few bites.

"Okay, I'll tell you what's on my mind. First, I want to tell you some basic facts, and then come to the main point. I hope you'll be patient with me, as always."

"Where can I go?" he says, raising his hands. "You have my ears."

"I have a friend, who is hiding here in Yerevan. She lives in fear that her own husband will again force her into prostitution. She cannot trust her own parents. There are young girls in orphanages here who will be homeless when they turn eighteen. They have no place to go, and they are prime targets of sex traffickers. There are poor and broken families, with a single parent, most often a single mother, who cannot provide the very basics to their children, let alone an education or protection from organized crime. During my own eighteen months of captivity, I met some others like me. They all live in fear, because they have no place to go." I stop and look at him for a minute. He shows no sign of disinterest.

"What I'd like to do with Viktor's three million euros," I continue, "of course only if it is possible for you to get your hands on it without too much trouble, is to open a shelter for such girls in Yerevan. A place where they can be safe, cared for, and they can go to school, learn how to support themselves and be independent. Ahmed, do you see how that would be the only correct way to spend Viktor's ill-gotten gains? Let's use it to help the victims of his crimes, both the existing victims and the potential victims, and I assure you there will be a lot of them."

He stays quiet for a long time. He watches me, looks away for a minute then returns his gaze to my eyes.

"Lara, I told you the money can be yours. Why don't you take it and do what you want with it? Open your shelter, if that's what you want."

"You don't know this country," I say. "I could never pull something like that off. An eighteen-year-old girl spending three million euros to open a shelter? They'll rip me apart in one day. The money will disappear in all types of complications, taxes, fees, rip-offs. You know how you said you can 'uncomplicate' things in Dubai? Well, the world's best experts in complicating things are right here. That's where you come in."

"How do I come in? Where?"

"*You* open the shelter." There's new enthusiasm in my voice. "They cannot touch you. It would even be better if your government lends its name to it as some type of sponsor. Then they really won't dare mess with it. A humanitarian gesture from you, supported by your government. I'm not asking you spend a penny more than Viktor's money. Just lend it your name. Visit once a year or send Manoj to check how things are going. Let the news cover it. Have the accounts audited, to let the vultures know that they cannot scavenge the shelter's resources. If you can, even appoint a manager of your choice from Dubai. A foreigner."

He looks tired just listening to me.

"What you're proposing is commendable. It truly is. But do you have any idea how much I have on my plate? Why do you think it took me a month to free up a few days to visit you? I'm on the board of ten companies and four government agencies."

"I'm sorry," I say, deflated. "I thought perhaps you could delegate this to someone, if not Manoj then maybe someone more junior. You were looking into business investment opportunities here, right? You'll have managers here to run them. You could delegate it to them."

"It is my turn to ask you to drop the subject for now," he says after a long silence. "Let me think about it tonight. We'll talk again before I leave."

"The subject is dropped!" I say, as he did last night. The difference is, I do not say *habiby*. Come to think of it, I have never called him that.

We leave the restaurant.

"Where can we go for a walk?" he asks. I remember my short walk with Anastasia near the Monument, and I try to give directions to the driver to go there. After a few wrong turns, mostly because of my own ignorance of the streets in Yerevan, we get there.

"You have to learn to get around this city, Lara," he chuckles. "You do live here, don't you?"

"Yes, Your Excellency," I say. "But in one day you seem to know more about this city than I do, and you're not a bad tour guide. If you ever want to change your day job, the Ministry of Tourism here will certainly consider your application."

We walk around the Monument, the Statue of Mother Armenia, and we stop at the edge of the park to watch Yerevan sprawled across the valley below. He puts his arm around my shoulder and pulls me to him, and I let myself be pulled, squeezed between his arm and the side of his chest. He gives the top of my head a kiss. "*Habibty*," he whispers. I fight the impulse to reciprocate with a "*Habiby*." The past is not yet dead enough for that kind of moment between us.

"I will take a taxi home," I tell him when we get back in his car. "Your car is arousing too much interest in my poor neighborhood."

"I can't let you do that at this hour."

"Ahmed, please, how do you think I got around before you arrived in Yerevan yesterday?"

"Very funny, Lara, and I hope you weren't wandering in the streets of this great city alone at this hour. But now I'm here, so things are different. Besides, we were both too good not drinking at dinner, we can't end the evening like that. We need to have a drink first. Then we'll figure out how to get you home."

We walk into the lobby and see Manoj and Edik sitting together at the bar. Several men in the lobby and at the bar watch me cross the room, oblivious to the fact that I appear to be with another man. Ahmed notices, and seeing how I ignore them, says nothing. From the looks of it, Edik and Manoj are having a great time. Edik is telling him a story, God knows from what part of the world, and Manoj is laughing his heart out. They both have snifters of cognac in front of them, and it doesn't look like it is their first drink. Edik finishes his story and raises his glass to a hysterically laughing Manoj when we approach them.

Manoj notices us and jumps from his chair.

"Your Excellency, Ms. Lara, a very good evening to you both," he exclaims.

"Hello Mr. Manoj," I say in English. "Edik jan, *bari yereko.*" Good evening.

Edik stands up and without any hesitation gives me a short kiss on the forehead. Then he turns to Ahmed.

"Good evening, Mr. Al Barmaka, I am Edward Laurian."

"*Barev*, Edik jan," says Ahmed with a smile. "Please drop the Mr., my name is Ahmed."

We must both look so surprised at his greeting that he continues.

"What?!" he says. "You think your language is so difficult that an old Bedouin like me cannot learn a few words? I've been here for more than twenty hours already!"

Edik bursts out laughing and I know right then and there that his problem with Ahmed as an enabler of the traffickers has been ameliorated somewhat.

"Lara here has kept me on the straight and narrow all evening," says Ahmed, throwing his arm around Edik's shoulder, and leading him back to his seat. "We've had dinner without a single drop of wine." He pulls out a chair for me. "We've talked about humanitarian issues," he says looking past me at Edik. "Now I need a drink, and I see you two are a few steps ahead of us."

Poor Manoj is forgotten to Edik's right. I'm squeezed between Edik and Ahmed, who are now talking to each other, even though I get the feeling that I'm the unspoken and unacknowledged catalyst in everything they say.

Then Ahmed asks Edik about his assignments in the Middle East, and that opens the floodgates of a boisterous dialogue between them. I no longer spark their conversation. In fact, I feel that I'm in their way, and I lean back so they can face each other more easily, leaning over the bar from either side of me. They talk about the civil war in Lebanon, the various Arab-Israeli wars, the emergence of oil as a political weapon in the early seventies, when Edik was still a teenager and Ahmed was around two years old. Edik tells him stories about OPEC meetings that he covered early in his career, about various oil Ministers of Saudi Arabia, Kuwait, Venezuela and Iran, some of whom Ahmed remembers. Edik lived in Beirut for several months and learned some Arabic, so they use Arabic phrases here and there. They talk about Beirut, which they both love as a city, and describe places and recount memories, even though they've been there at different times.

Over an hour and three cognacs later, they fall silent. The halt in their conversation is abrupt. They stare at their snifters, each absorbed in the thoughts and memories that their conversation has awakened.

"You know," says Ahmed after a while, "the oil boom changed how the world perceives the Middle East forever. And on the surface, it also changed the Middle East itself. But if you scratch the surface, the region has not changed much."

"That reminds me of what a Lebanese politician I once knew used to say," says Edik. "'The world today thinks of the Middle East as one huge oil reservoir,' he used to say. 'But people forget that, even in the Gulf, in the beginning there was no oil. That's not how it started, and that's not how it will end,' he'd say. 'In the beginning was the *desert*. Every brain cell of the endogenous population of the Gulf is conditioned by the desert,' he'd insist. 'Then came *religion*. But even the religion that came was conditioned by the desert. Later, much later, came oil, and when oil came, there was no less religion nor any less desert.'" Edik takes a sip of his cognac, and Ahmed leans over, surprised.

"A Lebanese politician told you that?" he asks. "He has understood the Gulf pretty well. Do you remember his name?"

"Of course I do. But wait, there's more," says Edik, "Then he'd discuss Lebanon. 'Some Western journalists come here and talk to me as if I was born with oil too,' he'd say. 'But in Lebanon there never was oil, nor any desert, nor much religion for that matter. In the beginning was the *sea*. Then came *trade*. And trade came *because* of the sea. Then came more trade, and with trade, came the *West*,' he'd say, showing a bit of disappointment. So you see, Ahmed, this man saw the long-term cultural history of the Middle East as the Sea-Trade-West versus the Desert-Religion-Oil dynamic. What a fascinating study of identity politics in the region one could do based on that!"

"Indeed," says Ahmed raising his glass. He looks at me, as if he has forgotten that I've been there all this time.

"Sorry Lara, I hope we didn't bore you. But you're taking history courses at the university, right? Some of this might have been interesting for you as well."

"The whole thing was interesting." Which, strictly speaking is not a lie, since I find the rapport between them fascinating.

"I need to get going," I tell them, checking the time. It is approaching midnight. "What do you want to do tomorrow?" I ask Ahmed.

"I managed to extend my stay by one day," he says. "So I have tomorrow and the next day. The following day early we have to leave. I want to see the Genocide Museum. Aside from that, let's ask Edik. What do you suggest?" he asks, turning to Edik.

"If you had two weeks," says Edik with a smile, "I would have suggested all types of trips. But for two days, I have only one suggestion. You take one day to visit Vardahovit, and the second to finish seeing a few places in Yerevan, like going back to that art gallery and a few other museums."

"Lara has told me a little bit about your place," says Ahmed. "Varda...?"

"Vardahovit," says Edik.

"Vardahovit." Then he turns to me. "What do you think? Maybe you'd want to seat me on that bench of truth and redemption and ask me a few questions?"

Edik bursts out laughing. "Anyone who knows about that bench is obliged to visit it," he says. "So it's done. Why don't we make a day trip out of it tomorrow? We can leave in the morning and be back here by evening. Then you'll have a full day for museums and the Genocide Memorial. Manoj," he says turning to him, "you're most welcome also. I think you've been in the desert too long."

"Thank you, Mr. Laurian." Manoj smiles his 'grateful' smile.

"If in the Gulf in the beginning was the desert, and in Lebanon the sea, what was here in the beginning?" asks Ahmed.

"The *mountains*, of course!" says Edik triumphantly. "In the beginning were the mountains, and *we* are our mountains." Ahmed does not understand the significance of the last phrase, but it sounds good to him anyway. I make a mental note to explain to him later that "we are our mountains" is the name of a monument symbolizing Nagorno Karabagh.

"Very well, Edward," says Ahmed, laughing. "Many thanks for the invitation. Shall we leave around ten?"

"Perfect. Now, may I take Lara home tonight?"

"No you may not," I jump in. "You've had far too much to drink. Besides, I already told Ahmed that I'd be taking a taxi home. See you gentlemen tomorrow at ten."

"That simply won't do, young lady." A slight slur is noticeable in Ahmed's speech. "Manoj's driver Armen is outside. He'll take you home. End of discussion." And Ahmed smiles benignly at me.

Chapter Twenty-Eight

A vo has come up with a new idea. He wants to keep honeybees and produce honey for export. How can they mess with that? he asks himself. I don't have to buy feed for honeybees; I take my beehives to a nice meadow, preferably by a mountainside, and the bees feast on wildflower pollen. Once a year, in the fall, I draw the honey from the frames in the hive. If we find a good export market, he says, Russia or Ukraine, maybe even Iran, then they cannot mess with that either.

Saralandj is a good place for beekeeping. His father kept a few hives a long time ago. But he stopped when Avo was still a small child. Avo does not know why. The old hives are still in the underground storage area—old, worn out wooden boxes, holding around a dozen frames each. He'll have to get a lot more, he reckons at least a hundred to start with. He'll also need smokers and extractors. They probably sell second hand ones in the big market in Yerevan. Eventually, as the business picks up, he'll need to have a brand, labels and unique looking jars.

Avo calls Lara to tell her about his idea.

"Honey smells better than the pigs," she laughs. "Avo jan, that is really a great idea. And the work is substantially less. I couldn't imagine you cleaning those pigpens much longer anyway."

"Do you remember Papa's hives?" asks Avo.

"Sure I do. And I remember how good our honey was!"

"Do you know why he stopped keeping bees?"

"I have no idea. We were young. Maybe Martha can remember. But it doesn't matter. You're doing the right thing. You see, something good *can* come out of a catastrophe. The pig farm was not meant to be."

Al Barmaka notices her excitement and looks at her expectantly, but does not ask.

"I just quoted you to my brother," she says, pleased with herself.

"You did? I can't imagine about what."

"That something good can come out of a catastrophic event, but this time, unlike when you said that, it actually is applicable." She smiles mischievously.

They have already left Yerevan. Laurian has taken Manoj in his car and is leading the way. Lara points to the right of the road to a sign.

"Remind me to tell you about *Khor Virap*. I don't want to forget."

"I'll try," laughs Al Barmaka. "I'll remember *Khor*, because it is close to an Arabic word, and you remember the second word, because I've forgotten it already. All right? Now tell me why your statement was more applicable than mine."

"Because it is exactly what I told you before, it is one business venture gone bad, but another and much better idea has now replaced it. Avo would never have thought of the better idea if the first one had not blown up in his face."

Al Barmaka waits for more information, and Lara starts telling him the story, reluctantly at first, but then she gets into it and describes the entire saga with the pig farm, Avo's initial enthusiasm at starting something new, how well the farm was doing at the beginning, then the way LeFreak manipulated both the feed market and the pork market, how over fifty small famers were driven out of business almost overnight, and how Avo was devastated, not just financially, but also emotionally. She skips over LeFreak's bloody fence and Avo's incarceration.

Al Barmaka is shocked. He understands monopoly power well. His country has a few big monopolists, and he himself is one of them. So that's not what he finds shocking. Illegally ruining the livelihoods of a large number of poor farmers is entirely alien to him. The monopolists in Dubai and the Emirates can exist without affecting the livelihood of any citizen, because the government has its own vast financial resources and does not collect taxes. To the contrary, it subsidizes virtually everything for the citizen. But here?

"Now you know why last night I asked you to spearhead the shelter," says Lara. "This, unfortunately, is what this country has come to."

"We'll talk about the shelter later. I have some ideas. By the way, did you tell Edik about the money?"

"Yes," she says sheepishly. "Sorry, but I needed his advice. He's a good friend. Actually, the shelter was his idea."

"I'm glad you did, Lara," he says. "I want to talk about what I have in mind with him and you together. But that's later. Now, coming back to Avo, one of my companies is in the import-export business. We mostly import consumer electronics, but also some unique foodstuffs. We import only natural, organic and high quality foods. It seems to me your brother's honey, from bees exposed to nothing other than wildflowers in mountain meadows, is ideal. If he doesn't mess with the purity of the honey, we will buy all his output."

"That would be incredible!" says Lara. "But please listen to me on a very important point, you do not have to do this for me."

"Relax, when it comes to business, I am purely business. I *am* looking for pure, clean, old fashioned, natural, healthy, foods that have no hormones and are not genetically modified. Do you know what one of the ironies of that search is? One cannot find that in advanced economies. They all are so far down the road with their 'advanced' agriculture that it is difficult to say what is what. But, excuse me, the more backward countries, and Armenia is definitely backward in that respect, have a huge advantage. Their soil and water and air have not yet been corrupted, even if their politicians can put the most corrupt people elsewhere in the world to shame."

What does he want? Thinks Lara. If he helps me with the shelter, and imports Avo's honey, we won't just go our separate ways and forget each other. Is that what he wants? To what end?

"So, I'll import Avo's honey without hesitation. But let me tell you this: If he deviates even one millimeter from the quality specifications that we have, we'll drop him so fast that he won't know what hit him. Now do you believe that I am not doing this for you? It is just business."

Lara is impressed. She had never thought of her village as Al Barmaka described it. Clean soil, clean water and air, dirty homes and stables, corrupt politicians. So at least there still is something worth holding on to, something that is pure, in this country.

"I believe you," she says.

"There is another point, which I have been debating whether I should even bring up. Avo thinks the oligarchs cannot harm his honey business, but the same man who manipulates the import duties can also manipulate export taxes. Do you have export taxes in Armenia?"

Every trace of optimism escapes from Lara's expression.

"I don't know," she whispers, "but even if there aren't any now, they'll slap one on right when we start exporting."

"Stop," says Al Barmaka. "It won't matter to us, because we're willing to pay top prices if the quality is how I described. You tell your brother that. Let him secure purity. That's worth more than the honey itself."

They drive in silence for a while, each lost in thought. Al Barmaka seems to be absorbed in the countryside. He stares out of the window, at the agricultural fields and orchards, he sees farmers tilling the land with ploughs pulled by oxen, he sees irrigation systems of a kind that are long gone in Dubai, with hand dug canals manned by farmers, redirecting the water with shovels, a system replaced by automated sprinklers in the Gulf more than thirty years ago. He sees a dark brown, rich soil, instead of the desert sand, and rivers and creeks cascading by the side of the fields. To his right, he sees the ever-present two peaks of Mount Ararat, keeping watch over everything.

They reach Surenavan, a small town along the road where Laurian always stops to buy fruits and vegetables from stalls lined up by the roadside. There isn't much in early May, but they find some apples and pears kept refrigerated from last year and some fresh vegetables grown in green houses. These roadside stalls would be full of fresh fruit starting in June, when the legendary apricots and cherries ripen, and all the way from July to early November, when every other fruit and vegetable comes into season.

In the spring, Surenavan has another attraction. It is the favorite nesting place of the storks. They are all over, filling the sky with a joyful commotion that conjures homecoming, because they are building their nests.

On top of telephone poles, poplar trees, rooftops of barns. Huge white birds with black and white wings gliding gracefully and descending with new twigs.

"They raise their chicks here, and then migrate in the fall. But they always return home in the spring," says Lara, pointing to the nests.

They pass Yeraskh, go around an ill-kept circle in the road, and start to climb up the mountain.

"That leads to Nakhijevan," she says, pointing to the right, "that's where Edik's ancestors come from."

"Really?" asks Al Barmaka surprised, "then why didn't he settle there?"

"It's a long story, Ahmed. The bottom line is, that thanks to someone called Joseph Stalin, Nakhijevan is no longer part of Armenia. I'll let Edik explain that to you later if you're still interested."

Al Barmaka looks at Lara, and then at his surroundings, in amazement. This is history in the making, he thinks. Wherever he has travelled through Europe and Asia, he has encountered a lot of history, but everything there is *settled* now. History has somehow slowed down, if not stopped altogether. After hundreds of years of wars, today France is France and England is England and Germany is Germany. But Armenia is not Armenia. Not yet. Nothing is settled here. History has not yet come to a stop. In all his travels, he has not seen anything like this, except of course in the Middle East, but even there, he has not been to the unsettled parts personally.

"You look so handsome when you're deep in thought," says Lara, with her mischievous smile.

"*Habibty.*" Al Barmaka makes a superhuman effort to control his urge to reach for her and kiss her passionately. Then he looks away, to the incredible layers of mountains unfolding in front of them, a watercolor symphony of purple, azure, green, and a hundred shades of each of those colors, across mountain after mountain in an unending chain clear to the horizon.

"In the beginning were the mountains," he says.

"We are our mountains," says Lara, and tells him about the Monument in Stepanakert, the capital of Nagorno Karabagh.

క్ క్ క్

Carla's study has turned into a war room. She presides from behind her desk, wearing a black pantsuit and white shirt. Her hair is short, recently cut. She wears no makeup, nor any jewelry. Her feet are not on the desk.

Yuri and two other men sit on the sofa and side chairs facing her. The other men do not look like Yuri. They look like the typical bodyguards kept by oligarchs—big, muscular, with clean-shaven heads. They don't feel at ease. They sit straight and stiff, unsure where to look and how to behave. One of them, named Ari, works for Carla. He's one of the two men that she's assigned to Yuri. He is the bodyguard that accompanied Yuri to Stepanavan to talk with Hov. He has a round face, with dark brown eyes and bushy eyebrows that seem to twitch every time he turns his head. Ari's here because he has killed before. He is one of Ayvazian's old soldiers, whom Carla has seen with her father several times. He is also another one of the lovers she's known in the past seven months, although she has not required his services in the bedroom as regularly as she's called upon Yuri.

The other, Samson, is new. He is one of Yuri's recruits that Carla approved without meeting him. His resume, as described by Yuri, was enough. He is one of LeFreak's top security men, assigned to the prostitution and trafficking part of the business. He's been with LeFreak for less than two years, initially based in Georgia, and recently relocated to Yerevan. Before that, he was in Moscow for some ten years, but Yuri does not know what he did there. It cost a lot of money to have Samson change sides, but in the end, it was not the money alone that pushed him over the fence. It was his lack of confidence in LeFreak's ability to manage the trafficking business properly. He also has a round face, but thinner than Ari's, and his eyebrows are so light that they are barely visible. He does not seem to have a neck, and Carla tries not to stare at how his chin seems to perch directly on top of his chest, and his earlobes hang low, almost touching his shoulders.

For the time being, the team seems coordinated enough, with Ari as the soldier, Yuri thinking of himself as first officer and of Samson as second officer, and all three accepting her as the commander. For Carla, having that power is exhilarating.

"Do you have the exact date of the meeting?" she asks.

"May 20. In two weeks. At twelve noon."

"You're sure LeFreak will be present?"

"Absolutely. He's called the meeting." Samson answers her question, but looks at Yuri.

"How many people will attend?" Carla knows the answers to most of her questions from prior reports from Yuri, but wants to hear directly from Samson. She feels the direct questioning reconfirms her status as boss, and speaking to him gives her a reason to look at him, still amazed at how his head sits directly on his shoulders without the slightest hint of a neck.

"Four, excluding me. Five altogether."

"Yuri has told me about the two options," says Carla, "but I want to hear your take on both. I understand you prefer one over the other."

"The bomb is too risky. It will rouse suspicion of an inside job. People will question why I left the room before the explosion. Besides, why kill all four, when we just need to get rid of LeFreak?" Samson knows that Yuri favors the bomb option, but he has not been able to present any convincing arguments. It is messy and unnecessarily complicated.

"The other option is a sniper hit when we're all in the room. They never catch snipers. A bomb will leave too many clues behind."

"Yuri?" asks Carla.

"Both are fine," says Yuri and shrugs. "I don't feel strongly one way or another. But maybe we want it to look like an inside job. I don't mean raising suspicion about you, Samson, but an inside job by someone who is not present at the meeting. That way they won't suspect us."

"I'll be the prime suspect. I'd be leaving the room before the explosion," says Samson.

"They may suspect you, but they won't be able to prove anything," says Yuri. "We'll arrange for someone to call you with an emergency, and you'll leave to take care of it. Everything can be documented. Your story will hold up."

"But why?" asks Samson. "If there was a benefit from blowing up the entire floor and killing all four, I'd say let's take that risk. But we gain nothing, and we lose three experienced men."

What neither Carla nor Samson knows, is that it is Yuri's plan to also get rid of Samson. Only Samson can plant the bomb in the room, so he needs him for that. But then, instead of him walking out and detonating the bomb from a safe distance, a second detonator will set off the bomb while Samson is still in the room. The risks and the threats will die with the human targets of the operation.

"Tell me how the sniper option would work," says Carla.

"The meeting is in one of their safe houses right outside Yerevan. He has the top two floors of an old building. They use only the tenth floor. He keeps the ninth empty so as not to have close neighbors. Below that live some poor families. He has a separate, locked elevator. No one without a key can get to his floors, because the staircase entrance to the ninth floor has an iron door, and it is also locked. The tenth floor is entirely refurbished, with wide windows overlooking the gorge." Samson stops for a minute and looks at Carla. He has never planned an operation like this for a woman before. She sits completely still, staring at him with ice-cold eyes.

"There is only one building nearby," continues Samson. "Some fifty meters away, also ten stories high, facing his, and from the top floor and the roof one can see directly into the meeting room. I have been there once to check it out for security. There is easy and direct access to the roof. Nothing is locked, and the elevator goes all the way to the roof. There are two apartments on each floor of that building. An old couple lives in one of the apartments on the tenth floor, the one that does not face LeFreak's building. The apartment facing LeFreak's building is empty.

"LeFreak rarely draws the curtains during meetings. The two side windows don't have curtains. A sniper on the roof of the facing building can take him. LeFreak usually sits in the large armchair facing the window, and he likes to stand up and pace once in a while. When he paces, he always goes and stands by the window. Even if for some reason the curtains are drawn, he opens them while standing there."

"I agree that the sniper option is cleaner, let's go with that," says Carla. "I want Ari to be the sniper. You take him to the roof of that building and let him study every detail. Then I want to see the exact plan. We'll meet again before the 20th." The three listen, nod and wait.

"You will each receive one hundred thousand dollars," continues Carla. "Work as one team. If anything goes wrong, no matter whose fault it is, none of you gets paid. On May 20, when it is done, you'll get half of your payment. A month later, if none of you is arrested or under investigation, you'll get the balance. If any one of you gets in trouble with the law in that period, none of you gets the balance of the pay. Are the rules clear?"

They look at each other first, then at her, and they nod.

"Good. Let me know when you're ready to show me the precise plan."

When Yuri leaves the meeting, he is convinced that someone is coaching Carla. How did she come up with that on her own? The one hundred thousand each, told to all three together, is unusual enough. But fifty when the job is done and fifty a month later if no one gets arrested? The only reason she'd add that condition is to ensure that the men do not undermine each other. Does she suspect him? Or perhaps she knows something about Ari or Samson that Yuri doesn't.

Yuri wonders if Ari and Samson are resenting the fact that he will get paid as much as they are, when he is not doing much. In fact, now that he has found Samson, his role is technically finished. Carla could have told him that she'd take it from here, and worked with Samson and Ari to plan and execute the operation. Why then was he in the room? Why is Carla, who is careful to fairly reward contributions to the business, giving him the same reward as the others, and letting them know about it?

Whatever it is, Yuri is now more convinced than ever that Samson has to somehow become a victim of the operation. He needs a new plan. A new plan without Carla's knowledge and approval will cost money. He'll have to pay the cost of getting rid of Samson. Yuri decides that at least part of his one hundred thousand would be worth spending on eliminating Samson. Chances are that Samson, if he stays, will end up running Carla's operations and costing him a lot more.

Chapter Twenty-Nine

I t was cloudy and drizzling when we left Yerevan, and Edik was worried that we might get rain in Vardahovit. "For me," he said, "any time of year, regardless of the weather, it is perfect up there, but for a first-time visitor on a day trip, I want a bright sunny day so you can get the full experience."

He must be relieved, because by the time we take the Getap junction road, the skies clear up.

"In around ten minutes," I tell Ahmed, "we'll pass through some typical villages. Poor and undeveloped, these places are in miserable condition, but I don't think their fields have seen any contaminants like agricultural chemicals."

"You're lucky to have a friend like Edward," he says, out of the blue, as if he did not hear my last comment about the villages.

"I know. He's a very good friend, but what made you think of that now?"

"I did not think of it now. I've been thinking about it since I met him. He's a good man."

"I knew you two would end up becoming friends the minute you called him 'Edik Jan.'"

"I want to tell you something, Lara, which probably should wait until we sit on that bench of truth and redemption. But I will not wait. The truth is, that I do not have a lot of friends. All the socializing that I do is with family members. All my other interactions with people are for business. I have many business associates, fellow board members, trading partners, employees, some loyal, others not so loyal, but no friends. Isn't that something?"

"I don't have a lot of friends either," I say. "Aside from Edik, there are only three people that I would consider to be my friends, in the sense that I would go out of my way to help, and that I trust. That's it. Four friends."

"You're only eighteen and you have four friends, that is something. I'm thirty-five, and I have none. There's a big difference."

"Have you ever felt the need for friends?" I ask. "I mean, your family is so extensive and tight, that maybe it has made friends redundant for you."

He looks at me with surprise.

"How come you know so much about me? Have I told you about my family?"

"Well," I laugh, "you've said very little. But girls talk, you know. I had a few chats with Sumaya."

He frowns at the mention of Sumaya, but says nothing.

"Ahmed, I want to ask you something, which I know is none of my business. May I?"

"About Sumaya?"

"Yes."

"Go ahead."

"When I was planning my escape, I used her. I lied about my intention to return after five days. And she helped me. She understood my desire to visit my family and my sick mother, and those were not lies, by the way. Anyway, she helped me, and she arranged for a driver to take me to Oman, she arranged all my tickets. I was feeling guilty for betraying her trust, almost as bad as I was feeling for betraying yours. But then I found out in

Istanbul that she had her own plans to send me away for good. I was supposed to end up somewhere in Russia and 'disappear.' What was that all about? Did you ever figure out the details of her plan?"

"Lara, *habibty*, you don't know how beautiful you are," he says, and I misunderstand him at first and roll my eyes. "No, listen to me, I'm not flirting with you. And that is one of the most attractive things about you. I mean that you don't know how beautiful you are. To me, that was charming. To them, that was threatening. They used your desire to visit home to scheme to get rid of you."

"Nadia was in on it too?" I've heard that she was, but I want him to confirm it.

"Yes. But let's stop talking about that. Did I answer your question?"

"Thank you, yes," I say, even though I still wanted to know what their plan was, what happened to them, what happened to Abo.

We fall silent for a long time. We reach the end of Hermon, and Edik takes the road to the right leading to Vardahovit. Ahmed's driver is not used to driving on dirt roads like this, steep, with huge potholes, and deep truck-tire ruts in the mud. We'll be climbing close to five hundred meters in just a three-kilometer stretch, with sharp curves. Had it not been for Edik leading the way, I don't think Ahmed's driver would even consider proceeding on this road. Of course Armen, who is following us, is used to worse than this.

"There's something else that I should tell you on the bench," he says, breaking the silence, "but I want to get it off of my chest before we reach Edward's place. All the women I've been with have been hired. I do not know anything else. Starting with Sumaya some eighteen years ago, and every single one since. I've paid for their time. I figured that when I decide to get married that would change, but why bother to 'date' someone in the meantime? What we've done in the past couple of days, what we're doing now, is new to me. No payment, no sex. Just being together. Just being normal. Please do not say anything. Just know that I am in totally new territory with this."

He does not realize how thankful I am that he asked me not to say anything. I wouldn't know how to respond to something like that anyway. He thinks I've had one normal relationship? If all his women have been bought, all the men I've known have bought me, including him. What am I supposed to say to him about that? Oh, Ahmed, I'm so sorry you've missed out on this great thing called a normal relationship? He thinks *he* is in new territory! After the talks of the last two days, after the deep remorse I saw on his face when I told him my story, how can he tell me this? Does he expect sympathy? Does he expect me to believe that he too, like me, has been deprived of the pleasures of a normal relationship? What a comparison, Ahmed!

But I don't like where this is taking me. Regardless of what has happened to me, he has not had a normal relationship either. My story does not diminish his. Even as I think these thoughts, something breaks loose inside of me. Ahmed loses a little bit of his charm.

Agassi opens the large iron gates to Edik's estate, and we drive in. Agassi has a new puppy, a mixed breed between *Gampr*, the famous Armenian hound best known for its ferocity in fighting wolves, and thus a favorite among shepherds, and an unknown type. His name is Cheko, and he looks more like a *Gampr* than like his mother. Cheko follows the three cars to the main house, and, recognizing Edik's car, jumps around with such exuberance that we're afraid he'll end up under the car.

It is past one-thirty in the afternoon, and everyone is hungry. We walk in through the back door, near the kitchen. Ahmed wants to wash up. Manoj and then I follow him. Then Edik leads us to the front terrace, where Vartiter has set up an incredible table.

"Sorry you had to enter my house through the back door," he says, "but check this out." As we walk out the front door, Ahmed's jaw drops. The scenery is truly breathtaking.

"This is my front yard!" Edik sounds like a spoiled kid who's just received a new bike for his birthday. But there's no denying the spectacular view that opens in front of us. A wonderland of highlands spreading as far as the eye can see. The mountain peaks are still covered with snow and the fields below are all green with fresh, lush spring vegetation, highlighted by bright purple and yellow wild flowers. "*Allahu Akbar*," utters Ahmed under his breath. That's when I know that he gets it. God is great. Only some divine presence could inspire the type of awe that nature inspires here.

We fall onto the food on Vartiter's table. She has outdone herself, if that is humanly possible. Everything except pork. Everything perfect.

"I have an interesting wine for you to try," Edik tells Ahmed. "The taste may not be anything special, but its story is. The most famous wine region in Armenia is right here, in Vayots Dzor. But this wine comes from somewhere else. There is a little town near Etchmiadzin, called Aghavnatun. Aghavnatun literally means 'home of the dove.' Do you know what dove that refers to?" Ahmed shakes his head, still seeing God's presence in his surroundings.

"That is the dove that Noah released from the ark to check if it was safe to disembark. The dove flew and the first place that it landed was on a tree in Aghavnatun. Hence the name of the village. Remember, the ark landed on Mount Ararat, and Aghavnatun is not far from Ararat. Then it returned to the ark with a green branch in its beak, and Noah knew that it was safe to disembark. Now, legend has it that Noah then came to the same spot where his dove had landed, and planted the first grape vine with his own hands. This wine, my dear Ahmed, is from the very same vines planted by Noah."

Edik is a master storyteller. He is so convincing when he tells that story that everyone expects a miracle when they touch the wine to their lips. But of course the miracle is already here, where we are. The magic has hit everyone already.

After we all take a taste of the wine from Noah's vines, Edik opens a different bottle.

"We've had the spiritual experience," he says laughing, "now let's try a really good wine." It is a bottle from his Bordeaux stock, a 1985 Margaux.

Manoj sits quietly at the end of the table, under the shade of the umbrella. The two drivers are next to him. The easiest thing to do is to focus on the food, and that is what they do. Agassi has joined the table, and sits next to Armen, and the two of them chat about their backgrounds and get to know each other.

"Ahmed," says Edik raising his glass, "I want to formally welcome you to Vardahovit. I am very pleased and honored that this opportunity presented itself, not only for us to meet, but for you to visit my home."

"The opportunity you speak of has a name," says Ahmed turning from him to me. "Lara, thank you for an incredible experience."

"Are you sure this guy is not Armenian?" asks Edik in Armenian. "Who talks like that?"

I think that's one of Edik's rare lapses in courtesy, because Ahmed knows he's talking about him. So I translate what he said, as closely as I can. To my relief, Ahmed just laughs.

"I myself am not sure that I'm not Armenian. Here's to the mountains that we are!"

244 ~~~ *Vahan Zanoyan*

Vartiter is busy freshening up the table. Empty plates are taken in and returned full, and cooling dishes are taken in and returned warm.

Ahmed stands up, walks to Manoj, whispers something in his ear and returns to his seat. Manoj talks to the two drivers, and Armen talks to Agassi. They all stand up. Agassi asks Edik if it is okay for them to go to the guardhouse for coffee, because the big guest wants to be alone with him and me. Edik nods. "Take good care of them," he says. Then the four of them go, leaving just Ahmed and me with Edik on the terrace.

"Before any of us have any more wine," says Ahmed, "I want to cover an important business matter. Let me warn you both," he adds with a chuckle, "once that matter is covered to my satisfaction and we resume drinking, I will not be responsible for my actions."

"Tell me," says Edik.

"It is about the shelter idea that Lara proposed. After hearing the story of the pig farm, I understand why Lara wants me to be involved. At the same time, I cannot accept a new commitment without being sure that I can do it justice. And a shelter for abused girls in Yerevan is so out of my realm that, no matter how sympathetic I may find myself to the cause, I cannot, with a clear conscience, pretend that I can personally do justice to it."

He sees the somber expressions on our faces, and stops for a second.

"So I have a non-negotiable proposal to you both," he continues. "I will help you set up the shelter, under my name and even under the patronage of my government, on two simple conditions. First, Lara will act as the executive director, and will run the operations of the shelter. She will be responsible for the staff as well as for who to accept as residents. She will be responsible for the budget and expenses. She will hire an assistant to handle administrative details with which she has no experience. Lara may delegate other tasks to the assistant, at her discretion, but she will be responsible to the board of trustees. I have some ideas about what the shelter should provide, but since those things are negotiable, I will not spend time on them now. My second non-negotiable condition is that Edward serves on the board of trustees, and formally represents me at all board meetings that I cannot attend. Formally, I will be the chairman of the board. But most probably you'll end up acting as my proxy at all board meetings. Finally, I will decide the monetary compensation of the executive director, and there shall be no argument about it. The board and Lara will accept whatever I propose. We'll put together the board later, a good mix from Armenia and the Emirates; the total should not exceed five people, so we need only three others. I suggest that they be women, but that too is negotiable, and we have time. The members of the board of trustees will not be paid for their time, sorry about that, Edward," he says with a smile and stops.

Edik and I look at each other for a minute, trying to read each other's reaction before speaking.

"I'll do it," he says. "I accept all your conditions that deal with my role." Then both men look at me.

"Ahmed, thanks for accommodating us like this, and for your confidence in me, but no one takes an eighteen year old girl seriously in this country. Even with your sponsorship, we'll have to deal with government agencies, and with the police department, to make sure the shelter receives the necessary protection. I will have neither the credibility nor the authority with these people to do the job of executive director."

"You will have the confidence of the board of trustees. That is all you need. We'll give you all the high-level backing that you need. You will also enroll in accounting and management courses at the University. In the meantime, my office will provide you with technical support to handle the accounting and budgeting tasks."

I look at Edik, and he nods and then says, "In practical terms, Lara is right. Her assistant should carry the necessary credibility with the authorities."

They wait for my nod. But my head is buzzing with a million practical questions—staffing, finding a house, creating accommodations for the residents, the logistics of everyday needs, security, finding the victims and convincing them to come to the shelter... I must be frowning, because they notice the angst on my face.

"This is way, way over my head," I whisper.

"It seems that way now," jumps in Edik. "But it actually is not as daunting as it seems. We need to hire a few key people at the beginning and we need to find a house, preferably a large old house with five to six bedrooms that can accommodate two to three beds per room. You have to think of a full time psychiatrist, someone to manage the kitchen, and of course security. The shelter will need a car and a trustworthy driver. Ideally, the driver should have a room on the same property as the house. These are the basics. You'll think of everything else on the job."

"You sound like you've given this some thought," says Ahmed happily. "Perfect. Lara, all you have to do now is give me an answer. Don't let the details distract you, they can all be sorted out later."

"How long do I have to commit to?" I have never had any responsibility of this magnitude. Come to think of it, I've never really had any normal responsibility in my life. At sixteen, I moved straight from Saralandj into Ayvazian's web.

"Lara, look at me," says Ahmed. "It's me you're talking to. Do you really think I'll ever make you stay somewhere and do something that you no longer want to do? Tell me, do you?" I shake my head. "Then stop worrying about how long. Right now, you're the most qualified person I know for this."

"Why? What makes me so qualified to run a shelter? I've never even seen one!"

"Okay, I'll tell you why. First, trust. You had a chance to take the money yourself, and you turned it down. I will not worry about you misappropriating any funds. Who can we trust more with three million euros than someone who could legally have taken it but offered to use it for this cause instead? Second, you've been there. Yes, you have not run a shelter before, but that kind of experience can be hired. All the required technical skills that you don't have can also be hired. Even influence with the authorities can be hired. You have experience in something much more valuable—you've felt the pain of the girls we're trying to help. You are credible. That, we cannot hire. Third, you may be eighteen, but you're more thoughtful than a fifty year old. You'll figure this out."

"I couldn't have said it any better," exclaims Edik, jumping to his feet. "Lara jan, stop fighting this. You're in."

"Fine," I say, but my voice is shaking slightly. "I'll do it."

"How far is this bench?" asks Ahmed and jumps up so suddenly that Edik and I burst out laughing.

"I'd say around twenty minutes, if you get used to the rough terrain quickly," says Edik. Then he turns to me, "Lara, do you remember how to walk there?"

I nod.

"Then I'll let you two go there alone, if you don't mind. I want to wrap up a few things here before we head back to Yerevan," he says and winks at me. Edik's consideration seemingly has no bounds.

"Edward, may I then be rude and ask for a bottle of wine and two glasses to take with us?"

"By all means," laughs Edik. "You have the right idea."

It takes us closer to forty-five minutes to get there, because Ahmed stops to study every shrub and flower. I try to explain to him as much as I remember from Edik, the poplar forest, the wild fruit trees, the bears, the rosehip bushes, how most of the wild plants are actually edible, and the villagers gather them and cure them.

In the last fifty meters the path passes very close to the ravine.

"Be careful," I tell Ahmed, imitating Edik, "walk exactly where I am walking. The grass can be slippery around the edge."

"Yes dear." I am leading and he does not see me smiling, finding this entire experience utterly ironic, an incredible twist of fate. The desert has come to the mountain; my captor is witnessing the very symbol of my liberation.

We get to the bench.

"Oh my God...." Ahmed cannot express it in any other way.

He opens the bottle and fills the two glasses. He looks at me, leans over and kisses my cheek, and lifts his glass to me. Without a word, we drink, and stare into the horizon.

I don't know how long we sit in silence. One loses a sense of time here. Sometimes, I even lose a sense of the bench itself, and get the sensation of floating into the vast space beyond.

Then I hear his voice. It is even, low and steady, but it resonates.

"I apologize for all the grief that I have caused you." He is still staring into the endless ruche of valleys and mountains, as if he wants them to witness his apology. Then he turns to me. "I cannot undo the past. But I won't repeat it. And you'll have your shelter. You have my word." I realize that this is how he has resolved the heart wrenching remorse that I saw on his face in the restaurant in Dzaghgadzor. As I accept his apology in my heart, a huge weight escapes from my chest and is swallowed by the void under our feet. I turn to him and gently kiss his cheek.

Chapter Thirty

It has been a few days since Al Barmaka left. It was not an emotional farewell, because Lara and he both were trying to avoid one. There were practical matters to go over, such as the honey trade and the shelter. Al Barmaka covered them again, telling Lara that it may take a few months before he could sort out the legal issues involved with the villa.

"The most important first step is to register a foreign-sponsored charitable organization," he told Lara. "Then you'll have to open a bank account in its name, so I can transfer money, which I'll do in stages. You, Edward and Manoj will each have signatory authority. Have you thought of a name?"

"Not yet. I've asked Edik for ideas."

"Don't delay. You need the name to start the registration process."

Al Barmaka then told her about her salary. "I have done some research on salaries in Yerevan, and I have decided that the salary of the Executive Director should be four thousand dollars a month."

"No one makes that kind of salary in Armenia, least of all someone working in a charitable organization. What type of research did you base that figure on?"

"Remember my non-negotiable condition. No arguments. That is the salary. When the bank account is opened, you will receive automatic payments every month. So don't delay. And don't delay finding a house."

In spite of the seemingly unemotional and business-like goodbye, his visit has left a deep mark on both of them. The absence of any sexual approaches by Al Barmaka during the three days was a relief for Lara, who still cannot tolerate physical intimacy with anyone. More importantly, it made her believe that perhaps it *is* possible to kill the past. The awkwardness of the memory of their three-month sexual relationship (which seemed to haunt Lara a lot more than him) notwithstanding, the time they spent together was meaningful and consequential in ways that would take each of them a while to understand.

Al Barmaka boarded his plane carrying with him two revelations. First, the phenomenon of friendship beyond family and beyond business. And second, as a bachelor who's fought to stay that way, the phenomenon of a romantic relationship with a woman whom he has not bought for sex. In the frantic pace of his everyday life, focused on business and multi-million dollar deals, with the little time that could be spared devoted to family and political obligations, he had missed out on both.

He has also made two decisions. First, he would stop the practice of retaining concubines. He'd send the Chinese girl back home, and stop the search for a manager to replace Sumaya. He is thirty-five years old, tired, and finally ready to settle down. Just as Lara managed to return home, he'd return too, and finally do the right thing within his family culture. He'd find someone and get married within the next few months. Enough of the wandering outside of the boundaries, he tells himself, and is surprised that instead of fighting the prospect of coming home, he is relieved by it.

The second decision he's made is that he won't wait for the final settlement of the Palm villa's status to open the shelter. Contrary to what he told Lara, 'uncomplicating' things in Dubai is not that simple, especially when it comes to seizing a foreign owner's private property. He can succeed in tying things up in court for years, to make sure that the Ayvazians don't get access to it. But outright confiscation, even with a legal basis, is far more complicated. So he will cover the costs of the shelter from his personal funds. Over time, if he manages to have the villa appropriated, he'll reimburse himself. If not, he'll write it off.

Although Al Barmaka is amazed at how profoundly this visit has affected him, the revelations and his decisions feel like they were meant to be, and their time had come. The changes that they augur for his life are fundamental, but they are also changes that he feels he can accept without any hesitation or regret. It is almost as if everything was ripe for these changes to occur, and the last few days simply gave them a nudge.

Lara tries to get back into her routine. Anna is a priority, given the appearance of her photograph. In fact, things have become even more complicated. During one of her lunch breaks in the back room, she puts on her eyeglasses to read a newspaper. They are not the thick-rimmed glasses in the photo, but Lucy walks in and sees her with them on. She looks surprised, but tries to hide her surprise, or so it seems to Anna. Anna claims that she kept looking at her all afternoon. Random, passing glances, but pointed and purposeful at the same time.

Before leaving Yerevan, Laurian meets one more time with Anna and Lara. It was a beautiful day, and they walk around the Swan Lake in central Yerevan, spend some time watching Arno Babajanyan's statue, the musician's flying hands and fingers casting their long shadow over the large stone piano, then they sit on a bench soaking up the sun.

Laurian tries to convince Anna to quit her job.

"Don't even wait until you find another job," he tells her. "If you're really that worried about Lucy, get out of there. I'm not saying this to scare you more, but for your peace of mind. Don't worry about money. I'll cover you until you get a new job."

Anna shakes her head. She cannot accept money from Laurian, and she's not sure how long it will take to find a new job.

"I'll start looking for a new job right away," she says. But both Laurian and Lara know that given her hours, it will be difficult to look while working at the store. Laurian does not press her any further.

He leaves them and walks back to his hotel to pick up his car and drive to Vardahovit.

ℒ ℒ ℒ

Yuri is stunned when he sees the photographs that his informant hands him. He kicks himself for not starting the surveillance much earlier. It cost him very little to have someone follow Lara and document everyone that she met with. He always considered her to be an important loose end in their search for Ayvazian's operations. He stares at the first day's crop of twenty photographs with amazement. He usually doesn't have much use for the Internet, but he turns on his laptop and Googles a name. After half an hour, he chooses four pictures out of the bunch and goes straight to Carla.

"I saw this man in a restaurant in Ashtarak a few weeks ago," he says pointing at Laurian. He was there with another man. I knew I had seen him before somewhere, and when I entered the room I got this eerie feeling that they recognized me. But I could not remember where I had seen him. When I saw this picture, I remembered that I had seen him in Arshaluys newspaper. He had given an interview about events in the Middle East or something like that. His name is Edward Laurian. He is a Swiss investigative journalist of some international fame. There are thousands of Google entries under his name, with a lot more pictures, the news stories he has written and some interviews. In one of his interviews, he talks about his house in Vardahovit. Do you know where that is?"

Carla just looks at him, waiting for him to explain. She does not like being asked rhetorical questions. She's also thinking, this better be important, because she is not amused by the way in which Yuri barged in and started talking.

"That's just twenty minutes from Sevajayr, where your father and my brother were killed. Now, look at this lovely girl sitting at the other end of the bench. She is none other than Lara Galian, whose father, as we know, also found his demise in Sevajayr. She's not only stunning, but must also be very smart for managing her escape from Dubai."

Yuri now has Carla's attention. She takes the picture from his hand and looks at the three people sitting on the bench at Swan Lake.

"Do you have close-ups of their faces?"

"That's what the other three pictures are." Yuri drops them on the coffee table. He wants to tell her who the girl in the middle is, but he waits.

Carla picks Lara's close-up photo first and stares at it for a long time. She can now clearly see what all the fuss is about. Either her father or

Viktor, or most probably both, surely raped her, she thinks. She fantasizes about sleeping with her herself. What an incredible turn of events would that be? Right in front of the picture of Martashen hanging in her study.

Then she studies Laurian.

"He is a Diaspora Armenian?"

"Yes. According to one of his interviews, his ancestors are from Nakhijevan."

She studies Laurian's face carefully, while the basics replay in her mind: Swiss investigative journalist, with a home in Vardahovit, twenty minutes from Sevajayr. Laurian's face is slightly tilted to the left, and he looks like he is talking. She picks up the picture of the three on the bench again, then back to the close-up of Laurian, and she figures that he is talking to the girl in the middle. She starts with the top of his head, isolating each segment as she studies it—hairline, forehead, eyebrows, eyes, bags under the eyes, nose, cheeks, lips, mouth, chin.

She then picks the third picture.

"Who's she?"

"And that, I was saving for last," says Yuri. "That one works at one of your stores. The one off Abovian. Some trio, wouldn't you say?"

Carla studies the third face. Something about it troubles her. Her mind makes a quick scan of all the women she's met recently, but nothing comes up.

Then, almost on a whim, she asks: "Do you still have the picture of the wife of that snitch of yours?"

"I think so," says Yuri checking his wallet. "Here it is. The one on the bench is much better looking."

Carla covers the eyes and forehead in the old picture and studies her nose and chin. She looks at the close-up, doing the same. She then looks at the eyes in the old picture, trying to disregard the thick rims of the eyeglasses. Then she covers everything on the close-up except the eyes. She turns to Yuri.

"I'd give it eighty-twenty odds that they're the same girl," she says. "Show this close-up to your snitch, and he'll tell you for sure one way or another." Then she starts looking at Lara's picture again.

Yuri cannot decide which is more shocking—finding Hov's wife at the store or Carla's incredible skills of observation. She had seen the old picture of Anna only once, for just a minute or two. How could she make the connection, almost ten days later? A chill runs down Yuri's spine. What else is Carla observing?

"On second thought," says Carla, "I don't like the looks of this. I'd keep the snitch away from his wife and away from the Galian girl. You keep your distance too. Until we figure out who the Swiss really is, it would be stupid to go after either. We have enough on our plate."

Yuri hates instructions that seem whimsical and arbitrary. He can appreciate the risk that Laurian poses as a friend, or even as just an acquaintance, of the girls, but Carla's style of first telling him to show the picture to Hov and then ordering him not to frays his nerves. She may have sharp skills of observation, and she may have observed many of his own thoughts, but she is an inexperienced, horny woman and she is ordering him around, changing her mind and her instructions at will, without even a second thought, as if turning the wheel of a car right then left just because she can.

The merits of her reasoning do not matter to Yuri at that point. He doesn't want to take orders from her any longer.

♉ ♉ ♉

Yuri decides to turn Ari first. Hov is less important and can wait. He invites Ari to an expensive restaurant on Amirian Street. He has reserved the last table to the right of the kitchen to have more privacy. This will be a serious talk. A lot will be determined tonight.

Ari arrives on time. Yuri has a bottle of vodka open, and has already ordered some appetizers—fried frog legs, imported from France, arugula salad with prosciutto and dried beef, and a plate of mixed cheeses. Yuri stands up to greet him. He has to put his best foot forward tonight and win over this crucial asset, who he knows is loyal to Carla.

Yuri has done his homework. He knows that Ari has worked for Ayvazian for over fifteen years, twice as long as he has. His main activities have been in Moscow and Yerevan. Anastasia has told him, based on a vague recollection, she suspects that Ari might have met Nicolai. She could not be any more specific than that. Nicolai remains an enigma for Yuri, but he hasn't had the time to focus on him yet.

"We have a better chance than at anytime to make it really big," he tells Ari, lifting his glass. "That is what this evening is all about."

Ari smiles, and downs his vodka. Yuri refills the glass.

"Here's to a new era," he toasts.

The waiter brings the appetizers and divides each order between them. Ari devours the frog legs instantly, using his hands, sucking on them until nothing but the thin white bones are left on the plate.

"To a new era," he says, lifting his glass. He wants an excuse for another shot of vodka.

Ari then attacks the prosciutto and dried beef, taking forkfuls of the arugula as well.

"They say it doesn't matter how tall your grandfather was, you have to do your own growing," says Yuri.

Ari has no response. He keeps eating.

"We used to have some pretty tall grandfathers," continues Yuri. He is talking fast, as if worried he'll lose Ari's attention soon. "But now the Ayvazians are dead, and soon, thanks to you, LeFreak will be dead too. The arena is wide open for new leadership. It is our turn to grow tall."

Ari listens, but he has no respect for Yuri. His thick hair, thin body, and manners that seem too soft to Ari, are objects of ridicule and mistrust. Ari is an old fashioned soldier—bold, big, muscular and bald. He is a killer, and the best in the field. He does not do nor trust 'slick'. And Yuri is nothing but slick. But he listens, more carefully than Yuri realizes.

"The Ayvazian operations are in a mess," continues Yuri. "I went to Dubai recently, and found that everything Sergei built there is in the hands of an old pimp, a woman, and is disintegrating fast. Moscow is lost to some guy that I've never heard of, even though I was based there for eight years. He just walked in and took over. LeFreak has made a mess of the Lori operation. And here we are, still working as if Ayvazian is running the show."

"But an Ayvazian *is* running the show, isn't she?"

"Is she? Let me ask you this, would Sergei have gathered us in a room and offered each of us one hundred thousand for the LeFreak job? Is it right that I get the same as you, when you're doing the job? Is it fair that even Samson gets the same as you? Besides, would Sergei ever let us know what each of us was going to get?"

Ari lifts his head from the table and gives Yuri his first direct look. His eyebrows twitch and his eyes narrow, to focus better. "Go on," he says.

"The point is, that right now Carla isn't much better organized or qualified to run the sex business than LeFreak. The only difference is that she has experienced people around her, us, and LeFreak doesn't. But if we follow her every order, what good is our experience?"

Yuri lets Ari mull that over. He refills their glasses, raises his to Ari and downs it. He starts to eat, while Ari, who has already finished his plate, waits for more food to come. His huge hands are on the table, his fingers almost twice as thick as Yuri's.

"Which of her orders you'd rather not follow?"

"If you were running things, how would you plan and execute the LeFreak job?"

Ari shrugs.

"Okay, let me tell you how Sergei would have done it. Aside from what I already said about the money, Sergei would have taken care of Samson along with LeFreak."

Ari's eyebrows do a dance, rising half way up his forehead and falling back to the bridge of his nose.

"Don't look surprised," says Yuri. "Samson is a long-term liability to us. Once we pull this off, he'll be looking around for a better deal. He changed sides once, right? Why not again? Besides, we know very little about him. Two years with LeFreak, but where was he before that? What was he doing in Moscow? He won't talk about it. So Sergei would use his knowledge to plan the operation, but would make sure he goes away with LeFreak."

"How?"

"If we go the sniper route, he'd tell you to take two shots. Shouldn't be difficult, they are in the same room, they'll probably be so taken by surprise by the first shot that you'll have good fifteen-twenty seconds to pull the trigger on a second target. If LeFreak paces the room as Samson says, you choose your moment when he's passing by Samson, and do one after the other within two or three seconds. Those would be Sergei's instructions to you. And he'd pay you at least one-hundred-and-fifty thousand, if not more, and you definitely won't have to wait a month for the second half of your payment."

They bring the main course. Yuri has ordered the entrecote for both of them. It is a large steak, topped with grilled mushrooms and onions, and there's a plate of fries for them to share. The timing is perfect, because Ari does not want to respond to Yuri quite yet, and he turns his full attention to his plate. Yuri notices that his eyebrows move up when he opens his mouth to take a bite, and twitch a little while he chews. The man could look quite comical, but if you know what he does for a living, it won't be easy to see him as a comedian, no matter what his eyebrows do.

"I need to study this," says Ari after a while. "First I need to see the room from that roof."

"Of course. When you go up there, you can ask Samson where everyone usually sits."

"How will you get me one-fifty if this works?" asks Ari, ignoring Yuri's last comment.

"I'll give you half of my share," says Yuri without hesitation.

"But she may not pay either of us, if she takes Samson's death as something that went wrong."

"She will, Ari. If LeFreak is dead, she will pay us. Besides, we'll be saving her the extra hundred thousand that she was going to pay Samson. She'll be happy, she'll pay."

෯ ෯ ෯

Yuri's next order of business is to have Hov come to Yerevan. He cannot take the time to drive up to Stepanavan again, which is a two hour drive each way, and does not have anyone he can trust to take Anna's picture to him. Besides, he wants to be there to assess his reaction.

He plans to make Hov his first personal recruit. When he finally gets some money of his own, he'll pay Hov's salary himself, without telling Carla. Things are finally beginning to look up. LeFreak will be gone soon enough, hopefully with Samson, Ari and Hov will work for him, then he'll claim Ano's operation in Dubai, and the villa. After that, it will be time to figure out who Nicolai is and put him in his place.

It takes Hov a few days to secure a one-day leave to come to Yerevan, on the pretext of having to visit a sick relative. Yuri decides to meet him in the outskirts of town, in Proshyan. He will meet with him in his car and send him back right away. If this Anna is his wife, Yuri does not want the risk of having him linger in Yerevan.

He directs Hov to drive to the cemetery, where they have the best chance of being alone. There is a direct road from Ashtarak Highway, which, although it passes through the small town, is relatively quiet. Hov gets there a few minutes before Yuri, and parks his white Lada by the cemetery entrance. Yuri parks his black Mercedes SUV behind him, and signals him to come over. Hov gets in the passenger seat and, unlike at their last meeting, shakes Yuri's hand.

"Thanks for driving all the way," says Yuri. "I won't keep you long. Do you know this person?" and he hands him the close-up of Anna's face.

Hov's face lights up.

"You found her!" he exclaims.

"She looks nothing like the picture you gave me," says Yuri.

"I knew she'd have different eyeglasses, but I never thought she's cut her hair, especially this short. Where is she?"

"Not so fast, Hov, I'm afraid this is a bad time to go after her."

"Why? What's the problem?"

"She doesn't know that she's been discovered, and I know exactly where she is, and can follow her every move. So you don't have to worry about a thing. But right now, there are much bigger problems to resolve."

"When?" asks Hov, uninterested in Yuri's explanation.

"Not long at all, I'd say around May 21. And I may have an added bonus for you at that time. Now go back and continue doing what you've been doing. By the way, she's changed her last name."

"Just don't lose her." Hov isn't interested in her name change either.

Chapter Thirty-One

t is Friday. I have class this afternoon, from three to five-thirty. I'm in my usual late morning routine, having had coffee and a light breakfast in the kitchen and returned to my room, when Edik calls.

"Have you seen the news?" He sounds out of breath.

"No, what's happened?"

"LeFreak is dead. Do you have a TV there?"

"Diqin Alice has one."

"Watch the First Channel. It is interesting."

I turn on the small TV in the corner of the kitchen to Channel One. It shows a crowd gathered in front of a building. The police have barricaded the entrance and are keeping reporters away.

"The police don't have much to say at this point," says the announcer, "but our sources say that this was a professional job, with a high velocity rifle. Mr. Aleksyan was shot once in the base of his head. One of our sources, who spoke by telephone with someone who was in the room at the time, says that the entry wound is barely visible, which makes some experts speculate that it may have been a six-millimeter slug. A police spokesman said that the shot most likely was made from the building adjacent to where Mr. Aleksyan was holding a meeting."

"They moved pretty fast," I mumble to myself.

"There were four others in the room when Manvel Aleksyan was shot. No harm has come to any of them." They show the faces of the others who were in the meeting. Lara does not recognize any of them. "They will take the body to the coroner's office first and then to the home of the deceased. Mr. Aleksyan is survived by his widow, a fifteen year old daughter and a ten-year old son," says the announcer.

There is a sudden commotion in front of the building. The camera shows a group of reporters running toward a woman. "Mr. Aleksyan's widow has just arrived," says the announcer. The camera tries to focus on the woman, who's screaming hysterically and trying to enter the building. "It does not look like the police will allow her to go up to the crime scene. We'll provide regular updates on this late-breaking news as soon as we have them." And the announcer moves to other news.

I turn off the TV and call Edik.

"This was fast."

"Gagik is working on the next phase. I hope it turns out to be as easy as this was. I'm coming down to Yerevan. I'll call you later." Edik hangs up.

For the first time it occurs to me that the walls of my room are gloomy. They are totally bare, and their old, grey color is depressing. The paint is chipped in several places, and there are a couple of places where even the plaster is coming apart.

I tell Diqin Alice that I will repaint my room a lighter color, a soft cream, with a white ceiling, and that I want to redo the bathroom, and also, at my own expense, upgrade the kitchen. She looks surprised, and a bit concerned.

"Lara jan," she says in her shaky voice, "why go through all that trouble, *bala jan?*" Diqin Alice calls me *bala*, meaning child. My father sometimes called me *balés*. My child. I love to be called by these names: kurig, balés, bala… they all have a homey ring to them.

"I don't know," I say, which is the truth. "But do you mind? Everything I do will be an improvement and will add value to your house."

"Ha jan," she says, "go ahead if you really want to."

I'm surprised at how excited I am about this. I want to make this room mine, even if it is temporary. I want a brighter room, pictures on the walls, nicer curtains and a few items of memorabilia on the small table in the corner. I have not felt this need before. I want a little bit of Saralandj here. And how I'd love to have a picture of Sevajayr. Edik has so many beautiful pictures that he's taken. One or two could grace these walls.

Edik has decided on a different business formula to help Avo. He has proposed a partnership, rather than an outright loan, to kick start the honey business. I was impressed with the way he explained it to Avo.

"Let's be very clear on the business arrangement," he told him, looking dead serious. "I am not lending you this money. You do not have to return it. Here, I am taking the risk with you. Fifty percent for the capital, fifty percent for the labor. What that means is that I put in the money, you put in the labor, and we own the business fifty-fifty. If it goes bust like the pig farm, you owe me nothing. If it does great and makes millions, half will be mine. Do you understand the new arrangement?"

"Sure I do," says Avo with a chuckle. "You want me to do all the work and give you half the profits."

"Exactly," laughs Edik, "do you understand why?"

"Because you have money and I don't." Avo is doing his best to give Edik a hard time about this.

"No, Mr. Entrepreneur, that's not why. I deserve half the profits because I am taking a risk giving all the capital to you, and trusting that you will not blow it, and I expect to be rewarded for taking that risk. It is so easy to take risks with other peoples' money, isn't it? If we lose everything, you don't lose a penny, you just lose the time and effort that you put into this. I, on the other hand, lose everything I put in it. Now, do you understand why *you're* the lucky one in this deal?"

"Maybe, but you'll have the best honey ever produced in the history of mankind," laughs Avo. "As much as you can eat, for the rest of your life, for free. Tell me who's the lucky one now."

This is an unusual way to seal a deal, but it is sealed, and even a divine intervention could not make either side renege on anything that they agreed. If I have any role in this venture, it is to assure both of them that Ahmed's promise to buy the honey is good enough to take to the bank, and, in my humble opinion, it is probably the most secure aspect of the venture.

I no longer wonder about Ahmed and me. That alone is a huge relief. Now I know that the sexual part is over. He will go his own way, and he'll expect me to do the same, even though I still cannot tolerate even the idea of intimate contact with any man. I now admit to myself that perhaps, under very different and special circumstances, Ahmed could have been, may have been, and perhaps would have been, an exception, but that is entirely academic at this point, and I am relieved and happy that that prospect is no longer in the cards. I am amazed at how many lingering issues Ahmed's visit resolved. I hope that it did the same for him.

I do not own a computer yet, but Edik has lent me one. He showed me how to connect to the Internet, using a special access code. I'm sure that the code costs money, which he is covering. The purpose is to research the various shelters that already exist in Armenia.

I am amazed at how many are here and in operation, including some recently opened. 'Mer Doon,' which means 'Our Home,' based in Etchmiadzin, opened this year. According to its site, it houses girls who are dismissed from the orphanages at the age of eighteen, and have no place to go. That is my age. Imagine me sheltering girls my own age. Then there is 'Houso Aygi,' meaning 'Garden of Hope,' in Yerevan, that shelters young girls from underprivileged families. There is Orran, which takes a different approach. It gathers the children begging in the streets of Yerevan and gives them schooling, three hot meals a day and a nurturing environment. The children who end up at Orran are ideal targets for traffickers. Then I see something more unusual. There is a shelter created and run by UMCOR, some church in America that I have never heard of, nor can I pronounce their name, but here they are, with a shelter for sexually abused and exploited women in Yerevan.

Every one of these organizations is in a constant struggle to raise funds to keep their operations running. Together, they have saved hundreds, if not thousands of lives. I, on the other hand, have been promised a budget which is probably larger than what these organizations work with, yet I have hesitated, and even now I waver about whether I can meet the challenge.

I make it my first order of business to visit these organizations. I start calling them and making appointments. It is not easy to explain who I am and why I'd like to visit them. Some are rightly particular whom they allow into their premises. They offer to meet me elsewhere first, to get acquainted, before inviting me to tour their home.

I'd love to take Anna with me on as many visits as her time allows. She may consider living in one of these places until we figure out her situation. Lucy's reaction upon seeing her with her glasses on has not stopped worrying her.

I turn on the TV one more time before leaving. The First Channel no longer covers LeFreak. I flip though the other channels. Shant has a music show on, Kentron has an interview with a writer, but Armnews is doing a special feature on LeFreak. I watch with some interest as they talk about his business achievements, while the screen shows his mansion, and the camera moves around the fence that Avo had to paint. The announcer lists some of his charitable contributions, this time showing the church that he built. That's another farce that any oligarch worth his salt cannot do without— building a church. Armenia must already have more churches and monasteries per person than any other country on earth, and they keep building new ones. Edik says if they want to spend on churches, their money would be better spent on renovating some of the old masterpieces.

I wait a few minutes for updates on the police investigation, but the program continues recounting LeFreak's life story. I turn the TV off and leave.

I take the bus to Vartanants Street to look for paints and plaster for my room, and to talk to someone about installing a water heater and a new sink in the kitchen. After about an hour, I take the bus to the University.

𝔏 𝔏 𝔏

Ahmed calls. I give him a brief report, both about Avo's progress and about the shelter. The conversation is businesslike, like it was when he left. He does not call me *habibty* once. I am relieved, and yet feel an unusual sense of loss. It is unusual because the sense of loss is sweet. A past that no longer haunts can be warm and comforting.

"What do you think of '*Apastan*'?" I ask him. "It means 'Sanctuary' in Armenian."

"Go for it. I'll have Manoj come over to register it as a foreign-owned charity. But you have to prepare everything in advance. He won't be able to stay more than a day. Hire a lawyer. He'll get paid as soon as we transfer the funds. And don't delay finding a house."

"I'll do my best, Mr. Chairman."

But Ahmed, typically, has already hung up.

Chapter Thirty-Two

Ari knocks on Carla's door and enters. She's on the maroon sofa, her bare feet resting on the coffee table. She looks good: trim, self confident, not pretty but handsome in a strange way that Ari finds appealing. He has known her for a long time, since she was in her late teens. She had once asked Ari to talk to her father about letting her into the business. Ari had smiled, and then ignored her.

Now she sits there in a white blouse and black leather skirt, with a stone-cold expression. Her new role suits her. Ari wonders if he did the right thing by not talking to Sergei on her behalf, but he never liked interfering in other people's family affairs. Besides, given the nature of their business, he knew that Sergei would throw him out. And yet, he watches as Carla walks into the role as if she had been in it all along. She is devious, intelligent, and she has a subconscious that works overtime on figuring out people long after her conscious mind rests.

After their first time together, Carla tells him about one of their henchmen whom she had asked to come over to see her.

"Something just didn't seem right about him," she tells Ari, who's lying in bed wondering how on earth he could have done what he just did with the dead boss's daughter. "It's not that he was nervous," she says casually, as if talking to an old classmate, "they all are nervous when I call them in the first time. There was something else in the way he talked and the way he looked at me, it was almost as if he was avoiding something. Anyway, I did not think of it again. When I woke up the next morning, I knew instantly that the man had turned. I could see him, as if I was actually in the room myself, taking money from LeFreak. I told Yuri to watch him, and sure enough, two days later he told me the man had turned."

"What did you do?" asks Ari.

"I had him beaten till his mother could not recognize him, then let him go. Wasn't worth the risk killing him."

Ari might have assumed that she'd tell a story like that as a warning to him, but he didn't. He believed that she was telling the truth.

She has slept with him twice. Ari was uncomfortable the first time, enjoyed the second time very much, and has been looking for a third time since, but she never called. Today he is happy that he had a reason to call and ask for a meeting.

"I'm glad you're here," she says, taking her feet off the coffee table and sitting up straight. "I was going to call you myself today. Sit down."

Ari takes the seat next to the sofa.

"That was very well done, Ari. I'm sure you know that already."

"Thank you."

"I hope you have not told the others about our arrangement."

"Of course not," says Ari dryly. She shouldn't need to ask him that.

Carla takes a thick envelope from the coffee table and hands it to him.

"That's your first hundred thousand," she says. "You'll get another envelope like that in two weeks. Once again, the others cannot know that I made a separate deal with you."

"You don't need to either remind me or ask me again if I've told anyone." His eyebrows twitch.

"Now, you said you had something to tell me?"

"Don't trust Yuri." Ari does not like to use a lot of words. The very process of talking is cumbersome to him.

"You have to tell me a little more than that," says Carla. "Speak up, Ari, I know not to trust him already, but I want to know what you know."

"He thinks you have no experience and we should not follow your every order. He says you'll run the business into the ground."

"That's all?"

"He wanted me to shoot Samson too. He offered me half his fee to do it. He is angry that I didn't."

"That son of a bitch!" Carla, visibly angry, stands up and starts pacing the room. Ari watches her tight leather skirt, buttocks moving invitingly, but half his brain remembers Sergei. He used to get mad like that, except he'd scream till his face turned red. She stands in front of him, legs apart, hands on her waist, breasts heaving, and is about to throw a tantrum, when she controls herself and sits down.

"So," she says with a calmer voice, "he wants to run his own operation behind my back. Now Ari, I want you to answer two questions for me. First, why did you refuse to do what he asked? Second, why did you decide to warn me about Yuri?"

Ari shrugs. "He's not one of us," he says, as calm and casual as one can be. "I don't like him."

"Is that the answer to both my questions?" she asks.

Ari shrugs and nods.

"And Samson?

"He is okay. Should be watched, but is okay."

"And me?" she asks, "am I one of us?"

"You're Sergei's daughter," says Ari, averting his eyes, "and I like you." His eyebrows twitch.

"You like me, eh?" she says, enjoying making a man more than fifteen years her senior nervous. "We both need to calm our nerves a bit, and we have something to celebrate. How about a cognac?"

Ari nods.

She fills two snifters and returns to the sofa, crossing her legs. She puts them on the coffee table, and taps the space next to her. He gets up and sits next to her on the sofa.

"Here's to a well executed mission," she says.

"Thank you," says Ari and takes a big gulp.

"And this," she says raising her glass again, "is to a new friendship. You will not regret what you did today, Ari. Here's to you."

"Thank you," he says again.

"Now, how about you show me exactly how much you like me?" she asks, standing up and taking his hand. Ari follows her to the bedroom, unable to keep his heart from racing.

Ari is past forty-seven and generally old fashioned and conservative. He has a wife, who knows very little about what he does, and two teenage boys. His tastes are simple, and he does not like to indulge in sexual activities that diverge from the essentials. He makes up for some of his prudishness by his strength and stamina, but still, neither his looks nor his performance do much for Carla. That is why she has not asked him back for so long. But today is a special day. She wants to seal his loyalty and their new alliance.

"You said Yuri was angry," she says when he's done. "What did he do?"

"He asked why I didn't shoot Samson." Carla is amazed at how nondescriptive the man can be.

"That's it?"

"Yeah, but he was mad."

"What did you say?"

"I said I could not get a good shot. He was way in the back of the room."

"Was he way in the back of the room?"

"No." And Ari and his eyebrows smile one of their rare smiles.

"How do you think I should deal with Yuri?" asks Carla, even though she has already made up her mind.

"He'll be trouble. Get rid of him." Ari wants to get up and get dressed, but finds the moment awkward.

"Get rid of him? How?"

"There is only one way to get rid of someone." He gets out of bed. He finds it surprising that he feels shy walking naked in front of Carla. He starts to get dressed.

"There is no way to put him to good use?"

"Maybe there is, but he will always be trouble. Get rid of him."

"I want to do this myself, but you will set things up for me." She does not sound like she is making a request; this is a new order.

Ari nods. "Thanks for this," he says patting the envelope. "I have to leave now. Let me know when you want me to set things up."

𝒫 𝒫 𝒫

Just when things were beginning to look up, Yuri finds himself with a deflated morale. Ari's non-compliance is one thing. Maybe Samson was beyond his sights, as he says. But for two days now he and Hov have been waiting for an opportunity to snatch Anna, with no success. The ideal location and time is when she comes off the bus at night on her way home. Her building is in the outskirts of Yerevan and relatively isolated. She does not have to walk far from the bus stop to her building, just three blocks, but the street is badly lit and usually deserted. They can grab her in that stretch, throw her in the car and drive away. Before she can scream more than once, they can gag her. All other options that he has studied are much more problematic.

The problem is, the past two nights have been unusual. The first night the Swiss journalist drives her and the Galian girl and drops them at the entrance of their respective buildings. The second night, two other people get out of the bus with Anna, and walk in the same direction. This has never happened before as long as Yuri has had her under surveillance. Hov has to hang around in Yerevan for a third day to try again, but his absence is already causing him a lot of trouble back in Stepanavan, especially given the assassination of LeFreak.

He is tempted to have Hov quit his job and move to Yerevan to work for him, but Carla has not paid him his fifty thousand yet. That is another major source of frustration. She has been too busy to see him. Yuri is livid. How can the horny bitch be too busy? Doing what? LeFreak is dead, and she is too busy?

It is the third night that he and Hov stake out Anna. He has parked his Mercedes SUV around the corner from the bus stop, in a spot where there is no streetlight. Hov is with him. The bus comes around every half hour until nine o'clock. They cannot be sure when Anna will arrive, but they know she leaves work at seven, so it is unlikely that she'll get there before eight. Eight, eight-thirty and nine are the only real possibilities. They have arrived ten minutes before eight, just to be on the safe side. Waiting in the car with Hov is demeaning to Yuri. He considers himself so much higher in the chain of command that it is painful to sit there with him and make small talk. But he cannot leave this one to him alone. Not yet.

At eight twenty his phone rings. It is Carla.

"This is an emergency. Meet me at the park near the Monument in twenty minutes."

Yuri is at the other end of town. It will take him at least thirty minutes to get there. And he is so close. Anna may appear on the next bus, in just minutes.

"There's no way I can be there in twenty," he says. "What is the emergency?"

"Yuri, I have no time to explain. You have to get here, in twenty or sooner. I don't care how you do it, just do it." And Carla hangs up. She sounded rushed, but not distressed. If she had been distressed, Yuri would have assumed that she is in some type of trouble and ignored her call. But what could the emergency be? He waits a few minutes, the tension killing him, and then turns to Hov.

"We have to call it off," he says. "Something's come up. Go back to Stepanavan tonight, before your colleagues begin to get suspicious. I'll call you when we can try again. She's not going anywhere, I assure you."

Hov is so mad that he punches the dashboard of Yuri's car and slams the door on his way out. How did I lose so much respect so fast, wonders Yuri. Hov drives away burning rubber. Yuri sits there for a minute and shuts his eyes. There is no reason for so much frustration, he tells himself. We got rid of LeFreak, Anna can wait, Carla finally called and wants to see me, I'll get my first fifty grand soon, maybe even tonight, so what is so bad about any of this?

When he lifts his head from the steering wheel and opens his eyes, he sees the bus leaving the station. He drives around the corner and sees Anna walking alone to her apartment building. Within minutes, she's inside the building, and the motion-detector lights at the entrance hallway turn on. He watches her as she calls the elevator and gets in. The elevator doors close, and a few minutes later the entrance hallway lights turn off again. It is total darkness in the building and in the street. Yuri starts laughing out loud and drives toward the Monument.

Carla meets him at the entrance of the public park, where Yuri hasn't been since his childhood, when his mother used to bring him for the rides.

"Park your car and get in mine." She is calm, but hurried, giving the impression of a real emergency.

"We may have a little problem," she says as she drives away on the main road. "His name is Samson."

"Samson?"

"The police have him. One of my sources tells me that he may be getting ready to talk. He may tell them how LeFreak was killed in exchange for amnesty. Ari is following the situation. In the meantime, I want you to talk to the source yourself."

"How did they get Samson?"

"Beats me. He was head of LeFreak's security. Someone has tipped the police off that this was an inside job, so the head of security is the first suspect."

"Someone has tipped the police?"

"It looks like it. We don't have all the details yet. But if Samson talks, we're all in trouble."

The scheme that Carla has devised is cleverer than Yuri realizes. The story about Samson is a lie, but it makes Yuri feel vindicated that Samson turned out to be a liability, just as he thought, no matter that the liability played out differently than what he had envisioned. He will now look into Ari's eyes and enjoy seeing him squirm. That is exactly what Carla wants Yuri to think. She cannot have him getting suspicious about where she is driving him.

"I always thought that Samson would be a problem in the long run," he says. "But I did not think we'll face it so soon."

"What kind of problem in the long run?" She has to keep his mind occupied for ten more minutes. They are already almost out of Yerevan. Yuri keeps talking about his suspicions, but she concentrates on the road. She has driven on Azatutyan Avenue until Tbilisyan Highway, and then on Yerevanian street towards the town of Abovian. Before entering Abovian, she takes Kotayk Street towards Nor Gyugh and then Kotayk, and makes a right toward Akunk. She stops the car in the middle of the deserted road between Kotayk and Akunk.

Yuri stops talking, and looks around him. It is dark. There is only a quarter moon, giving just enough light to cast mystical shadows everywhere.

Then, out of nowhere, Ari appears by his side and opens the door of the car. He has a gun in his hand.

"Step outside," he says.

Carla is out and around the car, standing next to Ari. She also has a pistol, with a silencer.

"What the hell is this?" Yuri's voice and hands start to shake.

"Step outside," repeats Ari, and reaches for his arm. Yuri tries to free himself, but Ari yanks him with such force that he stumbles and is nearly thrown onto the road.

"Let's go for a walk," says Ari, pushing him forward.

"Carla, what is this all about?" screams Yuri, and, to his horror, wets himself.

"Just walk," says Carla, adopting Ari's style of talking in short phrases.

They lead him to a grove of fruit trees. Ari has to push him several times to force him to move forward. Around twenty meters inside the orchard, they stop. Carla approaches him, the pistol primed in her hand.

"You chose the wrong person to mess with, Yuri." She walks behind him, aims her pistol at point blank range at his head and pulls the trigger. She is amazed at how simple it is. A kick from the pistol, a whoosh from the muffled shot, Yuri drops to his knees and then folds over, his body sprawls awkwardly on the ground, and it is all over. Done. Problem solved, liability removed, hundreds of future headaches averted. Aside from the exhilarating feeling of the kill, she feels nothing. No remorse, no regret, not even a sense of pride for having pulled this off. It is exactly as she imagined it would be when she was practicing.

She nods at Ari. They walk back to their cars and drive away.

Chapter
Thirty-Three

Edik sounds frustrated. "I can't finish it," he says. "I have one verse, but I cannot complete it."

"What are you talking about?"

"I've had this unfinished poem for seven months now. I have one verse written. I wrote it right before we met in Sevajayr. I can't finish it."

"Tell me the first verse," I say, hoping to be helpful.

"No!"

"If you cannot write it, maybe there isn't more to write."

"When did you learn to talk like that? Or have I asked you that before?"

"You've asked me that before, and, forgive me for saying this, but it is not the most intelligent question that you've asked me."

"Okay," he says, and I can hear the disappointment in his voice. "But it was easier for me to write before I met you. You are distracting me."

The problem is that Edik does not sound like he's kidding. It is not always easy to tell over the phone, but his voice is not light. He is serious.

"I will call you *Khev Edik* from now on."

"Then *Khev Edik* it is."

"I was kidding."

"So was I, but only a little."

"My Papa used to say there is a little joke in every joke. Meaning most jokes are meant to say something serious."

"Your Papa was right, Lara jan. Jokes are just a way to lighten up a serious subject."

"Okay, what other serious subjects do we need to lighten up with a joke?"

It feels great to hear him laugh. This conversation has been unnecessarily tense, about a subject that, at least for me, should not cause so much stress. I like his laugh.

"I take it that we don't have any other serious subjects," I say.

"Not every serious subject can have a fitting joke. Try to come up with one about Carla."

"If I understand correctly, Carla is a joke in her own right."

"Then you do not understand correctly," he says, his voice dead serious. "There is nothing funny about that character."

"Are we still on for Saturday?" I want to get off the phone and go back to Vartanants Street to look for more paint options. "Either way I need to go to Saralandj this weekend to look at Avo's plans for the beehives. I'll give Ahmed an update next time he calls."

"We're on. I'll try to come down on Friday evening, but it may be too late to meet. We'll leave Saturday morning. We need to confer about the next phase."

"See you Saturday, Edik jan."

That evening, he calls back.

"I have to ask again if you've seen the news."

"Now what?" He's out of breath again like last time.

"Yuri was found dead near Kotayk. I missed the news on TV. But there is a story with his picture on Arshaluys.am. Check it out. I need to talk to Gagik. We obviously need to revise phase two." And he hangs up.

I turn on my laptop and check the Arshaluys site. There it is. The story is titled "Murder in the Orchards." There is a picture of Yuri lying under a tree with a bullet hole in his head. I'm surprised the newspaper could get their hands on something like that. Next to it is another picture of Yuri in a suit, looking like a rich playboy. There isn't much information in the text. Just one paragraph saying the farmer who owns the orchard found him in the morning and called the police, and that the investigation has started, but so far the police have no leads. There is no mention of Yuri's association with the Ayvazians, and no information on his family or occupation.

Phase two of our plan was to have Yuri, and subsequently Carla, implicated in the LeFreak murder. We would arrange to give the police an anonymous tip about Yuri, claiming that he was seen with some of LeFreak's men and had been in the vicinity of the building the day of the murder. The police would have to investigate and bring him in for questioning. It wouldn't be difficult to uncover his relationship with the Ayvazians. Both Gagik and Edik thought that it would be more credible if the police arrived at the Ayvazian connection themselves.

Now Yuri's dead and the plan to implicate Carla in LeFreak's murder is dead with him. I can almost hear the confusion in Edik's mind.

I get to Edik's hotel earlier than usual on Saturday morning. We're out of Yerevan before nine o'clock, which is not easy for either of us, but we have too much to do in Ashtarak and Saralandj.

"Our problem is that we're in the dark," he says. "We don't know exactly how they pulled off LeFreak's murder. We need to have much better intelligence if we're going to eventually get to Carla."

"Or, maybe we should just let things run their course. It looks like a round of score settling has started. I like where things stand. Let the gangs keep each other busy."

"Not bad," he laughs. "Just sit back and watch them kill each other. But Lara, the mystery is killing me. Don't you want to know who killed Yuri? Don't you want to know how they killed LeFreak?"

"That is one important difference between you and me. I don't have to uncover every detail. They're both dead. That's enough for me."

"I don't believe you," he says turning to look at me. "You must be curious. Maybe not as much as I am, but curious."

"Sure, I'm a little curious; but I wouldn't go so far as setting up an intelligence operation just to satisfy my curiosity. One day, we'll know."

We arrive in Saralandj around ten-thirty. Avo has moved the dining table out to the wide, covered balcony across the front of the house. It will be possible to have meals here for at least five months, until the cold hits in mid-October. The removal of the table and ten stools has opened up a lot of space in the second room. They can now cook, do laundry and bathe more freely than before.

It is a beautiful day, sunny, warm, with a mild breeze. All the fruit trees are in full bloom. The cherry and apricot trees at the front of the house are especially heavy with blossoms; it is almost impossible to see the branches through the thick clusters of white and peach flowers.

Sona makes us Armenian coffee and joins us on the balcony, placing a plate of pastries on the table, made by her future mother in law. She looks better than I've ever seen her. She has plucked her eyebrows and has put on some light eye shadow. She has a red scarf around her neck, which makes her features stand out. She is pretty, and she looks happy.

"Sona, you're shining!" I say. "Is that a new scarf?"

"Yes," she smiles. "From Simon. It's silk."

"*Vay*, Sona jan, it's beautiful." I am so happy to see her like this, blossoming, content, looking forward to her wedding in just a couple of weeks.

She turns to Edik. "Paron Edik," she says bashfully, "we're taking your advice. The wedding will be in Ohanavank. Simon and I hope that you can attend."

"Your baby sister here calls me Edik. You are older, and are calling me Paron? If you drop the Paron I promise to be at your wedding!"

"*Shat lav*, Edik," says Sona, blushing.

Arpi and Alisia are inside busy preparing lunch. I walk in to say hello, and they too seem to be excited for Sona.

"Arpi, you're next, you know," I say hugging her. She seems even more reserved, shy, and distracted. She gives me a faint smile, but says nothing.

"Are you still reading Raffi?" I want to hear her say something.

"I finished."

"All ten volumes?"

She nods, and smiles shyly.

Alisia dances around as she goes about doing chores in the kitchen.

"Yeah," she butts in, "now you better hurry up and find someone who reads like you; I'm not waiting for you very long. What would it look like if your younger sister got married before you, eh? You'll immediately become an old lady." Alisia's laugh is contagious.

I hear Avo's voice and walk back out. He gives me a hug.

"Where are the boys?" I ask.

"I've given them some work to do in the garden. They'll be here by lunchtime."

"You have no conscience, Avo," I say, mocking him, "making your younger brothers work on a Saturday."

"It's good for them," he says. "They work well together. They've turned into a real team, and if I try to help them, they ask me to leave them alone!" He laughs.

Avo sits down and puts three sheets of paper on the table, with scribbles and random-looking notes all over them. It is his business plan.

"Is Gagik coming?" he asks.

"A bit later. Why don't you start," Edik then turns to me. "After the business plan, we need to talk about other plans. Can't do that with the family around. Maybe we can go somewhere else."

"A full hive costs around 40,000 dram," he says, pointing at some numbers on one of the sheets. "That's around one hundred dollars. I was initially thinking to start with one hundred hives, but maybe we should start with two hundred, given the interest from Dubai. We should also have empty hives handy, because it is possible to get new queen bees each year from each hive. The empty ones cost around forty-five dollars."

I notice Edik focused on Avo's notes. There is no apparent logic to them. There are random entries, some written sideways in the margins, some circled in the middle of the page, some with small letters, some large. I can't tell if Edik is studying the content, or the doodles.

"The maintenance costs are relatively small," continues Avo. "The largest is transportation. To maximize output, it is important to move the hives at least three times per year, usually higher up the mountainside. At higher altitudes flowers bloom later in the season. This can cost three to four dollars per hive. But it is worth it. Beekeepers here do not do this regularly, partly to save on cost and partly because they are lazy. But they average around eleven kilos of honey per hive. If you move them regularly and take good care of the hives, you'll get twenty five to thirty kilos per hive!"

"Avo," I interrupt, impressed by his newly acquired knowledge. "When did you study all this?"

"I talk to people," he says smiling. "And Aram got some books on beekeeping from the Aparan library. There is even a beekeeper's association in Armenia, but I have not contacted them yet. Domestic honey prices are much higher than international prices. I mean there is a *huge* difference, around double. That's why we don't export much."

"I'm surprised imports haven't killed local production," says Edik.

"The market here is too small," says Avo. "Small producers cover their local markets. You don't really have a national market. So importing gets complicated, because the most inexpensive foreign producers apparently are interested in large markets where they can export hundreds of tons per year. They cannot do that here."

"So do you want to focus on the local market?"

"No way," says Avo. "We'll sell some here, but the secure market will be the export route. Even if the price we get is lower, it will be more stable."

"What's the upshot, the big picture?" asks Edik.

"If we start with two hundred full hives and two hundred empty ones, we need an initial capital outlay of twenty nine thousand dollars. Plus the first year setup and moving costs, and the cost of a used extractor, say thirty thousand dollars in all. If we do this right, we'll harvest five thousand kilos the first year. We can sell five to six hundred kilos locally, at a minimum of seven dollars per kilo. We export the rest for around four dollars. So gross revenue the first year should be around twenty-two thousand dollars. We'll have around a dollar a kilo operating cost, so net income the first year is seventeen thousand dollars, or, more than fifty percent of the capital cost."

Avo is pointing at these numbers on his sheets as he talks.

"In the second year we should have double the hives, and so double output and double the income. The net total at the end of the second year will be over fifty thousand dollars," and Avo stabs his forefinger at a circled figure at the bottom of the page.

Gagik arrives ready to start talking about Yuri. But we tell him he has to wait. First the honey business, then lunch with the whole family, then the four of us will go somewhere to talk. I see the briefest shadow of disappointment pass over his eyes, but in a second, it is replaced by a wide smile, and his eyes regain their luster.

Sago and Aram arrive from the garden covered with mud; they wave hello and go to wash up. They're full of energy, talking non-stop and joking.

I remember when Avo and I were like that, playing in the fields and catching frogs in the irrigation canals. Aram returns with one of the slingshots that I had brought for him from Istanbul. I frown, but he does not notice.

"Kurig jan," he says, "do you remember this?"

"Sure I do." I give him a hug. "You haven't killed any of the neighbors' hens, I hope."

"Came close to hitting their cat once," laughs Aram. "Not one domestic animal has been hurt yet, but two dead crows testify to what a good shot I am!"

The night before I first left, I had tried to lighten the mood in our bedroom with my siblings by asking them what they wanted me to bring them back from Greece. Aram had asked for a slingshot. I remembered his request while being held in Istanbul by Abo. Abo was being very courteous. His associate brought three slingshots to me within a couple of hours. They made it back with me to Saralandj. Aram does not know the story, and probably thinks I bought them myself in Greece. All he knows is that I kept my promise. But they evoke different memories in me.

Lunch is cabbage dolma, yoghurt with garlic, and steamed Ishkhan trout. No wine or cognac, but, at Avo's suggestion, just one glass of vodka to open the meal with a toast. He pours for Gagik and Edik. Sona and I decline. He gulps down his glass with the toast, and, true to his word, puts the bottle away. Since we're sitting outside, he chain smokes, and I don't have the heart to ask him not to smoke at the table.

After lunch, Avo suggests we go for a walk instead of to a coffee shop in Aparan or Ashtarak. "It's a beautiful day," he says, "and a little mud on your shoes will be good for you."

We walk toward the village and turn right into the fields, on the dirt road that leads to two long, rectangular buildings, which are the stables where the villagers keep their animals in the winter. They are empty, since the animals are grazing by the mountainside. It is amazing how spring can transform these fields from the desolate, inhospitable winter landscape to an amalgam of life forms, full of color. It seems that every wild flower, every blade of grass, every butterfly has gone mad with joy. We walk to the stable where Avo keeps the grass and hay bales. They are almost all gone, consumed by the animals in the past winter. There are six bales of dry grass left, stacked at the entrance of the building. Avo spreads them around and we sit on them, facing each other. I can smell the aroma of spring, of fresh wild flowers and wet earth, and I do not want to start a conversation about Yuri and Carla and murders. The topic clashes with the atmosphere saturated with joy and celebration of rebirth and of life.

But apparently the men do not feel the same contrast. Gagik delves straight into the subject, impatient as always to tell us what he knows.

"I have an old friend in the police department in Yerevan," he says with a low voice, even though there is no one who can hear us. "He says they are clueless about both murders. The bullet was lodged in LeFreak's head. It was in fact a six-millimeter slug. That is tiny. It is not the usual ammunition used by snipers. Ballistics offers no leads. The police say they know of some sniper hits with similar bullets in Russia. These are professional rifles, high velocity and accurate up to around three hundred meters. So now they suspect that a Russian hit man entered the country, shot LeFreak, and left the same day. The deputy head of the team working on the case, a young detective, says it is futile to look for the killer in Armenia."

"Do you think Yuri or Carla had a hit man brought in from Russia?" asks Edik.

"Sounds a bit far fetched to me, but not impossible. Remember Yuri was based in Moscow. You never know."

"What about Yuri's murder?" I ask.

"Well, they have to think the two are related. Two murders, a few days apart, competing oligarchs... But they know nothing. Yuri has been shot at point blank range, with a nine-millimeter pistol. The bullet traversed his skull, and they found it some ten meters from his body in the grass. Again, ballistics cannot trace it. The pistol could have been smuggled from abroad. Their most logical suspect would be someone from the LeFreak team—revenge killing."

"So there's no way to pin any of this on the Ayvazian woman?" asks Avo.

"The police are not looking anywhere near her at the moment," says Gagik.

Chapter Thirty-Four

Hov does not dare attempt kidnapping Anna alone and without approval from a superior. His superior in LeFreak's organization is not approving anything. Everything has come to a halt, pending not only the murder investigation, but also the outcome of a desperate power struggle among the senior henchmen. The prevailing atmosphere is paralyzing for the underlings, who sense the chaos at the top, but have neither information nor any influence. In this environment rumors and speculation flourish.

Samson, the most senior person in the room after LeFreak, has been called a few times to the police department for questioning. As head of security, it was his responsibility to prevent what happened to LeFreak. At first his co-workers were happy to see him questioned. But then rumors spread that he is giving background information on others on the team. Everyone else who was in the room has been called for questioning once, and then released. Their account of the event has been recorded. They have signed the transcript of their testimony, and then they've been released. Samson has gone though all that too, but then he has been called back.

Hov has been told to stay put and wait. He has not been given permission to leave Stepanavan. He still gets his regular pay, but has lost the pay from Yuri and, more importantly, all hope that his continued presence in LeFreak's old organization will ever amount to anything. He now believes more than ever that LeFreak was a liability, who risked his own life, and put the lives of his subordinates at risk also. Even after his death, no one seems to feel safe. How ironic that Yuri, who warned him about that in the first place, is proven right, but has also died. This does not change Hov's determination to join the Ayvazian team.

The only person that he knows who also knew Yuri is the bodyguard that came with him to Stepanavan. He does not know his name, or his contact details, but he knows what he looks like. When Yuri gestured for him to bring over the envelope full of cash, Hov took a closer look at his face. It won't be difficult to describe Ari. Just describe his eyebrows. But Hov is at a loss about where to begin.

Then, after further stressful hesitation, he calls the number that Yuri had given him. This is the number that he used to call to give his reports about LeFreak's operations. He would call, and the person would answer *"dah."* He would ask if this was *Chicka.* The voice would repeat *"dah."* He would then quickly give a report on the latest operation and hang up. That was the arrangement. But with Yuri's death, the setup could be compromised.

Desperation can sometimes give people courage. In spite of the risks that he feels surround the old setup, he calls the number.

"Dah." It is a relief that the answer has not changed.

"Is this *Chicka?"*

"Dah."

"I want to speak with Yuri's bodyguard, the one I met in Stepanavan."

"State your business," says the voice.

"I want to meet with the bodyguard. I will talk only to him."

"Where are you now?"

"Stepanavan."

"Can you come to Yerevan?"

"I'll come if I can meet with the bodyguard."

"Meet me tomorrow at four p.m. in Zovuni," says the voice. Zovuni is a suburb north of Yerevan.

"Are you the bodyguard?" asks Hov, surprised, but at the same time chiding himself for being surprised. Of course it would be the bodyguard.

"You remember me?" asks the voice.

"Yes."

"And I remember you. See you tomorrow at four. When you reach Zovuni, wait for my call."

Hov ignores his orders to stay in Stepanavan and drives to Yerevan. He is nervous and excited at the same time. Somehow, the people he has not met yet seem to be more powerful than those he's met. The death of LeFreak and Yuri make the bodyguard look like he may be the real power, for no other reason than the fact that he is still alive. He is the constant, while LeFreak and Yuri have proven to be transitory. Maybe finally he has stumbled on the real center of power.

He parks along Yeghvard highway, the main highway into Zovuni at the northern tip of the suburb, and waits. He is early. He sits in his car and chain-smokes, waiting for the call that will change his life.

He gets the call at precisely four o'clock.

"A grey Lexus will pass you in two minutes," says the voice. "Follow it."

In two minutes a grey Lexus zooms past Hov's car. The windows are dark. He starts his car in a panic and follows. The Lexus exits the highway and heads to a secondary road towards Kanakeravan. Before reaching Kanakeravan, it stops in the middle of the road and puts on its flashing emergency lights. Hov parks behind it, his heart pounding. He feels reassured by the fact that it is still daylight. He wouldn't want to do something like this in the darkness of night.

Nothing happens for several minutes. Then finally the driver's door of the Lexus opens, and Ari steps out. He shuts the door and stands by it, staring at Hov's Lada. Hov recognizes the face and the physique. There is no mistaking him. He steps out of his car and approaches Ari.

"So we meet again," says Ari. "Now, state your business."

"I had an arrangement with Yuri," says Hov. "I know he's dead, but I want to implement our agreement."

"What arrangement?"

"He said LeFreak will be finished soon, and when he is, he said 'we will hire you directly.' You're the only person I've seen with him. And I believe I've been talking to you when I call to report. So, LeFreak is finished, and here I am."

"Come closer."

Hov takes a few more steps toward Ari.

"What would we hire you to do?"

Hov is not prepared for that question.

"Didn't Yuri tell you?" he asks, knowing that the bodyguard will not admit to anything.

"Yuri is dead. So you have to tell me."

"I want to be in the prostitution business. I have a perfect first candidate."

"I know about your wife," says Ari. "Forget it. It is too high risk."

"But Yuri agreed with me. We tried for two days to kidnap her."

"I'm glad you did not succeed. She will come with baggage. Not worth the trouble or the risk. Forget her."

"Just forget her?"

"Now pay attention," says Ari. "You cannot mix personal problems with this business. If you have a score to settle with your wife, you cannot work for us. If you're serious and want to be a real professional, maybe we can work something out."

"I'm not trying to settle a score with my wife," says Hov, but he knows he has already lost this battle. "I just think she's a perfect candidate."

"She's the furthest thing from a perfect candidate."

"Why?"

"Never mind why. Let's just say we don't want the complications that some of her friends can bring."

"Then why was Yuri keeping watch with me to kidnap her?" Hov's tone is angry and defiant.

"And look where Yuri is now." Ari's arctic tone sends chills down Hov's spine. *Could he have been shot because of our attempts to kidnap Anna? How could that make any sense?*

"What does his death have to do with kidnapping Anna?"

"You talk too much," says Ari coldly. "And you ask stupid questions. If you want to be in this business, you have to sober up."

Hov is quiet. Pride and ego are shattered. There is nothing he can say to save the moment. So he waits.

"You want to be in this business or not?" Ari sounds bored.

"Yes."

"Then go back and pack your things. I do not trust you here, with your marital baggage. I'm sending you to Moscow to meet someone. You will receive your plane ticket, and will have accommodations in Moscow. Plus you will receive two thousand dollars a month salary if we decide to keep you, which is *eight* times what you make here. But Moscow is more expensive. You will leave in a few days, as soon as I call you, for an initial meeting. When I call, you'll have a few hours to get to the airport. In Moscow, you will follow every instruction, to the letter, given to you by someone called Nicolai. His recommendation will seal your fate. I'll give you all the contact details that you need."

This is probably more than Ari has ever spoken in one stretch. But he had to get all the basics out. Hov is unable to process the new information as fast as he heard it. He has never been out of Armenia before. Two thousand dollars a month? That's probably more than the official salary of cabinet members.

"I need your answer now," says Ari, bringing Hov out of his reverie.

"I have some questions."

"Hurry up. I have to return to Yerevan."

"Who is Nicolai? What will I do in Moscow?"

"I will not answer your first question now. And Nicolai will answer your second question in Moscow. Anything else?"

Hov feels like he is shipwrecked and has nothing to hold on to other than Ari. "Nothing else. My answer is yes."

Ari takes an envelope from his pocket and offers it to him.

"Good decision. This is a down payment on your salary, even before we decide to hire you." Hov approaches and takes the envelope.

"I'll call you soon," says Ari, getting in his car. Then he drives away.

Hov walks back to his car and sits behind the wheel thinking for a long time. He checks the contents of the envelope—one thousand dollars. So a down payment is fifty percent. He starts to laugh, and immediately feels silly for laughing. He does not start the car. He does not want to drive all the way to Stepanavan, not yet. He watches the gorge of Zovuni and the meadows below. He is not sure how long he has sat on this deserted road. A few cars have passed by, but he has barely noticed. He checks his watch. It is just past seven in the evening. He starts his car and drives toward Yerevan.

Before he knows it, he is parked at the same location where he and Yuri staked out Anna. It is almost eight-thirty, and darkness has fallen on the streets. He waits, unsure of what will happen next. The headlights of a moving vehicle shine on the wall around the corner. The bus stops, and Anna steps down. He starts his car and crawls around the corner.

The bus drives away, and the street is dark again. Anna is walking in front of him. His headlights are turned off. He drives slowly toward her and then suddenly accelerates and knocks her down. He makes sure not to run over her; just send her senseless to the ground. Then he jumps out and carries her to the back seat of the car. She is in shock. She has fallen onto her face and her nose is bleeding. He quickly drives around the block and off the road and jumps into the back seat with her. He starts ripping her clothes off, and as she comes to and starts struggling, he slaps her hard a few times, sending her back into a daze. He pulls off her sweater and rips her shirt, then undoes the buttons of her pants. Her underwear comes off with the tight pants. He grabs her knees, pushes them up to her chest, and forces himself into her with such ferocity that even in her stupor her eyes open wide in shock. He slaps her again and again as he rapes her.

"So you think you can outsmart me, don't you, you silly bitch," he mumbles under his breath. When he is done, he opens the car door and kicks her out. Anna rolls out, naked, into the dirt. He throws her clothes and purse at her, walks to the driver's seat, spits in her direction and drives away.

It still gets cold in the evenings. Temperatures drop by several degrees immediately after sunset, and fall through the night. The cold ground helps bring Anna around. Her face is throbbing with pain, and she cannot breathe from her nose. She pulls herself to her knees and tries to stand up, but feels the ground spinning around her like a tornado, and sits back down. Then she feels semen flowing down her thigh, and realizes in horror that she is naked. She tries to look for her clothes and her purse.

She finds her sweater and slips it on; as it rubs against her face her nose turns into one excruciating ball of pain. She then finds her pants and slips in a leg at a time, still sitting, then pulls them up to her waist lying down, but a sharp pain in her lower back paralyzes her for a minute. She feels dirt and gravel stuck to her buttocks. She makes a heroic effort to ignore the pain and scrambles on her hands and knees looking for the rest of her clothes and her purse. She finds her shirt and underwear, then her purse. She finds her phone and dials Lara's number.

"Lara," she mumbles, her voice barely audible.

"Anna, what's wrong?"

"Please come. I'm two blocks away from your apartment." Anna's nose is full of clotting blood and her voice is so faint and garbled that Lara barely makes out what she said. She figures if Anna is two blocks from her apartment, she is either only a block away from her own place, or, if she is two blocks in the other direction, then she's five blocks away from her own place. It would save a lot of time if she knew.

"Are you between your building and mine?" she asks, keeping her voice as calm as she can.

"Yes, hurry."

"Coming. Keep your phone in your hand all the time."

Lara runs out of her apartment, flies down the top flight of stairs and calls the elevator. She almost gives up and heads back toward the staircase when the elevator doors open. She runs toward Anna's apartment. She sees her, sitting at the side of the road. She runs up to her and sits next to her. It is dark, but she can see her disfigured face and torn clothes. She does not have to ask what happened. She only wants to make sure it was not a random attack.

"Hov?" she asks.

Anna nods.

"Let's go," says Lara, helping her up to her feet. Anna feels a sharp pain in her lower back and buttocks. That's when she remembers the car hitting her. It is difficult to walk. "I can't let you go to your place like this. You're coming with me."

Lara grabs her purse and tries to put her arm around her waist to steady her, but Anna winces. She takes her arm instead, and they slowly manage to get to her apartment building. The elevator is still on the ground floor. Lara sees her in the light and for a second stops breathing. Anna's entire face is covered with blood. She holds her upright in the elevator, careful to avoid her waist and lower back. Going up the last flight of stairs is more difficult than walking on the street, but they manage.

"*Astvadz im!*" Oh my God, exclaims Diqin Alice as they enter the apartment. "*Bala* jan, what happened to you?"

"Sorry, Diqin Alice," says Lara. "This is my friend Anna. She had an accident. She needs a bath, and maybe a doctor. I will have her stay in my room tonight."

"Ha *balés*, what can I do?"

"Nothing, let her rest a little and then I'll help her bathe."

Lara calls Laurian, and hurriedly explains what has happened, keeping her voice calm and coherent.

"Just in case, do you know a doctor I can call? It is past nine o'clock, and she is in no shape to go to a hospital now."

"I'll give you a name and a number," says Edik. "I'll call him right now and explain everything. I'll give him your name and number. His name is Dr. Suren, and he is a good friend of mine."

"Thank you."

"Lara, one more thing. Take pictures of Anna, many pictures. Use your phone if you don't have a camera. Everywhere you see bruises and cuts, take photographs. Now, before she washes, and also after. Take pictures of her back and even her buttocks if they are severely bruised, don't be bashful. This will be important evidence later. We'll go all the way with this. The police cannot ignore something this serious."

"Ha Edik jan, let me go take care of her."

Lara snaps a few pictures of Anna with her phone, and then walks her to the bathroom. She brings a chair from her room and makes Anna sit in front of the sink. She washes her face as carefully as she can, softening the clotted blood with soap and warm water and then wiping it away. Her nose looks broken and crooked, and there are deep abrasions on her right cheek and the right corner of her forehead. Her head must have been tilted slightly left when she hit the ground.

There is sticky, clotted blood also in her hair, but that has to await the bathtub. She runs her fingers lightly over Anna's skull.

"Does that hurt?" she whispers.

Anna shakes her head. Lara is relieved that there are no obvious head injuries. She uses cotton swabs to clear blood from her nostrils. That is painful, but she manages to clean enough for Anna to breathe more easily.

"Let's see if you can bathe," she says, and starts filling the bathtub. A doctor will be here soon." Anna stares at her blankly.

Lara takes off Anna's sweater, careful to avoid any contact with her face. Her bra is still on, but her breasts are out of the cups. She undoes the bra and takes it off. She checks her shoulders and arms. The right shoulder is bruised, and both her elbows have deep scratches and cuts. She snaps pictures.

She gently leans her over and checks her back. There are no bruises on her upper back.

"I'll help you stand up for a minute," she says taking her arm. Anna stands up, falters at first, then steadies herself. "Let's take these pants off."

Anna reaches for the button, but Lara unbuttons the pants and slips them down to her ankles. They are full of dirt from the road.

From the lower one-third of her buttocks down to the middle of her thighs, there are black and blue and red patches.

"Sit back down," she whispers, helping her. She slips the pants off her ankles and takes off her shoes. Surprisingly, there are only light scratches on her knees. But there is a dark bruise on her left side. She looks carefully, and sees that the bruise has a vague, semicircular pattern right above the hipbone.

"Did he kick you?" whispers Lara.

Anna gives her a blank stare. Why on earth should the kick matter, given everything else that he did?

"I think so," she mumbles. "I think he kicked me out of the car, when... when he was done."

"Let's get you into the bath," says Lara. "I did not make the water hot, so it won't burn your bruises. Just lukewarm. It should feel good."

She walks her to the tub and helps her step into it. Anna winces as she sits down, and gasps for air as she reclines. Her back and buttocks are on fire. But she lies down and shuts her eyes. Lara pours water over her head, trying to avoid spilling too much on her face, and washes her hair.

Her phone rings and she jumps.

"Dr. Suren here," says the voice. I think I am at the entrance of your building. Which floor do I come to?"

Lara explains, and goes back to Anna. She quickly finishes rinsing the shampoo from her hair.

"I'll get you one of my nightgowns," she says. "We need to get you dry and in bed. The doctor is here."

Chapter Thirty-Five

Thanks to Dr. Suren's tranquilizers, Anna sleeps relatively peacefully most of the night. I borrow an old duvet from Diqin Alice, fold it in half, spread it on the floor next to the bed, and lie down on it, but sleep is elusive.

Every rape and beating that I have endured, and every horror story that I have heard from other girls returns and plays out in front of my eyes all night. Hov is gone, gotten away with what he did. The anger begins to well in my chest. It must be a Galian trait. This should not stand, my inner voice screams until it deafens me.

Dr. Suren puts my mind at ease that Anna's physical injuries are not life threatening.

"She could have been in much worse shape," he says. "The impact of the car is actually much smaller than the bruises would indicate. Scary as they look, the bruises are superficial. Had the car moved a little faster, it could have shattered her tail bone, it could have left her paralyzed for life, it could even have killed her. The car hit her under the buttocks, on the back of her thighs. Upon impact, her back jerked backward, and then her body was tossed forward, causing traumatic shock to the spinal column. Once her bruises get better, she's going to need to see a good chiropractor. I can recommend one, when the time comes."

"What about her face?"

"Her nose is broken. When I sedated her I straightened the bridge, but she'll need to see a specialist. I'll give you a name and number to call. The nose will heal. Her face will remain swollen for several weeks. The abrasions on her forehead are deep, but have not affected the skull. She may have a small scar, barely noticeable. Every physical injury will heal in time. She has to have the strength to heal herself emotionally."

He leaves painkillers, antibiotics and anti-inflammatory pills. He also gives me two other small pills. "These are strong sedatives. Give her one only if she is in a lot of pain and cannot sleep at night," he says. "These are not for regular use."

As he gets ready to leave, I ask him how much I owe him. He looks at me surprised.

"You owe me nothing, Miss Lara," he says. "I hope your friend recovers soon. You have my number. Call anytime if she gets worse or if there are any complications." And he leaves.

Then a horrifying thought crosses my mind. What if Anna did not know me? What if I did not know Edik, who did not know Dr. Suren? How many victims like Anna are there, who do not have a friend? How many die? How many are taken away, like I was, but never return? How many innocent lives are destroyed because a handful of criminals can operate with impunity? I remember Edik's story about his sister Sirarpi. There were no fatal wounds on her body, he said. She had died of repeated beatings, rapes and malnutrition. What a way for a twelve-year-old girl to die. *It should not stand!*

The idea of the shelter becomes more real as I think about this. I have not yet managed to visit any of the shelters. But I will. I still hope that I can take Anna with me.

Anna sits up and sips some tea. She has not eaten anything since yesterday's lunch, but refuses food. Her face looks gruesome.

"I am so thankful to you," she says.

"Hush, stop that talk. How do you feel?"

"My face hurts. My back hurts too, but I think less than yesterday."

"You have to eat something, because you have a few pills to take. Then I'm going to call a specialist to come and check your nose. Dr. Suren moved it back in place last night, but wants a specialist to look at it."

"I've put you through so much trouble, I'm so sorry."

"Anna, stop that. We still have a lot to do to sort things out, so you can't say something like that at every step." I smile encouragingly and go closer to check her nose. "At least it's not crooked like before," I laugh.

I help her walk to the bathroom. She freezes at the sight of herself in the mirror. She had not seen herself since the incident, even though she had been to the bathroom.

"You'll be prettier than ever. All this will heal and go away," I say, hoping that it's true. "Will you be okay alone in there?"

She nods. I shut the door behind her and go to prepare breakfast. She walks out after ten minutes, still looking shocked.

"How can I go to work looking like this?"

"You're not going to work for a while," I say. "I will ask Dr. Suren for a medical slip. The store will continue paying you, at least for a few weeks while you're on sick leave."

"I need to call and let Lucy know," she says, panicked. "She needs to find a substitute."

"We'll call. The store isn't even open yet. Come sit. You have to eat something."

I have some warmed up bread, honey and cheese on the table. She finds chewing laborious and painful. But she manages to get something in her stomach.

"I have to go to my place," she says. "I need to get some clothes, check things there."

"We'll go, don't rush," I say. "I want your nose looked at first. I'll go get clothes from your room. The doctor said you should not move too much until the chiropractor checks your back. 'She should not walk or go up and down the stairs unless it is absolutely necessary,' he said."

I give her an anti-inflammatory pill and a painkiller, and she goes back to bed.

Edik calls in the early afternoon. "I'm downstairs," he says, "Can I come up?"

I check on Anna. She is still in bed, but is beginning to stir. I have gone to her place and gathered some fresh clothes for her. No girl would want to be seen by a man in her current condition. But I know Edik has a lot planned, and is anxious to see for himself what I've been telling him.

"Give me a minute," I say. "I'll call you back."

I wake Anna up. "Edik wants to talk to you," I say. "I have your clothes here. Come, put these on."

"How can I see anyone looking like this?" she says in panic.

"Anna, it is okay. This is Edik. I *want* him to see you like this. Believe me, if I were you, I wouldn't mind it. It is really okay."

She still argues with me about being seen 'like this.' I ignore her. I lay her underwear on the bed. "Get dressed," I say. "He'll be up soon." And I leave to tidy up the kitchen. I return to the bedroom and help her with jeans and a sweatshirt with a wide-open collar. "I'm going to call him," I say. "Go comb your hair."

Edik does his best to hide his reaction. Showing alarm only increases their anxiety, he explained to me later. We sit at the kitchen table.

"I have spoken with Thomas Martirosian," he says. Anna looks confused, as if she does not remember the name. "Your lawyer," says Edik, "the one who's been working on your divorce. We will give him a signed account of the events of last night, along with some pictures of you. He will file a formal complaint against Hov with the police."

"I don't want to file a complaint with the police," Anna whispers.

"Anna, don't be silly. You have to do this." Edik is shocked, but he knows that most domestic violence cases do not get reported.

"I just want him to leave me alone."

"Then you have to file the complaint. In the very least, Martirosian will get a restraining order, so if he ever comes near you again he will be arrested. He'll also push forward the divorce papers. If we're lucky, Hov will also end up in jail, but I am not optimistic about that, given similar cases."

"Why wouldn't he go to jail for what he did?" I ask.

"Because we may not be able to prove that it was him. He'll deny it. It will be his word against Anna's. I didn't think to ask you to postpone Anna's bath until after Dr. Suren had seen her. He could have taken a vaginal swab, which would leave no doubt as to who raped her. Anyway, the judge will meet us half way and issue a restraining order, but he may not go as far as arresting him without proof."

Anna sits there, hands shaking.

"In the meantime," says Edik, "don't go back to work, and don't sleep in your apartment. We'll have to look for a new place for you. Still close to Lara, but a different place."

"Why don't I leave my place too," I say, "and we'll find a two bedroom apartment to rent together."

Anna's eyes light up, and she tries to smile. "Really? We can do that?"

"I'm sure some of these apartments have two spare bedrooms to rent out. We'll find one."

Edik questions Anna and takes notes, going over details of the incident. He spends some time on the identity of the attacker, reiterating statements testifying that she saw his face clearly, heard his voice, and that there could be no mistake about his identity.

"You couldn't have seen the person driving the car when it hit you," he says. "You probably were in shock and couldn't be one hundred percent sure of the identity of the person who then threw you in the back seat of the car. It was dark, after all." He notices that Anna is getting agitated.

"I am one hundred percent sure who threw me in the car," she says curtly.

"Anna, bear with me, these are the types of questions that his defense will throw at you. They'll make a convincing argument to the judge that it was dark and you were just hit by a car and had smashed your face on the hard ground. Now, inside the car, when he was raping and hitting you, you obviously had a clear view of his face from up close. They will still argue that it was dark and you were in shock, but their argument will be less convincing. I want to make sure that your testimony sounds plausible. Because if there is one sentence that does not sound reasonable, the entire testimony will lose credibility."

He works with her for over an hour, taking copious notes. Then he questions me as well, from the point where I went to get her. "I'll pass these on to Martirosian," he says at the end. "He'll draft the statement for your signature. Then we'll add Dr. Suren's report and the photos, and we'll have a pretty strong case."

On his way out, Edik leans over my shoulder and whispers. "I need to see you alone. It is urgent. Can you leave her for a few minutes and come down with me?"

I take Anna back to my room and go with Edik. We sit in his car. He stays quiet for a while, and I wait, watching him. He looks tired.

"You were right about something," he says at last. I wonder what I could have been right about. I don't recall saying anything about Anna that would make him say that.

"You remember how I was complaining about being in the dark, and you said let's sit back and watch how things play out?"

"You mean after Yuri was killed?"

"Yes."

"What does that have to do with Anna?"

"Nothing. I'm not talking about Anna. When I was waiting down here for your call, Gagik called. Carla is the prime suspect in Yuri's murder. She hasn't been arraigned yet, but is under house arrest until the police investigate further."

"Whoa!"

"Indeed."

"But how?" I ask, flabbergasted. "How did they build a case against her so fast?"

"The details are sketchy. But apparently a package arrived at the police station yesterday. It contained a CD and a note. The CD had a twelve second video clip, showing a woman shooting a man in the back of the head in an orchard. It is dark, and everything is fuzzy. There is a dark figure next to the woman, but his face is turned away from the camera. The note says: 'This is how Carla Ayvazian shot Yuri Avetisian.' They are analyzing the tape. If they can prove the woman is Carla, she'll be arrested."

Chapter Thirty-Six

Carla can think of only two possibilities of how the video could have been recorded. Either a nosey passerby that they did not notice, or someone planted there by Ari himself. She thinks of the angle—whoever recorded the twelve seconds was facing Yuri. She shot him from the back, and was facing the same way as Yuri. They were well into the orchard, at least twenty meters off the road. There was a dense line of tall poplar trees along the road. There were no houses nearby. She had not noticed any lights.

So the person who recorded the tape had to be inside the orchard, which rules out a random passerby. Who knew they were going to be there? That's when, against all her instincts, she starts suspecting Ari.

But Ari has been attentive and helpful. His explanation is that hunters of wild boar often keep watch from trees.

"It is easier and safer for them to spot approaching boars, and more difficult for the boars to detect their scent if they're perched in a tree," he tells her. "The picture is taken from above your level, which confirms this. He must have been there by pure coincidence."

"And by our dumb luck," says Carla curtly.

"I don't think we have anything to worry about," says Ari. "It was too dark. No one can be recognized from the tape. Even Yuri's face is not clear, let alone yours."

"So what about the note? How could this hunter name both me and Yuri?"

"Remember that he watched the whole thing from the tree, so he may have recognized you, even if your face is not clear in this twelve second tape. And I bet he read about Yuri's death. It was in the papers and on many news sites."

"What are the chances, Ari? Honestly, what are the chances of all that coming together?"

"I don't do chances, Carla. Relax. There's nothing we can do right now."

Carla doesn't like where she is at all. Ari has acquired a patronizing air, and some of her other underlings do not seem to respond to her as they used to. She feels her authority eroding and, with it, her sexual appeal. She misses the days when she used summon Yuri to her bedroom on a whim.

She calls the lawyer that used to work for Ayvazian to check on the progress of the police investigation. She instructs him not to discuss the case with anyone but her, which offends the lawyer. She does not want Ari to be in any way involved in her defense. The lawyer follows up with the police regularly, but has no new information. He is told they are using the latest technology to reconstruct the images from the tape. He has to wait. There is no way to rush a murder investigation.

Ari calls the next morning to say that he has to fly to Moscow for a couple of days.

"How can you leave in the middle of this?" she asks.

"It's important. Personal matter," he says dryly. "Will be back after tomorrow. Nothing will change in the next two days."

꧑ ꧑ ꧑

Thomas Martirosian has gone to the police with a large file. He has the signed testimonies of Anna and Lara, and a detailed medical report from Dr. Suren. His file also contains pictures of Anna's injuries.

He has pressed charges against Hov Samoyan on behalf of his client for aggravated assault, reckless endangerment and rape. He has also filed for a restraining order and presented the divorce papers signed by Anna.

The evidence is strong enough for the police to issue a summons for Hov to appear for questioning. But Hov is nowhere to be found. Stepanavan police have checked his apartment, and questioned some of his associates. No one has seen him for at least twenty-four hours. A check at Yerevan airport border security finally reveals that Hov Samoyan boarded an Aeroflot flight to Moscow the night before. Aeroflot records show that he had a round-trip ticket with an open return date. A request is sent to Moscow police to help find Hov, giving his identity card details, photograph and description. But they are not optimistic that Moscow will make this a priority. Had the crime been a high profile murder, or had it involved narcotics, it would be different.

ළ ළ ළ

In Moscow a young man meets Hov at the airport. He looks like a delivery boy. The car is an old Russian Lada 111 station wagon with the back seats removed, and looks like they have transported every conceivable commodity in the back. Hov tries to engage the driver in conversation to at least understand what comes next, but he is not talkative. He just shrugs. "They'll call you," he says.

The hotel room is prepaid, and includes breakfast. He walks into his room, which, aside from the single bed, has a narrow plywood closet in the corner. When the door swings open, it almost touches the bed. The bathroom and toilets are outside, at the end of the hallway. A single dim light bulb hangs from the ceiling, which barely illuminates the tiny room. The window across the foot of the bed is about one square foot, with a metal bar running across the middle. This might as well be a prison cell.

It occurs to Hov that the room reflects his status in the Ari's eyes. A momentary cloud of doubt crosses his mind about his prospects in Moscow. He is totally alone in this gloomy place, for the first time in Moscow, and all he can do is wait for a call from Ari. Even in his most desperate times, he has never felt so much at the mercy of someone else as he feels now.

He sits on the bed. A cloud of dust rises from the covers as the mattress sinks about twenty centimeters. He looks at his return ticket, and wonders if he should take a taxi back to the airport and try to get on the next flight to Yerevan. That's when his phone rings.

"Do you need anything?" Unlike the driver, the caller speaks fluent Russian with no accent.

"When will I meet Nicolai?" asks Hov.

"Be ready at ten-thirty tomorrow morning," the voice tells him. "Someone will pick you up outside the hotel." And he hangs up.

Hov is not used to luxury. His apartment in Stepanavan is Spartan in every way. But his stomach revolts when he enters the bathroom in the hallway. Rusty faucets leak, the floors are all wet, and the toilet is so dirty that he decides he will not go near it until it becomes a real emergency. He goes back to his room and lies on the bed, waiting for morning.

ᕵ ᕵ ᕵ

"How do you want to handle Carla?" asks Ari. They are in Nicolai's apartment in Moscow. It is a luxurious penthouse on Begovaya Street. The floor to ceiling windows in the living room open to a panoramic view of the Moscow skyline. Nicolai takes a sip of his coffee.

"I'm not sure yet. You have the more incriminating segment of the tape, right?"

"It is a twenty second segment where her face is clearer. There will be no question as to who she is. But this segment does not show her carrying her gun. It will be possible to tell she's standing in the same general area as where the shooting took place. The two segments together can make a much stronger case than what the police have now. With a good defense lawyer, she may manage to get away, but it's not very likely."

"The question is, can we control and manage her?"

"She thinks she's the only Ayvazian left, so she does not share power with anyone. But if she knew more, she may concede more."

"But you're not sure if she will."

"Can't be one hundred percent sure. But right now, her other options don't look that good."

"And they may look a lot worse if we show her the other tape," mumbles Nicolai to himself. "What are her weaknesses?"

"Power and sex," says Ari without a moment's hesitation.

"Sex?"

"She'll fuck anything." And Ari's eyebrows do the twist.

Nicolai looks at him incredulously. "You?" he asks.

Ari nods, and the eyebrows dance. "And three quarters of the staff. Yuri was her favorite in bed. Her authority over the men who work for her turns her on."

"Does she have any genes at all from her mother?" Nicolai mumbles again to himself, but looks intrigued and amused. "It would be a pity to waste her. Is she really worth the trouble?"

"She has access to a lot of Sergei's money. I know she is using the bank accounts, and I know Sergei always had a lot of cash stashed away, which she must have found. She has access to all the papers that Sergei kept at home, and she has searched Viktor's apartment and taken the papers from there too. So she has a pretty good idea of where the assets are. I'd say she's worth it, at least until you get your hands on all that."

"What type of fight will she put up?"

"She tried for years to convince Sergei to let her into the business. Now that she understands what we do, she loves it, and she loves her new role even more. She shot Yuri without a second's hesitation, in cold blood. It was her first kill. Calmer than I was the first time. She's smart, calculating and understands how to control people. So it's your call. If you want a competent number two who one day can kill you when you let your guard down, go for it."

"Ari, you're my competent number two, and I hope one day you won't kill me. You have to help me manage her. Give me a copy of that second tape, just in case."

"Sure," says Ari.

"Any basic advice?"

"Don't fuck her," says Ari without hesitation. "It will throw her off. She doesn't know how to handle anyone unless she sleeps with him. You'll have a much better chance of controlling her if you confuse her."

Nicolai bursts out laughing. "So the whole world can fuck her except me, eh?"

Ari's phone rings. He says a few curt "*dah*'s into the phone and hangs up.

"That kid I told you about is here. Shall we go talk to him?"

"The one who tried to sell his wife?"

"That one."

"Let's go," says Nicolai.

Hov checks into the same Aeroflot flight from Moscow to Yerevan as Ari. They have decided to hire him, but he needs to go back for a few days to sort out personal matters and his apartment. They get separated at Sheremetyevo airport. Ari checks in quickly and goes to the Business Class lounge, while Hov waits in the long line of economy passengers. Hov stands out from the other passengers only in one way. He has a small carry on bag, while everyone else is checking in huge suitcases, boxes tied with rope and suitcase-size bundles wrapped in protective plastic. He is intrigued by the physical commotion and the emotional anguish of passengers wanting to make sure their bags are checked. We watches the process with detachment and amusement, wondering what all these people were doing in Moscow in the first place, and what is it that they are taking back home with such ardor.

As Hov takes his seat in the back of the plane, he is torn in several directions. They have shown him the lowest state of existence by keeping him in that run-down hotel in Moscow for three nights. By contrast, the reception room on the ground floor of Nicolai's apartment, where they met, had been the most luxurious room Hov had ever seen—polished brass and glass and deep-colored wood paneling, paintings, the plush leather sofas and arm chairs, mahogany tables, and beautiful white marble statues of naked women gracing the room. What had made all that even more awe inspiring was the way the staff was treating Nicolai—he might as well had been one of Russia's Czars from the imperial days.

The burning question in Hov's mind is whether it is possible, really possible, to move from where he is to where they are. Does that happen? Living in Armenia these days no one would believe that it is possible for anyone to improve their lot. That type of hope is long since stifled by the unrelenting greed of the oligarchs and corrupt officials. But that hopelessness is for law-abiding citizens. The odds have to be better for the criminal class.

"We are not a family," Nicolai had told him. "Don't make the mistake of thinking you're joining a family. I run a secret and sensitive business organization. You'll have colleagues. Over time, you may even build a friendship or two, but don't count on it. This is a dangerous business. Once you come in, you cannot diverge one-centimeter from the established rules, because we have only one way of dealing with employees whom we no longer trust. Like Yuri was dealt with." Nicolai had stopped for a minute to allow the effect of mentioning Yuri to sink in. Hov had remained quiet, his face expressionless.

"Curiosity is not a virtue here," Nicolai had continued. "We're not conducting experiments in a science lab. You'll be given an assignment, and you will do it. If you get your nose into anything that does not concern the assignment you are given, you come under suspicion. Do your job, and do it consistently well. We will notice you, and move you up a notch. Then do the new job well, without nosing around. We will notice again and move you up again. That is the only way to move up. Any other way will get you killed."

The plane has reached cruising altitude. Passengers start bringing bags down from the baggage rack and putting them back for no apparent reason, and lining up to use the toilets. The cabin attendants are scurrying around among the passengers trying to start the meal service.

Hov cannot get Nicolai out of his mind. The gold ring on his finger must have weighed as much as his carry-on. The diamond stud on it must be worth more than Hov has made in his entire life. His ostrich leather shoes and matching belt must have cost more than all the clothes and shoes Hov has owned since he was born. But his apparent flamboyance belied the seriousness and the deadly determination conveyed through his eyes and his total concentration, which gave Hov a chill. Listening to him, Hov did not doubt for a minute that he meant every word he said.

But still, Hov does not believe that the prescription that Nicolai gave for success would work as he explained it. If you only do the job they give you and don't look around, they can take you for a fool. You'd be acting like a mule with huge blinkers on. If you get too nosy, they can kill you. So there has to be a middle road somewhere.

In the hustle-bustle of the crowded economy class cabin, as the plane begins its final descent into Yerevan, Hov makes what he believes will be a major decision in his life. He will join Nicolai's organization and find that middle road, he will rise though the ranks, and one day he will live like him. He already knows how to beat and rape women, and he has made a one-time fee selling his wife, so he understands the basics of running a prostitute. The rest should be easy.

Ari disembarks. He does not make much of the two policemen standing outside the plane, nor of the additional policemen standing at the entrance of passport control. He passes though passport control and customs and is in his car minutes after landing.

When Hov finally makes it to the doors of the plane, the two policemen approach him.

"Hov Samoyan?" asks one of them, blocking his way.

"Yes?"

"Come with us," says the policeman, signaling the way. The second policeman is on Hov's other side and they lead him to a side door at passport control, away from the rest of the passengers. They process his papers quickly, ask if he has checked luggage, and they take him away in a police car.

Hov sits in a small windowless room at the police station. Thomas Martirosian and a police officer explain to him the charges against him.

"Do you have a lawyer?" asks the officer.

Hov looks at him in disbelief. Aggravated assault, reckless endangerment, rape, divorce, restraining order, possible long jail term if he is convicted of the charges. How did that worthless piece of shit manage all this? His hands begin to shake. Mounting anger, mixed with fear, is nerve wracking. He looks at Martirosian for a long moment.

"She hired you?" he mumbles.

"That is not your concern, Mr. Samoyan," says Martirosian. "I represent Anna Hakobian, and these are the charges against you. As the officer asked, we'd like to know if you have a lawyer you'd like to contact."

"I don't have a lawyer."

"The charges against you are serious. You can go to jail for a long time. I think it is best if a lawyer represented you."

"I'd like to call a friend." They allow him the phone call.

"*Dah*," says Ari's baritone voice.

Hov explains where he is and why, skipping many of the details, but giving the basics.

"You attacked her, after I told you to forget her and go back home?" Hov is silent. "Are you really that stupid?" Now Hov is in a cold sweat. "I've made a big mistake about you. You're on your own. Never call this number again." And Ari hangs up.

Hov is given a large stack of papers to sign, acknowledging the various charges and notices.

"These," says Martirosian pushing a document towards him, "are your divorce papers. I strongly recommend that you sign them. There are no claims or demands made, so you don't need a lawyer. By signing, all you do is end your marriage to Anna Hakobian."

Hov leafs through the papers, without reading one word, and distractedly signs at the indicated places.

"Thank you," says Martirosian, giving him one of the signed originals. "That's your copy."

He shuffles through his files and produces another document.

"This is a restraining order issued by the judge. Do you understand what a restraining order is?"

Hov shakes his head.

"It says you cannot go within fifty meters of Anna Hakobian. Under any circumstances. If you are seen within fifty meters of her, anywhere, you will be immediately arrested. Do you understand?"

Hov nods.

"Sign here. By signing, you are acknowledging that you have received the order and understand it. It is in effect already, so you are warned."

Hov signs. Martirosian stands up, without a second look at Hov. He turns to the officer.

"Thank you," he says, shaking his hand. "My work is done here. The rest is in your hands."

"We'll see what we can do about his defense," says the officer. "In the meantime, he's staying in jail."

Chapter
Thirty-Seven

To Edik, everything seems in limbo. To me, we are in the best shape we've been for a long time. The difference is that he needs to understand everything, and I don't. From my perspective, LeFreak is dead, Yuri is dead, Carla is under house arrest and Hov is in jail and possibly facing a long sentence. All welcome news. But Edik wants to know who, why and especially how these things happened.

Manoj has come and we have registered *"Apastan"* as a foreign owned and sponsored charity, with the purpose of sheltering and rehabilitating victims of sex trafficking and domestic abuse. He had to stay one extra day to complete the procedures, even though all the legal documents were ready for his signature when he arrived. Nothing just takes one day in Armenia. Besides, we also had to open a bank account. The bank officer kept staring at me as Manoj, Edik and I signed all the paperwork. He could not believe that I was being given full signatory authority over the account, equal to the others.

Avo is back to being his enthusiastic self. They have registered a company—fifty percent Avo, forty percent Edik, and ten percent Gagik, who insisted on participating. The capital is in place, and Avo has already started buying the hives. He wants to be the best honey producer in Armenia—the most pristine and the most efficient. He is targeting thirty kilos per hive, when the average here is under twelve.

The other good news, at least for me, is that Sona and Simon have postponed their wedding. They are a bit disappointed, but they are not ready. As for me, there is far too much happening right now, and I know I wouldn't be able to give the wedding my full attention. Their initial date, at the end of May, is only a week away. It is a relief to have an extra month.

Anna's physical injuries are healing, as Dr. Suren predicted. But I still notice her withdrawing into herself. I know exactly where and what that is. That was an important survival tool for me too. Withdraw, heal a little, come back out, hurt again, withdraw again, heal a little more, until the hurt is less and more distant every time. No one who hasn't been there would understand any of it. Some girls withdraw like that and find it impossible to come back out. Their self-esteem is so shattered that they do not want to face the world, or even to heal. For them, withdrawal turns into an emotional grave, not a healing process. That's one of the main reasons why I did not want Anna to live alone.

Since Anna is not working, I manage to take her with me to visit the organizations that I had planned to visit. Her nose and forehead are still badly bruised, but that, in a way, helps melt the ice with the administrators, who do not understand the nature of my interest in their organizations. We spend a lot of time in each place. We learn about their programs, and we hear the stories of some of the young girls who board there. We speak to many of them and see their living quarters.

I have intensified the search for a suitable house for the shelter. Once or twice I asked Edik to come with me, because, as I had predicted, no realtor takes me seriously. We're looking at two-to-three story, older homes, with fenced-in gardens, five or six bedrooms, and large common living areas. To minimize cost, we're looking in the outskirts of Yerevan, but even there, homes like that cost upwards of half a million dollars. The realtors did not believe I was a credible buyer when they saw me, and would not bother to show me houses.

One day we go to the store where Anna works so she can get her pay. Lucy is in shock when we walk in.

"Anna jan!" she screams, "What happened to you? I saw the doctor's medical slip but never imagined something like this."

"It's a long story," says Anna. "By the way, this is my friend Lara." Lucy and I shake hands. "We don't have much time; I have another appointment with the chiropractor."

"Come in," says Lucy, leading us to the back room. She counts a few monetary notes from the drawer and hands them to Anna.

"I don't know what this world is coming to," she says. "First Yuri gets shot, then the manager of our sister store calls to say Madame Carla cannot make the rounds because she is under house arrest. Who are we supposed to report to? We have to file semi-annual audits with the tax authorities soon, and I have no idea who will sign the documents."

"I'm sure it will all work out," says Anna. "Thanks for the pay."

"No problem," says Lucy truly sympathetic. "I wish I could give you more, but I'll get in trouble."

"I understand," says Anna, and attempts a smile. "By the way," she adds as an afterthought, "do you still have the picture of that girl we were supposed to look for?"

"Sure," she says, pulling the drawer open. "Here, do you want it?"

"If you don't mind."

"Yuri's dead. Of course I don't mind. Good luck, Anna jan."

We leave the store with the distinct impression that Lucy has figured out that the picture was of Anna, but none of that matters anymore, either to her or to us.

"What made you ask for the photo?" I ask.

"I don't know," she shrugs. "Why should she keep my picture?"

Our next stop is not the chiropractor, but an apartment with two spare bedrooms to rent. The building is in the southern outskirts of the city, while our current rooms are in the north. This one is on the second floor of an old building. It is obvious that the place has seen better days. There are beautiful plaster designs on the ceilings, layers of oval borders with floral corners. The ceilings are higher than in our current apartments, and the dining room walls are finished with beautiful cherry panels. But everything shows the wear and tear of at least fifty years, if not longer.

The four-bedroom apartment is occupied by an elderly couple. Mr. & Mrs. Poghosian take two of the rooms for themselves, using one as their bedroom and the second as an office for Mr. Poghosian, who is a retired professor of philosophy. They thus have two spare bedrooms to rent. The apartment has two full baths, one of which goes with the two rooms, a large kitchen, which we are allowed to use as long as we keep it clean, and a large living room, which we also are allowed to use. They are in their late seventies and seem delightful. Gentle, soft-spoken, un-imposing. The rent is a little more than the two rents that we pay now, and the bus stop is a few blocks further away, but we fall in love with the place and decide to take it.

I tell Anna we'll do what we can to give the place a facelift. The apartment is far too beautiful to remain in such disrepair. I still have the paint, brushes and scrapers that I had bought to touch up my room, which I never used. We'll try to use them here.

I feel bad about abandoning Diqin Alice. I promise to pay her three months additional rent, and to do her shopping twice a month until she finds a new tenant. I also promise to advertise her place at the University.

Avo calls to say he has finished buying all the hives. He has managed to get ten extra hives for the same price. He has mapped the whole program of where he will start the hives and how he will progressively move them up the mountainside throughout the summer and into the fall. He has also ordered the steel drums in which the honey needs to be exported. The boys will take turns helping, watching the hives while he starts preparing the space where they will extract the honey in the fall.

Hermine has been visiting with Martha more frequently. She is sixteen, and as innocent and clueless as they come. She's pretty and somewhat unusual looking, with her light brown hair and dark blue eyes. She always wears trousers and long blouses that reach mid-thigh. Girls in the village do not like to wear skirts or dresses, because the only socially acceptable ones are the long gowns that reach their ankles. That is for grandmothers. Trousers are a compromise.

Martha likes Hermine and has taken her under her wing. Hermine loves taking care of her little niece, Ani, which helps Martha. When I see them together, I sometimes feel envious. Their mutual support is unconditional, inherently understood and accepted, never discussed or formalized, and never betrayed. No one has taught them to be that way. It is just the way it can often be in Saralandj. It has always been that way in our house.

Thinking about their relationship, I get a strong urge to visit home. Without calling anyone, I go to the bus station and catch the next bus to Aparan. From Aparan I take a taxi.

It is mid-afternoon. No one is expecting me. I walk in and see Arpi alone in the kitchen. The others are all in the garden or tending the animals. She's getting ready to start preparations for dinner. I'm glad to be alone with her. I start helping her wash the vegetables and boil potatoes. I know she will not say much, so I start talking, telling her about the shelter that we're going to start, about Edik and about the poetry that he often gives me to read.

Arpi listens but does not stop working. Then, she suddenly stops, wipes her hands on her apron, and leaves. "I'll be right back," she says. When she comes back she gives me a light blue notebook, the kind that students use to turn in their homework.

"What's this?" I ask.

"Let me know what you think," she says coyly, and goes back to washing the dishes.

"Arpi, did you write these?" I am shocked. Written in small and neat handwriting, the book is full of poems. Most of them don't have titles. One ends and a new one begins, often on the same page, with a line separating the two. I remember we had to do that to economize on paper.

I start to read randomly, and I am even more stunned. Her writing is exceptional.

"Arpi, how long have you been writing?"

"A while." She shrugs.

"These are unbelievable! Can I show them to Edik?"

She shrugs again, and nods. I can tell she wants me to.

"I can't wait; I want to read him one right now. Is that okay?"

She nods. I call Edik.

"Listen to this." I don't even ask if this is a good time for him.

a lone robin on the bare apricot tree
    meets my stare
    rasp of winter's voice in its song
doused in hesitance
I'm splayed beneath its feathers
    coveting its wings…

the soil soaks what I spill in doubt
my shadow withers plucked from its roots
but this is home
I decant myself on its threshold
    restless
    weary of its pull
    stone on stone

I can't settle inside its pulse

the kitchen drips
it drips laughter
my sisters' voices
    skip on river stones
    as mine spatters on current's foam

yet I turn the soil
I know the hunger in me
    will starve this land and more

palm against the blur of certainty
I search for an aperture to free this light in me

but at dawn there's yet another dead bird
under my grandfather's apricot tree

"That is deep," murmurs Edik when I finish. "I cannot place it. It is as powerful as the works of the great classics, but the style is unique. Who is it?"

I turn to Arpi. "Arpi, you were just compared to the great classical poets!" Edik hears me.

"No!" comes Edik's voice over the phone.

I spend that night in my parents' room reading Arpi's poems with her.

Chapter Thirty-Eight

Nicolai Sergeiovitch Filatov never forgets the day he confronted Sergei Ayvazian. It was fifteen years ago, and he was eighteen years old. It was January third, and Russia was still celebrating the New Year. Sergei was throwing a lavish party in a hotel ballroom in Moscow. He had some thirty select guests—politicians, businessmen, an oil trader from abroad, a few police officers, and other wealthy-looking men of less known professional backgrounds. There were also around twenty ladies, invited not as guests, but as paid companions. The men were in their most expensive suits, and a live band was playing classical Russian music, waitresses were passing champagne and caviar, and the ladies, scantily clad, were doing their best to act classy and available at the same time.

It was twenty degrees below zero and Nicolai's bones were freezing. His mother was sick in their tiny apartment in Moscow, burning with a forty degree Celsius fever and coughing blood. She had told him about Ayvazian before, and shown him pictures, but he was not allowed to meet him. She had raised Nicolai in that apartment alone. That's why she had stopped bringing clients home when he had turned five. She was thirty-five years old, and on her deathbed. She called Nicolai to her side, and gave him a piece of paper.

"This is where you can find him," she whispered. "You can now go and introduce yourself."

Nicolai asked a friend from the days when he had been a member of a street gang to drive him to the address on the piece of paper. They drove through the icy streets and parked a few meters from the entrance of the apartment building. Nicolai was rehearsing what he'd say to him. He was nervous and angry and yet he felt an unusual anticipation. He was about to get out of the car when Ayvazian left the building with three other men. He was wearing a thick, dark-gray winter coat with a black fur collar, and a Russian fur hat. They were talking and laughing, and got into a black sedan parked by the entrance of the building. One of the men got behind the wheel, Ayvazian in the passenger seat, and the other two in the back.

"Let's follow them," he told his friend, who was curious himself. He followed the sedan to the hotel. The four men left the car at the entrance and walked in. An attendant came to park the car.

Nicolai's friend parked by the curbside. He stayed in the car while Nicolai walked to the entrance of the hotel and watched through the huge glass doors as Ayvazian and his friends walked down the wide hallway and entered a room on the right. He waited outside for five minutes, in the freezing weather, to make sure that was not just a stop on their way to somewhere else. He did not have on the right clothes. His coat was light and very old, he had a simple wool hat and gloves that had tears in them, exposing his knuckles, which were turning blue.

He did not know what to expect in the room that Ayvazian had entered, but he did not care. The doorman tried to stop him, but he kept walking. "I'll only be a minute," he said, "I have to give a message to one of your guests." The doorman watched him walk into the ballroom and Ayvazian's party. He relaxed. That room was swarming with bodyguards.

Two muscular men were standing at either side of the door inside the ballroom. One grabbed Nicolai as he walked in. "You're in the wrong place," he said, "out!" The scene inside mesmerized Nicolai. Huge crystal chandeliers hung from the eight-meter high ceiling, crystal sconces were all over the walls and gold moldings decorated the walls, framing rectangular spaces where huge paintings hung. His eyes scanned the room looking for Ayvazian. People were mostly standing with glasses in their hands, others were seated in large armchairs. They all seemed to know each other.

"Out," said the bodyguard again, pushing him.

"I have to talk to that man," said Nicolai pointing at Ayvazian. "I have an important message for him."

"He does not want to hear your message. Leave, now." The bodyguard grabbed Nicolai's arm so hard that it hurt. He pushed him over the threshold and blocked his way. "If you don't leave now, something bad is going to happen to you."

"Ayvazian!" screamed Nicolai at the top of his lungs. "One word, please." The bodyguard slapped him so hard that he stumbled to the floor and his nose started to bleed. Nicolai was quick to get back on his feet. He wiped his nose with his sleeve and looked inside. He saw someone approaching him. Ayvazian was watching from inside.

"Who are you and what's your business here?" asked the man.

"Tell Ayvazian that Evgeniya's son is here with an important message. It will take only a minute."

The man walked back and whispered in Ayvazian's ear. Ayvazian walked toward the door, but to Nicolai he looked like a bull charging to make a kill. He reached Nicolai and pushed him a few meters into the hallway.

"What do you want?" he hissed.

"Sorry to interrupt your party, esteemed father," said Nicolai, "but my mother is sick. She'll probably be dead by the time I get back home. I thought you should know."

"Once again, what do you want?!" Ayvazian's face was turning red. The dying woman did not seem to interest him.

"I am your son!" Nicolai raised his voice. The last thing Ayvazian wanted is to cause a scene in front of his guests. He took a wad of cash from his pocket and threw it at Nicolai. "Don't bother me again," he hissed, and walked back inside, telling the bodyguards to shut the door and not let him in again.

Nicolai's mother died the next morning. She had been one of Ayvazian's early victims. He had just turned twenty-one and, eager to prove himself to his boss, he had beaten and raped her into submission, and she eventually accepted her fate as a prostitute. But she had managed to keep her pregnancy a secret until the seventh month. The doctor that the boss kept at the time had refused to perform an abortion at that late stage. She was seventeen when she gave birth to Nicolai. That was eighteen years ago; today Ayvazian would have forced an abortion even at that late stage.

She had challenged him to recognize Nicolai as his son. He had been livid. She was persistent, but so was he. In the end, he allowed her to work freely, for herself, and raise the boy. She gave him her maiden name, but she registered his father's name as Sergei.

"Don't bring him up again," he had told her. "I don't want to hear about him, or to see you again. You're free and you're on your own."

"I will tell him about you, Sergei," she had said, spitting at him. "One day, he'll want to know who his father is. And I promise you he will know the truth."

And Nicolai learned the truth. The whole truth, over time, as he was growing up, as Evgeniya told it to him. By the time he turned sixteen, she had told him about the rape, her profession and the person responsible for it all.

His mother was kind and caring, but miserable. He had never seen her happy. He watched her come home in the morning, sleep until mid-afternoon, spend the afternoons in her nightgown watching TV, and then get ready and leave for work in the evening. He, as a young boy, would watch TV all night while his mother was out, and sleep late like her. She would not be up to wake him up in time to get ready for school.

As he approached fifteen it became more difficult to continue this routine, but they had no choice. He was unemployable and no school would accept him, given his spotty academic record. It became very tense in the apartment. He could not stand watching her 'get ready for work.' Her clothes, her makeup, and most of all her 'attitude' as she got into the mood for her work annoyed him to no end.

A year later he joined a street gang. They'd sleep in abandoned buildings or break into empty apartments in inhabited buildings. They'd steal from stores, and sometimes homes, and mug vulnerable people on quiet streets at night. He was sixteen when his gang cornered a woman in the street and took turns with her. As the youngest, his turn was last. At that point they did not even have to hold her down. She was nearly unconscious. That is how Nicolai lost his virginity.

But Nicolai blamed neither his father nor his mother for this state of affairs. In a practical sense, both seemed exogenous to his condition, so blame was irrelevant. But in an existential sense, neither was exogenous. He had something from each parent, like any other human being. The question that was more relevant to him was who to identify with.

His mother offered nothing with which he wanted to identify. She was not only sad, but also defeated. He did not see in her a victim that needed to be understood and protected. He saw a weakling who had been beaten and made miserable; he saw a loser who did not fight. There was no moral indignation in him when he thought of what his father had done. He did not have the education or the understanding to react on moral grounds. He saw instead someone who had not lost, who was not defeated, who was probably happy, or at least happier than his mother. He saw strength and toughness, and most importantly, he saw success. And he had not even met him yet.

It took Nicolai two years of persistence after his mother's death to finally convince Ayvazian to take him on. He kept appearing at his door, only to be rebuked and kicked out, but he did not stop. Eventually Ayvazian relented. Nicolai was twenty, his mother was dead, and something in Nicolai reminded Ayvazian of himself. Maybe he could forge the kid into something he could use.

Nicolai worked with Ayvazian for thirteen years before Ayvazian was killed. During that time, he was restricted to Moscow, and there was no contact whatsoever with Ayvazian's family in Yerevan. Even Viktor, who worked closely with Nicolai the whole time, did not know who he was until the last year, when Ayvazian decided the time had come to take Viktor into his confidence about Nicolai's identity.

Nicolai and Viktor were Ayvazian's top two lieutenants in Moscow. Between them, they managed over a dozen henchmen, and ran around fifty prostitutes directly. But few of the henchmen knew both men. Those who worked for Viktor knew Viktor, and those who worked for Nicolai knew Nicolai. Yuri did not know Nicolai.

Among the very few who knew both Viktor and Nicolai were Nono the housekeeper, a few prostitutes, including Anastasia, and of course Ari. But none of these people except Viktor knew about Nicolai's relationship with Ayvazian. All Ari knew was that Ayvazian had grown fond of Nicolai over the years, and had begun to trust him more and more.

Perhaps that was the reason why, in Ari's eyes, Nicolai had risen over the years to become third in command, after Ayvazian and Viktor. And when he asked him to come to Moscow right after Ayvazian's death, Ari did not hesitate. That is when Nicolai told Ari who he was.

ꝛ ꝛ ꝛ

Nicolai Filatov enters the study alone. He does not want anyone else in the room when he first comes face to face with Carla. She is standing in front of her desk, in her black pantsuit and white blouse. Her face is stony and serious.

"Good to finally meet you," he says. Carla sees the resemblance immediately. His eyes are Russian, from his mother, but the shape of his forehead and chin are pure Ayvazian. So are his mannerisms. They sit on the maroon velvet sofa.

"So," says Carla in her most businesslike voice, "Papa had a boy three years before he had me."

"That sums it up," says Nicolai, showing the first hint of a smile.

"When did he find out?"

"He knew all along, from when I was born."

Carla looks surprised. "But you've been working with him for only thirteen years?"

"I met him for the first time when I was eighteen. I started working with him and cousin Viktor two years later."

It suddenly occurs to Carla that it was around thirteen years ago when she overheard her father say that he wished she were a boy. He must have finally relented and taken the bastard son in right around that time, when he so strongly felt the need for a son. She makes a mental note to tell Nicolai the story one day. For a second, she wonders how differently things might have turned out if he had taken her into the business. He might never have felt the need to accept Nicolai if he had.

"Did you make the video tapes?" she asks, coming to the main question on her mind. She had received the second CD under her door, with the twenty-second clip of the scene in the orchard that left no doubt about her identity.

"I ordered them made. As an insurance policy. I do not intend to use the second one, if we can work together. And if we cannot, well, then all this," and Nicolai waves his hand around the room, "becomes irrelevant anyway."

"You want us to work together?"

"Of course. Why would I be here otherwise?"

"How?"

"You keep running things in Armenia, but you coordinate with me. We split profits fifty-fifty. You also give me half of all the money Papa left behind, both in cash and in the banks."

"That's it? You keep one hundred percent of everything else, and I keep half of Armenia?"

"I spent thirteen years building what you call 'everything else.' Of course I'll keep it. You've done nothing to earn any of this Carla, and yet you keep half of Armenia. I think if any of this is unfair, it is in your favor."

Very well played, thinks Carla. Besides, he can send me to jail on a whim. He's not even mentioning that.

"We obviously disagree on the definition of fair," she says. "Besides, I don't think it is about fairness, is it? It is about when it would no longer be worth dealing with each other. So allow me to suggest a slight modification to the arrangement. You keep one hundred percent of Russia, which is probably by far the largest operation anyway, and we split everything else fifty-fifty, not just Armenia. That includes the Ukraine, Dubai and Istanbul, as far as I know."

"You remind me of Papa," smiles Nicolai. "Negotiating even when you don't have a leg to stand on. That is why I'll accept your suggestion, not because I have to. This is the one and only concession you'll get from me as my sister. From here on, it is pure business. Do not give me any cause to suspect you, in anything. I can bring everything you have tumbling down on your head."

Carla is finally released from house arrest on the basis of inconclusive evidence. However, the police order makes it clear that the case would be reopened if and when new evidence implicating her comes to light.

Chapter Thirty-Nine

Two momentous events took place this week, hopefully both harbingers of better days to come. On Monday, *Apastan* officially opened its doors. It is a beautiful three-story house in the Malatya-Sebastia district of Yerevan. It has the charm of the old homes, but is renovated and well suited to accommodate twenty boarders. There is a two-meter high wall around the one thousand square meter property, with a small garden at the back of the house. Most of the furniture has arrived, and although we still have a few pieces to procure, we decided to do the opening because Monday was the only day that Manoj could visit again.

Manoj gave me a small sealed envelope. It was a note from Ahmed.

"Dear Lara,

I'm sorry I could not attend the opening, but please accept my sincere congratulations. As soon as you have next year's budget finalized, I will transfer the next tranche of the funds. The Ayvazians' villa is still stuck in the court, but I will fund the shelter personally until the villa is sorted out and sold.

On a personal note, I want to thank you again for opening my eyes. My life has changed immeasurably because of you. As you soar over your mountain peaks, know that you have a friend for life here in the desert.
Sincerely, Ahmed."

There was no pomp and circumstance, no long speeches, no cutting of ribbons. Just us, and the few staff that we have hired, including my assistant, a guard who is also the driver, a psychiatrist, a housekeeper and Dr. Suren, who is on retainer. There were also two people from the government: the chief of police of the district and a representative from the Department of Justice. No reporters were invited. Manoj outlined the purpose of the foreign benefactor, Edik translated, and the guests toured the house. The ceremony lasted forty-five minutes.

Although Hov is still in jail, I gave Anna the option to move into the shelter or stay in our new apartment. She opted for the apartment. She will enroll in acting and literature classes, and will work part time at the shelter. Her job will be to engage the residents in reading from classical literary works as a recreational activity a few times a week.

The second event was the wedding of Sona and Simon in Ohanavank on Saturday. Everyone in Saralandj was there, in addition to a lot of friends and relatives from Aparan and Ashtarak. The main hall of the monastery was packed. The service was traditional and truly lovely. I had forgotten how beautiful Armenian liturgical music is. Sona looked beatific.

The most amazing thing that Sona and Simon did was to leave the church through the secret door, into the underground cave, and out on the other side of the gorge, where a horse-drawn carriage was waiting to take them to a car on the main road, which, in turn, took them on their honeymoon, to a small hotel outside Ashtarak. Everyone laughed when she removed her high-heeled shoes and handed them to Simon. The scene where they walked down the hidden staircase as man and wife, she in her flowing white wedding gown, he in his silver-grey tuxedo, and disappeared into the ground, captivated everyone. As they emerged from the cave at the other side of the gorge, forty-eight white doves were released, which is the sum of their ages, twenty-two and twenty-six. It was their idea to build a bridge between their wedding and the thirteenth century tale of the church. Edik had tears in his eyes, as did I.

Edik had found the time to pull Arpi aside during the wedding and commend her on her poetry. He was not exaggerating. He honestly believes Arpi is already an accomplished poet, and should be encouraged to write. "Just keep writing," he told her.

Edik remains an enigma. I cannot decide whether the cause of his deep interest in me is his feeling that my coming home, and his role in it, has been a vindication of the loss of his sister Sirarpi, or whether a more romantic feeling is in play. Had it not been for the age difference between us, would he have wanted a romantic relationship with me? I guess I'll never find out, unless I put him on his bench of truth and redemption and outright ask him one day. In the meantime, I'm happy to live with this ambiguity for a while longer. He is not only one of the most decent people I have ever known, but a true friend, and someone who has helped guide me through some of the most difficult conflicts that I have had to resolve. He'll have a life-long friend in me as well.

Anastasia is back to her routine in Moscow and calls once in a while. She is another enigma. She has embraced everything that I have rejected, and will never understand my inability to accept the life she has adopted, and yet we too have become friends of sorts. I know she would trust me with anything. I just don't know why. That too is something I am happy to live with.

On Sunday, everyone at home was still glowing with the memory of the perfect wedding. Even Arpi was livelier.

Before lunch, I went for a walk toward the forests of Saralandj. I had no intention of reaching them this time. I just wanted to relive that experience from my childhood. The intense awe and excitement that I had felt years ago were replaced by a serene familiarity with the surroundings. The forest is now home too.

When I returned home, I saw Aram with his nose buried in Arpi's poetry book. I could hear Avo whistling a tune while working in the back garden with Sago, just like Papa used to do. He has his first shipment of honey to Dubai already scheduled for the fall. Alisia was chirping around like a spring sparrow learning how to fly. And I could see and feel Arpi drifting back and forth between the present and somewhere mystical in her mind.

In the afternoon I took a bunch of white carnations that we had brought home from the wedding, and went to the village cemetery. I remember how we used to visit our family section in the cemetery on *Merelots* days; there are five in the Armenian calendar. Early on, the visits were a lot of fun for us. We did not personally know anyone buried there, and my parents used to turn the visit into a family outing. They burned *khung*, incense, and played *duduk* music, wanting to keep the memory of my grandparents and great aunts and uncles alive.

Of course, all that changed when Papa was killed.

Aside from the graves, there are two stones with crosses on them for my great-grandfather and for my great aunt, the legendary Araxi Dadik, whose ring I now wear. They both died in Siberia, and their remains are lost somewhere there. How many secrets are buried in this small cemetery, I wondered? Great-grandpa, who was tired of multiple exiles and came to Armenia in the mid-forties just so he could die in the Motherland, was instead exiled to Siberia, where he died. The beautiful Araxi Dadik had a miserable life. She left a man who was madly in love with her behind, ended up marrying someone else in Siberia and died of tuberculosis at a young age, alone, because they had quarantined her.

How I wish I could exhume the secrets that have found a final home in these graves.

I placed a white carnation on each grave and the two stones, starting with Araxi Dadik, showing her her ring, and working my way down, taking a minute to think about each person, trying to revive their memory like Papa used to do. I stayed longer at Mama's grave. I told her how sorry I was that I didn't make it home in time to see her. I told her how I never forgot our last night and her words of advice; I told her how I never forgot the sorrow that defined her. How many secrets did you take with you, Mama? Did you have any? Were they your prison or your sanctuary?

I placed the last carnation on Papa's grave, and could not control my tears. Thank you for not abandoning me, Papa. You were there helping me every step of the way. Somewhere in the Bible stories that you used to read, you read once that Jesus died for us. The only person I know who died for me is you, Papa jan. You died for me, and then you saved my life and brought me back home. I will not leave home again, no matter where I go.

Acknowledgements

ike its prequel, *A Place Far Away*, this book is dedicated to the thousands of young women who fall victim to international human trafficking every year and suffer silently trapped in a horrific world. It was my chance encounter with some of them and my first-hand familiarization with their plight that inspired me to write both books.

Ultimately, this is the story of the heroic attempt of a young victim of sex trafficking to go home again. It is a work of fiction. All characters, events and places have no connection whatsoever with actual ones. However, once again, I have tried to tell the story in a way that allows a sense of the true nature of the anguish of that journey to flow through the fiction. My most valuable insights in creating that link came from the many victims that I had the privilege of meeting and interviewing, some still in captivity, others in various shelters in Yerevan. By their trust and candor, they gave me more than I can hope to return.

I am indebted to many individuals who helped improve the manuscript: Jane Vise Hall, who patiently and expertly edited the manuscript; Armine Hovannisian, who made several invaluable suggestions which enriched the plot immeasurably; Silva Merjanian, who wrote Arpi Galian's poem; Artak Tonikian, who helped both with my research and with the cover design; Debbie Beadle of Ecpat UK, who helped with my early research. I am also grateful to several individuals who patiently read the manuscript and made valuable suggestions, including my wife Charlotte Zanoyan, Nora Salibian, Ussama Saffouri, Arax Pashayan, Dikran Babikian and Hera Deeb.